# LEGENDS OF LHIOSQUOR

## BOOK ONE OF AFTER EDEN

### TRENT COLEMAN

WESTBOW·
PRESS
A DIVISION OF THOMAS NELSON
& ZONDERVAN

WestBow Press books may be ordered through booksellers or by contacting:

WestBow Press
A Division of Thomas Nelson & Zondervan
1663 Liberty Drive
Bloomington, IN 47403
www.westbowpress.com
1 (866) 928-1240

ISBN: 978-1-4908-3180-0 (e)
ISBN: 978-1-4908-3181-7 (sc)
ISBN: 978-1-4908-3182-4 (hc)

Library of Congress Control Number: 2014905761

Printed in the United States of America.

WestBow Press rev. date: 4/28/2014

# AUTHOR'S NOTE TO READER

Welcome to the world of <u>After Eden</u>. I sincerely hope that you will thoroughly enjoy the first installment in this legendary fiction series. Before we begin, I need to emphasize that <u>After Eden</u> is purely a work of fiction. We have virtually no knowledge of the state of the world before Noah's flood, certainly not enough to re-create the setting of the pre-Flood world with any degree of accuracy. A few of the characters in <u>After Eden</u> have their names appear in the fourth and fifth chapters of the Book of Genesis in the Bible. The names of some of the other characters were taken from the Dead Sea Scrolls or from mythologies of various ancient civilizations. Beyond those few names, none of the other characters, nations or events in <u>After Eden: The Legends of Lhiosquor</u> have any basis in history. <u>After Eden</u> is not a history book but an imagining of an unknown world lost to history. The world before the Flood is lost to us, but the human condition remains unchanged. Decisions and situations faced by the characters in <u>After Eden</u> are similar to those we face today. Moreover, God hasn't changed. He is still the same as He has always been. He sees the end from the beginning as has a plan for every individual, every family and every nation, and He will bring His plan to pass.

Trent Coleman

# PROLOGUE

I am Noah, the father of all now living. These scrolls I have written give an account of the world of our ancestors, from before the great waters covered the earth. I am writing this account so that the memory of ancient times, particularly the accounts of the great city of Lhiosquor and of the prophet Enoch, my great-grandfather, will be preserved for future generations. So much has changed in this new world. Much of the knowledge of the old world is already lost and forgotten under the waters of the flood. It is my prayer that we learn from those who have gone before us; from the examples of those who pleased the Almighty One and from the mistakes of those who failed. Perhaps in doing so we can help build a new world that will be more pleasing to the Almighty One than that of our ancestors. Here follows an account from the most ancient of times.

# THE CITY OF WOE

## (40 AM – 1 EC)

Now the world was newly formed, and all things were yet fresh and green upon the earth in its infancy; nevertheless, the seed of iniquity had already been planted, and its full fruition was made manifest when the first two brothers born of woman had come into manhood. The elder son envied his younger brother's favour in the eyes of the Almighty Creator, whom the people of ancient times called Eloi. Abel, the younger, red-haired brother, had great piety and devotion toward the Almighty and all of his deeds were blessed. It was an evil day indeed when Cain, the elder, dark-haired brother, grew so envious of Abel that he took his brother's life. His was the first death of a man in the world. As God had promised when the first man and woman forsook his ways, sin had brought forth death upon the earth. Because of Cain's terrible sin, he was banished with Awan, his wife and sister, to the Dry Lands of Nod in the east, over the Kheruva Mountains. Here follows the tale of Cain, of his descendants, and of the City of Woe.

# CHAPTER 1

# THE EXILES
## (40 – 57 AM)

## 40 AM

Cain and Awan were banished from the tents of Adam forever by the decree of the Almighty One. Because of Cain's crime, they became, for a time, foragers on the roots and wild berries of the earth, for the earth would produce no crops for them. In the days before the waters came, it was forbidden to take the lifeblood of an animal, so Cain and Awan hunted no wild beasts. One night, a great wind blew across the plains of Nod. As Cain looked up into the sky, it seemed as if the curtain of heaven – the perpetual cloudy mist that enveloped the earth in those days – receded like a scroll being rolled back. Cain was astonished and marvelled at the countless points of light in the night sky. Stars were a rare sight in the days when the earth was young, before the world was changed. As he gazed at their brilliance in wonder, Cain heard the awesome voice of God thundering in the wind.

"Cain," called the Almighty One. Cain fell trembling to the dusty ground beneath his feet and gazed fearfully into the night. "I have placed a light in the heavens as red as the hair of your brother and as red as his blood that you took with your hands. Every time you see this light, you will be reminded of your exile and of the price you have paid and will continue to pay for your brother's murder. I have taken some of his spilled blood that cries out to Me from the earth to mark this light in his remembrance. This light will be known in his honour as Abelon, and the sight of it will cause you to weep for your sin. Others also will see this sign and remember your crime."

Cain cried out to God in anguish, "This is too much to bear, Almighty One. Is it not enough punishment that You have taken all that

I have and have exiled me in shame, far from the dwelling of my father, mother, and sisters? How long must I endure such severe torment?" Then Cain fell to his knees, buried his face in his hands, and wept aloud upon the ground.

"Dust you are, and unto dust you shall return." replied the Creator. "Yet you accuse Me falsely. You say that I have taken all that you have, but have I not in My mercy given you your sister Awan to be your wife? She is with child and will bear you a son, the first of many children to be born to you. In time, you will become a great and mighty nation upon the earth. However, there shall ever be strife and bloodshed between your seed and the seed of your brothers to come, for as I have said, Abelon will serve as a reminder of your deed and they will seek vengeance on your race." Then the thundering voice was gone, and the Curtain hid Abelon and the stars from view.

# 41 AM

The time came when Awan brought forth her son, and she named him Enokk. He was a strong, healthy boy with a complexion and hair as dark as his father's. Two months after his birth, however, great winds blew across the plains of Nod. These plains were also known as the Dry Lands. The life-giving mist could not produce fruit in Nod because the soil was poor and often blown away by the wind.

One night, powerful, swirling winds blew Cain's tent away, leaving Cain, Awan, the baby, and all of their belongings drenched in the mist that watered the earth. Enokk grew ill because of the night mist. Awan placed her son in one of the large clay pots that they carried with them, so that he could stay warm, dry, and comfortable. As the winds continued over the following weeks, Awan became ill from the night mist as well. She asked her husband to build a new kind of tent so that they would not perish in the land of Nod. Cain then built a tent entirely out of clay and mud, instead of branches and great leaves, so that his family would stay dry and healthy. It thus came to pass that, with the building of the first house, Cain ended his wandering and came to settle in one place. Cain named the settlement Enokk after his son.

# 57 AM

Now Cain was unable to grow crops to feed his family for God had cursed the ground. The soil of the Dry Lands would not yield grain for them. Nevertheless, because the Almighty One is gracious, Cain and Awan were able to find more than enough food to feed their family by foraging for wild berries and grasses in the fields. They learned which plants were good for eating and found that the large, prickly stalks of the Dry Lands held more than enough water to quench their thirst. As their knowledge about living in the Dry Lands grew, so did their family; by the eighteenth year of their exile, Awan had borne Cain seven sons. After Enokk's birth, the twins Jagdan and Tophar were born, followed by Mathtu, Nehobal, Casfal, and Kherethtu.

Even so, no daughters had been born to Cain as of this time. Eve had borne Adam many daughters, Cain's ten sisters, but only two sons by this time, Cain and Abel.

Cain gave little thought to this predicament until his son Enokk began to grow restless in his seventeenth year. Enokk was now a strong young man, the very image in appearance of his father, Cain. He would often wander very far away from the settlement and not return for days. Cain knew that he would need to find his son a wife, but that would mean returning to his father's house, where he was no longer welcome. He decided to send his son to find the tent of Adam in the Great Forest, to ask for a wife from among Cain's sisters. Upon returning from one of his foraging journeys, Enokk met his father standing outside of the house.

"My son," said Cain, "I have seen you wander often and I know that the time has come for you to take a wife. You must go into the Great Forest beyond the mountains and find the tent of Adam. Inquire of him whether he will give you one of my sisters as your wife." Now in those days, people lived for several centuries and aged very slowly. It was not uncommon for marriages to take place between people of different generations. Also, because there were yet few people on the earth, Eloi had not yet pronounced His proscription against marriage between family members.

Enokk replied "Yes, Father, I will search for the tent of Adam, but what if I am sent away? Am I not also exiled with you?"

"Pray to the Almighty that He will have mercy on you. He has said that it is not good for a man to be alone, and He will provide a wife for you. Now go, my son, find a wife and return to us."

Enokk then gathered provisions for his travels: a tent made from the hide of the carcass of a great quake lizard, wooden posts fashioned to hold up the tent, and enough food and water for several days. He then set out to cross the Dry Lands of Nod and the plain beyond it, to come to the Great Forest. Nod was a very treacherous place as food was scarce. Great eater lizards were known to wander there searching for lost and dying animals, even occasionally attacking the stragglers of herds of other great lizards. Although all of Eloi's creatures ate only plants in the beginning, great eaters had adapted to life in the Dry Lands by eating animals as well. In our time, meat-eating animals are far more common, but they were extremely rare in the early years of the old world.

Fortunately, when Enokk ventured out, the land in Nod had brought forth beautiful flowers and other plants, due to gentler winds which had again brought the life-giving mists. Enokk managed to find food to replenish the little he had brought, by using the foraging skills taught to him by his parents. Day after day he continued his journey northwest toward the mountains.

One afternoon, as Enokk was passing through the heart of the Plains of Nod, he began to feel a great trembling in the earth. A great cloud of mist, sand, and dust arose from the south, and Enokk hid in the mouth of a nearby cave to brace for a storm. Cautiously peering out of the cavern's entrance, Enokk saw that the cloud of dust was caused by a stampeding herd of great speed lizards, running as swift as a storm in terrified flight from a great eater. The floor of the cave rumbled as they passed by, and Enokk could hear loud crashes in the cave behind him as rocks fell to the cavern floor. As the last of the herd sped by, Enokk saw of the speed lizards stumble and catch its foot between two rocks.

The great eater was not far behind. It was an enormous monster the height of three men, with powerful hind legs, teeth longer than fingers, and a tail as thick as trees. The creature saw that its prey was trapped and leapt in swiftly for the kill. Turning its head to scan for rivals, the terrible beast caught sight of Enokk's face peering from the cave's narrow entrance. At the sight of him, the monstrous lizard cried a great and terrible roar that put dread into Enokk's heart. The eater left its prey and tramped furiously toward the cave, roaring once more and filling the cavern with its foul breath. The beast then lowered itself at Enokk to devour him, but Enokk grabbed his walking stick and struck the snout of the great eater lizard with all of his might.

The beast let out yet another foul, piercing cry of pain and fury. Its roar was so loud that Enokk fell to the ground. Enokk wounded himself on some sharp rocks near the entrance to the cave when he fell. The monster, smelling Enokk's blood, lowered its head again with its jaws agape, ready to eat him. Just in time, Enokk stood up and jammed his walking staff between the eater's jaws. When the monster shut its jaws to break the staff, the sharp end pierced the great eater's palate, thrusting itself into the creature's brain. Enokk stood frozen in shock as the meat-eating monster thrashed about in the throes of death. When the great eater had ceased moving, and Enokk was sure the beast was dead, he removed its teeth and claws and fashioned them into something to wear around his neck, to commemorate his victory over the terrible creature. He crushed some aromatic herbs he had found on his journey, applied them to his wound, and washed himself in a fresh spring he found in the cave. This spring became known as Enokk's Spring.

When Enokk emerged from the cave, he heard the cry of the trapped speed lizard. He slowly and quietly approached the beast, holding his palms facing upward to show that he was not a threat to the unfortunate creature. Enokk gently patted the great lizard's back and stooped down to inspect the trapped foot. When he released it the beast did not flee, but the great runner looked down at Enokk quizzically. Before he knew what he was doing, Enokk vaulted himself onto the speed lizard's back and told it to take him to the house of Adam.

The following afternoon, Enokk reached the Pass of the Kheruvim where two brightly shining angels met him. The speed lizard stopped in his tracks, Enokk's hair seemed to stand on end, and he was stricken with great fear.

"You are the one whose coming was foretold," said the angel on the left of the pass.

"You alone, of all the descendants of Cain, shall be allowed to pass here. Once your errand is done, do not attempt to return again or you shall die." said the angel on the right.

"Who are you, mighty ones?" asked Enokk, his voice trembling.

"We are the Kheruvim appointed to guard this passage." The first one said. "Do not fear us now, for today you are allowed safe passage." The lizard's feet loosened, and it darted away quickly through the pass, twice almost throwing Enokk from its back as the young man wrapped his arms around the beast's thick, scaly neck.

The rest of his journey passed quickly as Enokk rode the speed lizard through the Great Forest. After passing effortlessly between the dense trees, the great runner stopped at the edge of a clearing, and lowered itself to the ground. Enokk then dismounted, patted the creature's snout, and told it to return to its herd. The creature then stood up, raised its head crest, looked quizzically again at Enokk, then turned and ran back through the woods, moving swiftly with the same effortless ease.

Enokk, gazing upon the clearing before him, noticed a waft of smoke in the distance. As he drew nearer, he saw well-tended fields of grain, and could smell the scent of fresh bread being baked. He knew that this must be none other than the land of Adam, his grandfather. He approached closer still, and saw a large, circular tent of branches and great leaves of the forest, a pasture where sheep were grazing, and beautiful women in the fields tending the sheep and the grain. With the flock of sheep Enokk also saw a large, strong looking man whom he knew must be his grandfather, Adam.

When the women saw him, they did not know what to do or how to greet him.

"It's Cain!" one of them shouted. "He has returned to us."

Adam shook his head. "No, this is not Cain. This is the one Eloi told me was coming, the son of Cain and Awan."

Enokk, trembling with nervousness and the awareness that he was the son of an outcast, began to speak.

"I am Enokk, the son of Cain. My mother, Awan, has brought forth seven sons, of which I am the eldest. Awan has yet to bear Cain any daughters, and because of this my father has sent me here to find for myself a wife. If there is a woman among you who will consent to be my wife, I will take her with me to live with my family. I have traveled far and fought many dangers to reach this place." As Enokk said this, he held up the necklace that he wore made from the teeth of the great eater lizard he had slain. As God had set a ban on taking the lifeblood of any creature, the people gasped in horror at the sight.

"I slew this creature as it attacked me in its unnatural hunger." he said, showing them the wound in his side from its claws. "If I did not slay that beast, it would most surely have finished me. Now I plead before you, Adam, father of my father. I know that my father and his descendants are forever banished from your household, and I do not wish to challenge the will of the Almighty One by remaining here among you. However, I ask that you would grant my humble request to send one of your daughters back with me to my father's house."

Eve was troubled by Enokk's request, and she whispered to her husband.

"My love, we have already lost Abel to bloodshed and Cain and Awan to banishment. Should we do this and lose yet another of our precious children with whom the Creator has blessed us?"

Adam replied, "I feel for their loss no less than you, my love, yet did not Eloi command us to fill the earth? Surely all of us cannot remain here within the refuge of the mountains forever." Adam then turned to Enokk, his brow furrowed in thought. "Last night, I saw the sign of Abelon revealed in the sky, reminding me of the cruel murder of my beloved son, Abel." said Adam, shaking his head sadly. "However, Eloi spoke to me, and said to me to send with you the woman you choose. He also said that neither of you are permitted to return here afterward. The way here will be hidden from you to protect the sanctity of this place."

Enokk thanked Adam, who summoned all ten of his daughters before him. Enokk, having never seen any woman besides his mother, felt strangely uncomfortable. As he looked at each one, Enokk's eye rested on a beautiful young woman with brown skin, flowing chestnut hair, and silver eyes. She was taller than Enokk by the width of three fingers, and Enokk stood still, his eyes transfixed on her.

"I am Neema." she said, meeting his gaze. The young woman smiled at him before lowering her gaze. "I will gladly go with you if you would have me."

Enokk's heart leapt, and he knew that Neema was the reason he had come to Adam's camp. "Yes, come with me Neema, whose beauty surpasses that of the moon."

That evening, Enokk stayed in Adam's home where he ate, cleaned his wound, and rested, for he was very tired from his journey. The following day, Enokk and Neema said farewell to Adam's family, mounted the speed lizard, and after passing through the Great Forest, came to the Pass of the Kheruvim. At the pass, the Kheruvim reminded Enokk that the way would now be hidden from him. When Enokk and Neema had ridden through the pass and looked back, the Kheruva seemed to have grown in stature and brightness. They became dreadful to look upon, and the path that had led them out of the Great Forest had disappeared. They returned to Cain's household where they began a family of their own.

# CHAPTER 2

# THE VILLAGE
## (58 – 122 AM)

### 58 – 74 AM

A year after the marriage of Enokk and Neema, Neema bore her husband twin daughters, Cayra and Seelue. By this time, the mud brick house which Cain had built, where he dwelt with all of his family, grew too small. Enokk left his father's house with Neema and their daughters, and brought them eastward, a morning's walk from the house of Cain. There he built his own house along the fertile river Pishon. Along the Pishon, Enokk was able to plant and grow grain, but his father could still grow none because the ground was cursed as a consequence of his sin in slaying his brother. Enokk, however, often shared the bounty of his fields with his father's household.

Three years after Enokk built his house by the Pishon, Neema bore him a son and named him Irad, meaning strength, for Irad was a very strong child. In the same year Awan bore Cain their first daughter, Eulla, which meant petition. It was then arranged that in the proper time Eulla would become wife to Irad and that the daughters born to Enokk would marry his younger brothers, the twins Jagdan and Tophar.

The little village of Enokk grew rapidly. In the thirty-fifth year since the exile, Cayra and Seelue were wed to Jagdan and Tophar, and they built houses for themselves along the River Pishon. The river was so named because of the abundance of fish living there. One day Mathtu, Cain's fourth son, grew restless and went running along the riverside. In those days men did not tire easily, and when Mathtu finally stopped he realized that he had been running all day and night. He became very hungry and ate of the fruit trees that grew along the side of the river, yet he found that he was still hungry. He then bent down to drink of the water of the river, and he saw the multitude of fish swimming in the river.

As he was drinking from the river, a large, black and red serpent stole down from out of one of the fruit trees and slithered toward him. To Mathtu's amazement, the creature began to speak.

"Mathtu, the fruit of these trees will not satisfy your great hunger. Meat requires meat to live. Catch, kill and eat some of these fish which you see here, and then your hunger will be abated."

Mathtu could not believe his ears. "We are forbidden to take the lifeblood of anything that moves unless we ourselves are in mortal danger! Doing such a thing would make us no better than the eaters, those terrible creatures who thirst after the lifeblood of other beasts. Why do you say such things?" Mathtu asked the serpent.

"Who told you that you might not eat meat?" the snake replied. "This is nothing but a myth invented by your grandfather Adam. All he does is stay in his forest. He wants to reign over everyone with his rules." The serpent scoffed. "You, however, no longer belong to the house of Adam, do you?"

This angered Mathtu, for all of the sons of Cain were resentful of the banishment from the Great Forest, especially since Enokk returned with Neema telling of the great beauty of the household and the lands of Adam. In his fury he shouted at the serpent:

"I am not of the house of Adam nor have I ever belonged to it! I am Mathtu son of Cain. I live in Enokk, the home of Cain. Our house will spread across the earth and we will rule over the house of Adam!"

"Then why do you follow Adam's rules if you are not of his house? Kill and eat of the fish, satisfy your hunger, and then you will have the strength to return home. Otherwise you will not have the strength to return home and you will die."

Tempted by the serpent, Mathtu took a branch from a nearby tree, sharpened it, and stabbed a fish that was swimming in the river. Then, so that he would not be guilty of drinking its lifeblood, he built a fire and cooked the fish. Mathtu ate the fish, and then caught and killed several more before his hunger was satisfied. So although in that age it was still prohibited to eat anything that moved, Mathtu became the first fisherman.

After returning to Enokk, Mathtu spent much of his time gazing into the Pishon and watching the fish swim by. Occasionally, when no one was looking, he would catch and eat one. One day he noticed a leaf floating downstream with ants standing and moving on it. It was then that he had an idea to build a something that could carry him down the river. After pondering the idea in his mind, he brought it before his father and brothers.

"Have you ever noticed how ants, though among the smallest of creatures, have the knowledge to use a leaf or twig to float down the river to other places? We should learn from the wisdom of the ants, and build ourselves something similar that would carry not ants but people. Then we could travel down the river swiftly with little effort."

Cain looked pensive. "Mathtu, your idea has great merit, but the current of the Pishon is very strong. How could anyone return home after journeying down the river? It would be very tiring indeed to carry this floating tent, log, or whatever it is you propose to build all the way back to the village. I advise you to design a method by which you would return such a thing before proceeding further with its construction."

Mathtu was clearly dismayed, but then saw the wisdom in his father's decision. "Very well, Father, I will build something that can both travel down the river and be returned." Then Mathtu went home to think upon the work ahead of him.

## 79 AM

By the fortieth year of the exile, as preparations were being made for the wedding of Irad and Eulla, the men of Enokk had come up with a design for Mathtu's invention. They cut down two tall trees, cut the trees into logs, and fastened the logs together with ropes to form a raft. Then they used carefully crafted wooden shafts which were to be inserted into holes bored into the logs. The shafts had to be perfectly straight and smooth so that they would turn evenly. Many attempts on making the straight, smooth shafts had failed and the by-product was thrown into the fire to be burned. Finally, when the shafts were successfully completed, they were inserted into the logs. Shorter but thicker log segments were then attached which would turn around on the shafts when on land. These functioned as rollers and allowed the raft to be pulled across land on a return voyage with little effort and little damage to the raft. Thus both the boat and the wheel came to be invented by the people of Enokk.

The watercraft was to be tested immediately following the wedding of Irad and Eulla, when the new couple would take it downstream on its first voyage. The preparations for the wedding ceremony began at dawn as the women of the village picked fresh, fragrant flowers that were hung outside of each of the houses in the village. The flowers filled the early morning air with their sweet fragrance. Preparations continued throughout the morning as bread and other food was prepared for the wedding. At noon, all of the people in Enokk assembled by the river. Irad awaited his bride at the bank of the Pishon, standing beside the watercraft in expectation. After a time, Eulla emerged from the ornately decorated doorway of the house of Cain arrayed in the skin of a zebra. By this time, Mathtu had convinced Cain to revoke the taboo of the killing of animals. The zebra skin extended from Eulla's shoulders to her knees. Around her waist was tied a belt woven from vines and around her neck she wore a necklace fashioned from river shells.

Irad looked on in wonder, smiling absurdly from ear to ear, as his bride approached him and kissed him. All of their kinsmen cheered to see them as Irad took Eulla's hand and led her onto the watercraft. He pushed the raft off of the riverbank with a pole, and the new couple waved at the crowd as the watercraft began to drift downstream. Irad removed the belt of vines from around Eulla's waist, throwing it into the Pishon to the further cheers of the people as the watercraft carried them off. This came to be the traditional wedding ritual among the free Cainites for many centuries hence.

"Return swiftly with the watercraft, Irad, but not too soon!" teased his father as the couple drifted away.

Irad and Eulla travelled downstream to a grove of tall trees far down the Pishon, a short distance beyond where Mathtu ate his fish. There they remained for six days, symbolic of the six days in which Eloi had created the heavens and earth and all that was within them. On the seventh day, Irad and Eulla began the long journey home. The return journey should have taken five days, but because they were pulling the raft it took eight days.

When they returned, they were exhausted from pulling, and Eulla's once soft and delicate hands were covered in calluses. Eulla vowed never to travel on the river again, and Irad began coming up with ways to improve the design of Mathtu's watercraft. Although it was possible to pull the craft all the way back to Enokk, a new solution was needed for returning the craft over long distances. Nevertheless, the people of Enokk discovered, as they had each taken turns pulling while the other rested on the craft that a wheeled device was still very useful for moving things around which were too large to carry. Henceforth, carts became commonplace in the village of Enokk, often pulled by aurochs, young great lizards, or other beasts.

# 81 AM

Two years after their wedding, Eulla bore a son, Mahu-Jaol, to Irad. In that same year, Mathtu married Irad's sister, Taurei. Mathtu and Irad had redesigned the watercraft for Mathtu's wedding by attaching a pair of wooden planks to the sides of the craft, each of which narrowed into handles at one end. These planks allowed the watercraft to be returned upstream along the river by the means of rowing. The planks eliminated the need for the cartwheels on the bottom of the raft, making it lighter. The lighter weight of the watercraft enabled it to be carried around dangerous rapids in the Pishon. Mathtu and Taurei found the new design to be a great success, and before long the sons of Cain had built many such rafts by which they traveled up and down the Pishon River. In time, these primitive boats were adapted further by giving them a cup-like shape, which helped prevent them from being overwhelmed by the waters of the river. These were the first true boats.

By the sixty-fifth year of the exile, there were nearly two hundred people living in the village of Enokk. They had learned how to irrigate the land using water diverted from the Pishon, so that more plentiful crops could be produced than the meagre crops of earlier years. They began to use shells and shiny stones, as well as the hides of animals, for trading among themselves. Cain invented a system of weights and measures to be used for trade. With the old law against eating animals abolished, the people of Enokk found more ways of gathering food. When the crops failed, the people of Enokk could fish the Pishon or even hunt the herds of the plains.

Cain, the tribal patriarch, had changed his dwelling from a modest mud-brick hut to a larger, two story brick dwelling as the process of baking bricks with straw had become perfected. On the lower floor of his dwelling was a large hall. This was where important meetings would be held to discuss matters of importance to the village. Here all of the men over the age of forty convened to confer, forming the Council of Elders. In later years, the number of "elders" at these meetings became limited to twenty as the population grew. The reasoning behind this was that the human body had ten fingers and ten toes, and that a ruling body should have no more members than the body has digits. Cain himself was counted separately as the "Mechal", a word meaning "Nose" or "Leader".

By the same year, Mahu-Jaol the son of Irad had come to maturity, wed Shiriei the daughter of Mathtu and Taurei, and had sired his firstborn son, Mathtu-Saol. Mahu-Jaol often sailed downstream in his boat to the grove where abundant fruit could be found and collected. However, although he went further downstream than any of the others who went along the river, he dared not go to the land beyond the grove where hot steam rose from the barren hills on the other side of the Pishon. He feared that there was something wrong about that place — something evil — so he cautioned all travelers to shun the barren hills across the river.

# 123 AM

Mathtu-Saol often journeyed downstream with his father as a child to gather fruit and to fish. Mahu-Jaol had told him expressly not to go beyond the grove to the place where the hot steam arose. When Mathtu-Saol had become a man, he began fishing and gathering fruit down the river alone. Once, after a journey to the grove where he picked fruit, a great curiosity arose in Mathtu-Saol to discover why the forbidden land was so frightening to his father.

He took up the anchor-stone into the boat, and continued downstream where he saw steam rising from the barren hills on the far bank. Mathtu-Saol rowed the boat to the far bank of the river, pulled his boat onto it, and began to climb the hills. When he reached the crest of the hills, he found that the steam arose from a hot lake nestled in among the hills. A huge black and red serpent, longer than a man and with the head of a beast, entered the lake and appeared to beckon him. Upon seeing the creature, a feeling of dread crept into Mathtu-Saol, but without thinking he followed the creature, removed his lizard skins, and dove into the lake.

The water burned terribly! Mathtu-Saol knew that the creature had tricked him and that his father had been right about this place. He leapt out of the lake like an insect out of a burning log and lay on the shore in agony. Mathtu-Saol had been severely burned by the water, and his entire body was in pain. Fearing he would die, he thought of crying out to God, but then he remembered how many animals he had killed, how he had disobeyed his father by coming here, and how he broke his promise not to travel beyond the grove. Also, he belonged to the cursed house of Cain. No, he believed, Eloi would not listen to him.

The vile serpent that had lured him into the water crawled out of the lake unscathed. "Look at you!" it said to Mathtu-Saol. "You've disobeyed your father and received the penalty of death for your action. No one else will come here to save you, even if they hear you cry." The serpent lied. "No one lives here, only I."

"How do you crawl from that lake of fire unharmed?" Mathtu-Saol asked.

The creature laughed. "This lake is my home. I have the power to withstand its heat. If you will do as I ask, you too can have the power to be healed from its effects."

Mathtu-Saol did not trust this creature. Everyone knew that serpents meant evil. Adam and Eve were cast out of the Garden after being tricked by a serpent. Mathtu-Saol began to think of a way to leave. Just as he was about to rise, the creature spoke again.

"Without my help, you will die here by this lake."

Fear and hopelessness overwhelmed Mathtu-Saol at that moment. He stopped straining to stand and asked the serpent, "All right, what would you have me do?"

At Mathtu-Saol's question, the serpent changed its form and became a thick black cloud. "Swear to me that your firstborn son will be mine to do with as I wish. If you swear this oath to me, I will let you live. Otherwise, you will die right here by this lake."

Out of fear and desperation, Mathtu-Saol made his pledge to the loathsome creature hovering before him. "I will do it. My firstborn son will be yours."

The shrouded thing spoke. "Then it is done." The black cloud then dissipated and Mathtu-Saol heard high, screeching, triumphant, mocking laughter. The sound almost deafened him. When the noise had faded away, he looked down at himself to see that the burns were gone and his skin was as normal again, but Mathtu-Saol's son would bear the price of his healing.

# CHAPTER 3

# SONS OF LIGHT AND DARKNESS

## (130 - 187 AM)

## 130 AM

In the ninety-first year of the exile, Mathtu-Saol married Ceemrah, the ninth daughter of Nehobal, fifth son of Cain. In time, she gave birth to a son whom she named Lamekk. On the third day after the child's birth, terrible burns and boils began to appear all over the infant's body. The child became feverish, was in terrible pain, and never stopped crying. Mathtu-Saol then remembered the deal of desperation he had made with the accursed serpent-creature, and he knew that it was time for him to live up to his end of the bargain. He left the village of Enokk in his watercraft and, bringing the infant Lamekk with him, he left for the Lake of Burning.

When he arrived there, he pulled his boat onto the bank, climbed over the hills, and lowered his son into the boiling hot water of the lake. When he did so the entire lake turned as red as blood, but Lamekk was whole. As if out of the depths of the earth, Mathtu-Saol heard the voice of the serpent call out. "Remember, this child is no longer yours. He is mine to do with as I please. The blood in this lake is a testimony that he now belongs to me." In loathing of himself that he had sworn such an oath, but consoled because his son's illness was gone, Mathtu-Saol and the child returned home.

That night, Adam, the father of all men, looked up at the sky and once again saw the curtain of heaven rolled back. He heard the voice of the Almighty speaking to him like thunder, and he was afraid.

"O man, the offences of the sons of Cain grow year by year. Tonight, one of them has entered into an unholy pact with our dark enemy, the serpent Lucifer. A child has been born who shall bring great sorrow to many."

Adam wept as he remembered his own failure to resist the temptation of the serpent over a century before.

"Almighty Creator, what can be done? I have no other son to carry on in the place of righteous Abel. Who will stand against the wickedness of the house of Cain and be the instrument of Your justice on the earth?"

Just as Adam said this, Abelon became visible over the horizon. The voice of the Creator spoke again, "A year from now Eve will give birth to a son. Through his descendants I shall perform My purposes and prevent the sons of Cain from laying waste to the whole earth. Through his line, in the fullness of time, shall come the One who will redeem humanity and the earth from the curse that you have brought upon it."

At the proper time, as the Almighty One had said, Eve gave birth to a son whom she named Seth, meaning granted. God had granted her another son who would not follow the way of Cain. Seth was a strong, healthy, and mirthful baby. On the eighth day after the boy's birth, God told Adam to dedicate this child to Him to counteract the dedication of Lamekk to the serpent. He told Adam to take some olive oil and anoint his son's forehead, hands and feet with the oil. Adam did as the Almighty One had asked, and made a sacrifice of a spotless, male lamb from the flock of his daughter Siara, the shepherdess. As Adam sacrificed the lamb, he prayed for the Creator's blessings on his son's life.

As Seth grew, he became the very image of his slain brother, Abel. He had the same bright red hair as his brother, and the same piercing blue eyes. He brought great joy to his mother, father, and sisters. Adam spent a great deal of his time teaching his new son about the farm, about all of the different plants and animals, and about the Garden from which all people had been banished. He passed all of his knowledge on to Seth, including the story about his two brothers; how one murdered the other, and now lived exiled with his descendants beyond the Dry Lands of Nod far to the southeast of the Great Forest.

When Seth was thirty years old, God appeared to him in a dream. Seth could feel light surrounding him and passing through him. Under the gaze of the Almighty One, Seth knew that all of his thoughts and feelings lay exposed. "Seth, I want you to leave your father's fields and walk north and west to a place that I will show you."

Seth did not know how to reply. All he could say in response was, "I will go with You." He awoke and went to his father. "Eloi appeared to me last night in a dream. He is sending me north and west through the forest. I cannot say for certain for how long I shall be gone."

His mother overheard Seth's words and her heart was filled with amazement. She exclaimed as she entered the room, "Eloi is going to show you the Garden! Only your father and I have ever been in the Forbidden Garden, for it is there that we once lived before we were expelled from it. Be aware of the angel who guards it with a great brand of fire!"

"I will, mother. I am certain that the Almighty One would not call me out only to strike me down. I promise that I will return." Then, after speaking with his mother and father, Seth set out through the Great Forest. The following day he came to a great, brilliant gate made of the whitest stone he had ever seen. As his mother had said, there stood at the entrance a mighty angel wielding what appeared to be a flaming staff. Seth stood amazed in awe and wonder.

"Welcome, son of Adam," the angel addressed him, "I am Michael, a servant of the Almighty. He has told me that you would come here today and that I was to allow you passage into the Forbidden Garden. You may enter here if you wish, but you must not remain here. Know that if you choose to enter this place that you will afterward be filled with a profound, unending yearning to enter here again and look once more upon the beauty of this garden. You will be allowed to enter this place one time only and never again. The choice is yours whether you will enter here now or later." Seth weighed the angel's words in his mind. Although he had seen the great sorrow of losing the Garden in the eyes of his mother and father, he knew that he needed to enter, and see the height from which mankind had fallen.

"I will enter the Garden. I know that I must look upon it and weep. There is something that I must learn about this place."

"Very well," Michael said, "but when the sun is on the western horizon you must be gone from here."

Michael stood back from the gate and it opened. Seth entered into the Forbidden Garden where no man or woman had set foot in one hundred and sixty years. The natural beauty of that sacred place made him want to fall to his knees, but he stood motionless. He marvelled at the brilliant, emerald green of the lush vegetation and fruitful trees. The many and various creatures of the Garden seemed more at peace here than anywhere else Seth had been. Seth reached up and plucked an orange from the overhanging branch of a nearby tree. It was sweeter and more delicious than anything he had ever tasted before, and he felt great vitality course through him as he ate it. He felt strong, and his senses were sharpened.

The colours of the Garden were brighter and more vivid than anything that he had ever seen before in his life. Birds sang together in a chorus that spoke of the majesty and splendour of the Creator. As Seth listened to their song, he could almost make out the words. As he moved further into the Garden, he saw the Fountain of Life. The four great rivers of the earth; the Pishon, the Tigris, the Euphrates and the Gihon, all sprang from this fountain. Seth saw the Tree of Life set upon a great hill, guarded by a ring of angels all about it. As he looked, two of the angels moved aside, making a gap in the ring. The angels bowed as a man dressed in what looked like the whitest wool Seth had ever seen stepped forth from among them, and descended the hill toward Seth. His face was radiant like the sun, and Seth could not look at it without hurting his eyes. He felt the same nakedness that he felt in the dream he had before beginning this journey.

"Rise, son of man." spoke the majestic figure. "Through you and your seed, My purposes will be accomplished on the earth. You will become a mighty nation, exalted above all of your brothers both born and yet to come. From you will come the One who will crush the serpent, avenging the death of your brother, Abel, and forever breaking death's curse. Your brother cries out for justice and I will not withhold My justice."

Seth was perplexed by the figure's last statement. "My God, you speak as if my brother still cries out. Has he not died and been destroyed forever? What does this mean?"

The glorious man spoke, "Though his body is dead in the ground, the spirit of Abel lives. You cannot see him or speak to him because he has crossed over into the Garden of Paradise. The garden in which you stand now is a shadow of the one in Paradise. One day, Seth, you will enter that garden and meet the brother you have never known. For now, be content to know that death is not the end of human existence.

"Know also that there is more to be known than the things that you see with your eyes. This garden, these angels, and I are only visible to you because I have chosen to reveal these things to you. The nature of this invisible world can be seen in the things you see all around you every day. I make many of My secrets known in the things that I have made. I have written My purposes and My plans in the heavens, and if you will listen I will teach you how to understand these things. Then, when I roll back the curtain of heaven, you will lift up your eyes and understand My purposes. To you and your descendants I will make known My purposes for as long as you follow Me and remain faithful to what I have told you. If you abandon Me, you will be cut off and I will raise up another to accomplish My purposes. If you remain faithful to Me, your descendants will never be cut off, and they will surely subdue all nations."

The man, who was none other than God Himself, became even brighter until Seth could neither see nor stand, and again he fell on his face. When he arose, Seth could no longer see the man. Seth then noticed that the sun, which had marked the hour of noon when he had entered the Garden, was now low on the western horizon. Seth immediately remembered the angel's warning, and made his way to the gates of the Garden as fast as his feet would take him. After he had passed through the gates, Seth paused to look behind him. The Garden and its gates were gone, and only Michael was left standing where the Garden had been.

"Seth, you must now go and seek out Cain, your brother." the angel said. "Now that you have seen this place, the time has come for you to make yourself known. The Almighty has many things that He must show you among the Cainites, and you must learn what has become of the people that He has exiled." The angel then vanished.

Seth was greatly disturbed about all that had just transpired. He was unable to sleep, but lay awake all night in the Great Forest. He dreamed of a city high on a mountaintop, of which the radiance was as bright as the sun. There were many towers and great buildings in the city, all fashioned of white stone. The people of the city were joyful in countenance, and were arrayed in clothing of many colours. They all seemed to be living together peacefully. By noon of the following day, Seth had returned to the village of Adam, and told everyone of his experience.

"I am leaving to find my brother, Cain, to find news of him and his people." said Seth. He related some of the story that the Creator had told him. "The seeds have been planted for a terrible battle that will take place in times yet to come. I will not be gone for long; I will return shortly. May Eloi bless you all and care for you until I return."

Seth's favourite sister, Azura, was deeply moved. She had a profound love for her brother. "Must you leave, dear brother?" she asked. "Must you travel alone? Please take me with you, for wherever you go, my heart is there."

Seth replied, "My beloved sister, I promise to you that I shall return shortly. I hold you very close to my heart, but now I must go. Be at peace." Seth mounted his runner lizard, Yehspal, and rode out of the Great Forest, through the pass of the Kheruvim, into the Dry Lands of Nod.

Having lived his entire life in the bounty of the Great Forest, Seth was surprised to see such a desolate wasteland as Nod. Although there were no true deserts in the world before the Flood, few things lived in the Dry Lands. There were sagebrush and grasses, and many herds of animals which passed over this open plain, but no creatures made Nod their permanent home, except for the Cainites. On the third day of his journey, Seth came across the rotting carcass of a great fan-head lizard. It had died of thirst and heat exhaustion as its herd had passed over the plain. The sight and stench of the carcass caused Seth to vomit, and made him anxious to be on his way, despite his own weariness. Se·h then continued his journey eastward.

On the fifth day of his journey, Seth felt that he could no longer continue. His lips were cracked from the lack of water, and his tongue had swollen up to the point where it filled his whole mouth. Yehspal could walk no further, and would often sit down on the ground. It took great effort for Seth to convince the beast to keep moving. Seth finally dismounted Yehspal and led the lizard along by a rope that he had fashioned.

As the sun began to descend from its midday apex, Seth caught sight of a glimmer near the horizon. The previous day, Seth had seen a similar shimmering, but it had disappeared when he approached. Not so this time; soon Seth had left Yehspal and was running toward water. He had reached the Great Lake that lay to the east of Nod. The water was as clear as crystal, and sweet to the taste. Seth had never seen so much water before in his life! This was the lake into which the Pishon River emptied. Seth leapt into the waters of the Great Lake, laughing and splashing and pouring its cool water over his head.

Yehspal found her way to the lake, leaned over its bank, and drank deeply. Seth drank and rested a while along the shore of the lake, and after he had rested felt directed to head south along the coast. He mounted his speed lizard and journeyed southward until he found the mouth of the Pishon. From there, he journeyed south and west along the Pishon toward Enokk.

Now Lamekk the son of Mathtu-Saol had also become a man. He had taken to wife Adah, daughter of Jagdisu-Kaol of the clan of Jagdan. Adah bore Lamekk twin sons, Jabal and Jubal. In his youth, Lamekk would often go hunting for days at a time in the marshes downstream from the growing town of Enokk. On one of these hunting trips, while hiding in the reeds pursuing a herd of zebra, Lamekk saw Zillah the daughter of Tophar-Cain bathing in the Pishon. Zillah was very beautiful, and when Lamekk saw her he leapt from the reeds and took her.

For several weeks afterward, Zillah would not speak to anyone. She would not let anyone touch her, and would pull back in fear from anyone who reached out to her. She no longer went to bathe at all, let alone in the river, and she became wild and mute like a beast. In time, it became known in Enokk that Zillah was with child. As she was not married and had shown no prior interest in any men of the town, there arose a great confusion over who could possibly be the father of this child. No one would admit to the charge, and when questioned, Zillah could still say nothing at all. She would simply scream and run off.

One day, Zillah was in the millet fields with Machdal-Cain, her brother, and Lamekk approached. As Zillah went about her chores, Lamekk the Accursed stood at a distance and watched like a hungry wolf watches its prey before it comes in for the kill. When Zillah saw Lamekk, she flew into an uncontrollable rage. She began to growl, bearing her teeth menacingly like a wild animal, and flailing her arms in front of her. She curled her fingers into talons like those of an eagle, and she ran at Lamekk to attack him. Lamekk, startled, fled through the reeds. Seeing him flee, Machdal-Cain called to his sister. When Machdal-Cain saw the fury in his sister's eyes, he knew that Lamekk was responsible and that he was the father of Zillah's unborn child.

When Machdal-Cain told his mother, Rimlah, what had happened, Rimlah went with her son and daughter to the Great Hall of Cain, where Tophar-Cain, her husband, sat on the Council of the Twenty-and-One. Rimlah entered the Great Hall with a grim countenance and boldly addressed the Council.

"I, Rimlah, wife of Tophar-Cain, come to raise a grievance. My daughter, Zillah, was attacked and subdued some time ago by Lamekk son of Mathtu-Saol of the clan of Enokk. Now, she is with child and without a husband. I demand recompense for the loss of honour that Zillah, and indeed our whole family, has suffered because of this."

Rimlah's grievance had the Council in an uproar. Each councillor turned to his neighbour inquiring as to what should be done. This was the most serious crime yet to have occurred in Enokk, and the suspected perpetrator was in the line of the Firstborn! This matter could not be taken lightly, as having the blood of Firstborn Lamekk had been granted the most fertile and most extensive land in the village. After much discussion, Cain, robed in the skins of a great eater overlaid with the pelt of a dagger lion, arose and addressed the plaintiff.

"Because of the seriousness of this crime, the status of the accused, and because the girl, Zillah, has lost her sense and speech, we will bring the accused here tomorrow morning that we may address this matter further. Then, we shall hear the case of Rimlah, the wife of Tophar-Cain."

Tophar-Cain felt anger rising within him, but he dared not question the Mechal who held the power to expel him from the Council and evict him from his land. He would wait until tomorrow for vengeance against his family's dishonour. It was on this same day that Seth reached the mouth of the Pishon.

The following morning, Lamekk was brought before the Council of the Twenty-and-One. When Zillah, who had also been summoned, descried the face of her arrogant assailant, she leapt into a rage, running toward Lamekk to strike him. Mathtu and Casfal-Daol, two Council members, had to restrain her as she continued to struggle against them. She reached out, flailing her arms and curling her fingers, as she snarled and growled furiously at Lamekk like a wild beast.

Meanwhile, Lamekk's father Mathtu-Saol, who was a permanent Council member because of the right of Firstborn, felt profound guilt dragging down upon his spirit. He knew that his son was responsible for this atrocity. He knew the depths of Lamekk's evil that arose from the pact that he himself had made with the serpent. He knew that Zillah had become mad because of this same evil. At that moment, having pity on his son's victim, Mathtu-Saol felt compelled to testify against his own son.

Cain stood and called for order. "What is the meaning of so much hatred? Could this be nothing more than a ploy by the house of Tophar-Cain to extort wealth from my heirs?"

Tophar-Cain rose in anger at the patriarch's words. "Mechal, that is not true! I have served you loyally for many years! All that I have done has been for the good of our people. I only desire to see justice done and this grave dishonour removed from my household!"

No longer able to contain his guilt, Mathtu-Saol rose to his feet.

"I believe that the accusations against my son are true. I believe that he subdued the woman, Zillah, and is responsible for her present state. I made a dark covenant with the serpent before Lamekk was born. Because of this regrettable pact, he has become an evil man, doing everything for his own interests alone. I, Mathtu-Saol, before this Council, hereby renounce Lamekk as my son and remove from him the right of Firstborn. This is my final act as a member of this Council. Because of my own responsibility in this matter, I decline my seat in the Council. I have forfeited both my rights in the line of Firstborn and my right to this Council seat."

The Council was stone silent. Cain, the Mechal of the Council, sat thoughtfully before replying. "That is acceptable, Mathtu-Saol." he said gravely. "You have acted honourably in this matter. You may leave when you wish. Your brother, Irad-Jaol, will take your seat in the Council."

A somewhat more relaxed Tophar-Cain arose to speak once more. "Mechal, I realize that I have angered you, and for that I am sorry. However, this action does not absolve my family's dishonour. Zillah, my daughter, is with child, and she has no husband."

"There is nothing that can be done." replied the patriarch. "The perpetrator already has a wife and so may not take another. That is not the way of things."

Kashir-Ibal of the clan of Mathtu asked to speak. "Mechal, what do you mean that it is not the way of things? We know that no man has ever had more than one wife, but why? What difference would it make? Who was it that said a man may have but one wife?"

Cain was in sombre reflection. "It was my father, many years ago, when I was wed to Awan. He said that the Maker had ordained that one man and one woman were to come together and begin a family. It was so ordained that man would be fruitful, multiply, and fill the earth."

Kashir-Ibal spoke once more. "With respect, Mechal, the logic of the Maker appears flawed to me. Would men not multiply faster if they had more wives? Remember that these rules that you follow come from the same Maker that cursed the ground beneath our feet. As for your father, how many more sons has he produced? All the land should now be filled with villages such as ours. I recommend that we give Zillah to Lamekk as a second wife, and thus restore honour to the house of Tophar-Cain."

A look of resignation passed over Cain's face, but it soon gave way to a look of resolute vision. As he spoke, his voice rose with every sentence. "Kashir-Ibal, what you have said makes sense. The girl Zillah, daughter of Tophar-Cain, shall be wed to Lamekk, the son of Mathtu-Saol. Indeed, we must not allow ourselves to be led by the old rules of the house of Adam. As Kashir-Ibal has observed, where are the other sons of Adam? Are there any that would contest our mastery over the earth? My people, we shall be the ones who shall carry on the mandate to fill the earth where Adam has failed, and we shall do so in any way we see fit."

As Cain finished speaking, a tumult arose at the entrance of the Great Hall. Those gathered near the entrance stepped aside to allow the passage of a fair-skinned man with fiery red hair and dressed in a robe of brilliant white wool. The Cainites had never before seen white wool or a fair-skinned person, and they drew back as the man moved to the centre of the Great Hall. When he looked at Cain, the proud and haughty patriarch fell to his knees and covered his face with his hands.

"Abel, my brother, have mercy on me!" he sobbed pitifully. "Please do not repay me in kind for striking you down on that dreadful day so long ago. Why have you come? What do you want from me?"

Seth looked at the brother whom he had never met and put together the puzzling words of Cain. His voice was gentle, yet strong. "You are my brother, Cain the Exile, but I am not Abel whom you killed. I am Seth, the son of Adam, and I was given birth to receive Abel's inheritance and take his place on the earth. I have come to learn of you and your people, and to bring news of you and your village to our parents, sisters, and brothers."

Cain was dumbfounded. Before he could collect his thoughts, he addressed the brother he had never met. "This is our village, Enokk, so named after my firstborn son. This is where I settled with Awan after wandering through the Dry Lands of Nod. Until this day, I had known nothing of your existence. I do not understand your purpose here, brother, but I ask that you would spare me and my people. I ask that my tribe and yours may live at peace."

"I have no tribe." Seth replied.

Relief followed by a subtle grin came upon Cain's face as he realized that not only was Seth not as powerful as he seemed, not only was Seth alone, but that Cain could turn this situation to his advantage. "Then you come to seek a wife, brother?" he asked.

"No, Cain, I have not yet been released to take a wife." he said firmly, but gently. "I have only come to meet with you, learn about your people, and see how they live."

Lamekk had been listening, and he spoke up. "You have no business here. You think that you are better than us. If you and I stood man to man, I would kill you."

Seth appeared to grow taller and brighter, looking Lamekk straight in the eye. The wicked man seemed to grow smaller. With a commanding voice he addressed Lamekk. "You would add to your inherited curse by killing yet another son of Adam?" Lamekk appeared surprised and shaken, and spoke no more.

Seth turned quickly to face Cain. "I see that murder still lurks within the hearts of your wicked descendants, Cain. Because of this threat against my life, the judgement of Eloi has come upon you. He demands life for life for my murdered brother. He has been slow to anger, but now this very night one of your own people will be struck dead. This will not be by my hand; Eloi Himself will demand his life for Abel's. Also, that you may remember my visit; know that this man who has threatened me will one day be exiled from this village. He will be an exile from the Exiled, and his name shall be accursed. Furthermore, it will be you, Cain, who will exile this wicked man."

Cain then abruptly dismissed the Council and sent Seth away, telling Seth that he would speak to him the following day. At sunset, Seth set up his tent far outside the village and went to sleep. In the middle of the night, when all of Enokk slept, Kashir-Ibal, the woodcarver of Enokk, disguised himself in a wooden mask. Under the cover of darkness, Kashir-Ibal stole away to Seth's tent to kill him. As he approached the tent, Kashir-Ibal suddenly burst into flame. His body was burnt to a heap of ashes, and only the wooden mask that he had worn remained untouched. At daybreak on the following morning, one of the village farmers had gone to wake Seth to speak with him. When the farmer saw the mask lying by the heap of ashes, he let out a sharp cry of terror. Seth awoke suddenly and arose to find out what the noise was about.

"What happened?" asked Seth as he emerged from his tent. The farmer was speechless and had a look of dread on his face. "What has caused you to fear?" Seth asked the man. The farmer gestured to the heap of ashes.

"The...the woodcarver...he has been reduced to ashes, all but for his mask. I was in his shop the other day when I saw this mask and overheard him talk of his plan to kill you. I came to see if you had survived, and I see that Kashir-Ibal has been destroyed. What have you brought upon us?" the farmer pleaded.

"I have brought nothing upon you." Seth replied stoically. "This man brought death upon himself by seeking the death of another. Eloi, the Creator, killed him in retribution for the death of righteous Abel, whose blood still cries out from the earth." Seth looked at the ashes thoughtfully; wondering how much blood was yet to be shed on the earth. He then turned to the farmer. "I should arise now and speak with my brother. Will you take me to him?"

The farmer nodded and began walking toward the village. Seth followed the farmer to Cain's dwelling where Cain was eating breakfast with Awan and their younger children who had not yet reached adulthood. Cain saw his brother standing at the doorway and beckoned him to enter.

"We have much to talk about, brother. One hundred and twenty years have passed since the Exile, and no one has heard tell of the house of Adam since my eldest son, Enokk, returned from there with Neema. One hundred and three years have passed since the wedding of Enokk and Neema. Five new generations of my descendants have come since that time. What things have changed in the house of Adam, brother?"

Seth thought for a moment before speaking, "We have learned to store food in earthen vessels in order to keep it fresh longer, and to keep the animals from eating it. We use the wool of sheep to make our clothing, and have learned how to ride on the backs of runners, such as the one your son, Enokk, rode to find our sister, Neema, long before I was born. We also use oxen to help plough our farms. Six more sons have been born to Adam after me, and the number of people living in the tents of Adam is twenty-five. Needless to say, however, that your descendants are far more numerous.

We have also learned to make instruments and to sing and play music as the angels do. Whenever the curtain of heaven rolls back on special nights, when we see the stars, we gather together and sing songs of when Eloi made the world. When we see Abelon in the sky, we weep for our lost brother." Cain felt a sharp pain in his spirit at this statement. "Otherwise, life carries on from day to day, and change is slow. Things go on as they always have."

"For us, much has changed." replied Cain. "We live in these houses of clay. We travel up and down the Pishon in boats. When we need to carry heavy objects over long distances, we use carts drawn by animals. My people number roughly two thousand, Seth, and we no longer regard our father's rule of sparing the lives of beasts. As you see, we regularly wear the hides of animals, and many of my people regularly eat the flesh of animals." Seth's stomach turned at the mental image that this portrayed.

"We aim to fill the earth and subdue it, brother!" said Cain, who held up his half-eaten cob of corn, and shook it at Seth to drive his point home. "This is the duty of all men, as our father must have told you. Now, this compels me to ask you what you have done in this regard, brother. Why have you not yet taken a wife? Why do only twenty-five people live in Adam's household?"

"I am the first son born since Abel, brought into the world to carry the legacy that would have been his. One day, I shall marry and raise a tribe of my own, but as I have told you, I have not yet been released to take unto myself a wife. I am but thirty years of age, and there are many more things that I must learn before I am ready. I shall know the time when it comes, just as one knows when a harvest of fruit is ripe to be picked. Dorro, the next son of Adam and Eve born after me, has taken our sister Bilah to wife this past spring, and his was the first family to establish a new tent and a new camp, without the stigma of exile. Each of my younger brothers and I intend to build our own separate camps, and thus begin the long task of spreading across the earth. You, Cain, have many times over the number of people in Adam's tent, yet you all live in one place. As for me, as I have said, I must wait for a sign before I can take a wife, but when I do, I will go forth from our father's house to build a new village."

"How will you know this sign, brother? What will it be?"

"The Almighty will reveal to me the proper time. He speaks to me through the stars of times and seasons in His purposes. It was He who sent me here to tell you that one of your descendants will rise up and take your life. This man will be his own law, ruling over all the people of this town, bringing to them great sorrow. They will be forced to work, not for themselves, but for this lawless and accursed one who will bring death upon all who defy him. He will rule by fear and oppression, and this town of yours shall then be known to my people as Turnienquor, the City of Woe. Nevertheless, many of your people will escape from here, and their descendants will build great cities. The story of your people will be one of woe, brother, but in His mercy Eloi has pledged that the rule of this lawless man will never be complete and that it will also end in violence."

"Why are you telling me this?" Cain replied. "What have I to gain from this knowledge?"

"All knowledge brings wisdom to those who apply it." Seth answered placidly. "I offer you wisdom about how to prevent a terrible disaster, but it is your choice what you will do with it. There is nothing else that I may tell you at this time. I must return home, but I will come again when ten years have passed, and at that time the traitor will be revealed to you."

"I don't understand what you mean, Seth." answered Cain, his confusion turning to anger. "Since you arrived in my village, you have brought nothing but evil on my people. Perhaps I should have allowed Lamekk to kill you yesterday at the Council meeting."

Seth stood tall, and his voice seemed to deepen. "I see that you are foolish enough to add to the curse already upon you, so I will not give you the opportunity. I now take my leave of you and your people, Cain, but I shall return when the appointed time comes. Farewell, brother."

Seth turned and walked out of Cain's house, leaving Cain a seething mass of anger, an anger which served solely to cover over the fear of what he knew would come to pass.

# 170 AM

Ten years passed in the town of Enokk. Lamekk had wed Zillah who had borne him a strong son, Tubal-Cain, and a beautiful daughter, Naamah. Zillah became Lamekk's favourite wife, and her children were treated better than Adah's twin sons, Jabal and Jubal. Zillah had regained her speech, and began to love her husband even though her family had never forgiven Lamekk for what he had done to her. Machdal-Cain in particular hated Lamekk and one could see the smouldering rage in the eyes of Zillah's brother whenever her husband came near him.

One day, as the townspeople were trading in the marketplace, Machdal-Cain was at his booth in the market square as was his daily custom. There he traded various kinds of fruit grown on the family farm for beads, skins, and grain. Lamekk happened by and, seeing the fruit vendor, came and grabbed some figs out of Machdal-Cain's basket. Lamekk began to eat them right in front of the vendor's face without payment. When Machdal-Cain stood up to confront his belligerent brother-in-law, Lamekk lazily tossed a fig in Machdal-Cain's eye. Infuriated, Machdal-Cain took up a beam of wood lying nearby and swung it hard at Lamekk's legs, knocking him to the ground and injuring him. Lamekk then grabbed Machdal-Cain by the leg and pulled him to the ground. He then took his flaying knife and slit the throat of his brother-in-law. When the other people in the market saw what had happened, they began to panic. Men were shouting and women and children were screaming. Lamekk had been hit badly in his left leg, but he got up, with no thought of what he had just done, went his way, and returned home.

When Lamekk arrived at his house, he summoned his wives. "Adah and Zillah, listen to me." he began. "I have killed a man for wounding me. Now if Cain is avenged seven times, then I, Lamekk, will be avenged seventy-seven times." From that day forward, Lamekk son of Mathtu-Saol walked with a limp in his left leg.

The following day, Lamekk was summoned once more for trial before the Twenty-and-One. News had spread rapidly of the bloody deed done in the marketplace the previous afternoon. Many council members, led by Tophar-Cain, moved that Lamekk should be put to death. Others, led by Lamekk's uncle Irad-Jaol, moved that Lamekk be permanently banished from the town of Enokk. The sentence of exile was carried, and Cain decreed that Lamekk should never again set foot within sight of Enokk, or he would surely be put to death. A large boat would be built to carry Lamekk's family and all of their belongings down the Pishon. Sorn, of the clan of Mathtu, would accompany the exiles to ensure that the boat was completely destroyed once it had reached its destination. He would then return to Enokk by foot.

Several days later, after the boat had been completed and was put into the river to be loaded, a woman of the clan of Jagdan saw a man on a runner lizard. He was approaching from the north, following the river downstream. When Cain heard of this, he went to the northern part of town along the banks of the Pishon to see for himself who it was. He recognized the man by his white woollen robe and fiery red hair.

"It is Seth. He has returned as he said." Cain then quickly returned to the dock just as the boat was being boarded. Lamekk paused on the dock and looked Cain right in the eye. It was a look of such hatred that Cain never forgot it for the rest of his days. He now knew the identity of the murderer was in Seth's prophecy."

Seth came to the dock just as the boat was about to disappear around a northward bend in the river.

"Brother, I have returned as I promised. Who is that who leaves on a journey?" he said, seeing the boat disappear around the bend.

"That is Lamekk and his household. Lamekk took the life of the brother of his second wife, so I have now exiled him from this town just as I was exiled from the Great Forest. It has happened just as you said. I also know that Lamekk is the one who will take my life. What must I do so that my people are not all under his rule when he returns?"

"All of your eggs are in one nest, Cain." Seth answered. "The egg-eater will come, and all of your young will be destroyed. However, if you build other nests, these will survive. You must seek the meaning of this riddle, my brother, for in it hides the secret to the survival of your people."

"Indeed, brother, your predictions are true, but you speak nonsense with your words of nests and egg eaters." Cain grew angry. "Do I seem no more to you than a great lizard? Speak more plainly or you shall lose your tongue!"

Seth replied calmly, "If you would listen, you would understand. You do not listen because you hate me. You hate me because you fear me. You fear me because I have been sent by Eloi who holds the lives of all in His hands. Because you do not listen to Him, you do not understand me." Seth turned back toward the north. "I must leave again, and I will not return to this place. You will see not see me again, my brother. May you be wise with the time that you have left, for when that time has gone you will reap whatever you have sown." Seth then left toward the east, and never again set foot in Enokk.

# 187 AM

Lamekk's family settled in the valley just beyond the Burning Lake, not far from the place where the Pishon emptied into the Great Lake. Lamekk named the place Shaol, meaning destruction, declaring that he would destroy anyone who attempted to come there without his permission. During these years in exile, the hatred in Lamekk's heart toward Cain had grown. No one ever came to or left Shaol except when Adah's twin sons, Jabal and Jubal, left for Enokk to find wives. Afterwards, they returned to Shaol. Tubal-Cain had remained in Shaol and married his sister, Naamah.

Naamah was a very beautiful young woman, as was her mother, but she was cursed because she was the daughter of Lamekk. Because of the curse passed to her from her father, Naamah could bear her brother no children. One day Naamah was out in the field planting seeds when she saw a figure dressed in the black skin of a panther approaching. Naamah knew that if her father saw the man he would kill him, so she went to him. She thought that the man looked like Sorn and, after all, Sorn was the only person outside of Shaol who knew the location of Lamekk's settlement.

"Sorn!" she said. "You've come back, but why? What are you doing here? My father will kill you if he finds you."

"I have come for you, Naamah." said the man in a deep and sinister voice that was not Sorn's. Naamah recognized that voice from nightmares she had had as a child. Whenever she had heard it, it had terrified her, and she would wake up shaking with fear. As the man came closer, a feeling of absolute dread overtook Naamah.

"I have been waiting for you and watching you for many years as I have travelled about through the earth. I have sworn that you would be mine, and your father's master and mine has given you to me."

"No!" cried Naamah. "You are terror given form! Someone help me!" But no one was there to hear Naamah's scream. The dark figure vanished, and were anyone there to see, Naamah would have appeared to float across the field, carried by the invisible terror.

She spoke little for weeks after her return. One day, when Tubal-Cain had returned home from hunting the evening's meal, Naamah had news.

"Tubal-Cain, I am with child." she said.

Tubal-Cain's face broke out first into disbelief, and then joy as he dropped the freshly killed deer and ran and embraced Naamah. "At last! Praise to the powers of heaven, I will be a father!" he shouted, spinning Naamah around in his arms. His smile broke straight across his face, as he was overjoyed that he would finally be a father. However, when Tubal-Cain went to sleep that night, he had a dreadful dream. In the dream, Naamah gave birth to a terrible monster that breathed fire and consumed everything in its path. He heard a voice speak:

"The child is not yours, son of Lamekk, and never will be yours. He is mine, just as you and all of your father's family are mine and will always belong to me. He will be a great and terrible warrior who will destroy all who cross his path." Tubal-Cain then saw the terrible creature turn around and stare him in the face. The creature had the cold, dark eyes of his father. Then the creature breathed fire at him, and Tubal-Cain awoke from the dream trembling.

# CHAPTER 4

# THE USURPATION
## (192 AM – 1 EC)

## 192 AM

Tubal- Cain became a great hunter, and he was skilled in the making of weapons for the hunt. He had discovered that some of the rocks he placed around his hunting fires would become soft and melt when heated in a very hot fire. After years of experimenting, Tubal-Cain found that these soft, semi-molten rocks could be shaped into far better hunting tools than anything yet used. Thus, Tubal-Cain became the first to practice metalworking, and made many sorts of things out of copper, silver, and gold. He also discovered bronze by alloying copper with tin.

Now Tubal-Cain's son (or the son he believed was his) was named Hishirash. The boy grew very rapidly in mind and body, and at the age of five was already the size of a boy twice his age. He was also wild and uncontrollable, bringing much anger to his father and much grief to his mother. Lamekk, however, adored the boy and saw in him a way to overthrow the rule of Cain. He would often take his abominable grandson hunting with him, where he would bring down even the most deadly of game animals, the great eater lizards.

By this time, Cain had deciphered Seth's riddle of the nest, and had sent out his sons to build new cities. Enokk, which remained the largest city, was kept by the tribe of its namesake, Cain's eldest son. To the west, upstream along the River Pishon, Jagdan and Kherethtu founded the twin cities of Niragadan and Kheropheth. Northward on the coast of the Great Lake and in the sight of Mount Threthor, Mathtusekh was founded by Mathtu. Rethobal was founded by Nehobal still further north at the mouth of the Gihon where it emptied into the Great Lake. Following upstream along the Gihon lay the cities of Barudaol, founded by Tophar, and Casmithri which was founded by Casfal, built further upstream from and to the west of Barudaol. Thus were the seven largest tribes of the Cainite nation spread through the Pishon and Gihon valleys and along the western coast of the Great Lake.

# 214 AM

Hishirash had reached the height of four cubits, that of a full-grown man, by the age of eight. At age twelve, he stood six cubits tall. At twenty-one, he rose to the height eight cubits and continued to grow taller. Naamah bore other sons and daughters with the same traits of gigantism, brilliant intelligence, and diabolical ruthlessness as Hishirash. Lamekk began to prepare his grandsons for the eventual assault on Enokk. Hishirash designed all manners of weapons and armour from the bronze metal that his father had invented.

On the day that Hishirash and his sister-wife Ichsha had their firstborn child, the first of a second generation of Giants, a son named Gorgondish, Lamekk called his clan together for a family meeting of sorts. "We are growing in numbers and in strength, my people. We have sired a new race, the race of Giants, a race that will be rulers over all that they see and will destroy all those who oppose them. I tell you that one day soon, when our might is sufficient, we will return to Enokk from our exile. From that city we shall rule the world!"

At this, all of the Giants let out a terrible shout. A look of fierce determination combined with a lust for battle was on all their grim faces. They thirsted for blood, for revenge on the exile imposed on their clan, and for the day when they would rule over the lesser, small-minded race of mankind. Those of the households of Jabal and Jubal, the sons of Adah, trembled as they foresaw a dismal future in a world ruled by such as these.

# 1 EC

When Gorgondish had reached the age of sixteen, the Giants built three long, wooden ships to carry the warriors of the clan of Lamekk up the

Pishon to take the city of Enokk. The ships were to be propelled by the warriors of each ship rowing oars together as a unit. Lamekk demanded that all men of fighting age, numbering eleven Giants and twenty-five ordinary men, were to go into battle. After the grim warriors had sharpened their weapons of war and put on their armour, they departed from Shaol to conquer the city of Enokk. When Lamekk's ships reached the city, the people there did nothing but stand still and stare as men as tall as trees came forth from the river. Lamekk stood on the tallest mast of the lead ship and shouted to the townspeople. "Prepare for battle, all you sons of Cain. Lamekk has returned from exile to exact his revenge. Come forth, Cain the proud. Come and meet your destiny."

The Cainites were taken by surprise as the Giants began indiscriminately slaughtering all whom they could see, as war had yet been unknown in the world. The men of Enokk finally began to organize and fight back, but the superior size, armour, and weaponry of the warriors from Shaol were no match for them, even with all of their numbers. Gruogh, the least of the Giants, slew twenty men himself, and was the only one of the terrible race to be slain in battle that day. As he stood by the largest tree in the city, fighting off the unready and ill-equipped men of Enokk like swatting at flies, a small number of men came behind him and felled that great tree. It hit Gruogh square in the back of the head where he stood, and he fell to the ground and died, crushing three men underneath him as he fell.

Hishirash broke into the Great Hall where he found Cain hiding. He broke the patriarch's legs and dragged the astonished Mechal before Lamekk, laying him before the invader. Lamekk greeted his ancestor and former ruler with bitter contempt. "What has become of the mighty father of our race?" he shouted to all who could hear. "He has become like a cricket, one that buries himself in the ground, so that the burning sun will not find him. The Mechal of the Council of the Twenty-and-One now kneels before the man whom he exiled."

Cain protested at this. "You are a usurper, Lamekk. You are pure evil and a rebel with no law but your own. Do you think that my people will long endure your rule without rising up against you? And as for me, I kneel only because my legs are broken. I will never serve you." Cain whipped out a stone dagger that he plunged into the knee of Lamekk's bad leg. The usurper shrieked as he stumbled, and grabbed the Mechal by the hair as Hishirash held back Cain's arms.

Lamekk stood glaring at Cain with burning hatred. "You are right when you say you will not serve under me, Cain." said Lamekk. He paused to watch the expression change on Cain's face. "You will not live long enough." He then slit Cain's throat with his short sword and Hishirash then removed the patriarch's head. Lamekk climbed to the top of the Great Hall and lifted up the severed head of Cain. "Behold the head of the patriarch, Cain." he shouted to the men fighting in the streets below. "Today, I have killed him, and I proclaim myself your king. As for the Council, it is dispensed with and is no more, for I shall be the council. Anyone who disobeys me will suffer the fate of their father, Cain, and their bodies shall be fed to the beasts."

Every man, woman, and child who heard the terrible boasts of Lamekk cowered in fear. Each one who lived after that first terrible battle vowed to serve him, even Enokk the eldest son of Cain. Enokk, however, obeyed with his mouth but made plans in his mind. Later, he fled to the city of Rethobal with Neema and their youngest children. There he gave council to Nehobal his brother. Lamekk searched for him but did not find him. Lamekk greatly oppressed all who lived in the city, and it came to pass that the city of Enokk became known as Turnienquor - the City of Woe. Lamekk ruled like a terrible, wrathful god; becoming a god in the eyes of his hapless subjects, one who must be feared and appeased in any way demanded.

Even in the midst of the most terrible bloodshed the world had yet known, as war made its first appearance in a world that has seen no end to war, Almighty God had a plan to redeem mankind. Seth yet dwelt in the tents of Adam, and he had reached the age of one hundred years. On a night when the mists had rolled back to reveal the heavens, Seth saw seven bright stars and several lesser ones that together formed the shape of a Giant. Seth saw that the star Abelon was above the Giant, out of its grasp. The thundering yet melodic voice of the Almighty Creator then came to Seth.

"Seth, son of Adam, I have created you in the place of your brother who was slain. All that would have been his will be yours, for like Abel, you have done what is right and honourable in My sight. I will protect you all of your days, and no enemy will be able to touch you. Although Giants may come against you, you will elude their grasp. I will make you into a mighty nation, and from your descendants shall come the One who will redeem the world from the curse."

Notes of sorrow entered the music of the voice of the Creator of song as He spoke again. "I hear the cries of those who have been slain in the city of Enokk Turnienquor. My hand now moves to raise up a nation far greater than that of the Cainites. This will be a nation greater not in number, but in wisdom, in understanding, in fortitude, in justice, and in righteousness. This nation will have My favour forever and will be the defenders of all creatures great and small.

"Therefore, I now grant you your heart's desire; the time has come to take your beloved sister, Azura, as your bride. In time she will bear you a son, and you shall name him Enos, just as Awan bore Enokk to Cain. I will bring you and your bride, and any who will follow you, to a great mountain where you shall build a glorious city. In this city, after the birth of Enos, people will call upon Me. I will hear them, and from that city I will frustrate the plans of the enemy of mankind who is at work in the hearts of Lamekk and his accursed offspring."

After this revelation, Seth stood still with his gaze turned heavenward. For two nights and a day he did not move from where he stood. It appeared as if he had turned to stone. A look of pure joy rested on his countenance. Then, on the following day, the Almighty Creator moved the heart of Azura to awaken Seth from his trance with a song of such intricate, ethereal melody that an angel must have taught that it to her. As she sang, Azura took the hands of her beloved brother in her own and led him to Adam's tent. There, Seth ate and slept, but he could not yet speak for two more days. Whenever he opened his mouth to speak, exuberant laughter or loud whoops of joy burst forth from his lips. Azura watched her dearest brother with concern, wondering what strange thing had happened to him.

When Seth finally regained his ability to speak, he sought his father, Adam.

"Father, the Creator has revealed His purpose to me. It is time for me to take Azura as my wife, to leave the Great Forest, and to build a city for future generations. The Almighty One is to make of us a great nation."

Adam smiled broadly and embraced Seth. He said to his favourite son, "I shall send you with my deepest blessing. Any of your brothers and sisters who wish to go shall also be blessed to join you in your journey, to help bring forth the purposes of Eloi. Sadly, I am constrained to remain here, and cannot look upon your city, very fair though it shall become. Your mother and I have sinned greatly, and must stay hidden here in the Great Forest. However, let this be a time of celebration! Let us bring grain from the storehouses and food from the fields and have a feast as we celebrate your wedding!"

The wedding of Seth and Azura was filled with great excitement and jubilation. All of the people of the village of Siaghlamh were arrayed in dazzling blues, greens, whites, pinks, and yellows. They sang songs of great, overflowing joy, as they sang of the day when a descendant of Seth and Azura would redeem the earth from the curse incurred by the fall in the Forbidden Garden. They danced and made music on wooden instruments. All of the celebrations of the Cainites appeared dull, ugly, and awkward in comparison to this grand event. Six sons and six daughters of Adam and Eve joined them in the ceremony, making what was to be one wedding into seven.

Everyone in the village stopped working for the day to attend the celebration. In the middle of the village square, a banquet table was made ready, covered with fresh fruit and vegetables of every kind. The scent of freshly baked bread seemed to permeate the atmosphere. Everyone present, all of the sons and daughters of Adam and Eve who yet lived in Siaghlamh, and the children and grandchildren born to them, came in turn and blessed Seth and Azura. Even the birds in the trees rejoiced on this day, and the beasts of the Forest came to watch the ceremony (and undoubtedly to eat some of the sumptuous food that had been prepared).

When night fell, the curtain of heaven rolled back, and the celebrants sang joyfully underneath the stars. There was such singing as had never been heard since the Divine Song that had brought all things into being. As they were singing, a flock of great winged lizards landed in the midst of those assembled in the village square and sat placidly on the ground. Seth, Azura, and the twelve others who had been married that day climbed upon the backs of the magnificent beasts. The winged lizards then arose high into the night sky, carrying the seven couples eastward.

They travelled until daybreak, when Seth descried a great mountain with a summit so high that it pierced the clouds. This was Mount Threthor, the chief and easternmost of the Kheruva Mountains. The flying lizards landed upon a plateau on the top of the mountain. On the plateau was a blue lake as clear as crystal. Forests and fields of flowers covered the plateau, surrounding the lake. Mighty Mount Threthor thus became the site where the most glorious of cities would be built - Lhiosquor, the City of Light.

# THE CITY OF LIGHT
## (5 – 206 EC)

The name of Lhiosquor brings to mind to all hearers all that was good and noble of the old world while good still remained in it. The Fourteen Founders were seven brothers and sisters: Seth and Azura, Duirthei and Riodha, Ruadil and Baeathil, Honos and Tierkre, Cerchil and Laitha, Triethan and Firdhial, and Agradelai and Wistaea. From their descendants sprang all of the peoples of what became the realm of Threthoron, except for the Refugees of Shrivazh of whom the tale is here told. It was from the founding of Lhiosquor that the counting of time was reckoned among the Chosen People of the old world.

Here follows the tale of Lhiosquor in its infancy while it was yet hidden, before there was any king on Mt. Threthor and before the formation of the Old Alliance and the Second Battle of Turnienquor.

# CHAPTER 5

# ENOS
## (5 – 93 EC)

## 5 EC

Seth, Azura, and the twelve of their brothers and sisters who accompanied them to Mount Threthor built their new settlement on the mountain's summit. The summit of Mount Threthor was a concave circle, with a cool, clear lake at its centre. It was named the Crystal Lake. The fourteen founders built the foundation of what would become the glorious, fabled city of Lhiosquor, encircling the shores of the lake.

Now the Almighty One had promised Seth a son; however after four years had passed, Azura was still barren. Seth began to doubt God's promise, and his doubt grew into an inward grumbling against the Creator. In the fifth year since the foundation of Lhiosquor, the giver of dreams spoke to Seth in a dream and confronted him about his grumbling.

"Seth, why do you grumble against Me?" said the Almighty in a voice filled with compassion for His chosen servant. "Why has your heart grown hardened toward Me?"

Seth shouted his reply while angry tears coursed down his reddened face. "You promised me a son, but Azura cannot bear children. Why did You make a promise that cannot be fulfilled?"

"I have promised you a son, Seth. Why do you doubt? Why do you raise this complaint against Me? Already your wife has conceived the son I have promised you, but because you did not believe and have grumbled against Me, there will be tension between you and your son. You will envy him, and he will fear you. Still, I will fulfill My promise so that, when the time has come, I shall raise up a king for your people when this village has become a great city. Know, however, that neither you nor your son shall be the one whom I shall use to smite the sons of Lamekk. The son of your son shall I use for that task, and he will be My instrument of justice against your enemies."

Then Seth realized that he had sinned, and he fell down on his face and wept. He realized that the Creator was not slow in keeping His promises, but that this had been a test for Seth, a test that he had failed. When he awoke, he remembered his dream and knew that the Creator had indeed spoken to him. From that day, Seth tried with all his might to listen to God's wisdom before his own thoughts.

# 6 EC

In the days before the great waters destroyed the old world, there was no winter or summer, no springtime or autumn, nor even rainy seasons and dry seasons as there was, of course, no rain before the Great Flood. The years were marked by a windy season when the mists brought moisture and the season of harvest. Both came once every year. It came to pass in the windy season that Azura gave birth to a son. Seth's sorrow at failing his test turned to joy upon seeing his son come into the world. He named the boy Enos, just as God had commanded. Seth and Azura gathered the people of the village together.

"From this child shall come the One who will redeem the curse." he said to those gathered. Then the people built an altar to Eloi and from that time those in Lhiosquor began to call on the name of Eloi, the Almighty Creator, and present their requests to Him whenever they gathered together. Because of this, they prospered greatly, multiplied rapidly, and their flocks and fields were fruitful.

During this time, Lamekk ruled in Turnienquor as a ruthless despot. No one would stand against the Giants to challenge him. Now Lamekk fawned over his younger wife, Zillah, whose children were treated far better than the children of his first wife, Adah. Lamekk ignored Adah, and he had not lain with her since the conquest of Turnienquor. When Adah finally confronted Lamekk about his neglect of her and her children and grandchildren, Lamekk beat her, threatened to kill her, and cursed her and her twin sons, Jabal and Jubal. Adah was afraid, and she made plans with her sons to leave Turnienquor and the wrath of Lamekk forever. Adah left the city under the cover of nightfall. Her sons, Jabal and Jubal, their wives and children, these children also with their husbands, wives and children, also left at night and assembled together a thousand paces upstream along the Pishon. When they were all accounted for, they numbered seventy-three people. Bringing their possessions with them on carts, Adah's families left Turnienquor that night to seek out the village of Mathtusekh.

Hishirash the Giant had been keeping watch that night. He noticed the departure of Adah's people, and told his grandfather. "Great King Lamekk, your wife Adah, her sons, and their households have left the city!"

Lamekk shrugged his shoulders and replied apathetically, "Let them go. There is no one who will welcome them, and they are of no consequence to us. We will grow stronger without them."

Many days later, Adah and her sons and those of their households were travelling along the coast of the Great Lake on the road to Mathtusekh. The journey was difficult, as they were travelling in a large group, and they had a lot of small children with them. One evening, after they had set up camp to rest for the night and had gone to sleep, Adah heard a voice in a dream. The voice spoke to her and said, "Adah, daughter of Jagdisu-Kaol, listen to Me. Do not go to the village of Mathtusekh, for great fear will come on the people there because you are the wife of Lamekk. They will not allow you sanctuary, but seek to be rid of you because of your husband's curse. Rather, head westward from here toward the great mountain whose heights reach to the clouds. There you will find refuge, you and your sons and all of their households. There you will find rest and be safe from your husband's wrath."

After this, Adah awoke, and felt enveloped in great peace. She did not know whose voice had spoken to her in the dream, but she somehow knew that she could trust His instructions to be true and right. In the morning, Adah spoke with her sons, and they told her that they had both dreamt the same dream as their mother. Following the instructions from the dreams, they turned west into the Dry Lands of Nod, and travelled for several more days. After crossing the Dry Lands, the terrain became rougher and the land more rolling as they continued westward to the great mountain in the distance. Many of the children cried out in their thirst, and everyone wondered if they would ever find rest and refuge.

Finally, the weary travellers came to the base of Mount Threthor, and there they rested for three days and three nights. On the fourth day at mid-morning, Agradelai, the youngest of the seven brothers who had come with Seth to Lhiosquor, was ploughing his field on one of the mountain terraces which he had built. He peered over the walls of the terrace, and saw a group of Cainites encamped at the base of the mountain! Alarmed, Agradelai left his oxen in his field and climbed to Lhiosquor at the top of the mountain to find Seth.

"Brother Seth," he cried, breathing heavily after the difficult climb, "There are dozens of Cainites encamped at the base of the mountain. No doubt, they mean to destroy us and all that we have built. What shall we do?"

Seth closed his eyes, stood still, and steeped his fingers underneath his nose in deep thought. He appeared to be listening to some unheard voice. Then, he suddenly opened his eyes as if he had been told the answer to his question. "Let me go and see this sight, Agradelai. All is not always as it seems." Seth followed Agradelai to his terraced farm that overlooked the encampment. Puzzled, he told Agradelai what he thought.

"This is no army, my brother; look - there are women and children among them. These people have probably come here to seek refuge from the wrath of Lamekk. In that case, we should offer them whatever assistance we can give. I will go down and speak with them. Will you accompany me, brother?"

"Yes, brother Seth." replied Agradelai reluctantly, as he was still anxious in his heart about these newcomers. Seth and Agradelai lowered themselves down the mountain cliffs by large baskets attached to a series of ropes and stone pulleys. Seth had designed this system as a means of travelling up and down the mountain easily without making a path for an invading army. When the two brothers reached the bottom, they approached the encampment of the Cainites. A man came out to meet them, and fell to his knees trembling at Seth's feet.

"O terrible and mighty Seth, Avenger of Abel, please have mercy on me and my household." he pleaded.

Seth was taken aback. Clearly his brief visits to Turnienquor had left more of an impression than he had expected. "You have no need of fear with me, Cainite. Tell me who you are, and what brings you to Mt. Threthor?"

"I am Jabal, son of King Lamekk the Accursed of Turnienquor. My brother Jubal, Adah, our mother, and myself are fleeing the wrath of my father together with our households. My father loves the children of Zillah, but he treats us with contempt. We have been led to this mountain in our dreams, though we know not why. We seek refuge, but we have found no place where we may rest. Please be merciful to us and spare us!"

A moment of silence passed between them before Seth responded "You are all of the clan of Lamekk, and each one of you shares his curse. If I were to grant you sanctuary in our village, the blood of our people would be mixed with yours, and your curse would spread to us. We cannot allow this to happen." Seth paused again, thinking about how he could help these people who were surely no threat to the security of Lhiosquor.

"However, halfway up this mountain, there is a fertile plateau. Your people may stay there for as long as you have need, and I will help you in any way that I am able. Be aware nonetheless, that none of you shall be allowed to enter our village of Lhiosquor without permission, and your people must never be allowed to intermarry with our people."

"Thank you, great Seth." replied Jabal. "Shall we be safe here from my father?"

"Yes. Do not be afraid of your father and his army of Giants. Though they are terrible now, one day their kingdom will be destroyed and forgotten by men."

Adah then came and stood beside her son. "Mighty Seth, we know nothing of the ways of mountain life. What do we need to do to survive here?"

Agradelai turned to Adah. "We shall teach you our way of life. We will share our knowledge with you, and your people will know all that they need to know to live well on the mountain."

"We will also share our knowledge with you." replied Jabal. "If you teach us the ways of the mountain, we will teach you the art of making bronze, gold, and copper. When the day comes that you need to defend yourself against my father's army, you will be able to use bronze to make weapons and armour at least as strong as those used by my father's army."

"Thank you for your offer, Jabal." said Seth. "Although this mountain is our armour for the present, a day will come when we will be too numerous for this mountain. Then we will need to expand our borders beyond the protective strength of this place. Such armaments as those of which you speak may yet do us service. I do not look forward to bearing the burden of taking another man's life as Cain did, but I know that one day we will need to defend ourselves. Now, let us go. Bring all of your households, and follow us. We will take you up the mountain."

Seth and Agradelai led the Cainites up along a narrow, winding secret passage through an intricate labyrinth of natural caves and carved corridors deep in the bowels of the mountain, as there were too many people to bring them all up by basket. After passing through these dark, bewildering places, the households of Jabal and Jubal came to the plateau halfway up the mountain. They founded a settlement upon that plateau that they named Shrivazh, which means refuge. In the years that followed, the people of Lhiosquor taught the people of Shrivazh how to terrace fields, raise livestock, and even to play music. The people of Shrivazh taught the people of Lhiosquor how to work with metal. The friendship between the villages grew.

# 22 EC

In the intervening years, Enos grew in stature and in knowledge, and became the fairest child on Mount Threthor. He was not allowed to travel off of the mountain, but he spent a great deal of time in the Common Fields, the terraces between Shrivazh and Lhiosquor where people from the two villages would meet. Enos spent a great deal of time with Jubal, who had taken a liking to the boy. Enos loved to sing, and the Cainites of Shrivazh were amazed at the boy's ability, having heard nothing like it ever before. Jubal was so inspired by Enos's songs that he fashioned the first flute out of a hollow reed. Enos would sing, and Jubal would accompany the son of Seth on his flute. People from both villages would come to the Common Fields to hear the harmonious music played by two people whose fathers were sworn enemies. At this time, there was still plenty of arable land on the plateaus of Mt. Threthor, and both villages continued to prosper.

Seth was pleased at how well Enos got along with everyone, both the citizens of Lhiosquor and the refugees of Shrivazh. Seth taught his son everything he knew; about the creation of the world; of the forming of Adam and Eve in the Forbidden Garden, and of their subsequent fall into sin that resulted in their expulsion from that same Garden. He told Enos of the murder of Abel and of Cain's exile, of the sign of Abelon, the building of Enokk Turnienquor and the spread of the Cainites. Seth told him of the usurpation of Cain by Lamekk and his tyrannical rule, of the founding of Lhiosquor and the coming of the refugees to Shrivazh. Seth was amazed at his son's ability to learn and at how he excelled at all he did. Enos grew in stature and wisdom, and he became known to all as the beloved heir of Lhiosquor.

# 92 EC

By the ninety-second year since the founding of Lhiosquor, the descendants of Jabal the shepherd and the flocks of their animals had grown so numerous that there was no longer room for all of them. Jabal then requested of Seth that he and the Founders of Lhiosquor come to the Common Fields to hear his request to leave Mt. Threthor.

"Wise lord and elders of Lhiosquor," said Jabal, "my people have grown too numerous to remain on this mountain. We are grateful for your hospitality in allowing us to remain protected here, and for teaching us how to care for sheep. Nevertheless, my clan and I must leave here, and we must go with all of our flocks to seek wider pastures."

"I believe that what you say is wise." said Seth. "However, to where would you go? I beseech you not to travel southward, for your father's power there grows stronger by the day. To the north and west you may find the pastures you seek; there are fertile plains in the lowlands beyond the river Gihon, north of the Great Forest. That land is as yet uninhabited, and your people would flourish there."

Jabal replied, "I thank you for your wise counsel, Patriarch of Lhiosquor. I shall heed your advice, and lead my people to the land of which you speak. May there ever be peace and friendship between our two peoples, wise Seth of Lhiosquor." said Jabal, gripping Seth's arm in a gesture of farewell. "We shall never forget your kindness to us."

Jabal then left the Common Fields and returned to his people in Shrivazh. The families of Jabal packed up their belongings, and they headed north and west to the plains beyond the hills north of the Gihon. In time that land became known as the land of Jabal. The Jabalites became nomadic herdsmen and dwelt in tents in the land. The smaller clan of Jubal yet remained in Shrivazh, and Adah stayed with them. The Jubalites, being farmers and not herdsmen, required less land for their people, and remained in Shrivazh for some time to come.

Now Enos was eighty-seven years old, which in those days was still quite young, and the time came for him to choose a wife. Enos went to the door of the house of Honos, one of the fourteen founders of Lhiosquor, who was well known for his wisdom and integrity. Enos called upon and sought the hand of Honos' daughter Hona. Hona's intellect nearly matched that of Enos, and her beautiful weavings were very much in demand in Lhiosquor. All of the Elders were very pleased with the proposed union, and Enos and Hona were wed in the midst of a great celebration, reminiscent of the wedding of Seth and Azura. Seth blessed the couple and sacrificed a choice ram to God, in the tradition of his brother Abel. This most solemn and sacred of ceremonies was only performed in specific occasions of importance, and only Seth, as the patriarch, was allowed to perform it. Seth knew that the son of Enos and Hona would be mighty and blessed by the Creator, and that from him would come the One who would be the salvation of the world.

After the ceremony, the wedding party went down from Lhiosquor to the Common Fields where they would celebrate with their friends, the Jubalites. There were many of the people of Shrivazh there, and some were playing on flutes and stringed instruments. There was great singing from the voices of both peoples, as Enos was ever a friend of the clan of Jubal. Because of Enos' great knowledge and wisdom that was beyond his years, he was admitted to the Council of Founders that same year, even though he had not yet reached the requisite age of one hundred. He showed wisdom in all that he said, so much so that the Council began to call on his advice even more than that of his father.

Seth began to grow jealous of his son, and would often find himself trying to come up with better and more numerous ideas in an attempt to outdo Enos. One of Enos's greatest accomplishments in the early years was to devise the first form of writing ever invented so that events, laws, trade records, and contracts could be stored in written format for future reference instead of having to depend on fallible human memory. Shortly after this, Seth took the idea one step further and devised a numerical system based on his son's writing so that more accurate records of quantities could be kept. Enos's form of writing was taught to many in Lhiosquor who became scribes and kept records of all that took place that city. In this way, even the jealousy between father and son that the enemy of mankind intended for evil, the Creator of all used for good. Using his father's mathematical system, Enos later devised a calendar to keep track of days, months, and years, and to mark special days in the year. The Enosian Calendar started with Year 1 as the year of the founding of Lhiosquor. This calendar became recognized as a standard throughout the world and remained so for centuries.

# CHAPTER 6

# THE JOURNEY OF KENAN
## (96 – 136 EC)

## 96 EC

In the ninety-sixth year since the founding of Lhiosquor, Hona bore Enos his firstborn son and named him Kenan. Hona experienced tremendous, overwhelming pain in giving birth to Kenan, but an angel of the Almighty appeared to her to comfort her. His garments were radiant white, and his face shone with the light of Heaven.

"Do not be afraid." he said. "You will not die. You will live to see Kenan rise to be a great leader of this city, and to see Eloi grant him dominion over all peoples. The Spirit of the Almighty will be upon him to do many wonderful works, and he will be a beloved servant of the Most High Creator all of his days. He will become a king who will reign in justice and will bring down the power of Turnienquor. He will put to death the abominable generation of the Giants and will be given wisdom to judge all peoples. He will learn the laws of Eloi; he shall write them down and tell them to the people. However, if he does not keep the laws of the Almighty, his reign will not last, and another, lesser than he in godliness and greatness, will take his place. If he does not keep the laws that he will be given, the seed of Hishirash will rise again to lead a terrible army against Lhiosquor, and this city shall be destroyed."

After regaining her power of speech, Hona addressed the angel. "Certainly the fate of the whole world does not lie in the hands of this child, for that would be a doom which no one could bear."

The angel spoke again to Hona. "No, even if Kenan fails, Eloi will yet raise up from his descendants one who will not fail, whose reign shall never cease. This One shall have victory over the great enemy of mankind and redeem from the curse all that shall call on His name and come to him; however, this last prophecy concerns a time in the distant future. May Eloi keep you well, Hona." After he had said all of this the angel left her.

# 136 EC

Kenan grew up beloved by many in Lhiosquor, and he grew in knowledge and wisdom as he was taught by his father and his grandfather. When Kenan was forty years old, God appeared to him in a vision as a man in dazzling white robes, with hair white as wool, eyes burning like fire, a golden sash around his chest, and feet shining like bronze. Kenan was afraid, and fell trembling at the feet of the vision of the Almighty.

"Oh Eloi, Creator of all things and judge of all men, who am I that You should come to me? Help me, for I am very afraid."

"Be not afraid," said the Almighty One. "I have chosen you to be a great king, the first of your people, but I must first send you on a great journey. I will reveal many things to you that have been hidden until this time. I will take you to places that are important in My plan, and I will instruct you as to what you are to do. Tomorrow, you are to leave Mount Threthor and travel along the eastern slopes of these mountains until you come to the Pass of the Kheruvim. From there, travel into the Great Forest. You will visit the hidden village of Siaghlamh and proceed from there to other places which I will show you in time."

Kenan was overcome by his astonishment at the appearance of this majestic Being and by His words. "I don't understand." he said. "I have never set foot off this mountain. How will I survive and find food on this journey?"

"Do not worry about what you will eat. Do I not provide food for the birds of the air? In the same way, I will provide for you. Prepare what you will bring with you on this journey, but do not take more than you can comfortably carry, for there are many places that I must show you." A cloud like smoke or fog then filled Kenan's room, and then the vision ended.

The next morning, Kenan told his father, Enos, about his vision. "Never refuse the summons of the Almighty, my son." replied Enos.

"Go and seek the first man and woman who dwell in Siaghlamh. They are reputed to have great wisdom. Take caution, for the journey may be perilous. Do not stray far from the mountains, my son, and do not and travel far southward, or you will become lost in the Dry Lands of Nod. Those barren lands produce no food, and there are bands of Cainites loyal to Lamekk who wander in that region. They have even begun to build new cities, as Lamekk wishes to establish an empire that will engulf the world. Go swiftly, my son, and do not tarry when Eloi summons you."

Kenan inclined his head toward his father in a gesture of respect. "Thank you, father, for your wise counsel. I will prepare immediately for my journey. May Eloi bless our household while I am away." When Kenan had bid farewell to his father, he gathered some of his belongings into a linen bag and descended from Lhiosquor to Shrivazh. There, he bid farewell to Nosjubal, his fast friend since childhood. "I am travelling west to the Great Forest." Kenan told his friend. "I shall return, but I know not for how long I shall be away."

Nosjubal was dismayed to see his friend's departure. "I will go with you." he said. "The land ahead is said to be treacherous; perhaps it would safer to travel with a companion. May I accompany you, Kenan?"

Kenan felt uneasy about bringing Nosjubal with him for fear that something may happen to his dear friend. However, he reasoned the truth of Nosjubal's argument; that it was indeed safer to travel with a companion than alone, should trouble come. After giving thought to this matter, he relented. "You may come," he said reluctantly, concerned for his friend's safety, "but you must watch out for your own safety. I shall have enough trouble of my own on this journey, and I do not know when I will return. I would be glad to have you journey with me, but know that you are heading into lands full of deadly peril."

"It is decided, then." declared Nosjubal. "Do we leave now?"

"Yes." Kenan replied quickly. "Gather what you will, and meet me at the bottom of Mount Threthor. Be sure to be there before the sun reaches its height, for by then I must depart whether you come with me or not."

Kenan used the system of hanging baskets that crisscrossed Mount

Threthor to descend to the base of the mountain. Nosjubal was already there, his few belongings tied securely to his back. He carried two bags of food attached to each end of a pole across his shoulders. The two friends ate a light lunch of dried fruit and bread, and then set out on their quest. They travelled southwest, following the Kheruva Mountains toward the Pass of the Kheruvim. That evening, Kenan and Nosjubal camped in a wooded vale through which a stream which flowed down out of the hills. After their meal, Nosjubal began to play a melody on his lyre while Kenan sang. The son of Enos sang a song of a kingdom yet to be born, and his song filled the night air with wonder. Nosjubal could feel a holy stillness descend upon the small camp as if all Creation had stopped to listen to his song, and as if even the spirit of the Creator Himself was present.

That night, they both dreamed strange dreams of a time yet to come, but they could remember nothing of their dreams after awakening. In the morning, the gathered up their belongings and set out westward along a stream that wound between the foothills of the Kheruva Mountains. When they turned their gaze southward, they could see the northern reaches of the Dry Lands. Kenan and Nosjubal made as little noise as possible that day and took turns watching at night to avoid being taken unaware by a great eater lizard. The following morning, after walking for about two hours, they came upon the Pass of the Kheruvim where the shining angels stood guard. Awestruck at the sight of these terrifying yet beautiful beings, Kenan and Nosjubal fell to their knees.

The angel on the left spoke, and his voice seemed to come echoing from the very mountains of Heaven itself. "Arise, sons of men. You have come to the pass that leads into the Forest of Adam. You must give account of yourselves before you may go any further."

Kenan spoke, trembling. "I am Kenan, son of Enos, son of Seth the builder of Lhiosquor. We have come here on a quest. I seek the house of Adam."

After a pause, the other angel slowly nodded his head and spoke. "You are the one whose coming was foretold to us. You may enter, but who is your companion?"

Nosjubal spoke, his words broken with fear. "I – I am N-Nosjubal of the clan of Jubal. Kenan has been my friend since childhood, and I am his companion."

"You are a Cainite, then." spoke the angel on the right. "The children of Cain are forbidden to enter this forest. You must leave your friend and return home, or wait for him elsewhere."

"W-Would you please, then, watch after Kenan, f-fierce Kheruvim?" said Nosjubal, shielding his face with his arm from their penetrating gaze.

"No harm shall befall him here; I cannot say the same for you should you accompany him. Though your heart is good, Jubalite, you carry the blood of a murderer in your veins and thus share his curse. No one who carries the curse of a murderer may enter here. You must leave Kenan to continue his quest alone."

Nosjubal turned aside from the Pass of the Kheruvim and turned toward the south. Kenan entered the Great Forest of Adam alone. No sooner had he passed through the mountain gate and into the forest, than he noticed orange faces peering from behind the trees around him.

"Who's there?" he called. "Show yourselves."

A group of orange-skinned men clad in green and brown tunics appeared. One of them wore a necklace of gold. The man with the necklace spoke.

"I should ask you the same, as you are the stranger here." the man said, with a suspicious tone in his voice.

"Very well, I am Kenan son of Enos son of Seth. I come here to find the house of Adam."

The man's countenance changed, and he smiled in welcome. "The children of Seth are greatly blessed and are always welcome among our people." he said, heartily. "Your patriarch is well renowned, Kenan. I am Quarro son of Chirro of the tribe of Dorro. I welcome you as one of our own. Come with us to our city - it is not far from here." Quarro gave the signal for his men to stand down and return home. He beckoned Kenan to follow him through the Great Forest. Kenan went with the orange-skinned men as they passed swiftly through the dense undergrowth. Around midday, they crossed a bridge and came into a clearing, where

Kenan saw an incredible sight that made his eyes nearly leave his head - a city made of gold!

"This is our city, Dorronquor." said Quarro. "As you see, gold is plentiful here and our craftsmen are very skilled with its uses. All of our buildings are covered with gold."

Kenan was stunned and stood motionless gazing at this wonder. "I had thought Lhiosquor to be the most beautiful of all cities, but I see that I was mistaken. The workmanship of your craftsmen is clearly unsurpassed." As he spoke, Quarro and his followers went ahead of Kenan into the city.

Quarro looked back, and motioned to Kenan to come with him. "Come and stay with us, Kenan of the Chosen People, even if for but one night before you leave for Siaghlamh. Come and meet Dorro, our patriarch, and feast with him in his hall."

Dorro proved to be a gracious host. Almost every kind of fruit of the earth was prepared upon his banqueting table. Singers clad in bright golden raiment sang clear, peaceful melodies. In the midst of the feast, Dorro and Kenan sat on cushions made of cotton and talked at great length of the various happenings in their respective lands. "It is good to hear happy news of my brothers and sisters on the Mountain of Glory. You seem to thrive as we do." After a thoughtful pause, he added, "This 'writing' of which you speak is of special interest to me. Can it be used to carry words to other places and be kept so that the words are not forgotten?"

"Yes Dorro, we have found many uses for it in trade, in teaching, and in recording the deeds of passing years."

"Could you send some of your scribes to teach us this art, Kenan? In return I would send some of our finest craftsmen to Lhiosquor to make your Council chambers shine like the sun itself when it rises in the morning."

"I would be honoured, patriarch. However, you should know that I am not planning to return to Lhiosquor yet. I must go the Siaghlamh to meet with Adam, the father of all."

Dorro looked at Kenan intently. "Well then, Kenan, you must follow the road north of here for a night and a day to find my father's village. I am sure that he will be pleased to meet you and help you with whatever you need. Are you leaving in the morning?"

"Yes," said Kenan, somewhat reluctantly regarding the luxurious surroundings in which he found himself. "Though I greatly admire your city, and am honoured by your hospitality, my quest leads me elsewhere. I will return here someday, but I do not know when."

Their conversation yet continued well into the night. The next morning, after a short but restful sleep in the Hall of Dorronquor, Kenan arose, gathered his belongings, and set off on the road leading north out of the city, where Quarro met him. "My grandfather holds the best feasts in the world, does he not?"

"I was indeed impressed, Quarro. I am almost sorry to leave now, but leave I must. Will I see you soon?"

"I will accompany you to Siaghlamh, if you wish. I am taking this bag of gold to Adam to trade for some of his fine sheep. The sheep of Siaghlamh have the finest, softest wool in the world, worth its weight in gold." he said, glancing at the bag that lay across the back of an ox. Kenan noticed that the beast seemed burdened with the weight of the valuable cargo.

"You may find this interesting, Quarro. We have learned from the Cainites who live in the south how to build carts that can carry large burdens. When I send the scribes to Dorronquor, I will also send you cart-wrights to ease the burden of your oxen." The two of them discussed the various implementations of wheels, as they headed north along the leafy road that wound through the trees of the Great Forest. While they travelled along the road, evening approached. As night fell, they felt as if all of the animals in the forest, even the very trees themselves, were watching their progress through the wood. They felt as if a million pairs of unseen eyes were upon them. That night, as they camped along the forest road, Quarro lay on his mat and heard voices – high, gentle and clear but barely audible – whispering in the woods:

"He has been chosen to rule over all nations."

"He will bring the law of the Creator to his people."

"He will triumph over the Giants of Turnienquor."

"Lhiosquor will prosper under his rule."

"But he will become proud and pride will cause his downfall and the downfall of the city he loves."

"The whole earth will mourn the fall of Lhiosquor."

"But first, that city will enjoy a long age of peace, and on the earth its glory shall know no equal."

Needless to say, Quarro did not sleep easily that night. Kenan, in contrast, slept soundly, and did not stir until the morning light when Quarro awakened him.

"What? Where am I?" asked Kenan, momentarily forgetting that he was not in his own house in Lhiosquor.

Quarro seemed puzzled at Kenan's question. "You are in the Forest of Adam, on your way to Siaghlamh."

Kenan then remembered his journey, stood to his feet, and stumbled into the waking world. "Yes, of course. I am quite unused to waking in the middle of a forest. Let us arise and continue on our journey, Quarro."

As the groggy heir of Seth clumsily gathered up his belonging, Quarro untied his ox from the tree and hefted the large sack of gold onto the animal's back, at which the animal groaned in protest,

"Remember Quarro, wheels!" said Kenan as they broke camp and headed northward along the road once more.

Before the sun had reached its peak, Kenan and Quarro had followed the Forest Road into a very large clearing. In the clearing, they saw a pastoral town surrounded by fields of grain and vegetables. There was a long, narrow bridge-like structure coming down into the town from a spring in the hills in the northeast. At its end in the centre of the town, water poured out of it into a reservoir. Ditches led from the reservoir and carried fresh water to the verdant fields that surrounded the town on all sides. Kenan and Quarro were passing through by of these fields at the side of the road where some farmers were gathering grain.

"Welcome to Siaghlamh." one of them said. "What brings you travellers to our fair town?"

"I am Quarro son of Chirro from Dorronquor. I come to trade gold for wool. My companion is Kenan son of Enos son of Seth. He has journeyed here from Lhiosquor to meet with the father of all."

The man's smile broadened. "I am Nahlon. The wool merchant lives near the centre of town by the marketplace. My father's house is near there as well. I will take you both there. It is indeed a blessing to have a visitor of the noble line of Seth in our town today."

Siaghlamh was a smaller and humbler town than Lhiosquor or Dorronquor. The houses and streets were well cleaned and neatly kept, but the streets were only trails and the houses only small, humble dwellings made of brown mud-brick. Nahlon led Quarro along the narrow trails to meet with the wool merchant in the marketplace, which was rather quiet where marketplaces are concerned. Siaghlamh, being a small and hidden town, rarely had any travellers except their Dorronite neighbours. After meeting Yamo, the wool merchant, Nahlon and Kenan bade farewell to Quarro. They came to a brick dwelling resembling the other houses in design, save that it was made of a rich blue brick instead of the usual non-descript brown mud-brick. A large, muscular man with olive skin and dark, closely trimmed hair stepped out from behind the doorway. His dark brown eyes grew wide when he saw Kenan, and a broad, friendly smile appeared on his face.

"Ah, you are the one who was sent! Come in, come in and be welcome in my home." The man gestured toward the doorway of the house, and Kenan entered. He could hear the sound of children playing in another room, and could see still others playing in the yard behind the house.

"Are you Nahlon's father, sir?" asked Kenan.

"Yes, just as I am yours, Kenan. I am the father of all men, made from the dust of the earth at the dawn of the world. Eloi told me you would come. He also told me that you have been chosen to lead his people. I know why you have come."

Kenan was baffled, and gave a look of astonishment. "What do you mean? Even I do not know why the Almighty Creator has sent me here."

"Did you see the Forbidden Garden on your journey, my son?"

"No, but my grandfather has told me much of it."

"The Creator cast Eve and I out from it after we partook of the Tree of the Knowledge of Good and Evil. He expressly forbade us to eat the fruit of that tree. Because of our transgression, no one is allowed to enter there, just as no Cainite is allowed to enter this forest. It is because of our disobedience that the curse of death has come upon the world and that men and beasts kill one another. It is because of what we have done that women have pain in childbirth and men must work to bring food from the earth.

Yet, thanks be to the Almighty One for his mercy, for He promised us that one from the line of Seth will arise to redeem the curse of death. He will reconcile us to Eloi, and he shall bring an end to the dominion of the vile serpent Lucifer who controls the heart of the self-proclaimed king of Turnienquor. Because Eve and I believed the serpent instead of our Creator, we have forfeited the dominion that was to be ours. We have unwittingly handed the world over to the serpent, the enemy of both Creator and Creation, until the Chosen One comes. The serpent hates everything, and there is no love or light in him any longer, because his heart has been twisted by evil and will never be set aright. He is doomed to ultimate destruction when the Chosen One sets up His dominion over the earth." Adam paused, looking deep into Kenan's eyes as if searching for his soul. "Are you the One who is sent to end the dominion of Lamekk and his master?"

Kenan felt unworthy at such a suggestion, and he looked away from Adam's penetrating gaze. "I do not know, Great Father. I only know that I have been chosen to be a king upon the earth, and that the Almighty One has many other places and things that He will reveal to me after this."

"Then you should begin at the beginning, my son. Go to the Forbidden Garden. Seth was allowed to enter once, and you may yet be allowed to do the same if your heart is pure." Adam pointed out the window to the hills from which the aqueduct brought its water. "Up in those hills is a spring from which flows the River of Life. The River of Life flows westward through the Forbidden Garden, beyond which it parts into the four rivers which give life to neighboring lands. Follow the River of Life and you will find the Garden."

Kenan remembered his grandfather's tales of the Garden, and could almost imagine the beauty, wonder and awe of that holy place. "What am I to do when I get there? What is it that I must know?" he asked Adam.

"That I cannot tell you, I do not know. Eloi alone knows why He is sending you there, but that is where you must go to continue this quest."

Kenan was greatly puzzled. A look of perplexity came over his face, followed by one of determination. "I shall go to the Garden and learn that which Eloi chooses to reveal so that I may become a good and just ruler. I will answer the summons of the Creator." Kenan then prepared for his journey.

The following morning, Kenan followed the aqueduct up the rocky hillside to the cave containing the hidden spring. He followed the stream which flowed down the westward slope of the hill for a day and a night until it became a deep river. As Kenan travelled along the banks of the River of Life, the trees grew taller and thicker, and the wildlife more varied and abundant. On the afternoon of the second day, he reached a place where the river flowed under a wall of what appeared to be polished white marble. Just as Kenan arrived, the curtain of heaven rolled back and the white wall glowed with a blinding brilliance wherever it was lit by beams of sunlight that pierced through the thick canopy of trees. Kenan began to look for a gate through the wall, and immediately saw the White Gate of Eden guarded by a fierce angel with a flaming spear. The angel called to him.

"Kenan, son of Enos, come forth. The Almighty has granted you permission to look upon this Garden once and once only."

Kenan trembled. "You are the one my grandfather told me about."

"Yes, I am Michael. As your grandfather Seth before you, you have no need of fear with me because you have been chosen to come here and seek your destiny within. However, you must not stay in the Garden after the sun has set, no matter how enticed you are to stay, because man may no longer live here."

Kenan stepped slowly, gingerly, and purposely through the Gate. Before him lay the most beautiful sight he had ever seen, even more beautiful than the golden splendour of Dorronquor. The lush green of the trees, bushes, and other foliage made the green of all plants outside the Garden appear grey. Flowers wafted their fragrant perfume through the Garden, and these were clothed in colours so vivid that Kenan had to look away until his eyes adjusted to their brilliance. Songbirds were everywhere, arrayed in the same dazzling hues as the flowers. Their songs were like the songs of angels, and Kenan was filled with wonder.

He could not help feeling very small and insignificant at that moment, as if he had just stepped into the courtyard of Heaven itself. Then he heard the voice of the One who appeared to him in Lhiosquor, though this time that Voice sounded deeper, richer, and more majestic than before, if that were possible.

"Come this way, Kenan," He spoke, "and I will show you the offering stone that will be placed on the holy mountain where you will build My house." Kenan's gaze was drawn to a beam of light shining down upon a great stone, measuring three cubits thick, seven cubits wide, and twelve cubits long. He wondered how it would be possible to move such a heavy object. The Almighty One knew Kenan's thoughts, and He spoke again.

"Know that I am the one true God. Human hands may not move this stone. Come and stand on the stone." With trepidation, Kenan walked forward and climbed onto the smooth surface on the top face of the stone. A breeze blew against his face, and he looked into the sky to see four angels descending with the wind. Each angel took up a corner of the stone and lifted it effortlessly into the air, over the treed canopy of the Garden, with Kenan still sitting upon it. Carrying the great stone, the angels flew swiftly over forests, mountain, lakes, rivers and grassy plains, as they headed southwest.

The angels flew without stopping for two nights and two days. At noon on the third day, the angels finally stopped atop a solitary mountain. The summit of the mountain was flat like that of Mt. Threthor. The angels set Kenan and the stone down on the mountain's summit, and then the thundering voice of the Almighty One spoke to Kenan again.

"This is the place where I will establish My dwelling forever. It is here that you shall build My house so that the people may come and meet with Me. If you do this, you and your descendants will prosper greatly in all that you do. You will become My voice to the people, and many will travel here to worship Me on this mountain."

Kenan wrestled with a question that had tugged at him since he began his journey. "Great Creator, what shall I call this house? Is it to be called the house of Eloi, the house of the Almighty, the house of the Creator, or something else? What is the name above all of Your other names by which You would be called?"

A hush settled on the mountaintop where Kenan sat. The four angels had departed. No birdsong could be heard, nor could the sound of any bubbling brook, nor the sounds of leaves rustling in the wind. "It is no small thing that you ask, son of Enos. When your father was born, men began to call on My name, the name Eloi which was known to them. I Am the Beginning and the End, the Almighty Creator and source of all things. I Am the Lord of the Heavens and the Earth. The greatest name that I am to be called is I Am, which is Yah in the language of the men of this age. This house will be known as the Temple of Yah. Here, people from Lhiosquor and all of the cities of the sons of Adam will come to build My house.

However, of the descendants of Cain, only the sons and daughters of Jubal and Jabal will be welcome here. They have repudiated the ways of their ancestor Cain to follow Me, but no other Cainites must set foot on this mountain for they will surely betray you and lay waste to the sanctuary you will build for Me. For the Jubalites and the Jabalites, an outer court will be built, but they cannot pass beyond it into the sanctuary where the priests will perform their sacrifices. If they do so, they must be put to death, for the blood of Lamekk is in them, and his curse is upon them."

When the visions had subsided and Kenan was left alone on the mountain, he found a lost lamb in a nearby thicket. He took the lamb upon the great stone and offered it as a sacrifice to Yah as righteous Abel had done centuries before. Only in such a solemn sacrifice was it permitted to take the lifeblood of an animal; it served as reminder to the participant of the seriousness of the sin that had permeated the fallen Creation, and still lay resident in all men. The price demanded for breaking the holy covenant that Yah had made with Adam and Eve was death.

Kenan remained on the mountain meditating on God's words spoken to him for seven nights and seven days. During this time he ate nothing, but angels ministered to him, and they counselled him on how he might find his way home to Lhiosquor. On the eighth day, Kenan climbed down the north side of the mountain. Here he found a small village of people who had established themselves in this place. Kenan had no idea that there were settlements this far away from the Forest of Adam! The people of the village were equally amazed to see Kenan. They had seen no one in this land except their own people. They had not seen anyone ascend the side of the mountain, and because Kenan's face glowed so brilliantly from being in the presence of God, they thought that he was an angel. All of the people of the village came out of their houses to meet him. Their skin had a golden hue and their hair was black and straight. One man, apparently the tribal leader by the deference given him by the others, stepped forward and spoke to Kenan.

"What tidings do you bring us, shining one?" he asked.

Kenan realized by the reverent fear in the man's eyes that he had been mistaken for an angel. "I am Kenan, son of Enos, son of Seth, of the city of Lhiosquor." he explained, all peoples having heard of his illustrious grandfather and his great city.

"I have met with the Almighty Creator, Yah, who favours your people greatly. He has chosen your mountain upon which to build His dwelling place. Many people from different cities and different tribes far away will come here to worship Him on your mountain."

"It is good that you have come." said the tribal patriarch. "I am Tsayun, son of Adam, and I am the father of this tribe. We are herders and riders of the great runner lizards. We followed their wanderings across the uninhabited lands for years until we came to this holy place. Here we abide beneath the shadow of the Mountain of the Almighty One, he whom you name Yah. I have heard tales of your great and marvellous city. An angel appeared to me a fortnight ago, and he told me to watch for one coming down from the holy mountain. He instructed me to tell the one coming down the mountain to return to Lhiosquor."

Kenan looked worried. "Patriarch Tsayun, I tell you the truth, I was carried here on a stone brought by four angels. I do not know the way back from whence I have come. It is very far from here."

Tsayun looked toward the northeast. "Yes, it is very far, very far indeed, but you may reach it by the Great River that flows north of here." He pointed to an indeterminate point beyond the horizon. "My fifth son, Shaochi, lives but a short ride north from here on the bank of the river that flows toward the Great Sea. He is a builder of boats, and he wishes to trade with the tribe of Turvah who live on the great lake near Mount Chayat – which many call Mount Sentinel – at the southwestern edge of the Great Forest. From there, you should be able to find your way home."

Kenan nodded his head in a gesture of respect. "Thank you, Tsayun. I am grateful for your help and for passing on what was spoken to you. Your people shall be given a place of honour when I return to build the Temple of Yah."

Tsayun nodded back and spoke again, "Please stay here with us tonight. We are blessed by your presence, and we would like to hear more about the glorious city of Lhiosquor."

So Kenan stayed in the village of Tsayun that night and told the people as much as he could about Lhiosquor. Around a bonfire in the open place at the centre of the village, all of the children gathered at Kenan's feet, wide eyed with wonder, as he spoke of the city on the mountaintop. The next morning, Tsayun's eldest daughter, Kenshi, brought Kenan the best of the runner lizards in their herds to ride up the trail to the Great River. Kenan said farewell to the friendly people of Tsayun, mounted the runner lizard, and set off on the trail.

By sunset, Kenan could see the bright blue shimmer of the wide Rahav River on the horizon. He made camp that night and reached the riverbank early the following morning, after but an hour's ride. A strong brick house had been built near the banks of the river, and there were large boats tied to a dock not far from the house. Children were playing with a dog far down the beach, and seabirds seemed to be everywhere, plunging now and again into the water to refresh themselves. A lean, black-haired man, who looked so much like Tsayun that Kenan knew must be Shaochi, stepped from the house. When he saw Kenan, he stopped and looked at him suspiciously.

"Who are you? You are indeed not of the tribe of Tsayun! What are you doing here?"

"I am Kenan, son of Enos, son of Seth. My people are the people of Lhiosquor, the city of Seth on Mt. Threthor. I need to return home. Your father told me that you were a builder of boats and could help me find my way back."

Shaochi looked hard at Kenan and appeared to grow thoughtful. "So, my father's tales of the mountain people are true! I do not like the look of you, stranger, and although you ride one of my father's best runners, I have no way of knowing you did not steal it. However, there is a look of integrity and honesty about you, Sethite, and if what my father says about your people is true, then I can take you at your word. I am not leaving for Turvah for a few days yet, but you may stay here with my family until then, provided that you make yourself useful." Shaochi motioned to his boats. They were quite large and had curious poles about twelve to fifteen cubits tall sticking up from their decks. There were ropes dangling down from these poles. "Do you see my ships, Sethite?"

"Yes, Shaochi; I have never seen ships like those before. What is the purpose of those poles and ropes?"

Shaochi beamed. "The currents of the great River Rahav are very strong, too strong to row against. Also, strong winds often blow through the river valley. Rowing a ship along this river all the way to Turvah is a futile feat for the foolish, but come and see this."

Kenan followed Shaochi onto the dock, and then onto the deck of one of his ships. Shaochi pulled on the ropes, bringing down a very large piece of woven cloth, one end of which he tied to a beam on the front of the ship, while the rest of the cloth stretched the length of the pole. This gave the cloth a triangular shape. A gentle wind blew, causing the cloth to billow out.

"See how the cloth catches the wind, Sethite? With this cloth, I can use the force of the wind do the work of many rowers. I can reach my destination far faster than if a whole team of rowers were employed to move the watercraft. My boats are unlike any made before." Talking about his ships had calmed Shaochi's previous suspicion of Kenan and had made him jovial. He continued talking as he admired his handiwork. "If you will help me prepare this ship for the journey, you can come with me to Turvah, and from there you can follow the Kheruva Mountains back to Mt. Threthor."

"Thank you, Shaochi. I look forward to finding out more about these ships of yours." At that, Shaochi beamed with delight.

Over the next seven days, Shaochi and Kenan prepared Shaochi's newest ship, the Laomin, which Shaochi had named after his lovely wife. Laomin herself prepared fine food each morning and evening for her family and their guest. "It is not easy having Shaochi gone so much," she said, "but he always returns with beautiful gifts and interesting stories to tell. Shaochi loves the feel of a ship on the water. I used to go with him, but someone needs to remain here to look after all of these little ones. One day, when they are old enough to care for themselves, I will sail with him again." Laomin's dedication to her husband and children was laudable.

"One day I will count myself blessed to a have a wife as devoted to me as you are to Shaochi." said Kenan. "You must be very proud." he said, turning to Shaochi.

"Indeed!" he beamed. "I can never stay away sailing the river for long, for although I love to travel, my heart is here with Laomin."

On the morning of the eighth day, the Laomin set out for Turvah. The river Rahav was much wider than the Pishon, and at first there were times when one could see neither bank of the river if one was out in the middle of it. Shaochi and Kenan travelled for a fortnight, and the ship reeled and rocked on the waves. Kenan had difficulty sleeping at night because of this, and he would often feel ill. Often, Shaochi would playfully taunt him.

"What's wrong, mountain boy?" he would ask. "You look like you've eaten mastodon dung!" One night, the wind was very strong, almost pushing the boat over and bringing water onto the deck. Shaochi shouted earnestly to Kenan, "Help me bring down the sail and bail out the water! The wind threatens to overturn us!" The night was as black as coal, and the two men could barely even see the buckets in their hands. The spray from the raging river drenched Shaochi and Kenan to the bone. As if this were not enough, the waters of the river often spilled over the deck when the boat was tipped by the wind. With great difficulty and after many failed attempts, the men managed at last to untie and bring down the sail that had been torn by the forceful winds. It would need to be mended as soon as daylight came, if it ever came for either of them.

Kenan and Shaochi had just returned to bailing the water out of the boat when a sharp thud arose, followed by a shifting and sifting sound beneath the ship. They had run aground on a sandy beach. Both men were relieved and immediately jumped out of the boat into the waist deep water along the shore. They grabbed the ropes at the bow of the boat, and they tried to pull it far onto shore as possible so that it couldn't float away. When the <u>Laomin</u> was made secure, Kenan and Shaochi set up camp on the beach and fell asleep, exhausted and weary from their labours.

The following morning, the two weary travellers awoke to find that, although the <u>Laomin</u> had not set itself adrift in the night, the damage to its hull had been extensive. There were rocks beneath the ship that had broken through the wooden planks of the hull, and the boat would have sunk if it had not been pulled ashore. Shaochi and Kenan would have to find a way to repair the breach in the hull or continue on foot. They decided to separate; Shaochi would attempt to repair his boat while Kenan would continue his journey alone.

"We have come far up the river, Kenan. As you can see, the other side of the Rahav is now visible from here." Kenan looked out across the river, and the sight of the hills on the far shore confirmed what Shaochi told him. "Turvah cannot be more than a few days from here by foot. I must stay here and mend the <u>Laomin</u>, but you should continue on your journey."

"Can she be repaired?" asked Kenan, who had come to have an appreciation of the sailing vessel.

"Yes, I believe so. It will take some time, but it can be done. I should be able to complete the repairs myself. Go now, my friend, and return to your people." Shaochi threw his right hand out to the horizon in the approximate direction of Mt. Threthor.

"Farewell, Shaochi son of Tsayun. May Yah richly bless you, your lovely wife, and your children both born and yet to be. I will not forget you, and I believe that we will meet yet again."

Shaochi gripped Kenan with both hands on his shoulders. "Farewell, Kenan, son of Enos, son of the noble Seth. The strength and wisdom of your family runs strong in your blood, and now I know the stories of Lhiosquor to be true. Someday I will come to visit you on your fair mountain." At this, Shaochi turned to his work and Kenan went on his way.

Kenan travelled for four days, following the river upstream to find the city of Turvah. He finally arrived, knowing the city by Shaochi's description and by the large lake nearby. The city was neither very large nor very small, but strangely quiet. Few of the purple-skinned people of Turvah were found in the city itself, but Kenan could see many of them out in the grain fields, labouring heavily.

Kenan then noticed something that raised the hairs on his neck. There were a few Cainites in the field along with the people of Turvah, and these scourged the Turvese people with long whips, driving them to work harder and faster. Alarmed, Kenan shouted to one of Cainites who held a woman of Turvah by the ear and was shouting at her angrily. Kenan ran into the field to try to stop him, but as he ran a Giant grabbed him by the back the back of the neck and lifted high into the air.

The Giant, who called himself Okhar-Enokk, stood ten and one half cubits high, which was nearly the height of three normal men. "This city belongs to me." the Giant exclaimed. "You are not welcome here. You are trespassing in my territory, little mountain man, and I will kill you." Kenan tried to speak, but Okhar-Enokk's grip on his neck would permit no words. "I do not care what you have to say, little man." said the Giant, who seemed as disgusted at Kenan as if he had just picked up a handful of maggots. "You are on my land, you do not belong here, you are of an enemy tribe, and now you will die." The Giant was about to throw Kenan to the ground to crush him with his hammer, but was stopped short.

"Kenan!" shouted a voice from somewhere behind the Giant. Out of the corner of his eye, Kenan saw a bald and clean-shaven Cainite running toward the Giant and himself. "Okhar-Enokk", he said, "this is my dear friend, Kenan of Lhiosquor. Please let him go."

"Or what, slave? You won't sing anymore?" The Giant laughed, but his tone became menacing. "I allowed you, a trespasser, to live, because you are of the race of Cain. Do not forget that I am the master and you are the slave. Another word and you will join your lily-skinned friend in death."

"Nosjubal, is that you?" Kenan exclaimed in astonishment, when Okhar-Enokk momentarily loosened his grip on Kenan's neck.

"Yes, dear friend, though my hair and my freedom have been taken from me." Nosjubal nodded to his friend.

"Listen, slave." said Okhar-Enokk, impatient to exterminate the 'vermin' which he held in his hand. "This man is a trespasser. He is not of our people. He is nothing. He will die."

Kenan reached up and grabbed the huge forearm of his captor, gaining the Giant's attention, as Nosjubal grabbed Okhar-Enokk's enormous lance that lay on the ground behind him. He took up the lance and shoved the point deep into the sensitive joint under the Giant's right knee, and Okhar-Enokk tumbled over with a great crash onto the ground beneath. The Giant inadvertently released Kenan who, though dazed by the fall, got to his feet and ran, joined by Nosjubal.

"Get them!" bellowed the Giant, alerting everyone in the city with a shout that boomed like an avalanche. "Do not let them get away!" A band a of Cainites clad in armour made of iron, a new metal which Kenan had never seen, appeared from behind a nearby building and began to chase after them with swords and spears. The warriors were led by with three grim Giants clad in fearsome attire. Kenan and Nosjubal fled into the plains beyond the city, but soon their pursuers drew closer, the long limbed, lumbering Giants outpacing the rest.

They would surely have been captured had a dust storm not arisen and covered Kenan and Nosjubal. The Giants could see their quarry nowhere in the obscuring, irritating dust cloud. When the dust cleared, Kenan saw no sign of his pursuers. He looked behind him and there was Mt. Threthor, its top hidden among the clouds. Yah had come and swept Kenan and Nosjubal away, bringing them home. They were greatly amazed and gave thanks to their Creator. After this, they returned home and told of all the marvellous things that had taken place.

# CHAPTER 7

# THE TEMPLE OF YAH
## (139 – 185 EC)

## 139 EC

In the year 139 of the Enosian Calendar, word came to the people of Lhiosquor that a terrible disease of boils had fallen upon the Giants at Turvah and killed every one of them. The people of Turvah took had taken courage at this turn of events, and they drove their fearful and outnumbered Cainite masters out of their city. The people of Turvah were free once again, and Seth convened a meeting of the Council of Elders. He proposed a motion to send a messenger to the town of Turvah to establish friendship and co-operation between the people of the mountain and the people of the lake.

Kenan was not yet a Council member at this time, but he was already widely respected by the elders. The Council of Elders gave Kenan the chance to share with them his vision for the building of a Temple to Yah, the Almighty Creator known to most as Eloi. The Council unanimously agreed to implement Kenan's plan and moved to begin construction of the temple as soon as possible. Because Turvah lay directly along the route to Tsayun where the road was to be built, Kenan was selected to be the messenger to Turvah. As a result of Kenan's meeting with Dorro on his great journey, the Council also motioned that scribes be sent to Dorronquor to teach the Dorronites the art of writing. In exchange, goldsmiths from Dorronquor could assist with the construction of the temple. Within a few short months afterward, trade routes had opened up between Lhiosquor, Dorronquor, Turvah and Tsayun, as well as with the free Cainite cities of Mathtusekh, Rethobal, Barudaol, and Casmithri.

# 165 EC

Once a road had been built from Mt. Threthor to Lake Turvah, merchant ships began to move up and down the Rahav bringing supplies to Tsayun. Because of the continuous trading of large amounts of goods between different tribes and cities, the Council of Elders in Lhiosquor issued the world's first currency; a gold coin named the dorron after the city of gold. The dorron became the currency of Lhiosquor, Dorronquor, Turvah, and Tsayun. A town soon began to grow around Shaochi's docks where most of the ships would stop to unload their goods. Shaochi, who lent his name to the bustling port town of Shaochiquor, became a very wealthy man because of this trade, and contributed a large portion of this wealth - thousands of dorrons - to the construction of the temple on Mt. Tsayun.

The Temple of Yah was overlaid with gold from Dorronquor and regions of the Upper Pishon where gold was plentiful and Lamekk's minions had not yet conquered. By this time, Lamekk controlled the entire Lower Pishon valley. Over a period of twenty-six years, the Temple of Yah rose to a height of thirty cubits and measured thirty cubits wide and eighty cubits in length. The altar in front of the temple was inlaid with an abundance of emeralds, rubies, sapphires, diamonds, and other precious stones of various hues and sizes. These jewels came from the people of Tsayun who mined for these precious stones beneath the mountain upon which the Temple of Yah now stood. From Lhiosquor came a golden box made by the goldsmiths of Dorronquor who had taken up residence on the mountain. The purpose of the box was known to no one, but God had commanded that it be made and be placed in the inner sanctuary.

When the construction of the temple was finally completed, and sacrifices had been made to dedicate the new dwelling of the King of the Heavens and the Earth, the glory of the Almighty One descended like a cloud upon the building and upon all who were gathered. Everyone inside the building fell to ground as though struck dead, and many began to pray earnestly. A voice like thunder spoke from the cloud.

"You have obeyed the words I have spoken through My servant,

Kenan, and because of this I will greatly bless the fair city of Lhiosquor and make it the capital of a mighty kingdom. The sons of Seth will be mighty men of valour who will smite the abominable offspring of Lamekk and bring their kingdom to an end. I shall appoint a king in Lhiosquor who will be given dominion over all the inhabitants of the earth. Justice and mercy shall reign in the streets of that city, along with wisdom and understanding, for as long as the people of Lhiosquor will abide by the law that I give to them this day.

"The tribes of Dorro, Turvah, and Tsayun I will also greatly bless. No eaters will enter their cities to devour their people, and they shall enjoy great prosperity for as long as they acknowledge the king whom I will appoint over the earth in Lhiosquor. I also appoint one-twelfth of the tribe of Tsayun to care for this sanctuary, My dwelling, and to make the appointed sacrifices in the times and seasons that I will give them. Their blue robes and golden headdresses shall make them known. They must allow their beards to grow long and never be cut, for this is a sign that they are set apart to My service.

"If the sons of Seth are to prosper, they must follow the commands which I have passed on to them through Adam; a man must have only one wife for all of his life, and a woman only one husband for all of her life. They must remain faithful to each other for as long as they both live. If one partner dies and the other is still alive, the surviving partner is allowed to remarry, but under no other circumstances must this holy union be broken. Shed not the blood of any man or beast, but the blood of a beast may be shed to save the life of a man, woman, or child, or to be used as a sacrifice. If any beast kills a man, woman, or child, it must be put to death.

"The Council elders must cast anyone who kills another person down from the top of Mt. Threthor off of its steepest cliff; however, if a man kills an enemy in battle, that must not be held against him. Also, you shall not worship any of the false gods of Turnienquor or bow down before the Giants or their idols. You must not allow any of your sons and daughters to intermarry with the Cainites, for they will lead you astray and entice your children to follow after idols. Take only your fair share of what belongs to you, and take nothing from another without permission. Anyone who violates any of these proscriptions must be cast off over the steepest cliff of Mt. Threthor to his death.

"Respect those in authority. Do not lie to one another, but always speak the truth, living honest and upright lives before each other. Remember to rest from your labours, as I rested on the seventh day after making the heavens and earth and all that they contain. Love Me and love one another and this love will be the power which drives you to greatness. If you do these things, you will be prosperous and strike down your enemies. If you do not, I shall allow factions and bitterness to rise up among you, and I will raise the accursed sons of Hishirash against you."

Yah the Almighty One gave many other laws to each of the tribes represented, but most of them concerned the citizens of Lhiosquor who would bear the burden of leadership. After He had finished speaking, the cloud of His presence rose up into the heavens and the thunder faded. Kenan then selected Hualichi, the seventh son of Tsayun and a mere youth of forty-five years, to be the High Priest of the Temple. Kenan took a jar of scented oil and poured it over Hualichi's head. He was dressed in the priestly garments and a silver ring was placed on his finger. Then, Hualichi told the men of Tsayun to sit in twelve groups of equal number. Hualichi released a white dove that hovered over the crowd momentarily before resting among the division furthest to Hualichi's right. "These are the priests whom Yah has chosen to serve Him." he said. "Arise and become priests of Yah." The men came forward and were anointed by Hualichi in the same manner that Hualichi was anointed by Kenan. They received the same priestly garments to wear, but without the silver ring. When the priests had taken their places, Kenan walked down from the Temple stairs and the people began to journey home.

When Kenan and the rest of the delegation from Lhiosquor had returned, a great celebration was held. In the midst of the celebration, Enos announced the wedding of Kenan, his eldest son, to Muhalelet of the tribe of Cerchil. (Cerchil was the second eldest of the seven sons of Adam who came with their wives to found Lhiosquor. These were known as the Fourteen Founders.) Everyone cheered, and the homecoming celebration became a wedding feast. Cerchil brought forth his granddaughter Muhalelet. She was robed in a dazzling white robe, hemmed in a vibrant forest green that reflected the green in her eyes.

Kenan's heart beat quickly and strongly within his chest as he came forward for Seth to place a mantle of silver on his shoulders. The patriarch of Lhiosquor clasped together the hands of the new couple and spoke a blessing over them. Kenan and Muhalelet had loved each other for close to twenty years, but because Kenan had been busy overseeing the construction of the temple, they had not yet been joined in marriage. Now that the Temple of Yah was completed, the time had come for them to be married. As Kenan stood on the raised marble platform in front of the Council building facing his beloved bride, the realization that the time of waiting was finally over went to his heart. Such a feeling arose within him that didn't know whether to laugh or cry. Muhalelet's green eyes began to grow misty, and tears of joy began to flow down her face. After Seth had completed the blessing and the new couple descended from the platform, celebrations began again as a great banquet was held in their honour. The sound of singing and the playing of musical instruments filled the air. Everyone was filled with joy and hope for the future of Lhiosquor. As for Kenan and Muhalelet, they were oblivious to all of the feasting and dancing and were simply absorbed in their love for each other.

## 166 EC

One year later, when Kenan was seventy years old, Muhalelet bore him their first child, a son whom she named Mahalalel, whose name meant "a song of praise". Mahalalel was greatly loved by his father and prospered in everything that he did. Around the time that Mahalalel was born, over two thousand people lived in the city of Lhiosquor. A road was built from Turvah to Tsayun, creating a land route from Mt. Tsayun in the west to Mt. Threthor in the east. It became known as the Pilgrim's Road. The road soon teemed with pilgrims and merchants who brought much wealth to the cities of Seth's people. The spires and towers of Lhiosquor grew tall and strong and its walls of polished marble shimmered in the sun.

As a result of its growing wealth and prominence, Lhiosquor was no longer a hidden place. Word spread of the location of the City of Light, and when King Lamekk the Twice Accursed heard of the whereabouts of the glorious city, he amassed a terrible army of his strongest warriors among men and Giants. The Giants began to raise quake lizards, armoured lizards, speed lizards, horses, mastodons and elephants to transport their armies. The smiths of Tubal-Cain's forges perfected the art of iron working, and the iron weapons and armour made by the smiths of Turnienquor rendered bronze weapons and armour obsolete. The advantage given by the strength and sharpness of forged iron allowed Lamekk's armies to conquer the twin cities of Kheropheth and Niragadan, former colonies of Enokk, bringing them under his rule.

# 183 EC

When Lamekk's grim hordes were made ready and the day had come to go to war, King Lamekk gathered his army together and addressed his bloodthirsty warriors.

"My loyal subjects, we stand on the threshold of universal empire!" he boasted, to great bellowing shouts of acclaim. "Today, we will move north to take the city of Mathtusekh, but that is only a prelude to the glory that awaits us yet farther north. We will move from Mathtusekh to Mt. Threthor and lay waste to the pompous city of the despicable Sethites. With our new machines of war, we will bring the self-righteous weaklings of the mountain city to their knees. Seth and Enos will bow before me, and I will slay them with my own sword. Once Lhiosquor has been crushed beneath our might, we shall be the undisputed rulers of the earth!"

The warriors of Shaol were stirred to hot hatred and bloodlust by the speech of their patriarch. They called for the death of Seth and his people. When their battle fury was aroused to a frenzy, Lamekk shouted a command for his army to begin marching out of Turnienquor toward Mathtusekh. They marched northward in unison following Hishirash, the first of the Giants, in rows of six. Hishirash was the commander of Lamekk's army, and it was he and his sons and brothers who had designed the terrible siege engines to which Lamekk had referred in his speech. Now Hishirash was far more popular among the soldiers than Lamekk, and a conspiracy had been growing to dispose of the king. Two days before the hordes of Lamekk reached Mathtusekh, Gorgondish went to his father, Hishirash.

"Father, Lamekk would have us leave to take Lhiosquor with no time to rest at Mathtusekh and enjoy our victory there. He has become so obsessed with his vendetta against Seth that he has entirely forgotten the reason why we conquer cities - to plunder and enjoy the spoils. How can we enjoy the spoils of war if we are forced to keep driving on toward Mt. Threthor? Notwithstanding this, he thinks that he can destroy a mountain! Our weaponry is yet to reach that level. He is mad if he thinks that we can scale Mt. Threthor, hoist up all of our war beasts and siege engines, and sack Lhiosquor!"

Sherbutoth, a brother of Hishirash, added to his nephew's comments. "Your son is right. We need to rid ourselves of our little king. Tonight, brother, while Lamekk sleeps in his tent, let us slay him and raise ourselves up as the overlords of the Cainites. Our race, the race of Giants, shall one day rule over all of the puny races of men as is our right. We shall take Lhiosquor, but at a time of our choosing, when our strength is indomitable. Let us first take Mathtusekh, enjoy what is ours, and finish developing our new siege engine. It will be more powerful than anything we have yet developed. Only with this weapon can we hope to tear down a mountain, and it is not yet ready. For now, we should enjoy what we have and not risk it all in a senseless raid against the Sethites. Their time will come soon enough."

The Giants, including Hishirash, were in agreement with the plan of Sherbutoth. In the middle of the night, Hishirash arose and strode toward his grandfather's tent. The towering Giant grabbed both sides of the tent, pulled it out of the ground and, wrapping the screaming, bewildered king inside, clove Lamekk in two with Chabaq, his terrible, curved sword of iron. The entire camp was now awake and alarmed, startled at the sight. When a commotion arose, Hishirash blew on the horn of a great three-horned lizard and addressed his army.

"I, Hishirash, firstborn of the Giants, proclaim myself king over Lamekk's entire kingdom. If anyone wishes to challenge my authority, let him step forward now, and I will dispatch him as quickly as our sometime king who now lies in two at my feet. Tomorrow, we shall continue to Mathtusekh as planned. Once the city is ours, we will rest, enjoy the spoils, and return to assail Mt. Threthor at a more convenient time when we are ready. Sleep now, and dream of victory!"

# 185 EC

When news reached Lhiosquor that the army of Hishirash had taken Mathtusekh, the city's stonemasons raised massive stone walls to protect the fledgling settlements at the base of the mountain. The walls were preparation for the time when the hordes of Hishirash would unleash their fury upon Mt. Threthor. Although Seth and all his people abhorred bloodshed, it was agreed that a permanent defence force was needed to keep watch for the enemy and to protect the people. Kenan was chosen as its leader. About two years passed until news came that the armies of Turnienquor were approaching Mt. Threthor. Pocabal, a grandson of Nosjubal and a friend of Mahalalel, spotted a large army coming from the south. Heedless of the ban on Cainites in the city of Lhiosquor, he ran and found Mahalalel who was walking in the colonnade of Enos' new academy, talking with his grandfather. Pocabal told them all about what he had seen.

"The Giants are coming with great lizards and terrible machines to Mt. Threthor!" he gasped, breathless from running up the mountain.

"So, Hishirash the Abominable has finally come to test the strength of our people." said Enos.

"Yes, he is coming from the south with a vast army. We need to make preparations immediately." said Pocabal, forgetting that Jubalites were not allowed to enter the city.

"We must convene the Council at once." said Enos. At that moment, Pocabal realized that he was in forbidden territory, and wondered whether Enos meant to convene the Council to have him executed. He began to tremble and sweat profusely.

"P-Please do not have me executed! I was so afraid when I saw the armies that I ran here completely oblivious of the p-proscription." Pocabal stuttered fearfully.

"Considering that you came as fast as you could to warn us of a dire situation, and because you and your family have been friends of me and my family for generations, you shall be spared if you leave at once and man the walls in Triethu. Hishirash will probably attack there first. Mahalalel," he said, turning to his grandson, "you will come with me until the Council bell is rung and the elders are all accounted for. Then, go and join your friend in Triethu."

Pocabal departed as quickly as he had come, relieved that Enos had shown him mercy. People who saw him rush by were astonished and wondered why the young Jubalite was running so quickly through the streets of the city. At the highest point of the city, Enos's face was grim with determination as, with Mahalalel following, he swiftly crossed the academy courtyard with its well-tended flower garden. The sage's hurried manner caused students studying in the courtyard to look up from their scrolls to see where their master was going.

Enos hurried through the west wing of the academy building to the main entrance and crossed the Avenue of Justice, the cobblestone road that led through the heart of Lhiosquor. The Council Hall was directly across the avenue from Enos's academy, and because of the recent advances in architecture it was now a much larger and far more beautiful building than when it was built, many years ago, when Enos was a very small child. The old brick building had been replaced with an elegant marble structure boasting a colonnaded courtyard. Another of the additions to the new Council Hall was a bell tower, built along the north side of the Council courtyard, which one could ring in times of emergency. Mahalalel had never forgotten the severe scolding he had received from his mother Muhalelet when, at the age of nine, he had snuck out in the middle of the night to the bell tower and rang the bell.

Young Mahalalel had awakened the entire city, and all of the elders ran to the Council Hall in their linen bedclothes. Mahalalel laughed in spite of himself all the way home until he saw his mother standing in the doorway, cradling his baby brother, Konaryah, in her arms, her eyes full of fiery green wrath. She gave her eldest son so strong a whipping that he could barely sit down to breakfast the next morning. Mahalalel smiled to himself as remembered the Elders of Lhiosquor scrambling like frightened chickens awakened by the trumpeting of a small eater lizard.

This time, however, a real emergency threatened every citizen of Lhiosquor. Enos rang the bell, and all of the elders arrived at the Council Hall within minutes. All fifty-two elders were present, and each took the seat assigned to him in the hall. Any man who had reached the age of one hundred was eligible to sit in the Council of Elders, but his appointment must first be approved by two-thirds of the Council members. Occasionally, women were appointed to Council seats and ten of the Council members were women. The counsel of Azura, wife of Seth, was well respected both in and outside of the Council Hall. She had come today with her husband, who presided over the Council meetings. When everyone was gathered, Seth sounded the ram's horn and called the meeting to order.

"Elders of Lhiosquor, for many years this city has provided for us a safe haven. This mountain has protected us from the outside world. In recent years, we have built new cities far more visible and vulnerable than our capital, and now the whole world knows where we are. We have established prosperous trade routes with our neighbours, and many of us have undertaken long pilgrimages to the Temple of Yah in Tsayun. These travels, along with our influence with our neighbours, have caused our renown to spread across the world. It is because of our renown that we can no longer simply hide from our enemies. Armed confrontations, I regret to say, will be inevitable as there are those who despise us and scorn the law given to us by Yah. We can no longer hide here on Mt. Threthor and expect the Giants simply to disappear. Our daughter cities, huddled at the base of this mountain, and those lying helpless in the valleys beyond, require our protection.

As you know, we have organized a defence force led by Kenan, and built battlements around the foothill settlements to help in this effort. My eldest and wisest son, Enos, has told me that they have been completed just in time; Hishirash's hordes have been spotted, advancing from the south along the road to Mathtusekh. We must make haste to reinforce our new battlements, prepare our defence force, and construct watchtowers to mark the progress of the enemy. Lhiosquor itself is unassailable, but without protection our loved ones in the surrounding cities may soon meet the fate of righteous Abel who was murdered by his unrighteous, jealous brother. Let us now call upon Yah, the Almighty One, to protect us in this terrible day."

Seth began to pray, and the Elders joined him. "Great Yah, Lord of the Heavens and Earth, Eloi the Almighty One who brought the land out of the sea and gathered it into one place, hear the cry of Your chosen people. Go before us and protect us this day so that we will not be destroyed. We desire that generations yet unborn will see Your works and praise You. We ask that You would go forth today and fight for us against Your enemies."

After the prayer, there was a moment of awkward silence as everyone looked around the room, wondering who would speak next. Solgart of the tribe of Duirthei stood to his feet and spoke, "If we should gain victory over Hishirash and his forces flee, what are we to do next? Surely if we were to pursue them, they would turn and destroy us."

Enos replied to Solgart's question. "You are right, Solgart, to say that we should not pursue Hishirash. We will let him flee and then strengthen our defences for the next attack. We will also use that time to join our forces with those of others, such as the valiant Turvese and the free Cainites of Rethobal who have no love for the abominable spawn of Lamekk. Rethobal is already making preparations of its own against Turnienquor."

"Well said, my son." said Seth, anxious to close the session. "If there is anyone else with wise counsel for our city today, let him speak." The hall was silent. Moments later, Seth spoke again. "If there is no other counsel today, I dismiss this meeting, and advise you all to remain in the city. Do not venture down the mountain for any reason. Go to your homes and pray for the conflict to be ended swiftly." Then the Council was adjourned and the Elders of Lhiosquor returned to their homes.

In the meantime, Mahalalel had reached Triethu where his friend Pocabal was keeping watch from a large wooden tower. It had been hastily constructed near the southern gate of the fledgling city. "The enemy is getting closer, Mahalalel!" Pocabal shouted. "The Giants are in the vanguard, and they are dreadful to behold clad in their iron mail."

Mahalalel peered ahead into the distance at the approaching hordes. He was greatly dismayed to espy enormous catapults the likes of which had never been seen being dragged by quake lizards and mastodons. The ground shook at the approach of these great beasts with their ominous burdens. Soldiers with torches walked alongside the catapults. One of the soldiers put his torch to the head of a catapult, and its contents blazed like a bonfire. When the catapult's fiery load was released, the great ball of fire soared through the air until it appeared that the sun itself was falling from the sky in fiery wrath upon Triethu.

At that moment, Kenan sounded the ram's horn alarm, summoning the forces of Lhiosquor to gather before the city gate. Mahalalel and Pocabal climbed down out of the watchtower to join the assembling army none too late; as they ran to the gate, blazing fire came down upon the watchtower where they had been stationed. Set alight by the fire, the watchtower soon collapsed to the ground. Then, Kenan gave the order to open the gates, and the forces of Lhiosquor let out a great cry as they ran forward to fight the abominable hordes of Hishirash. As the defenders of Lhiosquor charged ahead, a great cloud appeared around Lhiosquor at the top of the mountain and began to descend. Both armies could hear the sound of trumpets and war cries coming from within the fog. Before the army of Lhiosquor could reach the hordes of Turnienquor, cries of terror arose from the army of Hishirash. Many of the enemy warriors were caught in terrible winds arising from within the fog. Wherever the fog passed across the Cainite ranks, Hishirash's men lay dead in the grass. When the terrible fog had cleared, all that the men of Lhiosquor could see of the remaining enemy was a greatly diminished force, fleeing in terror southward toward safety. The Battle of Triethu was over, and the people of the Mountain were safe.

That night, Seth called for a celebration and sacrifices were presented in the Council courtyard, giving thanks to Yah for defending

His people. Although none of the soldiers of Lhiosquor had perished in the battle, Kenan was honoured for being ready to face death for sake of Threthoron, the growing realm that surrounded Lhiosquor upon Mt. Threthor. Great cheers of jubilation and gratitude to God arose from the gathered multitude. The celebrations continued for six days. The people of Seth still celebrate the annual Feast of Thanksgiving today.

# The Flowering of Lhiosquor

## (196 – 281 EC)

In a time just short of two centuries, Lhiosquor had grown from a tiny settlement hidden above the clouds on the top of Mt. Threthor to a small but influential city of over five thousand people. Despite its small size, it was in those days the most glorious city in the world. Kenan the Just was its king, and he was also king over the entire realm of Threthoron where the tribes of Lhiosquor had settled. However, the empire of the Giant Hishirash was also powerful in those days, and his empire bordered on Threthoron. In these days, the Old Alliance was formed between the tribes of the Free Cainites, the Turvese, and the people of Threthoron. The Dorronites had a role to play as well, but few ever came out from Dorronquor for fear of the wider world beyond the shelter of the Kheruva Mountains.

Here the story is told of the golden age of Lhiosquor, of its most glorious heroes and battles, of the deeds of the sons of Kenan, and of a tragic seed of division that was sown but lay dormant yet for many years. It was a time of legends, the dawn of the Age of Peace, a time when the full sinfulness of mankind was yet held at bay and virtue and honour and the love of God filled the hearts of His chosen people.

# CHAPTER 8

# THE BATTLE OF BARIQUOR
## (196 – 201 EC)

## 196 EC

In the year one hundred and ninety-six of the Enosian Calendar and on the one-hundredth birthday of Kenan, Seth convened the Council of Elders for a very important meeting. Today, Kenan would take his place in the Council. When all of the Elders had gathered in the Council chambers and had taken their seats, Seth called the Council into session.

"Dear Elders of the Council of Lhiosquor, today we remember the day when we first set foot on Mt. Threthor, nearly two hundred years ago. Here, we built a sanctuary where all that dwelt herein could live in peace. Today, we are the leaders of a great city that has grown too large to remain hidden. In the early days, the dark powers in Turnienquor knew nothing of our whereabouts. This mountain provided all the protection we needed, and no defence force was necessary. Now, we can rely on Yah alone for protection, and we need His guidance more than ever. Today, my grandson Kenan who received the vision to build the Temple of Yah has come of age. He has shown great valour in his efforts to defend our people from our enemies. I motion a vote to elect him to this Council."

In those days, strife was yet unknown in the Council of Lhiosquor and Kenan was very popular with everyone. All fifty-four Council members elected him to be the fifty-fifth of their number. After the vote, Kenan's father, the philosopher Enos, announced a long awaited motion. "My friends and fellow Elders of Lhiosquor, much has changed since those long ago days to which my father refers. Our society has progressed and specialized, becoming increasingly larger and more complex, and the menace of the Giants to the south of us is a constant threat. Consequently, this Council has spent more and more time in session. We have been deciding on many matters both great and small, and spending more time weighing the impact of these decisions. We have need of a governing body endowed with the ability make important decisions quickly and efficiently, leaving this Council to deal with less urgent matters which need to be more carefully weighed.

To more effectively administer the affairs of this city and the realm of Threthoron, I motion that we elect a permanent Council leader who will have a final say on all decisions. He will be given the authority to take control of lengthy proceedings to reach a final vote in times of crisis. This man will also act as king in times of war and will lead the defence force. He must be a member of this Council, a descendant of the Fourteen Founders, and must have received training in the defence force."

Baeathil, a sister of Seth and one of the fourteen Founders of Lhiosquor, was the next to speak. "Elders of Lhiosquor, I believe that our course is clear. The newest of our number most surely fits all of the criteria to be our leader. We are all familiar with the prophecies that he will one day be king on this mountain. I nominate Kenan, the son of Enos."

"Kenan is nominated." said Seth. "Are there any others?"

Murassan of Agradelai spoke next. "Kenan is indeed worthy, and it is not out of a lack of love or gratitude that I nominate my valiant and worthy brother, Yotis the son of Agradelai, who ran with the vanguard in the Battle of Triethu."

"Yotis is nominated" repeated Seth. "Are there any others?"

After a period of silence, Enos spoke again. "Kenan and Yotis have been nominated. Let our vote decide who will be the first among us. All in favour of Kenan, raise your right arm." Enos counted fifty-two. "All in favour of Yotis, raise your right arm." Enos counted three. "By a vote of fifty-two to three, Kenan has been chosen as the permanent leader of this Council of Elders and shall assume the title of King of Lhiosquor when needed. This decision will take effect in seven days at which time this Council shall reconvene."

So began the glorious reign of Kenan the Just, the first and greatest king in Lhiosquor. His first act was to establish smaller councils in each of the small towns in Threthoron surrounding Lhiosquor so that local matters would not need to be brought before the Council of the Elders at Lhiosquor. Each of these towns would also send representatives who would meet with Kenan once a year or at times of emergency in a new building on the Common Fields which became known as the Colonial Council. The Colonial Council addressed issues that could not be addressed in the council of a particular town, and was mainly concerned with defence. The Council of Lhiosquor would now only be called upon for matters concerning the city of Lhiosquor itself, or for matters concerning the realm of Threthoron as a whole. Kenan renamed the Council of Lhiosquor the High Council of Threthoron.

At the first meeting of the Colonial Council, representatives had come from Shrivazh, Triethu, Ruwad, Cerciann, Duirthan, Agrad, and Numeshad. These were the towns of Threthoron, save Lhiosquor, at this time. Adah herself had come to represent her people, the Jubalites of Shrivazh. When it was her turn to speak, she told of the problem facing her people.

"Great king, honourable members of this council, the people of Shrivazh have again become too numerous. Some of our people have already left to build new cities in the west, but our race multiplies quickly, and quarrels have begun to break out in the city streets. It appears that the murderous spirit of my sometime husband, Lamekk, still dwells in the hearts of some of our younger citizens. As space becomes scarce and land more difficult to obtain, some have begun to cheat and steal from one another. They say that there is not enough for everyone to have their share, and that new lands are needed. Although I abhor their actions, I believe that we should go forth and join the cities of the free Cainites in the north, those that have not bowed the knee to Hishirash. We shall also join those of our number who have already left to found settlements beyond Lake Turvah along the Rahav and the Pilgrim's Road. Others still have expressed a desire to seek out their brethren, the Jabalites, who wander in the north beyond the mountains."

"If you go, Lady of Shrivazh, do you know that Lhiosquor cannot protect you there? Are your people willing to look after their own defence, away from the shelter of this mountain?" asked Kenan.

"Lamekk, my one time husband, is dead. We are ready, o king, to venture forth on our own. There are a few among our number, belonging to the house of Nosjubal, your loyal friend, who would remain behind in Shrivazh, but for most of us the time has come to leave Mt. Threthor. Do not think that we have begrudged or resented the kindness of your grandfather who gave us this land to care for that we may be sheltered from our enemies, but now my cruel husband has been dead for thirteen years, and although I love not the House of Hishirash, neither will I live in fear of his wrath. Will you now bid us leave to seek out these new lands and new homes?"

"Yes, Lady of Shrivazh, you have my leave. You may take your people and go wherever you wish, but for your sake avoid the Lower Pishon valley and the realm of Turnienquor."

In those days, because people did not seem to grow old and die, people lived a very long time and remained able to bear children for hundreds of years. Even Adam and Eve in Siaghlamh, though over four hundred years old, still bore children. Because of this, a couple of such advanced age may have a hundred children. Those of the Cainite race married young, in their late teens and early twenties, whereas even the hastiest of Sethites waited at least until sixty. Consequently, the numbers of the Jubalites had exploded in Shrivazh as did the numbers of the Cainites in other lands, and the number which left Shrivazh was close to forty-five thousand. Only four hundred remained in that town. In contrast, by this time there were barely over five thousand souls in the city of Lhiosquor.

## 201 EC

For two hundred years, Enokk, the eldest son of Cain, had dwelt in the city of his brother, Nehobal, exiled from his birthright by his own execrable descendants. In Rethobal, after hearing of the plundering of Mathtusekh, Enokk and his brother built a great fortress to withstand the attacks of Hishirash. His hatred grew hot against the abominable upstarts who would deny him his birthright. Enokk's wife Neema, however, counselled him to proceed with more forethought, and to seek an alliance with Kenan, the new king of Lhiosquor. Neema's counsel prevailed and, in the early years of Kenan's reign, while the king of Threthoron was gathering together the strength of his people, Enokk set out from Rethobal.

He was headed, along with Nehobal, the fifth son of Cain, and the army of Rethobal, to Mt. Threthor for an audience with King Kenan. They travelled south from Rethobal until they came to the city of Ruwad, which lay in the shadow of Mt. Threthor to the south. Ruadil, the governor of Ruwad, saw a force of Cainites coming from the north, but noted that they carried not the colours and banners of Turnienquor.

Ruadil went out with a small band of guards to meet with the visitors and find out why they had come. "Who are you?" he asked Enokk. "Where are you from, and what brings you to the city of Ruwad and the realm of Threthoron?"

"I am Enokk, the Twice-Exiled, eldest son of Cain. The unlamented Lamekk the Accursed of Turnienquor denied me my birthright. I seek an audience with your king, Kenan the Just, that we may join our armies together to eradicate the race of Giants from the earth. I will then reclaim what is mine, the kingship of Enokk Turnienquor."

Ruwad was impressed. "Are you indeed Enokk the firstborn of Cain? No one has heard tell of you in all of the long years of Lhiosquor. Now you come to us in full battle array to have an audience with our king! Tell me, how is it that you escaped the Usurpation? For surely, after Cain was killed, Lamekk would have sought you next."

"When the battle was lost and Lamekk had beheaded my father, I knew that I could not then raise a force to defeat him. Under the cover of nightfall, I fled with Neema and those of my children who were yet young and remained in my house, and came to Rethobal, the city of Nehobal, my brother. My eldest son, Irad, was of like mind and he fled far into the south beyond the Duobinar Mountains where he built a city, Iradu. The city is far away where the Euphrates turns south and flows into the Outer Sea. I had not known that he had survived until last year, when a messenger came to tell me that Irad was coming from the south to assail Turnienquor. He is now but a few days from here, and I have asked him to meet me."

Nehobal was the next to speak. "I am Nehobal, the fifth son of Cain. Two hundred years ago, my brother came to my city seeking refuge from Lamekk, and since then we have been preparing an army fit to do battle against the foul fighters of Hishirash. Nevertheless, even with the help of Irad, our forces will barely match those of Turnienquor, and are insufficient for a full assault on Hishirash's realm. The forces of Lhiosquor would tip the balance and also strike great fear into the hearts of our enemies, for it has been made known to us how the hordes of Hishirash fled in terror before the bright host of Mt. Threthor. Such an alliance would bring a great and lasting peace to the whole world, and none of us will need to fear the Giants evermore."

Ruadil weighed the words that were spoken and judged that the leaders of this fierce company spoke the truth. "You may stay in Ruwad tonight. I will send a messenger to Lhiosquor, and he should have an answer from the king in the morning." The army of Rethobal made camp within the gates of Ruwad, and the following day a great procession came down from the foothills of Mt. Threthor. Kenan had come to meet with Enokk and Nehobal.

"Welcome to the realm of Lhiosquor, rightful heir of Cain." said Kenan, dismounting from the back of the speed lizard upon which he rode. "I hear that you wish to aid us in bringing down the House of Lamekk. I welcome you, brave Enokk, Mechal of the Cainites, and you, Nehobal, patriarch of Rethobal. I have heard your entreaties, and I will soon call a meeting of the High Council in order to decide what course of action we will take on this matter. Should the High Council decide in favour of this allegiance, as I hope it will, we shall then together decide how best to liberate Turnienquor that you may have your rightful inheritance."

Enokk's impatience began to boil to the surface. "With all respect, mighty king, is all this talk necessary? We could muster our forces now, and then advance upon the gates of my once fair city before Hishirash knew what was happening."

Kenan replied soberly. "Enokk, you have seen with your own eyes the tragedy that occurs when one man holds sole authority over a great number of people. Though king, I do not rule alone. The people of Lhiosquor bring their petitions to the High Council, the Council assembles along with me, and we then make our decisions according to the holy law of Yah, He whom you know as the Maker. Were Hishirash presently assailing the cities of Threthoron, I would then act according to my own judgement because haste would be needed. However in times of peace, such as we are now in as we have not yet declared to march against Hishirash, all matters of great import must be heard by the High Council unless utmost haste is needed. Together, many wise citizens may make more prudent decisions, and many councillors may often see things of which the king may not be aware or may overlook in haste.

Even though the cries of your people suffering under the yoke of Hishirash have not been forgotten, we must also take time to carefully plan our concerted effort against the abominable tyrant in Turnienquor. We need to anticipate all of his possible moves and countermoves in order to win victory. It is important that the best possible course of action be found.

Enokk looked at Kenan with renewed respect, even though the desire for vengeance still burned within his heart. "I see that you value your traditions, Kenan, and not without good reason. That is a very admirable quality. Keep in mind, though, that the longer we wait here, planning our campaign, the longer Hishirash will have to prepare against us."

"I understand, Enokk. That is why we must direct our attack in such a way that he does not know we are coming until we are already standing at his doorstep. I return now to Lhiosquor to call the High Council into session. In the meantime, you and your companions have my leave to travel throughout Threthoron, only you must not enter the city of Lhiosquor. When the High Council has rendered its decision, I will meet with you in the buildings of the Colonial Council where a Council of War will be held. There we will make our battle plans. Until then, may Yah bless your time here, Enokk firstborn of Cain." Kenan and his company then returned up the road to Lhiosquor.

The High Council ruled in favour of an alliance with Enokk and Nehobal in a campaign against Hishirash. Word was brought swiftly to Enokk who then left Ruwad, with Nehobal and his commanders, to meet Kenan and his captains in the Colonial Council building. The architecture of the Colonial Council building was similar to that of the High Council, except that the interior was more austere. Much of the gold and colourful tapestries that adorned the walls of the main chamber of the High Council building were absent in the main chamber of the Colonial Council. The building was still very large; its ceiling reached a height of fifteen cubits. In front of the council building was a pillared portico where Enokk and Nehobal waited with their chieftains. When given leave to enter, Enokk crossed the portico and stood beneath the red lintel of the doorway. Kenan rose from his seat and greeted his visitor.

"Welcome, rightful heir of Enokk Turnienquor. I have glad tidings; the High Council has ruled in favour of an alliance with your people and has requested that a campaign be undertaken to liberate your city. Our objective is to completely rid the world of the abominable race of Giants and bring peace to all people. Once our forces are equipped and readied, those of us already in Threthoron will meet in the harbour of Cerciann, the city which lies by the lake at the base of Mt. Threthor, south and west of its summit. We shall then divide our forces to lead a two pronged attack; one army will sail in galleons from Lake Cerciann down the river Mashiren to the place where that river flows into the Pishon. There, as you know, Hishirash has built the fortress city of Bariquor to prevent any assault from that direction. He will be expecting an attack from that direction. However, Hishirash will not be expecting the second army, which shall arrive first in Mathtusekh to liberate the people there. He will be distracted by the assault on Mathtusekh and leave few forces behind in Bariquor."

Enokk appeared thoughtful. "I see. Capturing Bariquor, should it prove possible, would tip the balance of power in the Pishon Valley in our favour, and we will be upstream from all of the other major cities on Hishirash's empire. However, we could just as easily sail right past Bariquor and take Turnienquor itself. Then we shall have the Giants' capital, and I shall have redeemed my inheritance."

Nosjubal, now patriarch of Shrivazh and one of Kenan's chief captains, replied to Enokk's suggestion. "We have sent out scouts to assess the strength of Bariquor in preparation of this very day. It sits at the confluence of two rivers and is protected by many towers, tall and grim, from which archers may rain down flaming arrows onto ships passing by. While the walls of Bariquor make an invasion by land virtually impossible, the towers are the sole defence for the harbour of Bariquor. The bulk of the forces stationed there will assuredly be sent to the battle at Mathtusekh, but Hishirash will not be so foolish as not to leave a force behind to guard against an attack. Any ships attempting to sail past will surely be set ablaze by the arrows of the enemy and be unable to sail further. We would drown in the Pishon before reaching Turnienquor. We must disembark at Bariquor and then, having captured the fortress, we will hold the key to the entire region. Also, the walls of Bariquor will provide a defence in the event that we must make a hasty retreat from Turnienquor."

"Your campaign seems sound and well planned." said Enokk. "I would have one thing, however. When Bariquor is ours, I will lead the assault on Turnienquor, as no one else knows the land there as I do. Every hill and valley, wood and glen I know, and all of the secret hiding places around the city are known to me."

"Indeed, Enokk, your knowledge of the terrain surrounding your home city will be invaluable. You shall be given command of the assault against Hishirash in Turnienquor. Nehobal may lead the second army against Mathtusekh, if he so chooses, and should lead forth that party as soon as it is ready. The rest of us will remain here for a fortnight to give time for the forces from Rethobal to be mobilized against Mathtusekh."

"I so choose." said Nehobal. "I tire of having the Giants for neighbours, and the sooner my slain brother's kin are liberated, the sooner my city shall have rest from its weary watchfulness." Nehobal was referring to Mathtu the Fisherman, the fourth son of Cain and once patriarch of Mathtusekh, who had been slain in Hishirash's first campaign in the year 183. "I shall depart immediately to begin preparations." Nehobal, along with his chieftains, then left the council chambers.

As he left, Enokk said to his brother, "When you return to Rethobal, send the rest of my men to meet me in Cerciann, all but the tenth under the command of my second eldest surviving son, Hurgart. Those shall accompany you to Mathtusekh."

"I will do so, brother, and if all is well, I will soon celebrate with you on the streets of your once fair city." then Nehobal left the Colonial Council chamber and departed for his city.

Thirteen days after the War Council was held, as preparations were being made in Cerciann for battle, Irad son of Enokk arrived at Mt. Threthor. He had first come to Rethobal, where he heard that the allied forces were gathered at the mysterious mountain of the Sethites. With him were one thousand warriors clad in shining mail and the red and gold colours of the tribe of Enokk. A standard bearer to the right of Irad bore a standard, similar to the standard of Enokk's forces - a golden mastodon on a red background - but a distinctive mark was made on the banner. Above the mastodon was a golden seabird that Irad took for his own sign, as his city of Iradu lay by the Outer Sea. Irad himself, clothed in full iron battle armour, topped by a golden helmet with an extravagant red plume, stopped in front of the gates of Cerciann and shouted in a high, clear voice.

"We, the men of Iradu, have come from the far south to free the city of our fathers from the foul usurpers. We will give our swords no rest until no Giant walks the face of the earth!" The forces of Lhiosquor were gathered in the harbour of Cerciann at this time, where they readied their galleons for war. Kenan was standing on one of the docks, unwinding ropes for the rigging while he oversaw the preparations. He heard Irad's declaration and came to meet him.

"Welcome, brave Irad son of Enokk, to the kingdom of Threthoron from your home far in the south. I am Kenan, appointed king by the High Council of Threthoron. Your father told me to expect you and no doubt he will be happy to see your arrival. You and your men are welcome here in Threthoron and may stay here tonight and tomorrow. On the third day we will depart for Bariquor by ship."

"It is good to meet you, great king. When I and my men arrived at Rethobal, we met other men who had come from Lhiosquor. They spoke of you with great admiration. They said that they were heading toward Mathtusekh; I had believed that we would be joining them."

"We indeed sent a force to Mathtusekh, and they should be arriving there shortly." the king replied. "They will provide a distraction for Hishirash so that we may take Bariquor when there are few of the enemy there. With that mighty fortress in our hands, we will be all the stronger for the assault upon Turnienquor."

"Then so be it. I will meet with my father, and my forces shall rest here until the third day. Soon after, we shall together bury the bodies of our enemies at the bottom of the Pishon."

Two days later, the galleons of Threthoron left the harbour city of Cerciann and came swiftly to the confluence where the Mashiren River joined the Pishon. Before them, on the Pishon's far bank, loomed the fortress of Bariquor, its grim, dark walls impenetrable by any assault from land. Without warning, flaming arrows rained down in a torrent on the galleons of the mountain kingdom, as they rounded the bend of the river to enter the harbour of Bariquor. None of the ships of Bariquor were in the harbour; they had carried forces down the Pishon to Turnienquor, in order to aid Hishirash in repelling the assault on Mathtusekh.

The men of Enokk's army were the first to abandon the burning galleons, and they waded ashore where the surprised forces of Bariquor were only beginning to assemble. The harbour of Bariquor was the only undefended area near the fortress, and once ashore, the attacking armies could enter the city. However, as they approached the shore, archers firing from the walls shot down many of Enokk's men. Many more were met with swords when they came ashore. Fortunately, the forces of Bariquor were diminished because many of them were fighting at Mathtusekh. Those that remained were taken by surprise and were not yet rallied. When the forces of Threthoron joined Enokk's men, the allied forces quickly entered the city and took the towers of Bariquor.

Once the towers were taken, Enokk's archers began firing at the remaining enemy below, as Kenan's men fought up close with the enemy on the streets of the town within the fortress. As the army of Kenan approached the citadel in the centre of the town, ten fierce Giants came out from within it, and began to crush the men of Threthoron under their axe-blows. Fortunately, the Giants' armour could not hold up for long under the fire of Enokk's crossbows. Before long, the battle was over and the people of Bariquor surrendered to Kenan and Enokk. Seven hundred men were slain on the allied side, and on the other side nearly two thousand men, the entire force left to defend Bariquor, had been slain. The allied forces now prepared for the anticipated counterattack from Hishirash.

The raid on Mathtusekh did not succeed in capturing the city outright because the forces of Hishirash were swift to rally in response to the attack. Still, the allies dispatched large numbers of the enemy there and laid siege to the city. Both sides remained at a stalemate until news had come that to Hishirash that he had been tricked and Bariquor had fallen. So great was the distress and rage of Hishirash to this news that he simply withdrew his forces from Mathtusekh completely, abandoning it to the allied forces, and made swiftly for Bariquor. Upon his arrival, he saw the banners of Lhiosquor and Rethobal flying over the battlements.

The wrath of Hishirash was terrible to look upon as he approached the gates of the fortress. His face, which at any time was enough to strike fear into the hearts of men, was covered in red war paint, portraying the Giant king as furious and grim as death itself. His lips were raised in a snarl like that of a wild predator distracted from its freshly killed meal. He pounded three times upon the gates and then cried out in a terrible voice.

"Come out and fight me, mountain worm. Come out and meet your doom. Your flesh will be food for the birds of the air." he snarled in anger.

Enokk, with his guard, appeared on the top of the battlements. Although he seemed tiny next to Hishirash, king of the Giants, his voice was that of a king addressing his prisoner. "Go home, upstart," he said, "for soon I will be avenged for my father's murder and your crown, by right, shall come to me."

The wrath of the King of Giants soon turned to laughter when he heard the words of his ancestor. "Old man Enokk!" he taunted. "I thought you had been done away with long ago! You may live now, but not for long. You will find it very difficult indeed to adorn that puny head of yours with this crown. Instead, your severed head will adorn the capstone of the main archway to my royal palace."

As Hishirash spoke, a sole ship bearing the white and blue standards of Lhiosquor on its sail sailed down from the Mashiren into the harbour of Bariquor. Seth had come to congratulate his grandson on the capture of Bariquor and meet with all those gathered there. When he heard the bellowing boasts of Hishirash, he came and stood beside Enokk on the battlements and called to the King of Giants.

"Foul tyrant of Turnienquor, cease your taunting and return to that putrid palace of yours now, or today you will die."

Hishirash knew that Seth was a prophet and had heard tell of his deeds of when Lamekk was young. At first the Giant's words faltered, but then he returned to his taunts. "So, the great enemy of my people has dared to show himself in my fortress. Can you come down and back up your audacious words with strength, o prophet of the Maker? Know that the power of the Serpent runs deep in my veins and that my true father was not Tubal-Cain son of Lamekk but Hraw, lord of the Sun, one of the mightiest of the lieutenants of Lucifer when he fell to the earth. Come and meet me here and we will see whose god is stronger."

At this, the Spirit of God grew strong in Seth and he came out of the gates to meet the challenge of Hishirash. His clothes became dazzling white and his face was terrible to look upon. He carried no armour or weapon except the Spirit of Yah that rested on him. Hishirash towered over the Eldest of Lhiosquor and was clad in full battle armour, carrying Chabaq, his terrible sword. Hishirash laughed at Seth and vowed to destroy him. Seth however, knowing the courses of the heavenly bodies, knew of the sign which was about to take place.

"You claim Hraw, whom you say dwells in the sun, is your father. Now be amazed as the power of Yah, the Almighty Creator, is shown to be greater than that of Hraw." As Seth spoke, the moon passed in front of the sun, hiding the light of the sun and casting a shadow upon the land. Hishirash was profoundly distressed.

"Hraw, my father, where are you? Why does your light fail in the middle of the day?" he shouted to the sun. Hishirash turned his head this way and that, searching frantically for the light of the sun. Hishirash then channelled his fear into rage and swung Chabaq at Seth for a decapitating blow. However, to the surprise of all, Seth disappeared by the power of Yah and reappeared beside the angry Giant. Twice more Hishirash swung Chabaq, and twice more Seth was not where he appeared to be.

Seth, as bewildered as Hishirash at the unseen movements of Yah, began to pray earnestly. He stood directly in front of Hishirash as the Giant lifted Chabaq to swing at Seth a fourth and final time. All of a sudden, a sandstorm came down from the Dry Lands in the north and swirled around Hishirash. He dropped his sword, which landed upright against a tree, and he clawed at his face. The stinging sand went into his eyes and nostrils, and Hishirash squealed in terrible pain. Finally, Hishirash lost his balance in the sandstorm, fell upon Chabaq his sword, and died. The power of God was shown to be far greater than the power of Hraw.

# CHAPTER 9

# The Liberation of Enokk

## (201 – 204 EC)

### 201 EC

When the Giants who had been witness to the contest at Bariquor saw that their king was dead, they bore up the monstrous body of Hishirash and carried it back to Turnienquor to be burned in a great pyre. Gorgondish took the kingship of the Giants' empire and began to raise a war-host to assail Bariquor. However, the allied forces of Kenan and Enokk were swift to use the disarray caused by Hishirash's death to their advantage, and they marched to the gates of the City of Woe before Gorgondish was ready. Upon reaching Turnienquor, Enokk and Kenan stood side by side in the vanguard of the combined forces. Enokk then called out to Gorgondish.

"Lamekk is long slain, and now in these days Hishirash, your father, has joined his fate. Now you will join them as well, Gorgondish. Yes, you will follow your treacherous forbears to the place of the dead."

Enokk's challenge was met punctually by volleys of flaming arrows shooting down from the parapets of Turnienquor. Many brave warriors in the vanguard were slain, forcing the allies to move back from the city walls. The allied forces took up a defensive position behind a large hill to the south of the city. Dorro of Dorronquor, who had led a contingent of his people out of their hidden city to help bring down the Giants, had also joined the alliance and counselled for besieging Turnienquor. However, because Gorgondish's remaining forces in Mathtusekh were to return any day, it was agreed that the walls of Turnienquor must be thrown down and that the city must be taken swiftly. This was no easy task, for whenever anyone approached the walls they were slain under a rain of fiery arrows from the enemy. When Enokk saw that the gates of Turnienquor were not about to open and release hordes of enemy forces contained within any time soon, he devised a new strategy.

The allies felled cedar trees and made battering rams along with enormous wooden shields, which were then soaked in a nearby tributary of the Pishon. Strong men were chosen who would bear these huge shields over their heads as they approached the walls carrying the battering rams. In this way, the arrows would be less likely to hit the men attacking the wall, and catapults and crossbows fired from further back would keep the enemy archers on the ramparts occupied. The attack took place at night so that the forces on the wall would not see the battering rams approaching. When the rams reached the wall and the enemy forces were alerted, the fiery arrows that flew from both sides looked like comets in the night sky.

At daybreak, Gorgondish came forth with his armies from the gates of Turnienquor to battle the forces arrayed against his capital. The men with the battering rams had nearly succeeded in breaching the walls, but the emerging hordes quickly slew them, their overlarge and unwieldy shields preventing a successful stand. At this time, the rest of the allied forces came up over the hill behind which they had hid. Each of the allied divisions was clearly distinguishable: the forces of Enokk were on the western flank, the allies from Dorronquor and Turvah were on the eastern flank, and the army of Kenan came up the middle. All of them let out a terrifying war cry, and so great was the ensuing tumult that the weakened walls of Turnienquor began to crumble. At first, the enemy quailed and looked toward their city. The allied forces seized the opportunity and pressed forward, almost into the city, but the Giants were merciless fighters and slew many of the allies.

As the battle raged on throughout the day, the men on both sides grew weary from fighting and began moving almost mechanically. For those in the fiercest part of the battlefield, all actions and sounds became blurs, and only the fear of death kept everyone moving. Both Pocabal and Konaryah, the second son of Kenan, were fighting right in the thick of the battle, but neither even knew that the other was there as they were of separate divisions and the battle was raging. Pocabal swung his sword like a madman at all around him. He felt something like a swift breeze behind him and ducked quickly, avoiding decapitation by an enemy swordsman. The attacker instead was only able to slice off Pocabal's cloak that bore the colours of Threthoron. Pocabal, being of Cainite descent and in the middle of a battle in a division of Sethites, was now virtually indistinguishable from the enemy, and the enemy forces were thrown into confusion as Pocabal slew one of their number. They then began to turn on themselves as well as their attackers, not knowing who the traitor was.

Then Pocabal heard the bellow of a mighty warrior behind him and turned in time only to see a sword plunged straight through his armour into his chest. Konaryah had mistaken Pocabal for one of the enemy. Konaryah's eyes went wide in disbelief as his brother's friend swooned and fell to the ground. Konaryah, overwhelmed with grief, carried up the mortally wounded Pocabal, and retreated through the lines of the raging battle to the hill behind.

It seemed as if the Giants and their servants had rallied once more against the forces of Enokk and Kenan, for although many had been slain, they had been many in number and had pushed the weak eastern flank back almost to the hills. The allies who had remained behind, seeing the resurgence of the Giants on the battlefield, brought forth their catapults once again. The flaming burdens launched from the catapults easily struck their large targets as the enraged and bewildered Giants scurried about. Those that managed to avoid being struck by the catapults were overwhelmed by a regiment of heavy cavalry that came up over the hill in this moment of disarray. The Giants' rally became a rout, and finally Gorgondish was surrounded. He slew ninety-nine men who came against him, but at last the arrow of a crossbow pierced through his eye and into his brain, felling him to the ground with a mighty crash like a tree felled for lumber.

The allied forces captured Turnienquor and slew all of the remaining Giants. However, unbeknownst to them, the Giantess Ichsha, widow of Hishirash, was in Shaol at the time. When she heard of the fall of Turnienquor, she fled beyond the Duobinar Mountains far to the southeast along the Outer Sea. She was with child with Hishirash's last seed and in time brought forth Hurash, the posthumous son of Hishirash.

On a hill south of the liberated city were seen three men, standing as still as stones in the last light of the evening. One man lay dying, another was crouched over the body of the dying man, and a third stood at the dying man's feet as silent as a stone sentinel. Mahalalel had found his brother Konaryah and his lifelong friend Pocabal. Konaryah stood still, in shock that he had fatally wounded a childhood friend who was more of a brother to Mahalalel than he had been.

"Ma ... Mahalalel" said the dying man as he recognized his friend.

"Rest, Pocabal. Don't speak; I will bring you to Bariquor where Seth will heal you." Mahalalel counselled his friend.

"Mahalalel, my time is through. I see angels, and I see righteous Abel standing with them. Kodhris, Labar, and others who fell at Bariquor are with the angels, too."

"Pocabal, you can't die! Susira, your wife, and little Kheruva, your daughter, need you! Besides, you are one of our bravest warriors and my dearest friend."

"You ... please take care of them. See that they are looked after. When it is time, find a descendant of Adah who will be a father to Kheruva and a husband to Susira. We will meet again, my friend..." then Pocabal breathed his last.

Konaryah spoke softly to his brother, "His mantle showing the colours of Lhiosquor had been torn off. Everything was a blur. I saw Cainites fighting each other. His back was turned and I mistook him for one of the enemy."

"The battle was fast and fierce." said Mahalalel. "We can only react to what we see, brother." Mahalalel lifted his eyes to look on the battlefield where carrion birds had already begun to gather, going about their grisly business of picking through and cleaning the bodies of the fallen. "Today, though we have won a great victory, many of our friends and kindred now lie slain. Still more of the enemy's men lay slain, most of who no doubt went forth in fear of their masters rather than loyalty to them. We have slain many who would otherwise have been our friends but for fear of the abominable race of Hishirash." Tears welled up in Mahalalel's face, turning red as the sun set to his left. The Giants are now no more and the people of the city of Enokk are free again, but to me this city will forever be called Turnienquor - the City of Woe - because it was here that I lost a friend who was closer than a brother."

Those last words seared Konaryah's shame-filled mind like a cattle brand. On that day a seed of bitterness was sown in him against the people of Shrivazh and against his brother's house. Very slowly it grew, feeding on Konaryah's guilt over Pocabal's death, and it lay dormant for a great number of years. Nevertheless, the seed of doom sown that day would eventually bear fruit.

# 204 EC

After the liberation of the city of Enokk, the disheartened Giants of Niragadan, Kheropheth, and Shaol were easily and swiftly defeated. The liberated people of Enokk declared Enokk son of Cain their rightful king, and all of the cities of the Cainites from the Duobinar Mountains in the south to the Gihon valley in the north acknowledged his rule. Enokk named his realm Arattu after his second son who was slain during the Usurpation. Nonetheless Enokk, along with all the patriarchs of the tribes between Tsayun in the west and the Great Lake in the east, acknowledged Kenan as High King of the entire known world. Mahalalel and Konaryah were both awarded honours by their father for their bravery in battle. To each of them was given half of the armies of Threthoron to administer as generals under their father, the king.

Mahalalel kept his promise to Pocabal, and he made sure that Susira and Kheruva were cared for, sending Susira eighty dorrons a month. After Pocabal's death, Susira moved to Uarga with Kheruva. Uarga was a town in the Common Fields that had been built since the construction of the Colonial Council buildings. One morning, Mahalalel was in Uarga minding five-year old Kheruva while Susira was in the marketplace buying necessities with her eighty dorrons. Mahalalel and Kheruva walked past the shrine where sacrifices were made to Yah, and there Mahalalel saw the most beautiful woman he had ever met.

She was like something seen a vision from heaven. She had deep auburn hair that flowed in gentle waves like a river down to her hips. Her eyes were grey with a hint of green, and shone like precious stones. Her skin was the colour of quartz; white with hints of pink and cream. Her full lips were like rose petals and her voice was like music from Heaven. Mahalalel fell hopelessly in love with her the moment he heard her singing. The young woman was looking at the flowers in the garden between the shrine and the marketplace, singing away, completely oblivious to Mahalalel's presence. When she turned and saw him, their eyes locked and Mahalalel felt arrows of destiny pass between them.

"Good morning, I am Lilara of Lhiosquor. Aren't you General Mahalalel, the son of the king?" she asked. Her voice was musical even in speech.

Mahalalel was at a loss for words. "The very same." he squeaked, his throat constricted with nervous tension as he stood in the presence of the personification of beauty and gracefulness.

Lilara laughed loudly. "The mighty general who talks like a mouse!" she teased him. "Are you sure that you are the courageous warrior Mahalalel of whom many tales are told?" Lilara turned to Kheruva, still addressing Mahalalel. "Who is the little Jubalite girl with you?"

"This is Kheruva, daughter of Pocabal, my dear friend who perished in the battle of Turnienquor." replied Mahalalel, regaining his composure and his normal speaking voice.

"I have heard songs sung of that day, and of the death of brave Pocabal." Lilara bent down to Kheruva. "And where do you live, Kheruva?"

The little girl looked at Lilara. "I live on a house on Cerchil Street here in Uarga, fair lady, just Mama and me."

"I am minding her while her mother is in the market. I bring them eighty dorrons every month so that they do not go cold or hungry." replied Mahalalel.

"Does it not look strange, general, for the King's son to be caring for a Jubalite woman? What must the High Council think?" she asked, half-smiling.

"They know what has happened, and they know also of the promise

I made to Pocabal; however, I admit that the situation can be awkward at times. I have been endeavouring to find Susira a husband among the Jubalites, but her grief for Pocabal is still too great." A new thought entered Mahalalel's mind. "Perhaps you could help, Lilara. If you could spend time with Kheruva and her mother and take care of things for them when Susira is busy, I would gladly pay you whatever you deem fair."

She smiled again, "My father is wealthy man, Mahalalel, and I have no need of money, but I would take care of Susira and Kheruva as a kindness to the king's son."

"Who might your father be, Lilara?"

"My father is Yahreth, the grandson of Chiolas."

"Your father is Yahreth of the clan of Chiolas? Chiolas is the brother of Enos, my grandfather. My father recently placed him in charge of the Treasury. Yahreth is the most skilled jeweller in Lhiosquor."

"Yes, he is my father, a very good and noble man, and very skilled at his work. Now, might I be able to meet the girl's mother?"

Mahalalel brought Lilara to meet Susira, and Lilara began to mind Kheruva and take care of things whenever Susira was busy or ill. This continued for ten years until Susira finally remarried, but the bonds of friendship between Susira and Lilara grew. Mahalalel and Lilara also grew quite close over this period of time, and they were married eight years after their meeting, in the year 212 of the Enosian Calendar.

# CHAPTER 10

# YARED
## (230 – 281 EC)

## 230 EC

For many years, Lilara could bear Mahalalel no children. In the year 230 of the Enosian Calendar, Mahalalel and Lilara travelled west on a pilgrimage to the Temple of Yah. There they made sacrifices to God and prayed that they might have a child. Hualichi, the High Priest, saw the couple and came and blessed them.

"Are you Mahalalel, the son of the High King?" asked Hualichi after he had said a blessing.

"Yes, and this is my wife, Lilara. We have been married for eighteen years, yet have been unable to have children."

"I see." said Hualichi. Then, remembering something, he spoke again. "Many years ago I dreamed of this moment in a vision. I saw the two of you kneeling here in the temple. The voice of Yah came to me and said, 'This union shall produce a blessed servant whom you will train as your successor. Priest and prince shall he be, and through him I will do many miracles. However, his heart will be torn between love for Me and love for another, and this conflict will continue through his whole life. If he does not choose wisely, great disaster will not fall on him alone, but on the entire earth, and this house will surely be destroyed. Nevertheless, whether he is faithful or not, from him shall come those even greater than he, and from his line will come the One who will save the world.'"

Mahalalel and Lilara marvelled at the words of the High Priest. "We shall do all that we can to encourage our son to love and honour Yah. What would you advise us to do?" asked Lilara.

"Return here with him every seven years until he is old enough to make the pilgrimage on his own. Take him to Enos to be trained at the

University in all of the knowledge of the Creation. When he comes here, I shall train him in the knowledge of the Creator." answered Hualichi. By this time the students of Enos had started several academies in many cities, and the mother academy at Lhiosquor had become known as the University.

"We shall do as you have said, High Priest." said Mahalalel. "Thank you for your blessing and your prophecy. Will you accept a donation of two hundred dorrons to the work of you and your brethren here?"

The High Priest seemed shocked. "My services are not unto man but unto Yah. I would ask no fee of anyone. If you wish to make a donation unto Yah, there is a bowl inside the temple. Do not give it on account of the words I have passed on to you, for Yah gave them to me. To pay me for the words of Yah would be to rob the Almighty One Himself."

Mahalalel sensed the sincerity of Hualichi's heart and encouraged him, nodding his head in a gesture of respect. "Never have I met anyone with your humility, Hualichi. May you serve Yah faithfully for unending years. Indeed, word of you will reach the ears of the king himself, and you will never be found wanting of friends." Mahalalel and Lilara then put their donation in the bowl in the temple, and departed along the road heading east for home.

# 231 EC

One year after their pilgrimage to the Temple of Yah, Lilara bore Mahalalel a son and named him Yared, a variant of the name of her father, Yahreth. Yared, with his red hair and brilliant eyes, bore a strong resemblance both to his mother and to his ancestor, Seth, from whom he was descended on both sides. Seven days after his birth, a great celebration was held in the newly constructed palace of King Kenan. The king was enamoured with his new grandson, and he blessed him before all the people who had gathered in the palace courtyard.

"Behold, chosen people of Lhiosquor, a new heir is born to you this day. Yared, the son of Mahalalel, will become a great man." the king proclaimed.

Many of the members of the High Council had gathered that day, and Enos came forward to bless his great-grandson. "Yared will become very wise, and he will teach us new things that are yet to be discovered. His wisdom will eclipse mine and be known throughout the world."

Seth, the great patriarch and Chancellor of Lhiosquor and the realm of Threthoron also came forward. "Great things shall he do indeed, but I see a shadow here that I do not understand. Great may be the man, but greater still the fall. Nevertheless, he shall one day sire one greater than himself whose name will never be forgotten. May Yah watch over and protect Yared son of Mahalalel." Thus the prophecies of Hualichi the High Priest were confirmed by the greatest of the Elders of Lhiosquor.

In the same week as Yared's dedication, a wandering band of fifty Jabalite shepherds and their families came out of the land of Jabal in the far north. They entered Threthoron seeking Shrivazh, the city where their ancestors had once taken refuge. Nabeg, their leader, came before the council of Ruwad. "New tribes have come out of the Forest, and new nations are being built in the lands where we have wandered for many generations, tending our flocks. Many of my people have moved still farther north and into the distant east, but we have become weary of the wandering life and wish to settle in the city that our patriarch Jabal once called his home."

"It is Shrivazh you seek." declared Ruwad. It lies on a plateau halfway up the mountain, and it may be reached by the pulley-carts which ascend and descend from the mountain. There is also the Passage of the Sentinels whereby the merchants come and go to the cities on the mountain and the Mountain Guard keep vigilant watch, but that is very steep, too steep for small children. I suggest that some of you lead the sheep up the Passage while the rest of you take the pulley-carts."

That was how the clan of Nabeg of the Jabalites came to Shrivazh. Kheruva, who by this time was twenty-four, met and fell in love with Madeg the son of Nabeg. Madeg also became good friends with Mahalalel and Lilara who still visited the family of Susira often.

# 238 EC

In the 238th year since the foundation of Lhiosquor, as the years of the Enosian Calendar had come to be counted, Kheruva bore Madeg their third child, a daughter named Medgariva. The children of Madeg and Kheruva often played with Yared and his little sister Ona whenever Mahalalel and Lilara came to visit. It was in this same year that the time came for Mahalalel and Lilara to take their children on a pilgrimage to the Temple at Mt. Tsayun as Hualichi had requested. As they travelled the road from Turvah to Tsayun, they noticed many new settlements had begun to spring up along the great river Rahav, mostly ports for merchant ships.

When the travellers arrived at the Temple of Yah, Hualichi greeted them. "So, this is your son." he said, looking at Yared.

"Yes, this is Yared. He has not been able to keep quiet about this trip ever since he heard about it." said Lilara.

"Hello, High Priest." Yared said, staring inquisitively at Hualichi. "Is it true that all of the priests have long beards like yours?" asked the boy.

Hualichi laughed heartily. "Yes, dear child. Yah told us that it is a sign that we priests are set apart unto Him. We must allow our beards to grow long and never cut them. Well, what have you heard about this Temple, Yared?"

The boy wrinkled his forehead in thought. "Yah, the Almighty Creator, spoke to my grandfather the king and told him to stop calling Him Eloi because that wasn't his favourite name. He told grandfather to build Him a very big house because Yah is very big." the boy stopped and looked at the High Priest with a curious look on his face. "Is Yah bigger than the Giants whom my father fought against in the war?"

All of the adults were startled at the mention of the Giants, and said a quick prayer of protection against evil. The High Priest looked at the boy sternly. "You must never speak of the evil ones against whom the nations fought. This brings fear, and fear opens the door to doubt, worry, despair, strife, and many kinds of evil. To answer your question, Yah is very big indeed. This temple is called his house, but the whole world is only His footstool, and the heavens in all their vastness are but His throne. Even the highest heavens cannot contain Him, for Yah exists outside of the Creation; surrounding it, acting in it, yet separate from it."

"If He is past the edge of the world, surrounding it, then how does He come and speak to people?"

"Yah can be everywhere at once." The High Priest replied as he began to walk through the temple courtyard, motioning for the boy and his parents to follow. "He is not limited to being in one place as we are."

Yared had a difficult time understanding this. "If Yah is in more than one place, are there more than one of Him?"

The High Priest stopped abruptly, and looked shocked. "Certainly not! Yah is One! Though His presence may be felt by a Nahlonite in the far west and by a Jabalite shepherd wandering the vast grasslands beyond the Great Lake in the east both at one time, He still exists in unity with Himself. This may be hard for you to understand at this age, but you will gain wisdom as you grow older."

The discussion between the High Priest and the grandson of the king of Threthoron continued for a long time. The family of Mahalalel stayed at the Temple for forty days, and Yared spent most of his time asking questions of the High Priest, when Hualichi was not too busy with his priestly duties. After the forty days, Mahalalel's family headed home to Lhiosquor. No sooner had they returned home when King Kenan told Mahalalel of the messenger who had come from Iradu in the far south.

As people were becoming more numerous and spreading into lands across the face of the earth, Ichsha had been discovered in a great cavern far east of Iradu where she had built a home for herself. The widow of Hishirash had taken unto herself many husbands of a tribe which had come out of the north. She had born Giants to none of them. Each time she gave birth and found that the baby was of the race of men and not of Giants, she burned both the child and its father alive in a pyre. Ichsha kept this pyre burning continuously on the top of the mountain in which her cavern lay. Irad, the son of Enokk, had led forays against Ichsha, but no one who entered the cave where she dwelt had ever come out again.

Kenan told Mahalalel that when the messenger from Iradu had

come with this news, Konaryah took a band of one hundred men to journey to the cavern and slay the Giantess. Now, no one had known that Ichsha had been with child when she left Shaol, and her son, Hurash, had not stayed with her long, but had gone into the southwest where he now dwelt along the great river of the Nahlonites. The tale of Hurash will be told later.

# 240 EC

Konaryah returned to Lhiosquor two years after he had set out, bringing with him only five men out of the original one hundred, and accompanied by a very tall, fair-skinned woman with yellow hair. Her name was Wolja, and she hailed from a tribe that they had met on their wanderings. While on his journey, Konaryah had taken Wolja to be his wife.

Konaryah recounted to his father how his men had found the cavern of Ichsha, and how they had destroyed the shrine built at the mouth of the cave by a local tribe that had come to worship her. When Konaryah's men entered the cavern, wild beasts that dwelled deep in its dark recesses and hidden passages attacked and devoured most of Konaryah's company. After navigating through the dark, cold, damp, labyrinthine tunnels of the caverns for seven days and suffering chills on account of these conditions, Konaryah and his remaining men finally encountered Ichsha. The warrior widow of Hishirash fought fiercely, slaying twenty-five of Konaryah's men, but Seuso, Konaryah's strongest lieutenant, slew the Giant queen. As she died, she cursed Konaryah, Seuso, and the rest of Konaryah's men, telling them that they would be divided by treachery and slain by a new race of Giants yet to be born.

When Ichsha was dead, Konaryah commanded that Ichsha's body be taken to her own pyre at the top of the mountain to be burned. When the people of the tribe of Harifa who lived in that area saw that Ichsha was dead, they rejoiced greatly. The chieftain of Harifa gave his daughter Hirja in marriage to Seuso. Irad, son of Enokk, came from Iradu when he heard of the death of the Giantess, and was so overjoyed and relieved that Ichsha was no more that he offered Konaryah land upon which to build his own city. Konaryah declined, saying that he had to return to Lhiosquor, but he told Irad that the honour belonged to Seuso, who had slain Ichsha. Seuso accepted Irad's offer and settled in the far south near Iradu. There he built the great city of Susa, which though later destroyed and rebuilt again, stands today even though the world has changed.

Following the departure of Irad and Seuso, the remaining company of Konaryah accompanied their general home across the Seven Mountain Ranges and it was during this homeward trek that they met the tribe from which Wolja, Konaryah's wife, had come. The yellow-haired tribesmen were impressed by the iron weapons, armour, and tools of the men of Lhiosquor. Their chieftain gave Wolja, his daughter and the most beautiful woman in their tribe, to Konaryah as his bride in exchange for the knowledge of iron working. That was Konaryah's account of his quest against Ichsha, the widow of Hishirash, at least as much as he told Kenan. The tale remains today, although greatly changed by the passing of the centuries.

## 252 EC

In the year 252, the time came for Yared to make his third pilgrimage to the Temple of Yah. This time Yared journeyed alone, as he had reached the age of twenty-one. Upon reaching Turvah, he chartered a sailing vessel to take him to Shaochiquor, where he then disembarked and travelled on to Mt. Tsayun. Yared arrived during festival time in the city of Tsayun, and there was jubilant music throughout the city. People danced in the city square, and many lambs and bulls were sacrificed at the temple. Hualichi was very busy with duties related to the festival, so Yared simply joined in the festivities. A few days later, when the festival time was over, he went up to the Temple of Yah to see the High Priest. At first, Hualichi did not even recognize the young man who came to look for him. When the recognition dawned on him, Hualichi exclaimed, "Yared! It's really you, all grown up! Where is your family?"

Yared nodded to the High Priest. "I came by myself, Hualichi. I intend to stay here for a year before returning to my studies at the University. I am learning such interesting things there. I never knew that the world was as large as it is. I am continually hearing of new lands being discovered and new tribes and nations building cities beyond what was once believed the be the edge of the world. Tell me, honoured servant of Yah, does the earth have an end or does it go on forever."

"Nothing goes on forever, boy, except for Yah Himself. Everything that He has made has a beginning and therefore has an end, but it is not known just how big the earth really is. From looking at the stars, on nights when the curtain of heaven is rolled back, we can guess that there is still more of the earth yet to be discovered, but we can only guess at its size."

Yared spent the rest of the day in the temple courts speaking with Hualichi. In the evening, he was shown his room in the priests' quarters near the Temple where he would stay for the next year. He felt strange and lonely living away from his family and friends, but he felt a connection to the place, as if his destiny lay within those sacred walls. One night, as he was lying in bed, he felt a rushing wind enter his room. The air was filled with a golden light that made all of the dust motes in the room sparkle like tiny stars. A voice spoke to him from the midst of the light. "Yared, do you know who I Am?"

"Are you Yah, He who is, Creator of heaven and earth and all its inhabitants?"

"Yes, I Am He. I have chosen you, Yared, to be My voice to the nations of the world. One day, you shall be the High Priest and serve Me in My Temple. I will speak to you of many wondrous things and shall use you to do many wonders, if you will follow me."

Yared did not know what to think, but before a thought entered his mind he spoke. "Yes, Lord, I will follow You wherever You lead."

The all-knowing Creator knew that the young man spoke hastily, so He continued. "Do you truly know, grandson of Kenan, what it is to follow Me with all that is within you? There are many things in the world that a man may seek after, but only I Am the source of all these things. If you are truly following Me, you will seek after Me before all others, and I will add to you all else that you desire for everything is Mine. However, if you turn away to follow after the pleasures of this life, disaster shall surely come upon you and upon this house that bears My name."

Then Yared realized the gravity of his earlier words. "Almighty Yah, I want to follow You with all that is in me, but I know that things that happen around me distract my mind very easily. What must I do to see You before all else?"

"Abide in Me, and I will abide in you. Seek after Me more than gold and silver, for all of the gold and silver are Mine and far more besides. Remember that I Am your strength. It is in My presence that you will dwell. Apart from My presence you will grow weak very quickly and you will be easily swept away by the cares of this life. Remain in My presence continually, for it is only in My presence that you will have the strength to resist the power of the tempter. He is the one who roams to and fro throughout the earth, bringing destruction to men of all nations. Remember My words; abide in Me and I will abide in you." After this, the voice stopped speaking, the light faded, and Yared slept.

# 258 EC

Now, as I have mentioned earlier, the family of Mahalalel and the family of Madeg were very close because Mahalalel and Lilara had cared for Kheruva, Madeg's wife, and her mother when she was a small child. Yared had become close friends with Medgariva, the daughter of Madeg and Kheruva. They began to spend more and more time together, but because their families were so close, no one thought of this s strange. In Yared's twenty-seventh year, his feelings toward Medgariva began to intensify, and he often would find himself thinking about her when he was alone, even thinking about marrying her.

At first, he immediately banished these thoughts from his mind because he was of the house of Kenan and she was of the lines of Jabal and Jubal. However, as these thoughts persisted, he would often find himself distracted by them when he was about doing other things. Medgariva, as well, began to take more of an interest in Yared at this time, and they would often leave the city together for long walks alone and talk about many things. Both of them felt that when they were together their senses were heightened and that their blood ran faster. Things continued this way for many years, and Yared was torn between devotion to God and his love for Medgariva, while Medgariva was torn between her desire to keep the laws of Threthoron and her desire to announce her love to Yared.

# 280 EC

One day, when Yared was in his forty-ninth year, he was out on a walk with Medgariva. The two of them walked until they came to a point along the western ridge of Mt. Threthor overlooking the valley of the Great Forest within which lay the Forbidden Garden. The Garden itself was hidden because of the canopy of the forest, but the western point was nonetheless one of the most beautiful places on Mt. Threthor. There, beneath a tall cedar tree, Yared and Medgariva began to kiss one another. Medgariva then reached up to untie Yared's tunic, and he jumped back.

Yared cried aloud with tears in his eyes. "This has gone too far. Were we to continue, I would be sinning against Yah, against you, against myself, and against the entire city of Lhiosquor.". Yared then ran home, quickly gathered his things, and left the city of his fathers for the Temple of Yah before he could change his mind. This time, Yared did not return to Lhiosquor but remained at the temple on Mt. Tsayun. Yared was tempted seven times on his journey westward to return to Mt. Threthor and take Medgariva as his wife. The seventh time, he was on the final stretch of the Pilgrim's Road from Shaochiquor to Tsayun, and he could see the Mountain of Yah in the distance with the golden Temple glittering on it like a star.

At this point, Yared turned back to look at the road by which he had come, remembering his last moments with Medgariva. He began to walk back down the road, away from Tsayun. As he did so, chills overtook him and he found himself unable to move. The chills became convulsions, and Yared lay in the dust on the road feeling very helpless and afraid. In his fear, he cried out to Yah to spare him.

"Forgive me, Yah Almighty, for turning back on the road. Please do not turn me over to these spirits of the great enemy which make war on my soul and body. Release me from them, and I shall go up to Your temple to serve You there for the rest of my days."

Gradually, the convulsions stopped, the chills subsided, and Yared began to regain his strength. He turned around again on the Pilgrim's Road, and continued on his way toward the Holy Mountain. Upon reaching the Temple of Yah, Hualichi came out to meet the prince of Lhiosquor. "Yared, my son! You have come once again! No doubt this is a momentous pilgrimage indeed, for by my reckoning you are now forty-nine years of age, seven times seven years, and this is your seventh pilgrimage."

"Yes it is, teacher, and I intend this to be my final pilgrimage. From this day forward, I will abide here under the shadow of the Almighty. I will take refuge here in His presence from the thoughts that torment me. I give myself into His service, and into yours, for the rest of my days."

Hualichi perceived the sadness in his words, and he realized what must have happened. "Before you were born, Yared, Yah spoke to me in a dream about you. He told me that you would always be torn between two loves, the love for Him and the love for another. From what you have told me during your previous visits, your desire for Medgariva is very strong. It must have been very difficult for you to make the decision to come here."

Yared began to wail and tears streamed down his face. "Why is the Creator such a hard taskmaster? Why does He demand of us things that are beyond our ability to bear? Why must my heart be forever torn between these two loves? Can no harmony exist between the two? Will I never know peace?" Yared then crumpled into a sobbing heap at the feet of the High Priest.

"You know the answer, Yared. I have seen you worshipping in the Temple. When you are in the manifest presence of Yah, you are caught up into another realm. When I have spoken to you just after these times, it is as if you have become a different person. Then there is no struggle, no distraction, but the transcendent peace of the Most High rests on you. This is where you must live, day and night. You must live in His presence. That is where all of the other things will disappear."

Yared spoke weakly. "I know that everything you say is the truth, but I don't know if I really want to live apart from Medgariva. I know in my mind what I must do, I know that we cannot be together, but as you have said the love between the two of us is very powerful. When I am with her, I feel so alive and I feel that there is no obstacle that cannot be overcome."

"Then what drew you here? Why did you come here if your desire is with her?" asked the High Priest. The words cut Yared sharply, who began wailing again.

After he had stopped wailing, Yared spoke again. "I knew that this is what I must do. Yah has a great purpose for me, and I want to follow Him. I just can't understand why my heart is so divided. Nevertheless, even though He may strike me with every kind of calamity, I must serve Him. This is my reason for living. My life finds its source in Yah, and to search for any other source would bring nothing but death."

Hualichi smiled. "This is the beginning of wisdom, my son. Do not forget that He is your source. Pursue Him and His love above all other things and He will comfort you even in your darkest hour when you call on Him."

Teacher and student climbed up the steps to Temple, knelt at the altar, and prayed to God. Yared left his old life behind in Lhiosquor, and found a new life among the Temple priests. After a year had passed, he had completed his training as an initiate and took the vows of a priest, the first to do so who was not of the priestly nation of Tsayun. Among his vows he added a vow of celibacy. Although Yah had not commanded this, the vow of celibacy had already become common among the Temple priests. Although there were still many priests with families, an increasing number of young priests had chosen to take this vow. For Yared, this vow was a promise to the Almighty One that if he could not be with Medgariva, then he would never be with any woman. He chose to devote himself to God alone.

# 281 EC

On the same day that Yared took his vows and entered the Temple priesthood, Medgariva had a dream of Yared in priestly robes. When she awoke from the dream, she knew that Yared would never return to the realm of Threthoron to be her husband. Weeping, Medgariva hastily packed up all of her belongings, bade farewell to her family, left Uarga, and set off alone to find the edge of the earth so that she could throw herself off of it. She headed north and dwelt for a time among her father's kindred, the Jabalite shepherds. With them she wandered eastward beyond the Great Lake.

Medgariva continued until she reached the shores of another large lake that was yet smaller than the Great Lake of Arattu. She named it the Lonely Lake because of her sorrow. Two rivers flowed out from the Lonely Lake. One of these she named the River of Tears, and the other she named the River of Forgetfulness. She followed the River of Forgetfulness southeast and came to the land of the Harifa. These who were friends of Seuso, Konaryah's lieutenant, the slayer of Ichsha, who had established the city of Susa to the west of the land of the Harifa. Medgariva dwelt among the Harifa for many years, teaching them about the realm of Threthoron and all that she knew of Yah, the Creator, for the Harifa had been deceived by Ichsha in earlier years and no longer remembered the Almighty One.

The Harifa loved Medgariva and gave her a new name, Valiturnea, which meant Maiden of Sorrows. Medgariva loved the people of Harifon, as their land was known, but her great sorrow had brought a shadow over her. The beauty of her youth faded, and she spent most of her time in her cave, as the Harifa were cave dwellers and miners of jewels. Later generations knew that place as the Wailing Cave, for many who would come there in later years and speak in that cave believed that they could hear the cries of Valiturnea echo from the walls.

# THE PRIEST
## (284 – 393 EC)

In its final days, before the waters flooded over the earth, the old world was filled with every kind of wickedness imaginable. I have already described in the first of this set of scrolls how the descendants of Cain increased in wickedness with successive generations, eventually bringing about the rule of the Giants. I have contrasted the wickedness of Turnienquor with the righteousness that was Lhiosquor in the following scrolls, and recounted how the Old Alliance was victorious over the abominable race of Hishirash. In the days when my great-great-grandfather, Yared, was still a very young man, the whole world was at peace and most of the people of the earth still honoured the Almighty One. However, the days of peace did not last.

Here I will tell the story of Yared. I will tell you of his wisdom and his discoveries, of his torments and his failures, and particularly of his one decision which, as a stone that is dropped into a lake causes ripples across its entire surface, began a chain of events that ended the Age of Peace and began humanity's descent into the Age of Darkness.

# CHAPTER 11

# THE VOYAGE OF AFALO AND ATALO
## (284 – 292 EC)

## 284 EC

Yared devoted his first three years in the priesthood to interpreting the movements of the stars. Remember that in the old world this practice had not yet been turned to the evil that in our day has caused God to ban its use in the new world. The order of the world was different then, just as in the old world it was not permitted to eat the flesh of animals. In these days our Creator has repealed that proscription, as food is often hard to find in the frozen wastelands that now cover all of the lands north of the mountains.

Nevertheless, I digress and must return to tale of my forefathers. Yared had determined by the orbit of the heavenly bodies, when the curtain of heaven did not hide them from view, that there was indeed no edge of the earth as many had believed. He concluded that the earth, like the moon, was round. He postulated that if one sailed far enough eastward across the Outer Sea, beyond the place where the land ended in the east, and if one was so blessed as to survive the tempests and many sea monsters that dwelt in the depths, that one would eventually find himself sailing the westernmost lands. If one continued sailing in the same direction, Yared reasoned, one would eventually find himself returning to the place from which he came.

At first, many people laughed at Yared's idea as a ridiculous fantasy. Nevertheless, Yared kept his patience as he explained how a ship travelling upstream along the Rahav from the land of Nahlon would be seen at first only by its topmast. The sails would then come into view before the rest of the boat. Yared had the glassworkers in the land of Tsayun make lenses so that people could see farther, that they observe more clearly the phenomenon which he had described. Thus the first looking glasses were made, and with them Yared set out to prove his theory. In the fourth year of Yared's priesthood, the priests came together to discuss his findings.

"I was astounded when I looked through the glass and saw the ships approaching over the horizon." said Chinsofan, one of the priests. "If the earth is curved and not straight, then no matter how hard we search, we will never find the edge of the earth because it truly does not exist."

Another priest, Gaoyang, wanted more proof of this bizarre new theory. "How do we know that the light passing through the lens of a looking glass is not bent, as the lens itself is bent, thus only giving the appearance that the ship is rising out of the water?"

"Those with good eyesight, including Yared, have seen the ships come this way. No one ever took notice of this before now, and that is the only reason why so many tend to doubt these observations." said Hualichi.

"High Priest, I believe there is only one way to prove for certain that Yared's unconventional idea is indeed the truth." Gaoyang continued. "Someone must attempt a voyage across the Outer Sea. If they sail beyond the easternmost lands, head eastward across the Great Sea and then return from the west, we will know that the world is indeed round."

"Who would dare to undertake such a dangerous voyage?" asked Chinsofan in amazement. "Where would we find the dorrons to fund such an expedition?"

"I will present this case to my grandfather, the High King." said Yared. "There are many courageous men of renown in Threthoron. Should brave men be found to take up the task, Kenan could make an appeal to King Dorro of Dorronquor for any money that could not be raised in Threthoron. The wealth of Dorronquor is legendary, and my grandfather is a good friend of Dorro and his family."

Hualichi faced the young priest with a piercing gaze. "Is it wise for you to return to the city of your birth, Yared? You know the struggles that you have faced. You may go there and never wish to return to this temple."

As Hualichi spoke, Yared found himself fingering the necklace inlaid with carnelian that he always wore about his neck. Medgariva had given it to him, and as he held it, his thoughts turned toward the woman he had loved. "I know that this will be difficult. I cannot say for certain that I will not succumb to the temptation to tarry overlong in Threthoron, but I will make a pledge." Yared removed the necklace, his only physical reminder of Medgariva.

"Hualichi, most honoured among the servants of Yah, I give this necklace into your keeping. This necklace means a great deal to me, and it is my only reminder of one who is very dear to my heart. I wear it at all times, even when serving in the temple, as you well know. I give this to you as my pledge to return to Yah's temple, that I may continue my service to Him." Yared handed the necklace to the High Priest who then embraced him.

"You have my blessing, Yared. You have been as a son to me, and although I fear for your leaving, I trust in your safe return here." Hualichi embraced Yared who then prepared for his journey to Lhiosquor.

It was the year 284 of the Enosian Calendar when Yared arrived in the city of his birth to tell his grandfather, the High King, about his latest discoveries, and to inquire whether an expedition might be launched to discover whether his theories were true. As Yared travelled the road that led up to Mt. Threthor, he felt his pulse quicken as the mountain came into view around the Kheruva range. He began to think once more about Medgariva, not knowing that she had fled to the land of Harifon. When Yared entered the city of Cerciann at the foothills of Mt. Threthor, the people announced his arrival with excitement. "Prince Yared has come!" they exclaimed. Yared expected Medgariva to press through the crowd, or leap out from behind a tree, and hold him in her arms. Medgariva did not come.

Yared passed through Cerciann, surrounded by adoring townsfolk, until he entered a small warehouse built against the base of the great mountain. He opened the door and made his way to the back room. Here he found the entrance to the old pathway – the Passage of the

Guards - that led up through the bowels of the mountain through a series of caverns. He passed through one cavern after another until he came to the Chamber of Guards. The guards on duty recognized Yared, and they permitted him to proceed through the exit of the secret pathway into a quiet quarter of Lhiosquor.

The City of Light had grown greatly since High King Kenan the Just began his reign almost ninety years before. Lhiosquor now covered the entire summit of Mt. Threthor, surrounding the Crystal Lake on all sides. It had become home to over fifty thousand people, and could now grow no larger. A new passage, a wider, winding road named the Passage of the Merchants, had been carved into the mountainside now that the Giants were no longer a threat. Food and raw materials were carried up the mountain from the daughter cities of Lhiosquor; finished goods were transported down the mountain for sale in the daughter cities and beyond to other nations of the world. There were no longer any farms or pastures on the summit of the Mount Threthor.

Yared went immediately to the Royal Palace to meet with his grandfather, the High King. In the palace garden just inside the palace gate he met Lilara, his mother. Her eyes filled with tears of joy to see her firstborn son, and she embraced him tightly.

"You have come home, my son. It is good to see you and good that you are here. We had heard that you had taken priestly vows and that you would never return."

"Yes, mother, I have taken the vows of a priest. I have not come home to live, but to visit for a while and to speak with Grandfather. In the course of my studies at the Temple of Yah, I have discovered something wondrous. I believe that the world is not flat, as we have thought for so long. There are no edges over which an unfortunate ship sailing too far into the Outer Sea might fall into the dark Void. I believe, rather, that the world is curved, round like the moon if you will, and that a ship that sailed eastward across the Outer Sea would eventually travel around the earth and reappear in the westernmost regions of the world. A ship that sailed far enough would eventually end up right where it began. I want to bring this before Grandfather to convince him to send an expedition of his best ships to circle the earth and return to the place from which they came."

Lilara smiled wanly. "You have always been very bright, my son, but this is indeed something which no one has ever imagined. Please understand that if your grandfather cannot do this for you it does not mean that his love for you is any less. Heavy are the burdens which lie on the shoulders of a high king. He has the entire realm of Threthoron to consider, as well the maintenance of peace in all of the neighboring kingdoms."

"I understand, Mother, yet I must at least try. Yah has instilled a great desire in me to learn as much as I can about all that He has made. Who knows what else may yet be discovered? Who can tell what mysteries await to be revealed? So much hidden knowledge remains to be brought into the light, and by the power of Yah, these things can be made known if we do not lose heart." Yared then walked with his mother to the throne room of Kenan. When the High King saw his grandson, he ran up to greet him.

"Yared, you have returned to us! Welcome home." Kenan noticed Yared's beard and garments. "So it is true, you have joined the priesthood in the Temple of Yah."

"Indeed I have, Grandfather. I have learned great things while under the tutelage of Hualichi, the High Priest at Tsayun. Most recently I have come to believe that there is no edge of the earth."

Kenan appeared astonished, his jaw dropping to his neck. "No edge of the earth? Does it then continue on forever?"

"No, Grandfather, I believe that the world is actually curved like a ball. If one were to sail from the easternmost port on the Outer Sea and head east, one would eventually appear in the west."

Kenan began to see what his grandson was talking about. He grabbed his chin in thought and stroked his beard, following his grandson's logic. "Then, if one sailed far enough, he would end up right where he began."

"Precisely; however, I need to test this idea and find out whether or not I am indeed right. The reason I have come here, Grandfather, is because I want to send an expedition to discover if my theory is indeed the truth. You are the only man I know, with the possible exception of

King Dorro of Dorronquor, with the dorrons to fund something like this."

Kenan was thoughtful. "Can this truly be achieved? Everyone knows of the dangers that lurk in the Outer Sea, of all of the monsters of the deep. Most men would be afraid to try for fear that, should they survive attacks from the creatures of the deep, they would still fall off the edge of the earth. The men who are sent on this journey would have to be very brave indeed. Who knows whether or not they would return?"

Just then, Konaryah entered the room. Seeing Lilara, he immediately came to greet his brother's wife, for whom he had a secret affection. "Good afternoon, fair lady." he said, grinning from ear to ear, and bending forward to kiss her hand.

Lilara had always been wise to her husband's brother's ways and knew how he continuously competed with his elder brother for the favour of all, including Lilara. Although Konaryah was wed to Wolja and he had not yet given himself over wholly to his selfish ambitions, Lilara was the fairest flower in the whole world in those days, and her legendary beauty captured the hearts of many, even though her heart was given completely to Mahalalel.

"Greetings, good brother." she replied. "How are you, and how is Wolja your wife?" she asked him, causing him to straighten and collect his thoughts.

"Wolja has borne me twin sons today! I am a happy man. She is doing well after her heavy labour and will soon recover completely. Her people are known for their hardiness. I have come to bring you the news." Konaryah noticed his nephew standing beside the High King. "Ah, our wayward nephew has returned as a priest! Welcome, Yared. Will you be joining your family here in the court or will you tarry in Uarga, as is your wont?"

Yared bristled at his uncle's words. People had seen Yared walking with Medgariva in earlier years, and rumours had spread everywhere after Yared's flight to Tsayun. Konaryah, however, was always clever enough to avoid an outright confrontation. "Come, Nephew, and we will have a feast tonight to honour your return and the birth of my sons."

"Yared has come to me with a very interesting proposal, Konaryah." said the High King.

"Oh, has he? Let's hear it then." Yared told his uncle what he had told Kenan. Konaryah beamed at the thought of such a grand adventure. "The men who returned from that journey would win renown in the whole earth." His face then fell. "Unfortunately, I cannot go. I must remain here and help Wolja care for the babes. Two infant sons added to our brood of daughters will need their father around." Konaryah then thought of his friend Seuso in the south, the man who had slain Ichsha many years earlier.

"I do, however, know of a man who could undertake such a journey. He himself has two twin sons, older than mine, mind you, and full-grown. Seuso's city is not too far from the Outer Sea, and there is a river that runs through his town toward it. I will send a messenger to him, and we shall see if he will undertake this expedition."

"I will go." said Yared. "This voyage is my idea, so I feel responsible to do what I can to ensure its success."

"I will send some of my men with you to ensure that you find your way to Susa safely, for the journey is very long. You will need strong men with you." said Konaryah.

"I will receive them gladly uncle, for I know that there are dangerous creatures in the land that no man should face alone." said Yared, thinking of the great eaters and flying eaters that often waylaid unwary travellers. Then Yared prepared for his journey to Susa and Konaryah sent with him seven of his strongest men.

It took several weeks to traverse the mountainous terrain that stretched out between the northern kingdoms of Threthoron, Arattu, Turvalon, and the southern kingdoms of Susaron and Shinar. Many times great flying reptiles would swoop down from the mountaintops to try to carry off one of the travellers, but Konaryah's men were brave and fought off each attack but one. In that attack Minyar, a brave warrior married to Holraea, one of High King Kenan's twenty daughters, was carried off by one of these dreadful creatures never to be seen again. There were also many mountain lions and other such wild beasts in the region. Finally, the travellers came down from the last of the Seven

Mountain Ranges into the plains of the Kharkun Valley. When they reached the city of Susa, their arrival was announced at the city gate. They were told to remain by the gate and await the arrival of the king.

King Seuso of Susa, a man of great girth and height with a long, golden beard, rode out upon his speed lizard to greet the travellers. "My friends and kinsmen, it is good to see you! It is too seldom that I have visitors from Lhiosquor. Come and see this great city which I have built! Many tribes have come here to live among us, and they have made this city great. Come and eat with us tonight!" said Seuso. That evening a great banquet was held in Konaryah's honour in Seuso's palace. King Seuso's people had taken up the Cainite custom of eating meat, but the men of Lhiosquor refused to eat any, explaining to their host that it was not their custom.

"Yes, of course. I understand that you do not wish to eat meat, for it was not long ago when I too dwelt in the city of Lhiosquor. There are many other delicacies here that have been prepared for you, and you may eat as many of those as you wish." Seuso noticed Yared among their number, whom he did not know. He wondered why a priest would come on such a journey. "Brother Priest, what is your name?" he asked Yared.

"I am Prince Yared, the son of Mahalalel, the son of Kenan the High King of Lhiosquor."

"A prince in the robes of a priest? I thought that only men of the priestly nation of Tsayun could become priests."

"I was called to the priesthood from before my birth. Hualichi, the High Priest of Tsayun, prophesied this many years ago when my parents made a pilgrimage to the Temple of Yah."

"Konaryah, your uncle, never mentioned any of this to me. Of course, I remember the day of your birth. I was with your uncle in the palace that day when your patriarchs dedicated you to Ea. What brings you here with these men, Yared?"

"Konaryah has sent these men to accompany me on my journey to meet you. I came to Lhiosquor to tell my grandfather, the High King, about my theory that the world is curved. From observations that I have made, I have come to believe that if one were to sail far enough into the east or the west, one would not fall off of the edge of the world into the

Void, as is believed by many. The intrepid mariner would eventually sail around the other side of the world, and end up in the west if he travelled east, or in the east if he travelled west. If one sailed far enough, he would end up where his journey began."

Seuso clasped his belly, bent forward, and began to laugh heartily. His courtiers joined him in his laughter. When the king of Susa had recovered, he returned to the discussion. "No edge of the earth?" Seuso chuckled once more. "Tell me, priest, how then does one avoid falling off of the earth when travelling around its underside? Tell me what enchantment holds the mariners' ship to that ocean in the "under-world." What prevents the waters of the sea above from emptying into the sky beneath?"

Yared thought for a moment. "I do not know the answer to that question, but both Kenan and Konaryah believe that a journey around the world is worth the attempt. Konaryah said that he believes you are the bravest man he has ever met, and that if anyone would dare such a journey, you would be the man to try."

Seuso's pride began to win him over to the idea of a glorious journey. "Why then is Konaryah not here himself?"

One of Konaryah's men who had travelled with Yared, one Lognar of Cerciann who had slain many of the attacking flyers during the journey south, was tearing of a piece of bread as he spoke. "Konaryah's wife, Wolja the Yellow-Haired, has born Konaryah twin sons. He is staying in Lhiosquor to help care for them."

Seuso smiled a generous grin of white teeth. "Ah, he must be a proud father indeed. Send him my heartiest congratulations!" he exclaimed before biting into a leg of mutton. He then motioned to two strong-looking young men sitting at one end of the table. "Afalo, Atalo, come here! I want you to meet these brave travellers from the great city of Lhiosquor where your father was born." The youths came and sat closer to their father. "I also have twin sons. Afalo and Atalo have their father's bravery in them. Always each tries to outdo both me and each other in feats of strength."

Afalo, tall and slender, fair and vain, was the first to speak, and he addressed Yared while inspecting his own fingers. "I hear that you plan to sail off the edge of the earth, priest, to get to the other side. It sounds like a crazy expedition, but I would like to be the first to sail to edge of the earth, or around it if what you say is true."

Atalo, the more rough-hewn and earthy of the twins, looked like nothing like his twin brother, but appeared to be a darker and younger copy of his father. He added his voice so as not to be completely eclipsed by his twin brother, of whom he was deeply jealous. He jabbed his twin in the arm with his fist to get his attention while holding a flagon of ale in the other. "Imagine the songs that would be sung of our journey, whether or not we should succeed, Brother. Imagine the realms that would be ours on our return home! We will both be made kings like our father because of the renown of our deeds."

"As for myself," said Seuso; "I already have a kingdom here that I must tend to. There are many new people who come here all the time and I have to meet them all. It is a king's duty to know his subjects." There was a murmur of stifled laughter among the courtiers at Seuso's last sentence, for they knew well what he meant. Seuso was not faithful to Hirja, the wife of his youth, daughter of the Harifa chieftain and mother of Afalo and Atalo. This was suspected by many of his closest courtiers who often saw the king coming or going from different houses in the city late at night or early in the morning. As of yet, he had not taken a second wife in public as had Lamekk the Accursed, but this itself would not be long in coming. In Seuso's later years, the practice of polygamy became commonplace among the wealthy of Susa.

"I will send my two sons and many of my bravest men on this voyage. You men of Lhiosquor who have journeyed here are welcome to join us on this quest, but first we must build ships strong enough to withstand the storms of the Outer Sea. It may take a long time to complete the construction of such great ships."

Yared declined the offer to join the expedition. "Although the idea of a round world is mine, I cannot go on the voyage. I am needed in my duties at the Temple of Yah, and I have already been gone far too long. I will return to Tsayun by way of Iradu, where I can ride a riverboat up the Euphrates to the place where it flows near the Rahav. From there I will take the Pilgrim's Road. I will not pass through the Seven Mountain

Ranges and no one need accompany me." At this, Konaryah's men were glad. They could journey to the edge of the earth and also be rid of the dovish priest.

Yared remained in Susa for seven days, and then returned to Tsayun, travelling to the new cities of Badtibira and Sippar on his way from Iradu. Sippar had been founded by one of Irad's descendants, Enmenduranna, and none other than Tubal-Cain, the son of Lamekk the Accursed, had founded Badtibira. Tubal-Cain had lived in Shaol with his wife and sister Naamah and never returned to Turnienquor, which was once again the city of Enokk. He had lost his father and all of his sons and daughters to the sword, and Naamah had died of grief a few years afterward, sometime around the year 208 of the Enosian Calendar. Tubal-Cain, having nothing left to him, headed south around the year 214 to the city of his ancestor, Irad, who pardoned him. Tubal-Cain took a new wife from among the women of Iradu and began life anew, building the city of Badtibira. The Southlands were becoming more and more populated as people moved down into the fertile plain of Shinar that Irad had named after his second son. Mahu-Jaol, his eldest son, had been slain in the Usurpation.

# 288 EC

It took four years for the shipwrights of Susa to construct ships fit to voyage upon the Outer Sea. During those four years, many different designs were tested, but most failed miserably and the sailors of those vessels perished beneath the waves. Finally the shipwrights built the <u>Magras</u>, named for its primary builder, which sailed upon the Outer Sea for seven days and seven nights before returning to port. When the <u>Magras</u> returned, Seuso commissioned the building of four more ships like it, and then sent word to Konaryah in Lhiosquor that the expedition would soon be underway. When the day finally came for the grand voyage, Seuso gathered his people together.

"Loyal subjects, I announce to you today that my sons, Afalo and Atalo, have accepted the challenge to lead an expedition to the edge of the world. It has come to be believed by some that indeed there is no edge of the world but that one may sail around it, returning to their point of departure. This is the commission that I give the brave men who will travel on this voyage. Should they return, our city shall be of great renown in all the earth." Seuso continued speaking for some time, and when he concluded, he sent the sailors on their way. "May Ea, the god of our fathers, watch over you and protect you on your voyage."

It should be noted here that Ea was the deity worshipped in Susa in those days. Seuso, being originally from Lhiosquor, grew up hearing of Yah, but many of the tribes who had dwelt in the mountains between the north and south had turned to false gods, forsaking the way of the Almighty One. The new god, Ea, was supposed by Seuso to represent Yah, the true God, but Seuso's heart was wicked, and although he knew of God he did not truly know Him. Therefore, he set up an idol of his own making and altered the divine name to Ea. A fallen angel, a lieutenant of Lucifer, was given that name and was appointed to bring a cloud of darkness over the hearts and minds of men in that city.

In the same way Irad, the son of Enokk, had seen the miraculous liberation of his father's city during the Battle of Turnienquor. He set out to worship the Almighty One, whose name he knew to be Eloi. However, in the same manner as Seuso, Irad grew wicked and set up an idol which he named Elli or Ellil for his people. Thus another lieutenant of the great enemy was given that name and assigned to bring a veil of darkness over the hearts and minds of the people of Iradu. The demons Ea and Ellil are still worshipped to this day by the people who have moved into the land of Shinar to rebuild these ancient cities, even though the world has been changed.

Now Afalo and Atalo journeyed east along the coast of the Outer Sea so that they would not be swept into its depths. They determined to follow this course until there was no more land to be seen in the east. It soon came to pass that the travellers came upon Harifon, the land of the Harifa who dwelt along the Sea. There they visited their mother's family and were given supplies for their journey from their grandfather, the king of Harifon. Medgariva was dwelling in Harifon during that time, and heard of the arrival of the visitors. She came out from her cave to see who had come among the Harifa. Lognar recognized her and called to her.

"You there maiden, if maiden you be, did you not once sell fruit in the market of Uarga on Mt. Threthor?" he asked.

Medgariva turned slowly to look at him, tears welling in her eyes as she remembered her home. "Once I dwelt in Uarga and sold fruit in the marketplace, but no longer. I am now Valiturnea of the Harifa and I cannot return to Mt. Threthor. My beloved has left me, and I do not know where to find him."

"Who is this man you seek? You say he is from Threthoron?" asked Lhutar.

"He is none other than Yared the Prince, of the royal house of Kenan."

The men from Lhiosquor were amazed. "Prince Yared came with us to Susa. He has returned to the Temple of Yah." said Lognar. "Did you not know that he is a priest and has taken the vow of celibacy? What's more, maiden, you are a Cainite, and you would never be allowed to marry a man of Lhiosquor, much less one born of the royal house of the High King."

Medgariva began to weep bitterly. "All is gone, then. Yared has taken the oath of celibacy and I shall never be with him." The men of the expedition began speaking with the fishermen of Harif, the main city of Harifon where they were now docked, about their quest to find the edge of the earth. When Medgariva heard this, she turned to Atalo.

"Did you say that you plan to sail to the edge of the earth?" she asked.

"Yes, and we intend to continue sailing if we find no edge."

Medgariva took a deep breath and hesitated before continuing. "I would like to accompany you." she said. "When we reach the edge of the world, I will throw myself off into the Void, because I have no longer any reason to live." So it was that Medgariva, called Valiturnea, joined the expedition. The Harifa, who saw Valiturnea no more, believed that she did indeed throw herself over the edge of the world, never to be seen again.

Weeks later, the sailors came upon schools of fish as red as scarlet.

So thick and great in number were they that the sea almost appeared to be set afire. The shoreline was raised up to sheer cliffs, and a waterfall cascaded down the edge of the cliffs into the sea. One ship was sailed to the base of the waterfall, close enough for those aboard to test the quality of the water. The men on the ship tasted no salt in the mist from the falls, so Afalo ordered them to sail to the place where the shore lowered itself once more to the sea. There they camped; filled barrels with fresh water, and prepared for the next stage of their journey.

Sailing on from the Eastern Falls, the expedition of Afalo and Atalo continued until they came to a rocky point where the land began to bend away far into the north. Here they camped and gathered food for the next part of their voyage, not knowing what to expect when they turned away from land. At this time their numbers were sixty-one: twelve men on each ship, plus Valiturnea who travelled with Atalo. When they left the point which was the easternmost point of land in the world, they continued sailing eastward.

After two weeks on the open ocean, a terrible storm arose the like of which had never been seen. The men struggled to lower the sails and secure anything which might move about on the ships. Although the sailors took down the sails as quickly as they could, yet still the wind tore through two of them. These would need to be mended soon, before they could travel much further. Water sprayed over the decks in torrents, and the men frantically bailed as much water as they could back over the sides.

"We must be getting close to the edge of the world." Lognar shouted to Valiturnea as the wild ocean waves buffeted against the sides of the vessel. Aboard the Queen Hirja, Afalo shouted orders to his crew, but his men could not hear his commands over the roaring of the furious, white water. The ships lurched from side to side in the water, and some of the men were so disoriented that they lost their footing, slipped and slid across the slippery decks. The storm was so severe that one of the ships, the Konaryah, was lost when the wind and waves turned it completely over in the perilous, angry ocean. All twelve men on the Konaryah perished under the waves. After that, the wind died down, and there were now four ships and forty-nine souls who continued the journey eastward.

They had travelled for another month after losing the <u>Konaryah,</u> and had still not found the edge of the earth, when a great sea monster with a long neck like that of a thunder lizard ascended from the ocean depths. The beast was as long as any of the ships, and it thought that the boats were others of its kind invading its territory. The fearsome creature swam forward in anger and rammed its body against the side of the <u>Seusaron,</u> one of the four remaining ships. The sea monster's crushing weight snapped the timbers on the ship's hull, and it sank. All aboard that ship were then eaten by the creature, reducing the number of surviving travellers to thirty-seven. As the creature returned to attack another ship, the men of the three remaining ships took up longbows and opened fire. They shot arrows tipped with flaming pitch into the creature's jaws and neck. With a bellowing cry of pain, the creature dove deep beneath the ocean's surface to extinguish the burning missiles. To the relief of the travelling company, they never saw the creature again.

# 289 EC

Nine more months passed, and still no end was found to the earth. The men of the expedition, even the bravest souls, were beginning to lose heart and begged their captains, Atalo, Afalo, and Lognar of Lhiosquor, to return home the way that they had come. Some had said that the sea was endless, and that they would end up sailing forever until Ea unmade the world. All aboard could eat only the fish of the Sea, and even the men of Lhiosquor, whose law forbade the eating of meat, ate fish in order to stay alive. Seventeen men died of starvation and related illnesses on this leg of the journey because their food supply had been exhausted. There was simply not enough food for everyone, and the strongest took what they could while the weakest starved. At this time, Atalo took pity on Valiturnea and shared his portion with her.

Finally Afalo, whose eyesight was keener than that of any of the other travellers, espied land, but at first it was believed to be only an illusion brought on by famine. When they came closer and saw the land was not a figment of imagination, the twenty who remained on the three remaining ships were ecstatic. They disembarked on what they believed to be the westernmost land on the earth, but in actuality was a very large undiscovered island on the opposite side of the known world. The island was with filled with many good things to eat, and many believed that they must have sailed over the edge of the world into paradise.

Now Atalo had become ill before arriving on the island, and Valiturnea tended him in return for his kindness in sharing his food. When they reached shore, Valiturnea found some herbs and made a broth for Atalo, who revived and regained his strength. Atalo fell in love with Valiturnea, and although Valiturnea did not love Atalo, she had consigned herself to never seeing her beloved Yared again. She was very lonely - and tired from her grieving - and consented to marry Atalo. The travellers dwelt on the island for a year until Afalo decided that the journey must be completed. "We must continue on, people. It is time to return to Susa and to the welcome which awaits us. We shall have great honour in my father's palace." Many of the sailors listened to Afalo and began to prepare for the journey east to come into the west. Atalo, however, was not of like mind.

"For myself, brother, I will stay here with my bride, who is with child, and build a life here. This island will be my kingdom which Valiturnea and I will populate with our descendants. It shall be called Atalanti." Five of Atalo's men agreed with him and remained behind, leaving thirteen men to return to Susa. In time, these five men married daughters of Atalo and Valiturnea. Thus was founded the kingdom of Atalanti, among the last of the kingdoms of the old world to fall, yet now fallen nonetheless.

# 290 EC

Now Atalo kept the Magras with him in Atalanti, leaving two ships to return to Susa. One, the Queen Hirja, was captained by Afalo with eight men on board. The other five men were on the other ship, the Wolja, which was captained by Lognar. These were the five men of Lhiosquor who were still left. Only one of their number who departed on the expedition was lost. This man was Uligant who had been eaten by the monster of the deep. Again they sailed for many months, this time with the ships stocked with plenty of food from Atalanti, but of course most of this food grew rotten as the weeks passed. Once more the men were nearly overcome with hunger when they came upon a small island.

The men anchored the ships and swam ashore where they found an abundance of fruit trees and a spring of fresh water from the centre of the island. The men of Lhiosquor gave thanks to Yah who had provided them with food and fresh water. The following morning they reluctantly set out once more. Weeks later, after four months of sailing eastward from Atalanti, the travellers encountered a deep fog that came upon the sea. No one could see anything, even their very hands in front of their faces. Suddenly, the men on Lognar's ship heard a loud creaking, groaning, and snapping sound. The Wolja had hit something and was taking water quickly. Afalo drew the Queen Hirja near, and his keen vision saw through a brief break in the fog that Lognar's ship had hit a rock.

"Lognar!" he yelled through the fog. "You have struck land! Get your men out of your ship and into the water. We will swim to shore." The shore was only dimly seen through the thick fog, but the fog began to clear and the men of both ships came ashore. The Wolja was damaged beyond repair, but the Queen Hirja was whole and was anchored near the shore. The men camped on the shore and ate anything that they could find. Three days later, they scouted the land where they had come ashore and found themselves in an estuary. The shore extended as far as the eye could see both north and south. They could travel deeply inland without coming to yet another ocean. Inland further still were lush forests and majestic mountains which pierced the bright green forest canopy.

Remember that in those days all of the land was gathered into one place, and only Atalanti and a few small islands stood apart. The men of the expedition decided that they would sail south in the remaining ship instead of heading further into the Great Gulf. They knew that the river Kharkun led out from Susa to meet the Outer Sea at the southern shore of the land. Thus they returned by sailing south around the bottom of the supercontinent (which was simply called Lanti or "The Land"). They encountered far fewer troubles on this journey as they stayed close to land where they could stop and gather resources as they needed. Furthermore, sea monsters rarely travelled close to shore, and storms were far less frequent. It was thus that they travelled for the remainder of the journey through unknown waters.

## 292 EC

In the year 292 of the Enosian Calendar, the company of men who travelled in Queen Hirja returned to Susa from sailing around the earth. The first settlement that they came to was the island of Dilumu. This island was but a few days south of Iradu by ship. The Palace of Dilumu, one of Irad's sons, was made of white marble, and it reflected the sun's rays that early morning as the sun began to rise over the horizon. All aboard the ship were overjoyed that they had finally returned to a place that they knew. Dilumu received the heroes with great fanfare, clothed them, and fed them a king's banquet. The weary wandered rested for a few days in Dilumu and shared tales of their journey with fascinated listeners. Dilumu made the men honorary princes of his kingdom, and after this ceremony, the sailors returned homeward and searched for the mouth of the Kharkun River which would return them to Susa.

Upon sailing into the harbour of Susa, the returning voyagers again received a heroes' welcome. Seuso held a feast in honour of the return of his son and the men who accompanied him. Because Atalo had set up his own realm on an island on the other side of the world, Seuso now named Afalo heir of his entire kingdom. After two weeks of feasting and resting in the palace of the King of Susa, Lognar's men returned on their way to Lhiosquor to tell the High King of their journeys. After months of crossing the treacherous Seven Mountain Ranges that separated Threthoron in the north from Shinar and Susa in the south, the remaining men of Lhiosquor arrived at Mt. Threthoron and rode the lift-carts up to Lhiosquor. Lognar related the entire journey to Kenan, the High King. Kenan listened intently as the tale of the voyage was told, of how the fierce sea monster was fought off, and how Atalo found an island on the other side of the world where he set up his own kingdom.

"Yared will be pleased to hear that your expedition was a success. I am not sure what he will make of the news of Medgariva. Nonetheless, I will make a pilgrimage to Mt. Tsayun and tell him that the voyage was successful. You are dismissed to your home, Lognar." Lognar nodded deeply in respect toward the High King and returned to his home and family. Kenan then prepared his entourage for the journey westward. When everything was ready for the pilgrimage, he set off westward toward Mt. Sentinel following the Pilgrim's Road to the city of Turvah. Kenan visited with his purple-skinned allies for a few days before continuing westward along the Pilgrim's Road which now wound its way along the Upper Rahav.

In time, the royal carriage and the king's entourage arrived in Tsayun. From the Temple of Yah on the summit of Mt. Tsayun, Yared saw the carriage approach, and the young priest ran to meet his grandfather.

"Yah be praised! Welcome, Grandfather. It has been a long time since last you were here. I will tell my initiates to prepare our royal guest house immediately."

"Thank you, Yared. I bring you news that you will be glad to hear. Afalo son of Seuso has returned from his journey around the world. Your theory has been proven correct."

Yared had a look of wonderment on his face as he spoke, "Really? The men of Susa have returned? That is wonderful! I myself was uncertain whether anyone could survive such a taxing journey, but apparently it was a success. What news did they bring of their voyages?"

Kenan told Yared the entire tale of the journey of Afalo and Atalo, of their storms at sea and their encounter with the terrifying sea creature, even of the weeping Valiturnea who became Atalo's bride, but he did not mention that Valiturnea was Medgariva. Yared had no need to hear that name again, for it could tear old wounds wide open and set his mind wandering away from his devotion to God. Yared seemed too content in his resigned role as a celibate priest, and Kenan did not want the mention of his former love to shatter his newfound peace.

That night, as Kenan and Yared spoke together of many things, the curtain of heaven rolled back. The priest and the High King looked up together at the signs of the stars. Yared aroused the other priests from their slumber and bid them to help him interpret what they saw. They saw a disturbing portent; Abelon had entered the constellation of the Giant, and shooting stars appeared to come from the Giant's outstretched hand. Kenan, Yared, and the temple priests all agreed that this could only mean that the Giants were about to rise again to bring war upon the earth once more.

# CHAPTER 12

# THE RISE OF HURASH
## (299 – 381 EC)

## 299 EC

Hurash had arrived in the land of the Nahlonites in the year 214 of the Enosian Calendar. Over the past eighty-five years, he had taken many wives, mainly by capturing Nahlonite women. Hurash desired greatly to produce heirs in order to raise an army to avenge his parents and achieve dominion over the whole world. However, to his fierce disappointment, all of his wives produced only normal offspring - no Giants. What was more was that all of Hurash's children were daughters. Hurash was so furious that he had all of his wives slain in turn after giving birth to a daughter, yet he spared the lives of his daughters and placed them under the care of Nuhum, a man of the tribe of Nahlon who had allied himself to Hurash and had built a temple to Hraw in a cave far up the great river Nahla. Nuhum raised the daughters of Hurash as his own, and they grew beautiful in appearance and became priestesses in the Temple of Hraw.

It was about this time that the bravest of the Nahlonite men began to wander up the river, having heard strange tales of Giants, beautiful women and a golden temple. The beauty of the daughters of Hurash so captivated the men that came into Hurash's land that they forsook the worship of the Almighty One and worshipped Hraw instead, as their desire for the daughters of Hurash were so great and Nuhum allowed any man to lie with them so long as he made a blood sacrifice of an animal to Hraw. Only to these men whom had sold their souls to Hraw did Hurash, who had remained hidden in a stone palace carved into the side of a mountain for nearly a century, show himself. These men, their wills held captive by the daughters of Hurash, swore allegiance to him and worshipped him as a god. Then they went back to the towns of their kinsmen to spread the degenerate worship of Hraw and Hishirash further among their Nahlonite brethren.

The physical sensuality of the daughters of Hurash was so striking that not only were they noticed by the sons of men, but by many of the evil spirits who served under their commander, Hraw. Lucifer, the great enemy of mankind, had appointed twenty of his most powerful and most wicked demon chieftains to work under Hraw and carry out his bidding in the land of the Nahlonites. Led by Shemihazah, the general of the demonic elite known as "Watchers", each of these chieftains had ten more Watchers beneath him. One day when the blood sacrifices were being given in the temple of Hraw, the sun god's twenty chieftains entered the temple, took on the forms of men, and had relations with the daughters of Hurash.

The daughters of Hurash all became with child and gave birth to abominable Giants. These were the Nephilim, the second generation of Giants. When Hurash saw this, he sent Nuhum to Nubat, the chief city of the Nahlonite people, to rally those who had given themselves to Hraw. The men came with their wives, sons, and daughters and established the twin villages of Pe and Dep which were dedicated to the worship of Hraw and Hishirash. The minions of Hraw went among the women of Pe and Dep and fathered many more abominable Giants over the course of the next forty years.

## 339 EC

After forty years had passed, Hurash assembled a fearsome army of Nephilim. It was about this time that the Watchers began to teach their children in the black arts of sorcery. With the invention of gunpowder in the hills of the Upper Nahla, the Giants devised weapons which could shoot armour-piercing projectiles from far distances with greater deadliness than any arrow from a crossbow or longbow. In the year 339, Hurash assembled his armies and conquered Nubat, bringing the entire Nahlonite nation under his rule. Nahlonites in the smaller towns who rebelled were swiftly crushed by the armies of the Giant brothers Ohyah and Hahyah, chiefs of the Nephilim. A few of those still faithful to the Almighty One escaped and headed northeast to the Temple of Yah. They were received there by Hualichi who had recently stepped down as High Priest in favour of Yared.

"Yared's wisdom and favour with Yah surpasses mine." Hualichi had said. "His graciousness to all peoples is unsurpassed by all, and I would pass my title to him. As for myself, I wish to take a wife and raise a family. The duties of a High Priest will not permit me the time to do so, yet I will gladly serve alongside the other brethren in this house as a fellow priest."

Hualichi saw the Nahlonites coming and welcomed them. "Welcome, friends from the city of Nubat and land of Nahlon. Why are you in such haste and look so weary?"

"A terrible thing has befallen our people." said one of the women. "The Giants have arisen again south of our cities. With their black arts they have seduced many of our people to the worship of other gods. These rebels have joined the Giants, who call themselves Nephilim, and have taken the city of Nubat. Hurash has sworn that he will avenge his father's death and will not stop until Lhiosquor has fallen and the Patriarch Seth kneels prostrate at his feet."

As the Nahlonite woman told the tale, the colour drained from the priest's face. "It is as it has been foretold. It would appear that one of the Giants escaped the Battle of Turnienquor, even a son of Hishirash. However, there was never any record of Hurash, son of Hishirash."

"Hurash claims to be the last son of Hishirash and Ichsha, and purports that he was born in the land of Harifon, far to the east." she said.

A light went on in Hualichi's mind. "So, Ichsha was with child when she fled to Harifon. Hurash now leads these Nephilim to rule the strategic Nahla River, and will no doubt be heading this way soon. Come with me, I will introduce you to Yared. He is the High Priest now, and he is of royal blood. His fate and the fate of these abominable ones are entwined somehow, and he must know of this."

Yared was shocked when he heard of the fall of Nubat, even though the priests had known for forty-seven years now that the Giants would return to make war once again, but no one knew how or when. "I must send word to the High King immediately!" he exclaimed. "The people of Tsayun are a peaceful people and are unable to defend themselves. We will need to build a garrison town nearby to defend the Temple of Yah from these walking abominations." Yared sent Tsiling, one of his initiates, to go to Lhiosquor and request aid. When Tsiling arrived at Mt. Threthor, he told the city guard that he was sent on a mission by Yared, the High Priest of the Temple of Yah. The guards brought Tsiling to the palace of the High King, where Kenan was holding court. When he heard the news, the High King nearly fell off his throne in astonishment.

"Giants have enslaved the Nahlonites? That is grave news indeed! Where did they come from? Were not all the Giants destroyed at the battle of Turnienquor?"

Konaryah, who was standing the left of the High King's throne, leaned over and spoke to the king. "When Ichsha was dying, she mentioned that one day one of her house would avenge the deaths of her kind. We all thought that she was bluffing, the last ranting curses of a doomed Giantess, but there must have been one of her brood who escaped Turnienquor, one who was not with her in Harifon."

"They must be stopped." said the High King, thumping his fist on the arm of his throne. Kenan then summoned Mahalalel, his eldest son.

"Good morning, father." Mahalalel greeted the High King when he arrived. "I can tell by your countenance and the urgency of your message that all is not well,"

Kenan motioned to the young initiate who stood beside him. "This young man, Tsiling, was sent here on an urgent errand from Yared. The Giants have arisen again, and they have enslaved the Nahlonites. The Temple of Yah, not to mention Yared's life and the lives of all the Tsayunis, may be in peril."

Mahalalel was clearly dismayed. "That cannot be! No Giant could have survived our assault on Turnienquor. We searched under every stone and log, behind every mountain and in every valley in the land now called Arattu."

Tsiling spoke. "The refugees who have fled to the temple say that

Ichsha was with child when she fled to Harifon, and that she gave birth to a son, Hurash, who came and built his palace in the mountains south of Nubat many years ago. It is Hurash who now rules over the Nahlonites."

"I will assemble an army of twenty thousand of our strongest men to build a fortress around Tsayalam, the city which surrounds the Temple buildings. We will also build a garrison to the east of Tsayalam to protect it from any attackers. Another set of walls with guard towers will be placed in the southwest to protect the area, for that is the direction from which the attack is most likely to come. Do you have any other suggestions, father?"

"Bring as many builders and craftsmen as you can, as well as many blacksmiths. Also, bring merchants who can purchase anything you might need. I will provide you with two hundred thousand dorrons from the royal treasury to begin. The Temple of Yah must not fall into the hands of the servants of the great enemy."

"With your leave, Father, I will go and begin preparations immediately." Mahalalel then turned and went straight away to assemble an army. The courtiers all murmured about what had taken place, and the room was filled with buzzing anxiety. In the weeks that followed, the royal military quarter of the city of Triethu at the base of Mt. Threthor teemed with visitors from across the Northern Kingdoms. Many were men who had volunteered for military service. Others were skilled artisans; stonemasons, blacksmiths, braziers, carpenters, and many other guildsmen who wished to help in whatever way they could by contributing their skills to the building of the garrison and its armory. Mahalalel assembled an army of thirty thousand men and set forth to Mt. Tsayun. When they had arrived, Mahalalel sought out his son, the High Priest.

"It is good to see you again, Yared, my son. It has been far too long since my last pilgrimage to the holy Temple of Yah."

Yared embraced his father. "Thank you for coming here. Never before was your presence so sorely needed. Hurash, the Giant King, has so far let us be and has not sent his armies this way. His people remain along the great river Nahla where they have enslaved the Nahlonites. I do not doubt, however, that Hurash will soon come here, for he wishes vengeance for the death of his father and wants to take Grandfather's place as High King. There have also been reports of powerful new weapons used by Hurash's people. We will need to discover how to defend ourselves against them. Even more disturbing are the reports of the siege engines that were used to bring down the once mighty walls of Nahla. They can blast great holes in the strongest of stone. Apparently, there are no fortifications which can withstand them. Whatever kind of dark sorcery these Nephilim have concocted, a way must be found to fight it."

"Do not fear, my son. You should know, as High Priest, Yah is on our side. As long as we are faithful to Him, He will protect us and will surely not let us be destroyed by the abominable house of Hurash. My men are setting up camp southeast of the sacred mountain in the valley. We will post a watch on the hills to the southwest, and once we have built a fortress, we will begin the construction of a wall west of here stretching to the Rahav. The wall will serve as an advanced warning to alert us of any movement coming from the land of Nahlon."

Father and son continued their conversation about other things, about life in Lhiosquor, about Yared's brother and sister, and about Yared's studies of the many aspects of Creation. This was a time in which men learned very quickly and many new things were being learned, discovered, and invented in the world. Almost all of this knowledge has been lost in the floodwaters that destroyed the Old World. After their conversation, Mahalalel led his men to the hills and valleys south of Tsayalam where they set up camp. There they began the construction of the garrison town, Yarku, meaning watchfulness, which, though destroyed and rebuilt, still stands to this day even though the world has been changed. Over the next few years, Yarku became a great fortified city where all who wished to put an end to the Nephilim came from around the world. Although Hurash ruled as a tyrant in the land of Nahlon, he did not yet strike eastward as he continued to bide his time and build his strength.

# 367 EC

In the year 367 of the Enosian Calendar, the army of Ohyah of the Nephilim came against Tsayalam. By this time, Mahalalel had constructed a concentric series of three walls and three moats around the city. The area was well defended, but Ohyah had come with an army of one hundred thousand men and three and a half thousand Nephilim. The forces around Yarku numbered only twenty five thousand two hundred men, five thousand of those being heavy cavalry. Of those five thousand, five hundred were mounted on mastodons and another five hundred on great armoured lizards. When General Mahalalel heard that the armies of the Nephilim were approaching, he immediately ran up Mt. Tsayun to the Temple of Yah where he prayed earnestly.

"O Almighty Yah, who gave us victory over Hishirash in former days, who established the city of your chosen people on a high mountain to protect us from our enemies and gave us dominion over the earth, You who dwell in this temple yet cannot be contained here, hear the prayer of Your servant, the son of the High King whom You have chosen to rule the kingdoms of men. Your enemies are my enemies, for I fight for You alone. These enemies, the abominable Nephilim, are coming here with a force much greater than mine. Please protect Your servants and do not let Your holy temple be defiled by the sons of demons."

As Mahalalel prayed, the glory of God filled His temple. A voice like thunder spoke from the cloud.

"Do not be afraid of the Nephilim, those blasphemers who are destined for destruction. Did I not allow them to be raised up again? Does anything happen on the earth without My permission? Am I not the One who created the great eater lizards who roam the wilderness and can bring down and devour even the largest of great quake lizards? Am I not the same God who established your father's kingdom over the earth? I Am the Lord Yah, and I say that today your enemies will turn from you in terror just as in the day when Hishirash was driven away from Mt. Threthor. He fled as an antelope flees from a predator from the warrior angels which I sent forth on that day to do battle. I tell you the truth, not only will they flee, but you shall pursue the enemy to the city of Nubat itself, and the city shall be yours for a time."

Mahalalel was puzzled by this last statement. "O Almighty One, for how many years shall Nubat be kept free from the Nephilim?"

"The fate of the world lies in the hands of one man; your son, My High Priest. Look carefully to him, Mahalalel. Remember the words of the prophecy given to you by Hualichi, My servant. If Yared chooses My ways, the Emerald Crown of Lhiosquor will never leave your line and will be passed from your father, to you, and to Yared. However, If Yared follows his own path the Emerald Crown will be taken from your father. It will later be taken from the usurper's line by a man who does not know Me or serve Me, but will be a worshipper of false gods. After that, Lhiosquor will surely fall before the Nephilim. They will rule the earth and your lineage will be reduced to a remnant. Nevertheless, even then shall come many great men of renown from that remnant, men who will revere My name. For the sake of the remnant, the days of the Nephilim will be shortened to less than five hundred years. Before five hundred years have passed, I will lift the yoke of oppression from the people of the earth and bring them freedom once again."

Mahalalel was confused. "How can I help my son? How will I know when the day of decision is upon him?"

"I will give you a sign." said the thundering voice. "Look for the Weeping Queen from the Island Kingdom. When she comes to My temple, it will be time for Yared to make his decision whether or not he will obey Me. Now arise, mighty warrior. You must go and lead your men into battle. Do not be afraid of the Nephilim, of their great size and strength, of their numbers, of their fearsome war lizards or their terrible siege weapons, for I Am giving them into your hands. Go now and take courage, for I Am with you. I will go before you and behind you, above you and beneath you, to the left of you and to the right of you, and I shall smite your enemies." Then the cloud of glory left and Mahalalel hurried down the mountain to Yarku to gather his forces.

The appearance of the approaching enemy forces on the horizon was like a huge dust storm coming out of the west. Mahalalel's forces had built a high wall stretching south of the Rahav for twelve miles, and upon it were stationed cohorts of archers armed with the best longbows and crossbows. Catapults were hidden behind the walls of the fortress ready to launch fiery rain upon Ohyah's army. As the enemy came within range, Pikal the herald sounded the ram's horn and the archers fired. The catapults released their burdens, and the infantry and cavalry flew through the gate.

As this was happening, great clouds appeared in the sky, in front of the forces of Mahalalel, and the cavalry halted. Lightning and hail came from the sky and struck the forces of the Nephilim. From the clouds there appeared a great pillar of cloud which stretched down to the earth and destroyed all in its path. The pillar of cloud was surrounded by great winds, and it pursued Ohyah's army all the way back across the river Kapis, the twin river of the Nahla which marked the eastern border of Hurash's realm. Not one soldier of Mahalalel's army was harmed. As the Giants fled, there arose a great cheer from the men of Threthoron who returned to Yarku to celebrate long into the night. The following day, prayers of thanksgiving and sacrifices were made at the Temple of Yah, and all of the people rejoiced in God who had spared them from the swords of the Abominable Ones.

# 381 EC

In the following years, the forces of Yarku made the entire territory of Tsayun into a network of fortresses, particularly toward the west and south of Tsayalam. In the year 377, Mahalalel liberated the Nahlonite city of Nubat and gave the kingdom to Hamin, eldest of the remaining sons of Nahlon who were not killed when Hurash took the city. Nahlon had been captured during that earlier conflict, and was then executed in one of Hurash's brutal displays of power. Hurash still ruled the upper regions of the Nahla in the south from the twin cities of Pe and Dep, but for now his power was contained. In the year 381, one of Yared's younger brothers, Soduryah, joined the priesthood as an initiate. He had served in his father's army from the age of sixteen; however, as the army of Mahalalel had brought a relative peace to the region, Soduryah's inquisitive nature yearned for knowledge. He entered the priesthood after having served five years with his father.

One evening, the curtain of heaven was rolled back, and Yared looked into the heavens with an improved looking glass that he had invented. Soduryah came to see his brother on the roof of the Temple of Yah where Yared was staring through his looking glass in astonishment.

"What is it, my brother?" asked Soduryah, who was never one for formalities. He called his brother by his high priestly titles during ceremonies, but now he could speak to him as Yared.

"Almighty Yah has given me a revelation through these lenses. I have come to believe that the earth is not stationary, but travels around the sun as do the other planets. Only the moon travels around the earth. I have also seen that Plaricon, the largest of the planets, has smaller planets travelling around it just as the moon travels around the earth. I do not know what I will do with this knowledge, but it is wonderful."

Soduryah peered through the telescope where Yared had been gazing and saw a comet pass through the constellations of the queen, the fishes, the priest, and the great eater.

"What is the meaning of this sign?" he asked his brother. Yared thought silently for a moment before replying, "From what I can tell, a queen will pass over water. There is a priest on the other side of the water, and their meeting shall bring about a catastrophe." At that time, Yared had no thought at how that portent might come to pass.

# CHAPTER 13

# YARED'S CHOICE
## (384 – 385 EC)

## 384 EC

Medgariva had found peace for a season in the early years of her life with Atalo in Atalanti. Atalo had built a palace with his own two hands, and his sons added to its splendour as they came of age to work alongside their father. However, as the years passed, Atalo's love for his wife grew cold. Sometimes, he would be given to uncontrollable fits of rage, and at that time he was a danger to anyone near him. Medgariva began to think about Yared, the only man she ever truly loved. On night in the year 384 of the Enosian Calendar, the ninety-sixth year since the founding of Atalanti, Cloys, one of Atalo and Medgariva's youngest daughters, came to the queen's room. Her clothing was torn, she was bleeding from a cut under her eye and on her right arm, and she was weeping profusely.

"What has happened, my dear one?" the woman known as Queen Valiturnea asked her maiden daughter.

She looked sorrowfully at her mother as tears filled her dark brown eyes. Cloys was held by many to be the most beautiful woman in Atalanti, and many men sought her hand in marriage. Atalo was fiercely protective of his daughter and deemed no man worthy enough to marry her.

"I have fallen in love with Joreb, the farmer, but Father did not approve of him. Joreb and I could not bear to stop seeing each other, so we continued to meet in secret. Joreb was in my chamber tonight when Father entered and slew him right before my eyes." Cloys wept profusely, her tears running like rivulets down her cheeks into her dark hair.

After a moment, she continued in tears. "Then Father flew into a terrible rage, threatened me, beat me, and then he ..." she wept again before continuing, "He sent me screaming from my chamber." she sobbed. Medgariva understood the meaning of the words her daughter could not bring herself to say. She knew the rages that could grip her husband, but she never expected that Atalo, the man who had comforted her so many times when she wept for her lost home, the man who had praised her beauty and written it in a song, would ever treat their daughter this way.

Medgariva held her daughter tightly, and the Weeping Queen began to weep with her broken daughter. "I will take you far from here." she told Cloys. "I will take you to a place where you will be safe, but you cannot tell your father. If he knows what I am about to do, his wrath upon us could be terrifying."

Medgariva sat down at her great loom and began to weave an enormous cloth. She wove for weeks on end. When she was finished, the cloth measured thirty cubits by forty cubits. She arranged to meet with one of the original settlers, none other than Magras, the man who had built the only seafaring vessel on the island. "Magras, I need your help. I need the use of your ship. I have woven a new sail for it so that it may go about upon the open sea once again."

Magras was surprised. "My ship hasn't sailed in years, my queen. Whatever would you need it for?"

"Magras, I know that I can trust you, as you have always been a kind friend to me. If I tell you, you must promise to tell no one, not even the king. Only my daughter, Cloys, knows of this."

"I must know what it is that you wish me to do, Valiturnea." answered the shipwright.

"I have made a new sail to replace the tattered old one on your ship. I give it to you freely, but I need you to prepare the ship for a long journey. Cloys and I are leaving the island."

Magras was aghast. "Leaving Atalanti? My queen, where would you go?"

"I want to go home. Atalo no longer loves me and Cloys is in danger here. I cannot say more about her ordeal, but it is serious. We need to leave as soon as possible."

"I may be able to have the ship ready and seaworthy within three weeks. There is much that needs to be done. You will also need a crew, Valiturnea, to man the ship."

"Pick men who are the most honourable and trustworthy to be our companions who will not be tempted by my daughter's beauty."

Magras laughed heartily. "There is no such man on the face of the earth!" Magras thought for a moment. "However, if you are looking for honourable men who will not harm you or your daughter, I may be able to help you.

"There are a group of holy men; fishermen that live on the Rocky Isles off the northwest coast of the island. This time of year, when the tides are low, the largest of the three islands can be reached by land as the shoals come above water to form a causeway. These men devote themselves to prayer and meditation, writing and learning, and of course, fishing." No one in Atalanti knew of God's proscription of meat, as even the original settlers who came on the <u>Magras</u> hailed from Susa, where the law was unknown. Magras continued. "They know how to steer a ship, albeit small fishing vessels along the coast, but I believe that they will help you. No doubt many of them would love to embark upon a pilgrimage to the Temple of Yah in Tsayalam."

"As would I." said Medgariva, her eyes turning misty and distant as she imagined Yared, alone in the Temple, sacrificing bulls and lambs and praying for her. She wondered if he still remembered her after more than one hundred years.

Although the people of Atalanti were yet very few, the island was quite large. It was a journey of three days from the fair town of Ataliquor in the south to the windy north. In the afternoon of the third day, Valiturnea and Cloys crossed the causeway onto the Isle of Contemplation. They found a small stone building with smoke coming from the chimney, accompanied by the sound of men singing. A man dressed in a brown robe and wearing a wide brimmed hat came up the road from the other side of the island where the fishing docks had been built. He carried a long wooden pole across his shoulders to the ends of which were tied nets full of freshly cleaned fish. He saw the ladies approach, and seemed about to send them off until he recognized the queen.

"Queen Valiturnea, to what do we, the humble brethren of the Isle of Contemplation, owe your Majesty's visit?" asked the fisherman.

"We were told, kind sir, that your brethren may be able to help us in our quest. My daughter and I have need of men who can navigate a ship."

"You have come to the right place, your Majesty. How many men will you need, and when?"

"We will need twelve men in eighteen days. Please know that I intend to leave my husband's kingdom and return to my homeland."

The fisherman frowned. "Twelve men, you say? There are only thirteen of us. One man alone cannot stay behind to keep our house of prayer in order and to sell fish to the southerners. I am afraid that we cannot help you, your Majesty."

Medgariva noticed that the singing had stopped, and a man in a tan-coloured robe stepped out of the small stone building and came toward them. "My queen, it has been many years since we last met. Welcome to our house of prayer." She recognized the man as Garnan, one of the men who chose to stay behind with Atalo. Medgariva remembered that Garnan had had a disagreement with Atalo and moved into the north. He had always been a devout man. Garnan had visited Lhiosquor as a boy and had turned from the worship of the false Ea to the true God, Yah. Many believe that it was his prayers to Yah that allowed the Magras to reach Atalanti and not be swallowed up in the sea.

"Garnan!" she exclaimed with joy. "It is good to see you again. Are these your disciples?"

Garnan nodded. "They are my pupils and my brothers. I overheard some of your conversation with Moti." he said, indicating the man to whom Medgariva had been speaking. "I believe that all of us could benefit from a pilgrimage to the Temple of Yah in Tsayalam, and I would gladly accompany you. I will discuss it with the brethren at dinner tonight. You will eat with us tonight, won't you?"

"Cloys and I would be grateful, noble Garnan. You should also know that I have spoken with Magras, and he has offered us the use of his ship. He tells me that it may be ready in three weeks." Medgariva paused thoughtfully for a moment. "I know that you have little love for

Atalo, being that he believes Yah to be a false god, and in light of that I would make one more request."

Garnan appeared puzzled and anxious. "What might that be, my queen?"

"Atalo has become increasingly wicked. Though I have loved him and am bound to him as his wife, I must leave him. He has threatened Cloys, his own daughter, with death and killed someone very dear to her. I do not want the king to know where we are, or he may punish us severely. May we stay here until Magras sends word that his ships are ready?"

"You may, your Majesty. Here you shall be safe from the king's wrath." Medgariva and Cloys dwelt among the brethren for three weeks. The Isle of Contemplation was a very peaceful yet mysterious place, and it seemed that when fog descended, as it often did, the very presence of the Almighty One was in the fog. The brethren lived a simple life of fishing and prayer, yet all were excited to hear of a pilgrimage to Mt. Tsayun. All of Garnan's pupils had been born on Atalanti and had never sailed out of sight from its shores. All were eager to travel to the other side of the earth, except for Moti. Moti began spending more time alone, and in the third week of Medgariva's visit, he disappeared. No one knew where he had gone, but Garnan suspected that Moti had left to tell the king of the plan to leave Atalanti.

At the end of the third week, a messenger from Magras arrived in a small boat. "Magras says the ship is ready, but you must be careful on the road to Ataliquor. Someone has informed the king of your plan, and he will seek to capture you."

"Thank you. You are a faithful servant of Yah, young one." said Garnan. Turning to Medgariva, Garnan addressed her. "Your Majesty, we should leave as soon as we can. We must take the hunting trails through the woods and avoid the main road."

The brethren packed their few belongings and loaded their bags onto the pack lizard which served as their beast of burden. When all was ready, the company set off on foot southwards along the wooded trail. The brethren walked on all sides of the two royal women to protect them if necessary. On the morning of the second day, the travellers heard voices coming from the road. They hurried off of the trail into the deep woods to avoid detection from whoever was approaching.

Not long afterward, they came upon a forest glade about as wide as a farmer's field. In the glade, the company saw a man on a speed lizard clad in highly polished, full body armour. On his shield he bore the crest of the king, and he was accompanied by three hunting dogs. The armoured man stopped his lizard, dismounted, and lifted his faceplate. He removed his plumed helmet to reveal locks of brown hair which reached to his shoulders. The young man's skin was dark like his mother's, but his eyes were the same hawk-like piercing blue of his father. Cloys gasped as she recognized her brother, Ferdeo. The dogs heard the gasp and began barking, alerting Ferdeo to the presence of the company. The prince saw the group in the trees.

"Come down from there and surrender the women." said Ferdeo. Medgariva now knew the excuse wrought to bring them back to the palace. After Moti's report, she reasoned, Atalo must have murdered the treacherous fisherman and told the search party that the queen and princess Cloys had been taken captive by Garnan and his brethren. She came to address her son.

"Ferdeo, we are not being held against our will." she answered. Then, as the rest of the travellers came out from hiding, she related to Ferdeo all of what had been done to Cloys. Cloys began to weep as she relived the trauma in her mind.

Ferdeo, seeing his sister distraught, became wroth. "I would not believe such a tale about my father, though there are many of the like in the streets of Ataliquor, but that I had heard it from you, dear mother, and seen the pain in Cloys's eyes. I swear it, I shall defend your honour and that of my sister against the man I have called father." As Ferdeo spoke these words, the dogs began to bark again as the retinue of King Atalo entered the grove in response to the earlier bark. The king rode in the vanguard.

"There they are, seize them!" he cried. However, before the guardsmen could respond, Ferdeo cried out.

"No! These men have done nothing! The king has lied to you. Our queen sought them out for protection."

Atalo became red with rage and bellowed at his son. "Ferdeo, how dare you contradict my orders? I am your father, the king. Would you join these traitors?"

"To defend the honour of my mother and my sister, I would." he answered, defiantly.

"Then you shall die with them." he said, lunging his mount forward with his sword outstretched to chop off the head of his rebellious son. However, Ferdeo was quicker and rolled under his father's speed lizard, slicing open its belly. Atalo was thrown to the ground, and Ferdeo held the point of his sword at his father's head.

"I should kill you, but I would be committing both parricide and regicide and would thus be barred admittance into the courts of Ea when I die. Instead, I will place you in chains and throw you into the dungeon where you threw the traitor, Moti. I will take your crown from you and the people shall decide who will rule over them."

Atalo was afraid and outraged. "Kill him!" he shouted to his guard. The twenty guardsmen, all as one, looked blankly up at the prince, then to the king, and they bound up the king with the ropes which were to be used on Garnan's men.

"Too many tales have spread through your kingdom about you, Father." Ferdeo said the last word as if he had the taste of bile in his mouth. "Only a very small number of our people remain loyal to you. Most would like to see you dead." Ferdeo looked thoughtful for a moment, and then looked again at the bound king, writhing to be loosened from the ropes. "You have told me how the cornerstone of the palace has been loosened by captives in the depths of your dungeon who have tried to escape and that the foundation of the palace is no longer secure. I have found a solution; your sentence will be to hold up that stone until you are dead or until the palace collapses or is destroyed. In this way, you will help to maintain the palace which you have built." So began the legend that Atalo held up the foundations of the earth, as Atalanti was on the opposite side of the earth from the main continent of the old world.

Thus Medgariva, Cloys, Garnan, and his brethren travelled back to Ataliquor free in the company of Ferdeo. The people of the city came out to see the strange sight of their king in chains. At first they stood dumbstruck, but then they began to cheer. When they reached the city square, Tertero the head guard, came to place Atalo's crown on Ferdeo's head, but Ferdeo declined.

"Atalanti will not have another king." he declared. "Worthy men shall be chosen from among our citizens, thirty of them, and they shall make decisions. We will have a Council like the fabled city of Lhiosquor, upon which my mother had looked in her youth from her home on Mt. Threthor. Two of these men shall preside over the council each year, and at the end of each year they will return to the thirty and two new councillors shall preside." Thus began the Republic of Atalanti. Medgariva, nonetheless, still did not wish to stay in Atalanti.

"Atalo is gone now, and I am free to go and find the one my heart loves." she said.

"But mother, Atalanti will need you now more than ever. You are their inspiration. You are the voice of wisdom from the Mountain of Wisdom itself." said Ferdeo.

Medgariva looked kindly at her son. "Dear Ferdeo, have you not seen? The people find in you all the inspiration they need. I am going to Mt. Tsayun with the dear brethren of the Rocky Isles. I must find Yared, the priest."

"You have told me of him many times, mother. You have done much for me and taught me well. May Ea ... excuse me, may Yah watch over you and bless you, mother." said Ferdeo, as a lump formed in his throat.

Medgariva embraced her son. "You and your friends are now the leaders of Atalanti. Remember that he who governs least governs best. The more faith you have in the citizens of Atalanti, the more faith they will have in you. Teach this wisdom to all who will join this new Council. Do not let the mistakes of your father be repeated."

"I will not mother, I swear it."

"Then I bid you farewell, my son, and may Yah, the Almighty Creator, watch over you all of your days." Medgariva then joined Cloys, Garnan, and the brethren aboard the <u>Magras</u> and sailed away across the Outer Sea.

# 385 EC

After four long months at sea, the <u>Magras</u> came upon the foggy Westerlands. Landing somewhat further north than the men of Afalo's voyage, they soon found the Western Sea into which the Rahav emptied after its long journey. It should be mentioned to all who will read this account that since the Flood the Westerlands have disappeared. The Rahav has since widened to become the Inner Sea, which should not be confused with the Western Sea of the old days. I fear, however, that as mankind continues to forget the knowledge of older times, they will probably never venture farther than the Inner Sea, nor will they care about the rest of the earth. It is likely that, a century after I am gone, there may not even be anyone left who is able to read what I have written in these scrolls.

Never minding that, I will return to the story. The pilgrims travelled more slowly now, keeping within sight of the shore. They would often make camp on land and forage there for food as they travelled eastward. When they came upon the eastern shore of the Western Sea, after travelling along the northern shore for three months, Garnan built an altar to Yah and offered a sacrifice to Him of a deer that was caught earlier that day. As the sacrifice burned on the altar, Garnan felt a strong wind come up from the Sea. In the wind of the Sea, Garnan heard the thundering, resounding voice of the Creator God.

"Garnan, I have known you from before you were born. I chose you to be My servant when you were still in your mother's womb. I knew you when you were a young man serving the sons of Seuso in Susa. You alone of all who came to Atalanti, save the queen, knew My true name and sought after Me in that land where all follow the false god of Ea as Seuso taught them. Now I am bringing you to a new land, and here you must learn My laws that your fathers abandoned. You have been faithful with the little light you have been given, but I require holiness of all who call on Me."

Garnan did not know what to say. "What must I do, o Lord? You know that I love You and will follow what You ask of me."

"When you reach the land where you are going, you and your

brethren will no longer live on the fish of the sea. One of the laws I have given to My people is not to take the lifeblood of any creature except to save one's life. Until now I have allowed you and brethren to do this, but as you come to dwell among My chosen people, you must learn to obey everything I have commanded them that your fathers have forgotten."

Garnan was amazed. He had never heard of this commandment, as Seuso had abandoned the ways of Lhiosquor, and his sons had no knowledge of them. "I will obey you, Almighty Yah." said Garnan.

"I call you My friend, because you have sought Me, and you will obey what I ask of you. Because you are My friend, I will tell you that the day will come that the old law of the letter will pass away, and those who serve Me will have My laws written on their hearts. In those days, whatever men eat or drink I will not hold against them, so long as they do not allow their desires to have mastery over them. In those days, the ones whom I will call My chosen people will no longer only be those who dwell in the City of Light, but they will be all who call on My name. They shall be called My sons and daughters, and I will raise up a people for Myself from all nations, yes even of those who have the blood of Cain in their veins.

In those days, there shall be no distinction between the tribes, nations, and races of men, for I shall call My people out from all of them. Then men will no longer offer Me the sacrifice of the blood of sheep and bulls, but they themselves shall live as living sacrifices to Me. Until that day, however, those whom I have called must be careful to obey all that it written in My law. When you reach the place where you are going, you will read what is in My law."

The wind and the voice disappeared, and Garnan realized that night had fallen while he had been speaking with the Almighty One. He returned to the camp and told the others of what he had heard and they were amazed. The following day, as they continued on their pilgrimage, the <u>Magras</u> entered the mouth of the wide and mighty Rahav. It should be told that they had now been travelling for seven months. It had not been long after the company had left Atalanti that Cloys discovered she was carrying Joreb's child. She had become weak after many months of travelling on the sea, and it was expected that, if she survived the rest of the journey, that she would give birth in a month's time. Moreover, her heart was sick with grief over the death of her beloved.

The company now travelled quickly, hoping to reach a town or village along the shore of the Rahav before Cloys gave birth. As the expected day came upon them, they came to a settlement of Nahlonites at the place where the river Nahla emptied into the Rahav. There the pilgrims rested as the pains of labour came upon the young princess of Atalanti. Garnan and the brethren offered prayers as the Nahlonite midwives attended to Cloys.

"I am afraid it is not good." said Nefera, the chief midwife. "She is weak with sickness. We will do what we can, but I do not know whether she or the child will live." Later that day, Nefera returned to Medgariva. "Your daughter has given birth to a son. The child will live, but what had remained of your daughter's strength left her and went into the child. She has died, my lady." Nefera brought Medgariva to the birthing place to see Cloys's lifeless body.

At the sight of her daughter's body, Medgariva wept bitterly. "I should not have come on this journey. It was because of my flight that Atalo pursued me and became a prisoner forever. I had left my sons, daughters, and all the people who are in some way my descendants in Atalanti. Now, I have lost the only daughter that I brought with me. She was as dear to me as my own heart. Truly I am Valiturnea, she who weeps." Medgariva began to wail in despair over the dead body of her daughter. Nefera stayed to comfort her, but to no avail. Then she left and sent Garnan.

"Do not despair, dear lady." Medgariva had told the brethren to refrain from calling her by her royal titles, as she had left the life of the palace behind her. "When we reach the Temple of Yah, all will be well."

Medgariva shook her head. "No, it will not. I left with Atalo to Atalanti because I was forbidden me to marry the priest, Yared. I must tell you that it is because of my forbidden desire for him that I have come on this journey, and because of this ungodly passion I have lost so many that I loved."

"Dear Valiturnea, I must tell you that Yah told me in a dream that He was bringing the brethren here, that He would bring them to complete the pilgrimage to His temple. Although what you have done you did for your own reasons, Yah is using it for His purposes. I am to remain in this new land, but I will send back brethren to Atalanti who will teach the people of the laws of Yah."

The words of Garnan comforted her little. Medgariva did not even go to see her new grandson until the next day. "I will name him Mattu-Seth." she said. "He will be like me, one not at home anywhere, and he will travel on a journey even longer than mine." The pilgrims stayed in the Nahlonite village for seven days after this, and they buried Cloys. After this, they journeyed up the Rahav to the bustling port of Shaochiquor, which was now defended by high towers. The people of Shaochiquor had built an island in the middle of the river. Here loomed a great tower manned day and night by watchmen who kept watch for any sign of the Nephilim who yet dwelt far up the Nahla. When the Magras came to the harbour of Shaochiquor, which had been barred by a long chain stretching across it, a small ship manned with soldiers came alongside.

"I am the harbourmaster of Shaochiquor. Where do you come from, and what is your business here?" asked one of the soldiers.

"We are pilgrims from a distant land beyond the sea. We are going up to the Temple of Yah." replied Garnan.

"What news do you have of Hurash and the Nephilim?" the soldier asked suspiciously.

"I tell you the truth, we have never heard of the people of whom you speak. Are you at war with them?" asked Garnan, noticing the fortifications.

The soldier's stoic aspect broke with a smile at the abbot's obviously innocent question. "You are indeed of distant lands if you have never heard of Hurash or the Nephilim. Yes, we are at war with them. They are of the race of the Giants, and they have returned to do battle against all the faithful. From what you say, they must still be hiding in their twin cities far up the river Nahla. You may enter the harbour as soon as we raise the chain. Welcome to the kingdom of Tsayunos." With that, the small ship sailed away. Shortly afterward, the chain was pulled away from the harbour, and the Magras came to rest in the port.

The pilgrims stayed in Shaochiquor for three days, and met with

Shaochi himself, who was now called the Duke of Shaochiquor. From him they learned all that they could about the state of affairs in the western kingdoms. When they were certain that the remainder of their journey could be made safely, they departed for the Holy City of Tsayalam.

Yared was overseeing the temple sacrifices when Tsiling came to him to tell him of the new arrivals. "There are people here from the kingdom of Atalanti, on the island on the far side of the world, who have come here on a pilgrimage. They know you by name and wish to meet with you."

Yared followed Tsiling to the temple courts. As he descended the main stairs of the Temple of Yah into the courtyard, Yared saw Medgariva and their eyes met. At that instant, all of the memories that he had fought so hard to erase over years of meditation and devotion to God returned like a flood. Both had changed over the past hundred years, Yared's long red beard was tied around the sash of the robe of a high priest. He gait had become slower and more fluid, giving him a more austere, priestly aspect. Medgariva's countenance was lined with a hundred years of grief and woe. Now, however, with just one glance, they knew that the intervening decades had done nothing to dim or quench their desire for each other. Medgariva placed Mattu-Seth in Garnan's hands and ran to embrace Yared.

"I had never expected to see you again." she said, holding him tightly. "Nor I, you." replied Yared. Releasing himself from her grip, he continued. "I have taken a vow of celibacy and have become the High Priest of Yah in His temple. I am no longer the man you once knew." Both knew the lie of these last words as soon as they were spoken.

"I, too, have changed." replied Medgariva. "After you left Lhiosquor, I fled to the land of Harifon where I was discovered by Afalo and Atalo on their voyage around the earth. Atalo comforted me during that time, and when we reached the land which became the kingdom of Atalanti, I stayed with him there as his wife and bore him twenty sons and thirty daughters. Over the course of the years, however, Atalo grew less and less fond of me, and eventually his desire turned toward our own daughter, Cloys. When he forbade her to marry her true love, she met him in secret. Atalo found them in Cloys's chambers, killed the boy, beat my daughter and threatened her life."

Yared raised his eyebrows in surprise. "You are the Weeping Maiden of Harifon? I had heard tell of Afalo and Atalo's voyage; indeed, it was I who went to the High King to recommend the voyage to prove that the earth was round. I never suspected that you were Valiturnea of Atalanti." Yared glanced at Garnan carrying Mattu-Seth. "Is the child yours?" he asked.

"No, he is Cloys's son. I brought her with me on this voyage to escape her father, but alas, Cloys died giving birth to her son. I have named him Mattu-Seth." Medgariva gazed deeply into the grey eyes of the man she had loved for so long. "I knew that I would find you here, my heart. Even though so many years have passed, and so much has changed, my love for you remains. I had to see you again, even if it meant crossing the Outer Sea once more."

Yared's heart felt torn in two at these words, for he knew that his feelings for Medgariva had yet to be expunged. Yared also realized that he could never entirely rid himself of all desire for her. At that moment, as the High Priest was deep in thought, Mahalalel came to the place where the Atalantians were gathered in order to speak with his son. At once he saw Medgariva and stared at her in disbelief. "Medgariva, how did you come to be here?"

"This is her Majesty, Queen Valiturnea of Atalanti." said Maichil, one of Garnan's followers, as if to correct the general.

Medgariva shook her head. "No, I am no longer the Queen of Atalanti, and will resume the name given to me at birth." she said to Maichil before turning to the general. "Hail, General Mahalalel. It has been many years. What news of my family?"

"They do well, and many generations have been born while you have been away. Your mother, however, was never the same after you disappeared. She will be glad to see you again."

"I am sure she will." she replied. At that point, Mahalalel remembered the word of prophecy given to him of the Weeping Queen. He froze right where he stood.

"Father, are you all right?" asked Yared.

"I'll be fine, Yared," said the general through his strained throat. "However, I need to talk to you alone about a vision that I was given years ago."

Yared turned to the new arrivals from Atalanti. "I welcome you all to the holy city of Tsayalam. I have some urgent matters to attend to, but Soduryah, my brother in blood and brother in the priesthood, will show you your accommodations." Yared did not like having to send Medgariva away like that, but he was glad to get away from her for a moment, and he knew she needed to rest. He went with his father up to the temple, into the sanctuary where the priests performed the sacrifices, so that they could speak freely.

"Yared, I had a vision from Yah eighteen years ago about a decision that you would have to make when the Weeping Queen came to meet you from across the Outer Sea. I did not know that this Weeping Queen was Medgariva whom you had once loved."

"Still love, father," he corrected, "and she feels the same about me. She cannot stay here, or I will not be able to continue as High Priest. I love Yah more than anything, and this illegal desire for a Cainite woman – as that is what she is as much as I would like to deny it – must be purged from my mind."

"You must make your decision and act quickly, my son, for Yah has said that the entire fate of the world hinges upon it."

Upon hearing his father's words, Yared felt the weight of the responsibility of the entire world. He let out a long sigh which slowly grew to become a ghostly wail. As Yared's cry grew louder, Medgariva, who was praying in the outer courts, heard Yared wail and thought perhaps that he had been badly injured. She ran from the courtyard into the sanctuary to see what happened. When Yared saw her, he tore his robes and shouted in sorrowful anger.

"Get out, foolish woman!" he cried, his face red and eyes filling with tears. "Don't you know that the penalty for a Cainite entering into the sanctuary is death? Get out and fly back to Atalanti before it is made known what you have done!" Medgariva broke into tears and sobs, then quickly ran out of the sanctuary, out of the temple courtyard, and through the main street of Tsayalam heading westward. Yared also wept bitterly now, and Mahalalel tried to comfort his son, but to no avail.

"Father, do you not realize what I have just done?" the High Priest asked, his voice broken with tears. "According to the law, Medgariva must die. I sent her away instead. In doing so, I have become a lawbreaker. I, the High Priest of the Temple of Yah, have not upheld the laws of the one I worship. Duty dictates that I resign my office as High Priest and go away from here." Yared then ran out down the Temple stairs and passed Hualichi on the way. With his eyes streaming with tears, he neither recognized nor acknowledged his old mentor, and he kept on running. Hualichi entered the sanctuary where Mahalalel was praying.

"Your son is deathly distraught. What happened, and who was the Cainite woman I saw running down the stairs from the Temple courts?" the old priest asked. Mahalalel then told him the story of what had happened, and Hualichi's face took on the grim aspect of death itself. "So this is how the end begins." he said.

# CHAPTER 14

# THE FULFILLMENT OF THE PROPHECY
## (386 – 393 EC)

## 386 EC

Yared returned the office of High Priest to Hualichi and departed into the Southern Wilderness, also known as the Dry Lands of Ravi, where he sought to escape the effects of his failure. There the mists were lighter and warmer, and so Yared often slept out beneath the curtain of heaven. Still, after living in the Southern Wilderness for nearly a year, he had only seen the curtain roll back twice. One night, the wind picked up out of the north and drove hard. Yared found a nearby cave and went to take shelter there. As he found a place in the cave that would be reasonably comfortable, he heard a faint sound from somewhere nearby. He had heard tales of small, fast eater lizards, no larger than a man yet deadly nonetheless, that dwelt in caves such as these and devoured those who entered. Yared's body tensed, braced in an instinct to defend itself from a ferocious attack. Before he could think of what to do next, Yared screamed. He heard another scream, human, in response to his. "Who goes there?" he asked.

"A weary traveller descended from an accursed tyrant who is not welcome in this world." said the voice. A female Cainite of the line of Lamekk, like Medgariva, he thought.

"Where did you come from?" he asked her.

"I was raised in the shadow of the City of Light, from whence I fled unto the hills of Harifon. From there, I was carried to the other side of the earth where I found contentment for a season, but my joy turned again to sorrow and my desire to return home was great. When I came back, I became marked for death, and I have been driven into hiding."

"My love, do you not recognize my voice? It is I, Yared."

"No, you are a dream. Perhaps you are a demon sent from the enemy of mankind to torment me. Yared is the High Priest of the Temple of Yah, and he would not come to me here in the wilderness."

"Even so, it is I." Yared had been carrying a lamp with oil in it for the times when he needed to shelter in caves. He lit the lamp and saw his beloved standing in front of him, squinting in the lamplight. "I have made my choice. I have already broken the law of Yah by allowing you to live. Now that you are here with me in this place, it is clear to me now. My days as a priest are over, and I want to spend the rest of my days, good or bad, with you." As he said those words, Yared felt as if a terrible burden had been lifted off of his shoulders. "You understand, though, that we will not be accepted in my grandfather's realm, for the punishment in Lhiosquor for intermarriage between Sethites and Cainites is death."

"Who, then, will perform the ceremony? Is it not custom for an heir and his bride to be married by the patriarch of his tribe?" inquired Medgariva.

"We need to find a holy man, devoted to serving Yah. Hualichi would not do it. He would be breaking the laws of the temple. No priest of the Tsayuni priesthood could marry us." Kenan noticed that the child Mattu-Seth was not with Medgariva. "Where is Mattu-Seth?" he asked.

"He is with Garnan and he is safe." A thought entered her mind. "What about Garnan? He could perform the ceremony. He is a holy man."

"If Garnan is still in this part of the world, and if we can find him, I would be honoured to have him perform the ceremony, provided that he learns the form of a proper Sethite wedding ceremony."

Then Yared and Medgariva came up out of the desert and returned to Tsayun at night, and there they met Yared's young brother, Soduryah the priest, walking in the colonnaded streets. "Greetings, dear brother, I see that you have remained in the priesthood."

"As I wish you could have, dear brother, but I understand why you had to leave." he said, glancing at Medgariva. "I could not have brought myself to kill one I loved dearly if I were in your shoes, either, as I doubt most could."

"Nonetheless, I became a lawbreaker and I had to leave. Things will not be the same for me, and there are few who will now accept me and what I will do." Yared came to the matter at hand. "Soduryah, I am looking for Garnan. Is he living here in Tsayun, or has he left for somewhere else?" Soduryah looked at Medgariva. "My lady, your servant Garnan and his disciples went off to Mt. Threthor with the baby to meet your family there, and to tell of what has happened to you. I believe that they intend to stay there."

Medgariva lowered her head. "This could make things difficult. If we go to Mt. Threthor together, we could be in danger."

Soduryah was puzzled. "Danger? Why would you be in danger? Yared, Grandfather would love to see you again, and Medgariva, you ... oh no." The realization of what his brother and his Cainite friend intended to do suddenly struck Soduryah. "You mustn't! We have laws against such things that carry stiff penalties! If Grandfather finds out..."

"He won't know. We will travel in disguise to Uarga to seek out Medgariva's family. They should know where Garnan is. Please do not tell anyone we were here. We are leaving for Mt. Threthor immediately, but we will be in touch." Before Soduryah could say another word, Yared and Medgariva had disappeared down the streets of Tsayalam. "Be careful, Yared." Soduryah whispered as a prayer.

Journeying alone together was very awkward and difficult for Yared and Medgariva, especially after being separated for over a century. They focused their energy on getting to Uarga and finding Garnan without being recognized by anyone in the Royal Guard or anyone else close to the High King. When they neared Mt. Threthor, Yared found a patch of blueberries, and he smeared as many as he could find all over his head, neck, and arms so that he would appear to be a purple-skinned visitor of the nation of Turvah. The pigment wouldn't take on Medgariva's dark Cainite complexion, so she used some of the extra cloth that they had brought and draped herself in a veil. To this day, it is the custom of many of our brides to fully veil themselves on the wedding day before the wedding in remembrance of Yared and Medgariva.

Disguised in this way, they entered the city of Cerchil at the base of Mt. Threthor. Cerchil was the market city of Mt. Threthor, and was the largest of all the cities of Threthoron; its population was five times that of Lhiosquor, the capital. From Cerchil, Yared and Medgariva climbed the Passage of the Merchants leading to Uarga near the City of Light. When they arrived, they sought the house of Madeg, and Medgariva's parents were astonished to see their daughter return. Yared pulled the hood of his robe hood over his face so that only his purple-stained arms were showing.

"Dear Medgariva," cried Kheruva, her mother, "it has been far too many years. It is good that you have returned. Who is this man with you? Is this your husband?"

"No, this man is from the land of Turvah. Centuries ago, when his village was ruled by the Giants, he spoke against their rule. The Giants burned off his lips and cut out his tongue." The sentence of cutting off the tongue was a common punishment used by the Giants against those who attempted to stir up dissension against them. "He is well schooled, however, and if he needs to communicate, he will write on papyrus." Yared took out a roll of papyrus and wrote in carefully scripted Enosian characters:

λℵ⅄ ‘ℵ  ⅄⅃△OΔ ⲅ △‘Oʘ ‘ℵ△
△ⴑ⅄ ʘꟼ △ⴑⳒ1Δ △Ω“ Δ“ʘⴑⴖ△Ʊꚛⴑ
ⳒꚛOⴑⴖℛΔⴖ 1Ⳓ Δ‘ℵꚕ ⴑ ⵑℵ “ʘ△ⴑꚛ ꟼ1ς
Δʘꟼⳑⴑ ⴑⴖℵꚛ ⅃△ⴑꚛʘ‘OΔ ⴑꚕ ⴖꚛΔθ △ⴑ⅄
△Ω“ Ʊ‘O⌂ 1Ⳓ Δⵑ“ς⅄ △ⴑ ‘ℵ ⅰ‘O1 ⴑꚕ ꟼ1ςⴑ
ⵑⴑⵑ△Oꟼ △Oℵ ꟄOΔℵ△ °Ꚗʘⴑⳓⲅʘ‘O1Ʊⴑ

For those who have lost the lore of these ancient times, I have provided a translation. The script reads thus:

"My name is Deraj. I have accompanied your daughter on her long journey as a guide to protect her from the dangers that abound along the way. I am pleased to make your acquaintance, Madeg and Kheruva."

"He keeps his face hidden because the Nephilim torturers disfigured him." said Medgariva.

Madeg looked over the mute curiously. "Something about him seems familiar, but I don't know what that might be."

Medgariva changed the subject. "I am looking for my friend, Garnan. He journeyed with me from across the Outer Sea. I was told by one of the temple priests that he had come this way."

"Yes. Garnan and his brethren now have a cloister on the other side of the summit on this same plateau, facing the east. It was once part of old Shrivazh, but it has now been designated land for the use of the monks. Garnan has told me all about how you were a queen in Atalanti, and about your journey. He told me of how you lost your daughter, Cloys, as she gave birth to her son, Mattu-Seth. The babe is with us and is sleeping soundly now. I am afraid that he probably will not recognize you." Kheruva paused. "Garnan also told me how you fled from the Temple of Yah after meeting with Yared." Medgariva and Yared both stiffened upon hearing her mother's words. Fortunately, Garnan did not know why Medgariva had fled the temple and let Garnan believe that it was because Yared had spurned her love. If the High King ever found out what had happened, she would have to be put to death. She returned to talk about Mattu-Seth. "May I see my grandson?" she asked. Kheruva led Medgariva and the shrouded Yared into the nursery.

"There he lies", she said, "oblivious to the world about him. He has been with us ever since Garnan arrived here."

Medgariva looked upon Mattu-Seth once more. He had definitely grown in the year since she last saw him. "Indeed, he will not recognize me. May I, then, leave him with you, as you have raised him and have grown fond of him? I know that Cloys would have approved."

"Yes, we will care for him, but why do you speak of leaving again?" asked Madeg.

"I must leave and go to Garnan, because my friend is ill, and only Garnan knows the cure for this disease. It was discovered on Atalanti."

"Very well, Medgariva," said Kheruva, "but please come back to us. We could not bear to lose you again."

As Medgariva and Yared left the house of Madeg, Medgariva felt like she wanted to die after telling all of those lies to her parents, and even worse after their parting line. She knew that she would not be able to stay anywhere in the High Kingdom after she married Yared. She did what she had to do in order to spare their lives. She wanted right then to kneel down and pray to Almighty God for forgiveness, but that would seem hypocritical as she and Yared were about to break one of the most sacred laws of that time; the law against intermarriage between the descendants of Seth and those of Cain.

When they came to Garnan's cloister, after Medgariva had donned her veil again to walk through Uarga unrecognized, they found the holy man out ploughing a field of grain. "Garnan, we must speak with you."

Garnan turned to the cloaked couple. "Do I know you?" he asked. "Wait...that voice! Valiturnea, is it you?"

"Yes, Garnan, it's me. My friend here and I need to speak with you privately. It is very important."

"Very well then, let us go inside." Garnan set down his plough, and Yared and Medgariva followed him inside. "It is good to see you again, my lady. Who is your Turvese friend, here?" he asked.

Yared pulled back his hood. "It is I, Yared."

Garnan's jaw dropped. "The High Priest! What has happened to you? Your skin is purple like the people of Turvah! You will need a physician immediately!" Garnan ran frantically about the chamber searching for the proper medicine, and then went to call one the brethren, but Yared smiled wanly and held up his hand.

"I stained my skin with berry juice so that no one would recognize me, just as Medgariva has veiled herself. We wish to be married, but if my people learn of it, we will both be killed. Sethites are forbidden to intermarry with Cainites."

Garnan then understood why they had come. "You wish me to perform the rites." he sighed. "I have heard my lady, here, tell me over and over again how much she loves you, and I believe that your love for her is equally as strong; otherwise fear of an illegal marriage would not have driven you to the priesthood and up the ranks so quickly. You realize that I, too, could be executed for enabling this union?"

"Yes, dear Garnan, I know that. I sought you out because you know, better than anyone I know, how to keep a secret." said Medgariva.

"I thank you, my lady. When would you like this done?"

"Are you familiar with the wedding customs of Lhiosquor?" asked Yared.

Garnan smiled. "Yes, I have attended the wedding of your cousin, Ayrus the son of Konaryah. He and his lovely bride were married in the royal palace. It was a splendid affair, and his bride, Upara-Ditri, was the most beautiful woman I have ever seen, after your mother, Lilara. She came from the people of Ayrus's mother, Wolja. Unfortunately, I am not Seth or Enos, and you are of royal blood. This ceremony should be performed by one of your patriarchs, is that not true?"

Yared shook his head. "I myself have performed numerous weddings at the Temple of Yah. You are a godly man, Garnan, and my bride trusts you. You will do well."

"What about your relatives? They obviously cannot come to such a wedding."

"Could you marry us here, Garnan, in your chapel? Could you marry us now?" Medgariva asked.

Garnan was unsure of what to do. "I believe so. My lady, I must tell you that you are quite unlike any of the Cainites that live in Arattu. Many that I have met are quarrelsome, devious, and treacherous. Though you have the skin of a Cainite, you have the heart of a Sethite."

"Indeed, she has mine." Yared said, smiling at his pun as he placed his arm around his beloved's waist.

"Then it shall be done." said Garnan. He brought them to the chapel of the cloister, and read the rites of marriage from a book that Seth had written in the early years of Lhiosquor. He sprinkled them with water from the Crystal Lake in Lhiosquor, and prophesied over them.

"Know that this union is outside of the laws of Yah, yet for some reason He permits it to bring about His own mysterious purposes on the earth. This union will bring about the fall of Lhiosquor, and will return the Giants to the land. In seven years, Hurash will retake the kingdom of Nahlon, and you will give birth to a son who will be the mouthpiece of Yah to all people, Sethite and Cainite alike, for the time of racial divisions will soon come to an end as all must unite against the Nephilim. When seven more years have passed, the Temple of Yah will be overtaken by the Nephilim and destroyed. They will then rule the earth for nearly four hundred years and enslave many, but from your descendants leaders shall arise to drive the Nephilim off the face of the earth."

All three of them were in tears after Garnan had finished telling them the prophecy, and Garnan finished blessing the union. "I now charge you with the charge given to Adam and Eve by Yah Himself. Go forth, fill the earth and subdue it. Be fruitful and multiply." With those words, the ceremony was ended, and the new couple retired to a room provided for them by Garnan.

The following morning, Yared and Medgariva awoke in each other's arms as the morning sunlight streamed through the window. Because of the curtain of heaven, it was more of a hazy, weak light than the bright beams of today. As they lay gazing into each other's eyes, half asleep, half awake, the noise of fanfare from out on the road alerted them into full wakefulness. The trumpeters announced that the High King had come to bless the brethren with a gift. The new couple quickly dressed and remained as silent as possible. Yared peered out of the doorway where he saw Kenan conversing, in his usual, exuberantly jovial manner with Garnan. "I have brought golden lampstands for you, and a new printing press. It is my father's invention; the old sage is always coming up with something new. With it you will be able to make as many copies of as many books as you want in a relatively short period of time."

Garnan had his back turned to Yared, and he only wished he could see the expression of the hermit's face. "Really?" he asked, his voice full of wonder. "How does it work?" Yared listened to try to hear his grandfather explain the device, but the abbot and the High King walked out to the cart to bring the machine into the scriptorium.

"My grandfather has arrived with one of great-grandfather Enos' latest inventions." Yared whispered to Medgariva. After he leaves, I want to take a look at it." Yared had an insatiable curiosity for new inventions. There were many new machines being invented these days, some, like the telescope, he had invented himself. He developed further ideas as the decades passed and more new inventions were needed to fight the armies of the Nephilim. As Yared listened from his room, he soon heard voices coming back to the main building of the cloister.

"I have a golden lampstand for each of your brethren. They will be able to read and write by this light. If you like, I can put one in every room." said Kenan.

"That is very kind of you, Your Majesty. I thank you, but..."

Kenan interrupted the hermit. "Garnan, are we not friends? I expect nothing of you in return. I see you as a friend, and I am honoured that you have chosen to live in this land, for the land is not mine but the property of whoever tills it. Unlike the Cainite kings, I give all of my citizens, my citizens are not subjects, ownership of their own land." Kenan turned toward the room where Yared and Medgariva were staying, and Yared quickly moved away from the door. "This guest room could use one of the golden lampstands. All who stay here will be able to use its light to read the works printed by the brethren on their new printing press."

"Your Majesty," Garnan said nervously, "there was a wedding here last night, and a couple stayed in that room. I have not had a chance to clean it, and you must not..,"

Kenan laughed. "Brother Garnan, you are worried about many things. I may be the High King, but I don't need to be impressed by everyone. I'll just..." Kenan opened the door and saw Yared and Medgariva hiding in the corner, looking at him with the sentence of death already written on their faces. Tears welled up in the High King's eyes as he saw his grandson and his new bride. "Yared, Yared my dear son. What have you done?" The High King wept, for he knew that duty called him to execute his grandson. He called Garnan into the room. "You did not tell me of this!" Kenan shouted as he fought for composure. "Does anyone else know what has happened here?"

Garnan was trembling; the fear of death was on him as well. "No, Your Majesty. Only I and the couple know, and now you."

"The law commands me, the law of Yah commands me, to have all of you executed, yet He has given this land to us, to our people, and has appointed me in authority over it. I believe that the decision of what happens to the three of you is mine to make." He turned to Yared and Medgariva. "I know of your love for one another, and indeed I love you both and cannot bring myself to execute you. Go now, leave Mt. Threthor. Be careful not to be seen. Go and live in the Southlands or the Westerlands, far from here. You must never set foot in this land again, for if anyone discovers that I have allowed you to live, I will surely lose the Emerald Crown to another."

He turned to Garnan. "Brother Garnan, I know that your heart is true, and I know that you love Yah and have been a faithful servant to Medgariva, who was once your queen. Remember what I am about to say: no one in the High Kingdom must ever learn about this union. I adjure you to complete and perpetual secrecy on this matter. In return, you will continue to have my friendship and respect, and you and your brethren will live peacefully here for as long as I rule. If the truth of this matter is ever known, I will not reign long after." Kenan looked to the company who awaited him outside the cloister. "I must leave now, and the two of you must leave tonight when it is dark. Go whither you will." With that, before anyone could say farewell, the High King abruptly left the cloister and rejoined his retinue.

# 393 EC

Yared and Medgariva travelled south and settled in the city of Unuk, also known as Uruk, in the kingdom of Iradu. Unuk was ruled by King Unuk, whose name was a variation of Enokk, the name of Irad's father. Unuk was a son of Shinar, the second son of Irad, and had been told the tale of the Battle of Turnienquor where Irad fought alongside Mahalalel, Yared's father. Because of this, Unuk welcomed Yared and Medgariva even though Unuk's people worshipped the false god, Ellil. The people of Unuk also believed that this Ellil had a consort whom they named Ana, and they worshipped her as well.

While living in Unuk, seven years after their wedding, Medgariva gave birth to a son, whom she named Enoch, yet another variant of the name of the king of those lands. Where Yared was very fair-skinned like his mother and Medgariva was very dark, Enoch was a median between the two. He had dark hair and dark eyes like his mother, but his skin was the colour of bronze rather than the deep, almost black, brown of his mother's. His hair, though black like his mother's, was straight like his father's. He looked almost like one of the people of Harifon, but somewhat lighter skinned. Enoch's parents determined to raise Enoch in the ways of Almighty God, and they made a pilgrimage to the Temple of Yah to have him dedicated.

When Medgariva placed the baby in the arms of the High Priest, Hualichi looked upon the child and wept. "This child has been foretold." he said. "Soon, the dark time will be upon us, and this house will be destroyed. The Nephilim will multiply and spread everywhere, and they will commit abominable acts against those whom they rule. This child will be a light of hope in a dark time, as one not born of this age but of an age to come. Enoch will never know peace in his lifetime, as he will be a prophet. He shall see into the things that are not yet more than anyone who has ever walked this earth. Know also that he will be spared the worst of the calamities to come if he keeps his heart pure before Yah."

"Thank you, old friend." said Yared. At first, I did not return here for fear of death, but I came for Enoch's sake. Medgariva and I have been spared Yah's punishment for the purpose of raising this child to be a light to Sethites and Cainites alike, as well as any other nations where he may visit. Thank you for your blessing, dear friend, it means much in days such as these."

"Remember that a blessing becomes a curse to those who do not follow the path set for them, as you know all too well. Teach your son what you have learned. If he learns from you, he will be strong in the power of Yah, and he and his son after him will continue the work that you have begun."

High King Kenan could not sleep well ever since the day he found Yared and Medgariva in the cloister of the brethren. For seven years he slept fitfully. One morning, Muhalelet turned to him, and asked him why. "For seven years now, my love, your sleep has been fitful and I have borne no children since that time. What is troubling you?" For seven years, every time his wife would ask that question, Kenan had told her his health was bad. Now, the passing years and constant questioning weakened the High King's resolve to keep the secret, and he told the queen how he came upon the newly wed Yared and Medgariva in the cloister.

"My love, you did what was best. Would you have felt better if you had had them killed? Garnan is one of your chief advisors. Where would you be without his counsel?"

Kenan sighed. "I do not know whether what I did was right, but what is done is done, and I pray that my grandson will be happy, wherever he is. I also did it for Mahalalel and for the High Kingdom. If it were known what had happened, Konaryah would be the heir to the throne, and he is reckless and does not follow the ways of Yah as he should. He is a great and courageous warrior and an able general, but he does not have the qualities needed to rule the High Kingdom."

At that moment, there was a knock at the door as one of the servant girls brought breakfast to the royal couple. "Your breakfast is here, Your Majesties." the servant girl said, and left the food at the door of the royal bedchamber. Kenan did not know that the servant girl was Bheregah, one of Konaryah's youngest daughters, who had awakened early that morning to find that the usual servant girl had not yet risen, and no one in the palace yet had their breakfasts. When she came from the kitchen to the door of the royal bedchamber, Bheregah heard voices from the chamber and listened intently. She could not believe what she heard, especially the way the High King talked about her father. She did not believe her father to be such a man, and she went right away to tell him all she had heard.

Konaryah had little love for Cainites, even less for the descendants of Nosjubal. One hundred and ninety-two years had passed since he accidentally struck down Pocabal, Medgariva's grandfather and Mahalalel's best friend, and the rift that began that day between the High King's two eldest sons never fully healed. Over the years, Konaryah had hardened his heart to escape his guilty conscience. He had convinced himself that he had slain a filthy Cainite who had stolen his brother's friendship, and who would have betrayed him to the Giants had the outcome of the Battle of Turnienquor been otherwise. He counted his brother a fool to place friendship in one of the descendants of Lamekk the Accursed rather than in his own brother.

When Bheregah had told her father what she had heard and what the king had said about him, he flew into a rage. Bheregah was terrified and flew from the room so that she would not be beaten. Konaryah then dressed himself in full battle armour and went out of the palace to the Hall of the High Council of Lhiosquor. He rang the bell and summoned a meeting. Within the hour, all of the now one-hundred High Council members were accounted for.

When the last of the councillors had taken his seat, Konaryah addressed the High Council. "Elders and leaders of Lhiosquor, I call this Council with a heavy heart. Here in this room, someone has betrayed the ancient laws which we hold dear." Most of the members of the High Council thought that sounded ironic coming from Konaryah. There had been many rumours that he had been unfaithful to his wife on many occasions, but he was never caught, and he could not be executed on the basis of rumours.

"I present to you my father, Kenan, the High King of Lhiosquor." he said in a mocking tone. The Council Elders talked excitedly among themselves, in utter shock and unbelief at what Konaryah had done. Aghast, Seth stood to his feet, and the councillors grew quiet as the patriarch, whose power was second to that of the High King and who was respected by all, raised his hand.

"It is a serious matter to accuse the king. If what you claim is untrue, keeping in mind that your own integrity is suspect and dubious, then you will be charged with treason and we will have no choice but to have you executed, even though you are of royal blood. Before you continue, do you understand this?"

"Yes." Konaryah said with defiance in his voice. No 'Yes, noble Patriarch' or 'Yes, honorable Seth'. He continued his tirade. "Everyone knows that many years ago Prince Yared, the son of Crown Prince Mahalalel, left the royal courts of Lhiosquor to pursue the life of a celibate priest because of his illicit love for a Cainite." Konaryah spat the last words. At this, Kenan knew the secret had been discovered, and looked over wide-eyed to Garnan who was seated two seats to his right on the other side of Seth. Garnan looked back at him innocently, and was just as surprised as the High King. Kenan knew that the hermit had not betrayed the king's confidence.

Konaryah continued. "This morning, my young daughter, Bheregah, awoke to bring breakfast to the High King and Queen because the servant girl was fast asleep. She overheard the High King confessing to the Queen how he had found Yared with the Cainite woman in Garnan's cloister, after they had been wed by the hermit the previous night. He released the outlaw couple and bid them go to a far off land." Konaryah turned to the king. "Is this not so, Your Majesty?" he said, giving the royal title a sardonic edge.

Kenan wept. "My son speaks the truth. My love for my grandson overcame my duty as High King. I became proud, believing that my word as High King was as good as that of Yah, and I exiled the lovers. Where they are now, I do not know, but if I must give up the Emerald Crown to another because of my poor judgement, I will do so. No king must ever believe himself to be above the law of Yah." He looked at his accuser as he said those last words, hoping that Konaryah would realize their weight for him in his own life.

Seth arose again to adjourn the High Council meeting. "You have all heard the testimony of our High King. He has disobeyed the law of Yah, but do not forget that what he did, he did out of love for his grandson. He risked this very thing, losing his kingdom so that Yared could live. Consider also the implications of these accusations for the succession of the throne. It is this man standing before you, impudently accusing the High King, who stands the most to gain, as the succession would pass from his brother Mahalalel, the father of Yared, to Konaryah.

"Also take into consideration what has been said about the moral conduct of this man and how he has behaved today in this Council." Those words held a double meaning, and it could be construed that Seth was speaking of Kenan, who upheld the law in spirit though breaking it in letter and showed his honesty and integrity by confessing the truth. They could also be construed to refer to Konaryah's unproven but suspected indiscretions, along with his brazen, defiant, and almost gloating attitude when he accused the High King.

Seth continued after letting the Elders chew on the double meaning of his words. "Tomorrow, we shall gather again, and the High Council shall judge who should be the High King of Lhiosquor and Threthoron, Kenan or Konaryah." With that, the patriarch left the room and the other councillors followed. Konaryah then thought of how he would ensure his victory in the vote tomorrow. There were one-hundred Elders in the High Council, not counting the High King. Konaryah himself would not be able to vote, leaving ninety-nine votes. The fifty-four of the oldest Elders who had sat on the Council when Kenan was elected king would surely vote for him, or would they? The party of Agradelai voted for Yotis, one of their kin, in that ancient day. If the resentment over the loss still lingered, or could be rekindled, Konaryah could gain their votes.

Konaryah knew that he could win (or buy) the support of the forty-five younger Council members who had joined in more recent years. That left a vote of fifty-one to forty-eight for the High King. He needed to persuade two more Council members to win, but then there was Garnan. Garnan had joined more recently but was a friend of the king. The vote would be fifty-two to forty-seven. Konaryah then decided that Garnan must die for marrying Yared and the Cainite. He would take care of that tonight.

Another of those who would vote for the king would surely be Mahalalel, his brother, but he was conveniently away fighting an uprising of the Nephilim in the land of Nahlon. That would leave a vote of fifty to forty-seven. Konaryah would need to persuade two more Council members to vote for him, or four more Council members would need to be disposed of, in the same way that Konaryah would dispose of Garnan … no wait. If anyone knew about that, he would not be king, but executed instead. Garnan's murder alone could he justify according to the law. He could invite four the other Council members to dinner, drug their food with sleeping medicine, and tie them up in the dungeon so that they could not attend the High Council. This was exactly the course of action that Konaryah pursued. Abbot Garnan was believed to have died when his abbey caught fire due to a fallen candle.

The following day, Seth called the Council and noted that beyond

Mahalalel's expected absence, Garnan's seat and four others were also empty. This disturbed the patriarch, and he delayed the vote for three hours. When the missing members failed to arrive, Tarcheng, a nephew of Seuso and one of Konaryah's most vocal supporters who had been among the few to return from the slaying of Ichsha, spoke up. "I propose that we wait no longer. Will we wait here all day until sundown? Let us vote now."

Seth realized then that something must have happened to the missing Elders and conceded. "Very well, we will hold the vote." He stood to his feet at pointed to Kenan on his right. "All in favour of Kenan raise your right arm and salute the High King." Seth counted forty-six, including himself. "All in favour of Konaryah," he said, pointing to the man on his left, "raise your left arm and salute him." Seth counted forty-seven. Konaryah would be the new High King of Threthoron.

The Battle of Nubat had been fierce, and Mahalalel's army suffered many losses against the Nephilim before retreating and leaving the city to the Giants. They trudged their way back in defeat to Tsayalam and went to the temple to beg Yah to grant them victory the next time and preserve the holy city. Mahalalel arrived at the same time that Yared and Medgariva were there dedicating Enoch. Although the dedication ceremony itself had already been performed, they had remained in Tsayalam for two weeks afterward to meet with old friends before returning to Shinar. Mahalalel saw them and wept. "Yared, it has all happened as Yah has said. You have married Medgariva and the Nephilim have grown strong." he looked to Enoch, a babe cradled in his mother's arms. "There is still hope yet, nonetheless. My dear son, I urge you to take care of this child of yours. He is the hope of our bloodline. Protect him at all costs."

"I will, Father." Yared replied, nodding deeply. At that moment, the noise of approaching carriages came from the north.

"It is Ohyah!" Mahalalel exclaimed in anger. "He has broken through the defences at Shaochiquor and has come to destroy us all." Mahalalel was mistaken; it was not Nephilim who came. The men who came were led by Kenan himself, and were fleeing Konaryah's purge which was already beginning. Mahalalel noticed that his father wore his old battle armour bereft of all of his royal insignia. The old High King greeted his most beloved son and embraced him.

"Father, where is your crown?" asked Mahalalel. Why do you wear your old armour?"

"I am no longer king, my son. Konaryah, your brother, has overthrown me by treachery, and his army has taken control of the city while yours has been fighting our enemies. Now I know the true reason why he did not send his army to your aid."

There was bitterness in Mahalalel's words. "We needed Konaryah here. With his army joined to mine, we could have defeated Hurash once and for all. Now, the foul Nephilim have retaken Nubat with their cannons and new hand-held cannons and have decimated us. It is only a matter of time before they decide to come here, too. If Yarku and Tsayalam are taken and this temple is destroyed, what will stop Ohyah from reaching the Northern Kingdoms?"

"We must do what we can, my son." Kenan turned to Yared and Medgariva, holding Enoch. "You cannot be blamed, dear ones. These events were set in motion before the world was formed, and we see only part of what is real. Yah is still in control, and He will not let us be completely destroyed. Though our enemies may triumph, a hope remains that one day He will make the world anew, and those days will be more glorious than the best years of Lhiosquor.

"For now, we will rebuild. We have chosen a site for a new city on Mt. Sentinel. Seth tells us that it will be like a new Lhiosquor. We will have a new Council and light and wisdom will shine from our new city long after the light of Lhiosquor has been extinguished. When the battles here are over, come and join us on the Council, my son. We will need your experience to direct us in strategies to defeat the Nephilim."

Mahalalel bowed slightly to his father. "I would be honoured to join you again when my task here is done. Thank you, Father."

Kenan passed the infant Enoch back to his mother and bowed slightly before leaving the temple courts. It was his last visit to the Temple of Yah which he had built.

# THE YOUNG PROPHET

## (400 – 449 EC)

In this scroll, I will tell of my great-grandfather, the blessed prophet Enoch. These were the sunset years of the Northern Kingdoms and in that time the wickedness of men grew great. The foul Nephilim spread across the face of the earth like an infestation and gained supremacy through conquest, fear, sorcery, and deception. The High Kingdom was divided and weakened, and the once glorious city of Lhiosquor descended into decadence and civil strife. Light still shone in the new city of Ahfeneyah on Mt. Sentinel, but a terrible, dark shadow had been cast across the earth and would not be removed. It was into this world that Enoch came bringing a message of repentance. He urged the peoples of all nations to turn from idolatry and debauchery, and to return to the law of Yah, or Yah would destroy the earth and all its inhabitants. Enoch travelled widely with the message given to him by the Almighty One. Those who listened and believed learned true wisdom, while those who did not believe increased in wickedness. Most did not believe.

In those days, knowledge increased, and the Nephilim developed great and terrible sorceries that they learned from their fathers, the demons known as "Watchers." This knowledge men were not yet ready to use, for the all-wise Creator had intended it for a much later age, but the Nephilim used the knowledge stolen by demons to create dreadful machines of war. With these powers, and with the heirs of Lhiosquor divided, they prepared to extend their rule over the entire earth.

# CHAPTER 15

# THE CALL OF THE PROPHET
## (400 – 423 EC)

## 400 EC

Some of the events described here may also be found in Enoch's <u>Memoirs</u> from which most of this tale has come. The story has been translated from the old Enosian characters into the new Northern tongue so that it may be better understood.

Yared and Medgariva remained in Tsayalam while Enoch was small, and the prophet's earliest memories were of his discussions with the temple priests. Young Enoch grew quickly in knowledge and wisdom; however, in the four hundredth year since the founding of Lhiosquor, Yared and his family were forced to flee the holy city. The naval armada of the Nephilim commanded by Hahyah, the brother of Ohyah, sailed eastward up the Rahav and obliterated the tall, proud ships of Shaochiquor. General Mahalalel led his forces northward from the fortress of Yarku which protected the Tsayalam to halt the southward march of Hahyah's forces which came up from the great harbour city.

When the defenders came upon Hahyah's men, the Nephilim fled, bringing Mahalalel's men into pursuit. Not until it was too late did Mahalalel realize it was a trap. Ohyah's forces came at Yarku from the southwest while the army of Mahalalel was in the north. The steel cannons of the enemy obliterated the walls of the fortress of Yarku, allowing the invaders to flood through the breach. By the time the defenders of Yarku had returned, the entire city of Tsayalam was in flames. When Mahalalel returned to Tsayalam, he fell to his knees and wept at the sight of the ruins where once stood the glorious Temple of Yah. Not a timber or a pillar had been left standing.

"Yah has indeed removed His favour from us. Who can now stand against the coming darkness?" Mahalalel saw the accursed banner of Hurash with its great eye flying over the ramparts of Yarku, and he could tell by the extent of the damage that the enemy host was very great. His army would be no match for this horde, especially after their exhausting pursuit in the north. Feeling the weight of defeat, General Mahalalel led his armies northeastward toward Turvah to regroup.

Meanwhile, Yared had fled Tsayalam with his wife, his son, and seven of the temple priests. Determined to put as much distance between themselves and the Nephilim as possible, Yared led them to the city of Unuk where Enoch had been born. There, outside of the city, they built a small shrine to Yah in remembrance of the Temple which had been destroyed. It was there in that small building that the priests taught Enoch about the ways of Yah. Enoch learned quickly and displayed all the intelligence of his father Yared, and of his ancestor Enos.

One of the priests who had fled with Yared was Niul, a servant of Yah who had come with Garnan from Atalanti. Niul had escaped from Lhiosquor when Konaryah slew the kindly abbot Garnan and burned the monastery. Konaryah circulated a tale that Garnan had set the fire because he no longer wanted to live after illegally marrying Yared and Medgariva, but no one in Lhiosquor really believed him. In the days of Kenan, the High Council could have challenged the High King when they knew him to be wrong, but the Council no longer had any real power. Furthermore, the old patriarchs - Seth, Enos, Kenan, as well as the Founders of Lhiosquor, who had set a moral standard for the people to follow, were gone. They found that they had virtually no influence on the new leadership and were greatly hindered by Konaryah's royal guard. The Founders and the wisest councillors left Lhiosquor to found the new city of Ahfeneyah, a name meaning the Shelter of God, on Mt. Sentinel.

Although Yared taught Enoch a great deal, it was Niul who was a tutor to the boy, teaching him all of the knowledge of the known world whenever Yared was occupied with other matters. Niul taught Enoch his letters, his numbers, and of the living things on the earth. Enoch's father taught him about the history of Lhiosquor and the wars with the Giants, about the law of Yah, and about the movements of the stars. On any of those rare nights when the curtain of heaven rolled back, Enoch would gaze up at the night sky through his father's looking glass which he had placed on the roof of the family home in Unuk, and would wonder about what was out there.

# 418 EC

Enoch continued to grow in knowledge as he grew in stature. By the time Enoch had reached the age of twenty-five in the year 418 of the Enosian Calendar, he was already well schooled in many sciences. Now he was apprenticing under Enmerkanda, the chief architect of Unuk. Enoch used the money earned from his labour to pay for new equipment that he and his father and the priests at the House of Yah needed for their studies of the natural world. As with everything else that he had learned, Enoch excelled at the designing of monuments. He wished to be able to rebuild the Temple of Yah on Mt. Tsayun as soon as that holy place was liberated from the armies of Hurash. He aided Enmerkanda by designing the walls of Unuk that were commissioned by the king. Everyone hoped that the new, complex system of walls and moats would be strong enough to withstand the cannons of the Nephilim. The people living in the valley of Shinar – Iradu, Unuk, Dilumu and the other city-states – had developed their own cannons by this time. In Unuk, these were mounted on the walls of the city to impede the progress of any approaching army.

Soon, there were rumours coming from the fishermen of Dilumu that the fleet of Ohyah was sailing up out of the southeast; they had sailed around the great southern peninsula which had become known as the Irad peninsula after the king of Iradu. Enoch realized that his new walls may be tested sooner than expected. The people of Unuk began to make preparations for what seemed to be an imminent attack, but the expected onslaught did not come. Instead, the frigates of Ohyah sailed up the river Kharkun to Susa where they laid waste to that city. King Seuso was slain to avenge the death of Ohyah's great-grandmother,

Ichsha. The Nephilim claimed dominion over Susaron, thus bordering the kingdoms of Arattu, Threthoron, and the city-states of the Shinar valley on both the east and west. Prince Afalo escaped with a remnant from Susa and fled to Lhiosquor and King Konaryah. The new High King of Lhiosquor received the hero of the voyage of the Queen Hirja as if he were his own son, without questioning how Afalo had managed to escape when the rest of Susa was destroyed.

Meanwhile, the patriarch Seth in Ahfeneyah perceived by the Spirit of Yah that the shadow in Lhiosquor was deepening. He had learned from Mahalalel the prophecy that had been spoken about Enoch, and he made the journey into the land of Shinar to meet Yared. Four months after the sacking of Susa, Seth arrived in Unuk with a retinue of twelve guards, and the Patriarch of Ahfeneyah marvelled at the mighty walls that had been built around the city. The gates of the city were shut for fear of the Nephilim who ruled Susa in the east. Seth called to the gatekeeper.

"I am Seth, Patriarch of Ahfeneyah. I come in friendship to meet my grandson's grandson, Yared of Lhiosquor, who lives in your city."

The gatekeeper opened the gates quickly, and as Seth and his companions entered the city, they saw the streets lined with awe-struck onlookers who had come out of their homes to see a living legend, the famed founder of legendary Lhiosquor. Seth addressed the masses.

"I have travelled from the city of Ahfeneyah to seek Yared of Lhiosquor. Does anyone know where I may find his house?"

Enmerkanda was in the crowd. "O great and powerful Seth, prophet and builder of Lhiosquor, I know the house of Yared." he said. "I am Enmerkanda, chief builder of Unuk, and Enoch the son of Yared is my apprentice. Even now he is building a new temple to the god, Yah. I can take you there, if you wish."

Seth and the men accompanying him followed Enmerkanda to Enoch's building site. The new temple was far smaller than the old one on Mt. Tsayun. It was only ten cubits high, ten cubits wide, and twenty-seven cubits long, but Enoch did not have at his disposal all of the workforce and material that Kenan had had when he built the once glorious Temple of Yah on Mt. Tsayun. When Enoch saw Seth approach, he came down to meet him, although he did not know who he was.

"Enoch son of Yared, I am Seth of Ahfeneyah from whom you are descended. I have come seeking you and your father's household. Would you direct me to your dwelling?"

Enoch was stunned. Of all the people who might visit him, he never imagined that Seth, the builder of Lhiosquor, would come to call on him. "Noble Patriarch, I am honoured that you would come." he said, with a nod of respect. "I will take you to my father's house." Enoch then led Seth and his retinue through the streets of Unuk to Yared's house. Medgariva saw them approaching and was greatly surprised. Why had Seth come to visit them? Were she and Yared to be judged after all these years?

Seth saw the worried look on Medgariva's face and calmed her. "Fear not, Medgariva. I have not come to pass judgement but to speak with your husband. Terrible forces are at work in the world, as you must have heard. The Council of the Wise in Ahfeneyah fears that the shadow of the Nephilim will continue to grow stronger, and we are beseeching the help of Yah. Your husband is one of the wisest of men on the earth, not unlike my son, Enos. I would have counsel with him.

"My husband is eating his noontime meal, but I will tell him you are here, great patriarch." Medgariva said with a deep nod to Seth. Moments later, Yared emerged from the doorway of his home, and then nodded his head deeply in respect to his grandfather's grandfather.

"Patriarch Seth, welcome to my home. I would be honoured to have you as a guest in my house today. What is the news from Threthoron?"

"Threthoron is divided, Yared. Konaryah, your uncle, rules in Lhiosquor in the east, and the Council of the Wise rules in the west. We have not chosen a king, but I preside over the Council as I did in the early days of Lhiosquor. The cities around the base of Mt. Threthoron have formed a single great city which surrounds the mountain like a ring; it has been named Faoriquor, the Ring City. Still, the reason for my visit is because Yah has shown me that darkness will soon fall upon Lhiosquor. The Council of the Wise believes that Enoch will be the greatest prophet yet known, and I would like him to return with me to Ahfeneyah to be trained under Enos at the university there."

Yared thought deeply. Enoch was of mixed race and the product of an illegal union. Would he be accepted among the students of the university, or would he be shunned because of the colour of his skin? "Noble Seth, I am grateful for your wisdom, and I want my son to fulfill the call of Yah on his life, but will Ahfeneyah be safe for a man of mixed blood? Would he not be despised and cast out by all who looked upon him there?"

"Enoch may have the blood of Lamekk the Accursed in his veins, but my blood also runs through his heart. Enoch is in the line of my firstborn, as are you, Yared. Your sin may have cost you your place in the bloodline, but your sin is not passed on to your son. Furthermore, he is of the seventh generation. Adam is the first, I am of the second, then Enos, Kenan, your father, yourself, and now your son. The Wise have great hope in Enoch. We believe that the light of Yah will flow through him to drive the darkness out of our lands once again. We believe it is important that he learns the wisdom of his people."

"Enoch has had a thorough education here under Brother Niul and me. He has excelled at everything that we have taught him..." Yared trailed off into a thoughtful silence. Seth said nothing, but waited to hear what Yared would say. "Wise patriarch, if Enoch wishes to go, I will send him with you. He has learned all that we can teach him here, even though he is but a youth. Other teachers may be able to extend the knowledge we have imparted to him beyond what we ever could. Please forgive me for my lack of humility. I was concerned for the well-being of my son."

"We will care for him in Ahfeneyah, as I am sure you know. He may still choose to remain here with you, and he is free to make that decision. Yet I would be grateful if you would tell him the news yourself."

"I will go with you." said Enoch, entering the room. "Once I have completed my work on the new temple, I will accompany you to Ahfeneyah. I have seen it in my dreams, and I am aware that some part of my future is tied to that city." Enoch had overheard the entire conversation between his father and the patriarch as he had stood by the doorway. "I want to see the City of the Wise, and I wish to learn how the citizens of Ahfeneyah live. I have heard much of the world, yet I wish to see it with my own eyes."

"If you believe that your destiny lies there, my son, please do not stay here on my account." Yared replied. "Yah's call on your life will take you farther than anyone has yet dared to go. Pursue your calling, Enoch, and follow the voice of Yah wherever He leads you."

Seth turned to face the young architect. "Ahfeneyah will be but the first destination in the journey which lies ahead of you, Enoch. Take the time that you need to prepare. I and my guardsmen will wait here in Unuk until you are ready to go." After they had discussed their preparations, Seth and his men left Yared and Enoch and visited the palace of Unuk. Unuk welcomed the renowned slayer of Hishirash, and he requested his aid.

"Great Seth, it is an honour to have you as a guest in my city. Have you heard any news of Ohyah and his army? My people have become greatly distressed since the realm of Susaron fell to the forces of the Nephilim. Irad, my grandfather, is calling for a mustering of soldiers from across the Shinar Valley to assemble and march forth against Susa, a city which is now in the hands of the Giants. I understand Irad's urgency, yet my people are mainly farmers and traders. We have very few soldiers. It is true that our vigilance has increased since the sack of Susa, but our militia are unorganized. There has been no war in over two hundred years, and our people do not know how to fight."

Seth looked at the concerned king thoughtfully. "War will come to you whether or not you go to it. You must prepare. When I return to Ahfeneyah, I will send General Mahalalel, Yared's father, to you to train your men to fight the Nephilim. To fall into their hands would be to lose your freedom and your lives. You must fight them with everything you have, or they will take everything you have."

The king thought about this nervously, and thanked Seth for any help he could offer. He prepared guest rooms in his palace where Seth and his men could stay until it was time for them to leave. Fifteen days after Seth's meeting with Unuk, Enoch completed the new temple of Yah and Seth dedicated it with the sacrifice of a lamb. Curious citizens of Unuk passed by and wondered about the strange god of the mountain people. They followed mostly Ellil and Ana, and knew nothing of Yah. In time, a few became dedicated followers of Yah and were ministered to by the priests who were once brothers in Garnan's monastery. Still, most of the citizens wanted nothing to do with a foreign god, and some scoffed at the peculiar laws of the followers of Yah, but for the most part the people of Unuk did not bother the followers of Yah. After all, they said, there were many gods that one could worship.

After the ceremonies had been completed, Enoch gathered together his belongings. He set off, mounted on a runner lizard, travelling with Seth and his guardsmen toward Ahfeneyah in the far northwest. They travelled north along the new road which ran along the Euphrates River. After a week's journey, they came to the village of Shuruppak where they purchased supplies and rested before travelling on. Now the road to Mt. Sentinel ran along the Tigris, not the Euphrates, but they did not travel along the Tigris as Ohyah's forces had built many fortresses along the eastern banks of the river. They did not turn from the Euphrates until a week after they had passed through the village of Sippar. Then they reached the northern Tigris and headed straight north along the river for three weeks. After that, the terrain became more mountainous as they approached the first of the Seven Mountain Ranges. Fortunately, since they were heading to Ahfeneyah and not Lhiosquor, they could travel Tigris Valley. Still, their progress was slow as they followed the Tigris to Lake Turvah from which it flowed. Terrible winged lizards that dwelt in the mountains swooped down to attack the travellers, but one of Seth's guards set off a firecracker, scaring them away. It was then that Enoch realized how far away from home he really was.

"In my country, there are no mountains and no fierce beasts such as these." he remarked. The guardsmen remained silent, knowing that Enoch was merely stating the obvious. He was so amazed at the majesty and terror of the mountains that he did not know what he should say.

It was a two month's journey through the Tigris Valley, as there was much uphill climbing and the ground was uneven. At long last, they arrived on the plateau where Lake Turvah lay glistening in the sunlight. The company camped by the lake in sight of Mt. Sentinel, knowing that their journey would soon be at an end. Enoch sat by the lake that night, staring into the water, wondering what his future held for him. He had had many fantastic dreams about his future, and he knew that his dreams were usually portents of things to come. He wondered what would happen to him in Ahfeneyah.

Seth saw Enoch sitting and contemplating. "You have a great mind, young Enoch. A great mind harbours great power, because knowledge is power. In Ahfeneyah you will learn wisdom. Wisdom is the ability to control that power. Hurash, king of the Nephilim, has great knowledge, but he uses his knowledge to destroy, to conquer, to kill, to enslave, and to bend the minds of others to his own. You must learn to be wise and to use your knowledge in ways that will do the most good to the most people. That is what the students at the Enosian University learn. They learn the law of Yah and the principles upon which that law rests. Your training will prepare you, Enoch, for the time when more powerful revelations than you have ever experienced will come to you from the Almighty One. Although we near the end of our travels and sit under the shadow of Mt. Sentinel, this is only the beginning of your journey."

"I have left all that I have known to come here and pursue wisdom. I know that I shall find more than I expect, yet I feel anxious about the future." Enoch said. "What will I do now in this strange land?"

"The Wise built Ahfeneyah as a shelter from the darkness that is spreading across the land. Here you will find rest and peace, as long as you make Yah your refuge. When difficult times arise, remember the calling for which you have been chosen. You will be the mouthpiece of the Most High to the nations of the world. Those who will listen to you will be saved, those who refuse you will be condemned, because they are refusing the words of Yah, the Almighty One. Be encouraged and strengthened, as He watches over you with unfailing love."

## 423 EC

Enoch studied at the Enosian University for five years, during which time he matured in his knowledge. It should be noted here that when the Wise left Lhiosquor in opposition to Konaryah, the descendants of

Nosjubal left also, but they departed for lands in the north and the tents of their Jabalite cousins. None of the descendants of Nosjubal came to Ahfeneyah, in part to prevent the possibility of intermarriage between the two races. No one wanted to see the mistakes of Lhiosquor repeated. Because there were no Cainites in Ahfeneyah, and because of the dark complexion that he inherited from his mother, Enoch was looked on with suspicion by some of his fellow students at the University. Most of the students were enlightened enough to understand that the colour of one's skin did not affect one's devotion to God and respect for His laws, but a few of the less brilliant students were jealous of the rate at which Enoch learned and of how well he applied himself to all disciplines.

They began to insult him regarding his parentage, as everyone in Ahfeneyah knew the story of Prince Yared and Medgariva. Enoch, being of a fiery spirit, quickly condemned the other students, warning them that they would not be spared the judgement that would soon come upon the earth. He said that Giants would come and carry them off to the land of Nahlon to force them to labour as slaves, building monuments for the Nephilim. The jealousy of these students then turned to anger, and they hated Enoch. Enoch's tormentors were only five out of twelve hundred students who attended the University, but they were enough to make his life there terribly burdensome. To make matters worse, these students told their teachers what Enoch had said, and in the year 423, Enoch was brought to answer before Enos along with his accusers.

Enos the Wise sat in his great, high-backed wooden chair, and addressed the situation. "I suppose you are all wondering the purpose for which I have brought you here." The five hooligans stared at the ground guiltily, and Enoch looked at Enos with a look of puzzlement on his face. "Horalyah, Elthiris, Machred, Velotis and Enveryah, you are brought here because your conduct toward Enoch the son of Yared is unacceptable. You have apparently learned nothing from your time here, and none of you have shown any notable achievement in any of your subjects. I built this University to be a place of understanding and enlightenment, of which you have shown none in your treatment of Enoch.

"Furthermore, your academic abilities in all subjects have shown to be less than satisfactory. Your cruel treatment of Enoch reflects only your envy at his superior abilities. Envy, jealousy, mockery, and cruelty have no place in this institution; therefore, I hereby expel you from this University on the grounds of being unteachable and incorrigible. You shall gather your things and leave the University premises immediately."

The five rascals skulked away, and Enos turned to Enoch. "Enoch, the grandson of my grandson, you have shown extraordinary talent and ability during your five years of study at this University. I know that the Spirit of Yah is often with you, teaching you deep and unsearchable truths. You continue to excel even in the face of adversity, but I believe that this University may not be the place where you will find your answers. Your fiery temperament, though often understandable, ill-becomes a scholar. A student needs to keep a cool head, a calm spirit, and a logical mind.

Nevertheless, I admit that logic and learning have their limits. You have learned all that we can teach you here, and the deep mysteries that you seek to unlock lie beyond the limits of human understanding. The answers you seek can be revealed by revelation alone, in other places and in other methods than by objective study. Last night, I had a dream, one of a very few which I have ever remembered. I saw you embarking upon a quest, much like my son Kenan did in his youth before he built the Temple at Mt. Tsayun. The answers you seek lie elsewhere. I do not know where you should go, but follow the Spirit of Yah who is so often with you. Let Him lead you into all truth."

Enos placed a yellow skullcap on Enoch's head which represented enlightenment and placed a scroll in his hand that represented learning. He spoke in a loud voice "You have completed your studies here at the University, Enoch son of Yared. Go forth into the world, and let your light shine before men." With this brief ceremony, Enoch completed his academic studies. He had planned to work as an architect in the city of Ahfeneyah, but that night he had a dream unlike any he had ever had before.

In the dream, an angel appeared to him and told him to go into the Great Forest, to Siaghlamh, where he would receive the answers that he had been searching for. He then saw the City of Lhiosquor rising like a fortress, full of soldiers. Even women and youths wore armour and carried weapons. Then, he saw the armies of the land of Shinar, led by Irad, contending with the armies of Ohyah. The Nephilim prevailed, and the armies of Shinar were overwhelmed. The temple that he had built in Unuk was destroyed, and in its place was built a monument to Hishirash. He saw kingdom after kingdom fall to the Nephilim, and finally he saw Lhiosquor burning; its flames rising up to heaven. Enoch awoke with a start, and remembered every image of the dream as if it had been real. He gathered together his belongings, and then set out from Ahfeneyah.

Enoch descended the north side of the mountain where the upper Tigris River entered Lake Turvah, and from there travelled upstream to where the Tigris met the Pishon. The two rivers formed the shape of a wishbone where they exited the Great Forest. Three angels stood on the banks of the rivers, one on each riverbank, and they were mighty and terrible to behold. They regarded Enoch sternly and spoke as with one voice. "Are you a Cainite, or a Sethite? We see the blood of two races in your veins - one line is the line of Kenan the Just, the other is that of Lamekk the Accursed. Whom do you serve, you who come out of the City of the Wise?"

Enoch was terrified and trembled. He could not even open his mouth to speak. Just then a fourth angel, one mightier and more glorious than the other three, stood on the water at the point where the rivers met. His face shone like the sun, and Enoch could not look upon his glory. Enoch fell on his face as one slain. The fourth angel carried a scroll in one hand and a sword of light in the other. His feet were red like iron being brought forth from a blacksmith's furnace and his voice was like that of a multitude.

"This man is the one whose coming was foretold to us. He will be given a message for all nations that will be like a sword dividing the wicked from the righteous. Those who hear his message and obey will live, but those who pay no heed will surely die. The Almighty One will direct his steps and lead him to the places where he shall go."

Enoch struggled to his feet and the three angels on the bank remained, but the one with the scroll had gone. "You may enter the

Forest of Adam, prophet of the Most High." The angel on the farthest bank said.

The angel on the nearest bank pointed to a road which led into the forest, a road that Enoch had not noticed when he arrived. "This pathway leads to Siaghlamh. Follow it, and you will come to the city of the Eldest Ones. May you find the answer to which you do not know the question in that city." Enoch said nothing, but set his feet upon the road ahead of him that led into the Great Forest. As he entered the forest, he remembered the stories that he had heard from Kenan while he was in Ahfeneyah. Enoch now understood what the old king had meant when he had spoken of millions of hidden eyes watching him and trees whispering to one another as he passed. The forest seemed alive with awareness, filling Enoch with anxiety, as he continued along the leaf-strewn forest road.

As night approached, Enoch could hear the whispering more strongly, and he thought that he could even make out some of the words, just as Kenan had done centuries before. It was as if he was dreaming again; he heard whispers about terrible wars to come, and portents of the dominion of the Giants spreading across the face of the earth. He set up camp along the road, but he did not sleep that night as he continued to hear messages carried on the wind. As he listened, he began to piece together the destiny that was laid out for him from the beginning of the world. He knew where he must go and what he must do, but he felt inadequate to accomplish even a fraction of what he was being called to do. The following morning he arose, gathered his things and continued on his way.

Enoch travelled along the road until he saw fields of corn under an open sky in a large clearing. The winding, leaf-strewn pathway became paved with stones and straightened out, pointing to a small city on the horizon. As Enoch passed by the farms, the workers looked at him strangely, and people standing outside quickly went indoors. From there, the farmers and their families peered at the dark-skinned stranger from a safe distance. No descendant of Cain had set foot in the Great Forest since King Enokk of Arattu had travelled there one-hundred twenty-seven years before the founding of Lhiosquor to find Neema, his bride.

Five and a half centuries had passed since Enoch's namesake came to Siaghlamh seeking a wife. Siaghlamh had no city walls as it rested under the protection of the Kheruvim, but as Enoch followed the road, the houses grew closer together until the farms stopped at the point where the city proper began. The houses of Siaghlamh appeared humble but sturdy. They were built of wood and stone, and most were only one story high. As Enoch was noting the architecture of Siaghlamh, he was met by a silver-haired man. Enoch had never met anyone in his life with such unusual hair, as people aged very slowly in the time before the floodwaters came.

"Welcome, young visitor. I have been expecting your arrival." said the man.

Enoch was surprised. "How did you know I was coming?"

The silver-haired man laughed heartily. "An angel appeared to me and told me to look for a dark-skinned man. Cainites are forbidden entry to the Great Forest as a rule, so I must assume that you are the man."

Enoch was taken aback. "Sir, I am a descendant of Seth in the line of the Firstborn. My mother is a Cainite, but she is devoted to Yah. My father is Yared, he who was once the High Priest of the Temple of Yah. Now that you understand the colour of my skin, may I ask you about the colour of your hair? I have met people with red hair, black hair, brown hair, and have even heard tell of people with yellow hair in some parts of the world; however, I have neither seen nor heard of anyone with silver hair."

The man smiled. "I am Adam, the father of all people on the earth. I have seen the earth travel in its great course about the sun six hundred and fifty-two times. In my five hundred and ninety-second year, my hair began to lose its colour as a reminder that one day I will die. One day, everyone who lives on the earth must die because of my sin many centuries ago. Every day, I wish that I could find a way to return to that ancient day and prevent what happened, to somehow undo the damage that I have done, but I know that everything is a part of Yah's plan. Even you being born of a mixed marriage, though it is against the law of Yah, is yet part of His plan. I cannot hope to understand the mystery of His will, but I know that one day, by His own hand, people shall be free from the curse that I have brought upon the world. Even so, I know that I shall not live to see that day. I will die one day, and return to the earth from which Yah formed me."

Enoch's attitude toward the man changed when he knew to whom he had been speaking. "Ancient Father," he said quietly, "I meant no disrespect in what I have said to you. It is you whom I was sent to find. Much has changed, and is changing, in the world outside the Great Forest. A shadow is falling across the whole earth, and Yah has appointed me to speak against it. I do not know what I will say or do, only where I must go. I have heard so much about my destiny, but I do not know how I can accomplish the task that Yah has set before me. I have seen visions, terrible visions, of things to come. The nations of the world must understand what will happen to them if they follow after false gods."

"Yah has placed His message within you, young prophet; that much is obvious. The Spirit of Yah will help you to articulate what it is that you see so that people can understand." Adam paused and looked at Enoch. After a moment he spoke again. "What is your name, son of Yared?"

"I am Enoch. I was named after the King of Arattu who helped my great-grandfather, Kenan the Just, to overthrow the Giants of Turnienquor long ago."

Adam gazed past Enoch, reflecting on an earlier memory. "I remember the King of Arattu when he was very young, a mere youth. He was the only Cainite ever to enter this land; it is fitting that you bear his name. He sought the hand of my daughter, Neema, in marriage. Enoch, when you travel to the city of Enokk, please tell my daughter Neema that I send my love. It has been far too long since I have last seen her." Adam closed his eyes for a moment as he remembered his beloved daughter. When he opened his eyes, he looked at Enoch again. "Young Enoch, you have much to do in the time Yah has given you, so I advise you not to tarry in Siaghlamh. I will pray a prayer of blessing over you that Yah will be your constant guide and companion."

Adam closed his eyes again as he began to meditate on the mystery of the Almighty One. He rested the palm of his right hand on Enoch's head, and prayed softly. "Mighty Creator, I Adam, whom You formed from the soil of the earth, call upon You. Please be with Your servant, Enoch son of Yared, as he begins the work which You have prepared for him to do from the beginning. May the full mantle and anointing of a prophet rest on him, and may You guide him every step of his way. Let not a word be uttered from his mouth that does not find its source in You, Most High. Fill him even now with Your Spirit of power which You will pour out in fullness in a time very far removed from now. I release the blessings of all the generations before him to rest on him now. May all Your promises to him come to pass as You have said."

When Adam's prayer of blessing was finished, the two men opened their eyes. Enoch now knew exactly where he had to go and what he had to do.

"I must beg your leave, Father of all Nations. I must find my half-nephew, Mattu-Seth, who dwells among the wandering Jabalites. I will need his help with the task that is ahead of me now." Enoch nodded deeply to Adam to show his respect.

"I will leave you with this prophecy, Enoch. There will be two judgements that will destroy the entire earth. The earth will be destroyed once by fire and once by water. May those who are wise understand the words of this prophecy." Adam also nodded to Enoch. "Go then, Enoch, and may all who receive your message be blessed." said the Eldest One. With that, Enoch left Siaghlamh and continued on his travels.

# CHAPTER 16

# The Heirs of Lhiosquor
## (428 – 431 EC)

## 428 EC

Enoch travelled north from the Great Forest, following the Gihon River, until he came to the Great Plains of Jabal. From there, he journeyed northward across the plains for seven days. One day around noon, Enoch met his nephew travelling with the nomadic Jabalites. They were grazing their herds in the grasslands far beyond the Gihon along the river that they named Bolkash. The tribes of Jabal had migrated further north over the centuries as new tribes had come and built their cities along the Gihon. Enoch dwelt among the shepherds of Jabal with his nephew for five years, learning the ways of the Jabalites and how to tend sheep. One night, he had a terrible dream. In the dream, Enoch saw the city of Lhiosquor shining in the sunlight as the rays of the sun reflected off of the white marble walls of the city. Next, he saw an enormous flying eater lizard swoop down and dig its talons into the side of Mt. Threthor. The monster's shadow was so wide that it blocked out the sun, and Lhiosquor was in darkness. Then the creature breathed fire on the City of Light and it burned as it did in the vision that Enoch had received many years ago. Next, Enoch saw the fire spread out to the ends of the earth. Not one green leaf or blade of grass remained, and smoke from the devastation blocked out the sun.

Enoch awoke from his dream with a start. His body was drenched in sweat and his hands trembled. He then felt Yah speaking to him in his mind, and listened as the Almighty One spoke to him the prophecy that he was to bring to Lhiosquor. "Konaryah has listened to the voice of an idolater and has forsaken My law. I love the people of Lhiosquor, but the king has allowed the worship of false gods in My holy city. If this remains unchanged, I will completely remove My favour from Lhiosquor, and the City of Light will be judged. My chosen people must understand that I am their god, and no other. If they give themselves over to the worship of evil spirits, those demons will have dominion in the city, and Lhiosquor will fall to the Nephilim who are themselves the spawn of evil spirits. Enoch, you must go and confront Konaryah. You must warn the men and women of Lhiosquor of the judgement that they will face if they give themselves over to the worship of false gods."

Enoch was silent as he allowed the living words of Yah to resound in his mind. He wanted to go, he knew that he had to go, but something was holding him back. How would he get to Lhiosquor? What would he say when he arrived there? What would happen to him if his message angered King Konaryah?"

As Enoch finished these thoughts, the voice spoke again. "Mattu-Seth, your nephew, will accompany you on your journey. He knows the way to Lhiosquor, and he will take you there. I also want you to teach him everything that I am teaching you. Enoch, do not worry about what you will say in Lhiosquor. I am sending you, and when you speak, My words will come forth from your mouth. Konaryah and the leaders of Lhiosquor must hear the message that I will bring to them. I Myself will be with you; I will send My Spirit with you, and you will be protected from the wrath of the king. I will not allow one hair on your head to come to harm."

When Yah had finished speaking and His presence had departed, Enoch realized that he had not indeed awoken until that moment. He dressed himself, arose from his tent, and sought out Mattu-Seth. His half-nephew was already approaching him from across the camp. "I have had a dream, uncle." Mattu-Seth said with a beaming white smile that showed all his teeth. "Today, you and I will go to the City of Light." Enoch was surprised at his nephew's statements, but said nothing and made preparations for his journey. This happened in the year 428 of the Enosian Calendar.

On the day that Enoch and Mattu-Seth arrived in Lhiosquor, High King Konaryah was holding court in the old High Council chambers, which he had made into his throne room. The second son of Kenan was seated high up on an ornate, golden throne. The throne was of such enormous size that the king, a heavy-set, robust man arrayed in all his biggest and brightest regalia, seemed dwarfed by it. Konaryah's throne faced across from the main doorway at the far end of the hall so that the king could see all who entered, and that all who entered could see the king. Konaryah wore the Emerald Crown upon his head. He held the Sceptre of Justice in one hand and the Orb of Wisdom in the other. His robe was deep purple, with square, puffed shoulders. Eagles were woven into his robe with golden thread. He was celebrating the thirty-fifth anniversary of his reign as well as the wedding of Astaris, his eldest and favorite daughter, to Afalo the son of Seuso. The courtiers of Lhiosquor and governors of all the provinces of East Threthoron were gathered in the Royal Hall of Council, (the new name of the building), wondering what grandiose announcement the High King would make.

Off to one side of the circular Royal Hall of Council, about sixty degrees to the king's right, a large band of musicians played together on a wide variety of instruments. This new style of music featured many different instruments harmoniously playing long, complex arrangements of music in several movements. It was very popular during the reign of Konaryah throughout East and West Threthoron, as well as in several other nations. As his court assembled, Konaryah did not pay much attention to the gathering nobility. His attention was caught up in the music. The nobles socialized, and gentle laughter could be heard arising at times among more serious discussions in the council hall. People gathered news of other regions of the High Kingdom and reacquainted themselves with friends not seen in years.

All of a sudden, Konaryah stood to his feet and began the speech that the courtiers had been waiting to hear.

"Assembled friends and governors, kinsmen and councillors, I have called you here today to be witnesses of the marriage between Prince Afalo the Brave, son and heir of the late King Seuso of Susaron, and my talented and brilliant daughter, Astaris. Afalo's father was as dear to me as a brother, and was the man who slew the Giantess Ichsha so many years ago. I still mourn when I remember hearing how Ohyah killed King Seuso, laid his city to waste, and enslaved his people, but Afalo has escaped and carries his father's courageous spirit. Afalo was he who sailed around the earth and proved that the earth was round. No greater feat has ever been done by man, and I am honoured to give him in marriage to my lovely daughter.

"I have gathered you here for this wedding, and also to tell you that I have chosen Prince Afalo to be my chief advisor. His authority in the High Kingdom will be second only to mine." There were a number of murmurs at this, for many of Konaryah's subjects mistrusted the son of Seuso, although they feared to say anything openly in front of the king regarding him. Konaryah stood to his feet and stretched his right arm out over the crowd to calm them. "I know that many of you are concerned because Afalo does not follow Yah, the god of our fathers. Today, before the wedding begins, Prince Afalo will participate in the rite of conversion by passing through water. We will now proceed from here to Lake Threthor where my new chief advisor will announce his vow to serve Yah. Then, once he has passed through the water, the wedding will begin."

Trumpeters arrayed in blue tunics and white trousers – the colours of Lhiosquor – wearing richly plumed hats of the same colours, and bearing the golden eagle insignia of Konaryah. They stood at the main portico of the Royal Hall and raised their trumpets. These were adorned with the standard of Lhiosquor; a white mountain on a field of sky blue, bordered again in white. The royal trumpeters sounded a short series of notes on their trumpets and began to proceed slowly in formation along the Avenue of Justice. Konaryah, Afalo, and Astaris arose from where they had been seated, causing all those who were seated to arise as well. The High King proceeded out through the main doorway, followed by the bride and groom, and after them came the throng of assembled governors and courtiers.

The royal procession led toward the shore of pristine Lake Threthor, the Crystal Lake. The sun was not as bright in those days as it is today, and its heat did not burn the skin, yet its silver disk could be seen through the curtain of heaven; enough for the Crystal Lake to shimmer faintly. At the water's edge two men waited, standing up to their ankles in the water of the lake. One of the men had the appearance of a Cainite, and the other of an unknown people, though clearly not of Lhiosquor. Konaryah halted the procession before reaching the two men.

"Who are you, and how did you enter my city?" the king bellowed. "Answer me before I have you thrown into the dungeon!" Konaryah's guard advanced to the front of the procession, but did not yet attempt to lay a hand on them.

The Cainite spoke. "I am Enoch, the son of Yared, the son of your brother, Mahalalel..."

Konaryah interrupted Enoch. "If you have come to claim your birthright, you are wasting your time. No Cainite is allowed on this mountain, mongrel. Go back to the Dry Lands of Ravi from whence you came, exile."

Afalo cleared his throat, and spoke softly into the High King's ear. "My lord, they might be spies from Ohyah or Hahyah. Would it be wise to let them live and return to their Nephilim masters?" At that point, the waters of the Crystal Lake of Mt. Threthoron were aroused from their renowned stillness as a great wind arose off the lake. The wind billowed out the robes of the two visitors, and their long, untied hair streamed out from their heads like rays. Gasps were heard from among the onlookers, and Enoch addressed the High King.

"Konaryah, is it wise to sleep with a poisonous serpent in your bed?" Enoch did not wait for the king's reply, as the High King's face was still frozen in shock. "In the same way, is it wise to let this two-tongued man into your family as a son and into your deepest counsels? He professes that he now follows Yah, but in his heart he has not relinquished Ea, the power of Susa. You know this to be true, o king, yet as ever you only wish to see the letter of Yah's law obeyed, regardless of the meaning behind that law. There was once a High King in Lhiosquor who held the law in his heart, not on his lips only." Konaryah glowered at the mention of his father.

Enoch continued in spite of the High King's icy gaze. "Yah says to you, Konaryah, you who care not for your own family but have rejected them to wear your father's crown; turn your heart to Yah, the god of your father. Turn to Him, and all of your people with you, or this city that Yah loves more than all others will fall under the shadow of the Nephilim and the dark powers that sired them. Tear down the shrines of false gods from your land, and you will live, and Lhiosquor will prosper and Threthoron be reunited. Refuse the words of Yah, and your pet serpent will bite, and you will die. Your children and your children's children will either be slain or corrupted by the Nephilim. Even your snake will be trod under the feet of the sons of Hurash. Only for the sake of His name will Yah spare one of your descendants. The armies of the Nephilim princes shall besiege Lhiosquor and it shall be destroyed by fire. Not one stone or timber will be left standing. When the light of Lhiosquor has been snuffed out, men will lose hope, and all will fall under the shadow of darkness.

"Your duty, o king, is to restore this city to the glory of its former days, when your father was High King of Lhiosquor. Let Yah alone be worshipped, lest His enemies triumph. Rid yourself of the viper in your household, and come before Yah with weeping. Rend your heart, and He will protect you."

Konaryah said nothing in response, for he was deep in thought. Most of the citizens of Lhiosquor were as yet devoted to Yah, and the High King could not take a stance that would be interpreted as going against the will of Yah. At the same time, he did not want to be seen as bowing his knee to a wandering mongrel. He must appear strong and decisive. However, before Konaryah could come to a decision, Afalo snapped. His plans exposed, he felt like a trapped animal and, seizing his betrothed at the point of his blade, he backed away from the High King.

"You will grant me safe passage out of Lhiosquor, with Astaris, or I will surely kill your beloved daughter." Konaryah was stunned.

"Afalo, don't do it! Do you think that I believe a madman from the desert who claims to hear from Yah? I do not! Release Astaris, and be restored to my favour."

Mattu-Seth spoke to Konaryah. "You have rejected the words of Yah's prophet and you will be subject to the curses which he has spoken. Your remaining span of years will be shortened and your life will be cut off. We take our leave of you." Enoch raised his staff, and the two men vanished. Konaryah's eyes were then opened, and he realized that these men had spoken the truth. His heart was gripped with fear as he understood that they had been right about Afalo. Afalo had released Astaris as he stood dumbfounded; his eyes transfixed on the place from whence the two strangers had vanished. Konaryah ordered the men to seize Afalo and throw him into the dungeon. Afalo howled in protest as the guards chained him, and he struggled with all of his strength, but the guards were too many. He was taken away to be imprisoned until the High King could decide his fate.

# 431 EC

Konaryah did not have Afalo put to death as the law demanded because of his respect for Seuso, but the king kept him chained in the dungeon. This was the first time that Konaryah publicly transgressed upon the letter of the law, and this lost him favour in the eyes of his people, particularly Prince Ayrus, heir to the Emerald Crown of Lhiosquor and General of the armies of East Threthoron. He was one of the twins born to Wolja on the day the Yared came to Lhiosquor to announce that the world was round. The other, Hebystos, was crippled from childhood after a fall from a tree. Ever since, he walked with much difficulty, with a terrible, twisting limp. Ineligible for the throne because of his condition, he devoted himself to learning the armourer's trade, and was now the head of the armourers' guild in Lhiosquor.

In contrast to his crippled brother, Ayrus was the very model of a prince in his appearance. He had his mother's fair, yellow hair and fair skin, and was beloved by all of the young women of Lhiosquor. His wife, Upara-Ditri, was also considered to be the fairest and most beautiful woman in Lhiosquor. Many compared her beauty to that of Lilara, the mother of Yared. Ayrus had been trained to succeed his father ever since Konaryah had ousted Kenan, and he had no love for Afalo whom he saw as a threat to his own succession. Ayrus was beloved of the people of Lhiosquor, and in the year 431, the prince rallied the discontented around himself to make his case against his father, the king.

"My father, the king, has become a lawbreaker. Should a man without regard for the law of Yah rule over His chosen ones? Konaryah might have given his throne to Afalo, or the deceiver would have taken it, leaving Lhiosquor in the hands of a godless, grasping traitor. The king was about to give my sister Astaris, who now despises Afalo, to this disciple of demons in marriage so that the snake could legitimize his claim to the throne. If my father wishes to remain king, he must act like a king and dispense justice in his kingdom where justice is needed. Afalo must be sentenced to a public execution so that the people of Lhiosquor will know that justice and the law of Yah still reigns in the City of Light."

A man in the crowd cried out, "Let us bring back the true High King from Ahfeneyah. Let us bring back the wise fathers that Yah would bless us again."

Ayrus spoke in a melancholy tone. "If they were to return, they would have come already. Ahfeneyah has abandoned us; we must see to our own affairs." Ayrus continued, "Do not forget that Kenan, however noble he was, and for all the wonderful things that he did for the City of Light, also transgressed the law when he failed to execute Yared, the son of Prince Mahalalel, for marrying a Cainite. We need a High King who will not fail the law and the people. We need a strong king who will make Lhiosquor great again and lead us to victory over our enemies.

Ayrus hung his head slightly and lowered his voice. "I have pleaded with my father to allow our armies to go forth and drive back the abominable hordes of the Nephilim." he said sorrowfully, glancing at the stone stairs beneath his feet. He looked up and continued, allowing the slightest hint of anger to enter his voice. "He says that war would be too costly, but will it not cost us more when Hahyah and Ohyah come, enslave our men, kill our children, and take our women to Hurash? We cannot stay hiding up here on Mt. Threthor, growing fat and lazy, while our enemies draw nearer and nearer. If I were High King, I would lead our armies straight to the land of the upper Nahla, to temple of Hurash himself, and destroy the abominable Giant King."

Many of those gathered, particularly the younger men, cheered at Ayrus' speech, but Prince Hebystos grew jealous of his brother's popularity. When the general concluded his speech and sent the people to their homes, Hebystos made his way back to his workshop thinking of how easily he was not recognized in the crowd. Few people even noticed his characteristic limp when they were hypnotized by his brother's speech. People always cheered when Ayrus spoke or even walked by, but they turned away whenever they saw Hebystos limping along the road. Yet although he was a cripple in his body, Hebystos' mind was as sharp as the rapiers which his smiths made in the royal armory. He knew that if he wished to counter his brother's influence, he would an ally whose speech was as convincing as that of Ayrus.

Hebystos sent a servant named Sumiseno to the dungeon to speak with Afalo, who had been confined there for three years. No one knows what words passed between them, but Sumiseno gave Afalo a mixture of herbs before he left. An hour later, Afalo swooned and fell to the floor. The prison guards could feel neither a breath nor a heartbeat, so they believed Afalo to be dead. They carried him out of the dungeon to the western shrine where burials were performed. Sumiseno met the guards at the shrine disguised as a priest of Yah. He took Afalo into the shrine to prepare him for burial, but when the prison guards had left Sumiseno poured a draught down Afalo's throat which revived him.

It was customary to allow three days for a burial to take place and, as there were very few burials in Lhiosquor in those days, Sumiseno and Afalo were the only ones in the shrine until Hebystos visited the following morning. He placed a dark cloak around Afalo's slight frame and led him out of the shrine to his house. "Have you heard that the prince, my brother, is calling for your execution?" he asked.

"I have not heard any news, but I am not surprised." Afalo muttered, his voice still weak from three years of solitary imprisonment.

"He also calls for my father to step down. I released you to help us. The High King gave you mercy when the law called for death. Would you stand with him now against my brother?"

"What does Konaryah say? Does he know that I have been released?"

"No, he does not. I will let him know that you live, and that you plead for pardon. Because of your friendship, he may pardon and restore you, but you must know that my brother has many followers who want you dead. Personally, I wish that Ayrus had been imprisoned in your place. The people adore him, but he has become too ambitious. He is very skilled in the crafting of words, as you are, which is why the High

King and I need your help. If you received the king's pardon and became his defender, Konaryah would be emboldened to make a case against Ayrus and hold his ambitions in check."

Afalo laughed out loud in spite of himself. "How can I make a defence of the High King when I am the source of contention? If the High King pardoned me, would not your brother's followers start a revolt? What would your father do then? He would have to kill me or lose the Emerald Crown. I would be a fool to put myself in such a ridiculous situation."

Hebystos paused in thought, steeping the fingers of his large, calloused hands. His sharp mind devised a plan. Hebystos spoke quickly and excitedly, gesturing with his hands and pacing the floor as he told Afalo his idea. "Write your defence on parchment, and I will deliver it to the High King. Write in such a way that its eloquence will convince him to pardon you. If it succeeds, he may read it to the people to defend his position against Ayrus. All matters would then be dealt with at once; you will be free, my father's authority will be reconfirmed, and my brother's claim will be thwarted."

Afalo agreed to Hebystos' plan, and proceeded to write a lengthy defence in which he apologized to the king and proclaimed his loyalty. Afalo was so skilled with words, and knew the High King's heart so well, that the defence nearly brought Konaryah to tears when Hebystos delivered it to him the following morning. In his defence, Afalo stated that he never intended any harm against the king or his daughter, but had reacted in a momentary panic against the words of the supposed prophet from Ahfeneyah. He wrote that he was afraid that the prophet held the hearts of the people, which had caused him to feel cornered. He apologized profusely to the High King for any apparent threat he had made against Astaris, for whom he professed undying love.

After reading Afalo's defence, the High King sent for his old friend that same afternoon. When Hebystos returned to the Royal Hall of Council with Afalo, there was an angry crowd gathered outside on the Avenue of Justice. They shouted curses at Afalo and demanded that he leave Lhiosquor. Afalo ignored the angry faces glaring at him and looked straight ahead with no sign of emotion on his face as he entered the Royal Hall. The High King's councillors had all gathered inside, along with the twin princes Ayrus and Hebystos. They shouted at each other across the floor of the council chamber as Ayrus' party argued with that of the High King, led by Tarcheng, the cousin of Afalo. When Afalo entered, Konaryah called for order and the councillors ceased their ranting.

"My loyal councillors, I have gathered you here today on a matter of great importance. "Afalo the son of Seuso has repented of all previous wrongdoings, and I have pardoned him. I offer him once again, should he accept, the privilege to sit in this council. Two months ago the Nephilim took Badtibira, and slew King Irad of Iradu in battle, along with Shinar, his second son and heir. Irad was the leader of the united armies of Shinar that stood against the Nephilim. His third son, Alulim, has succeeded him in Iradu, but the cities of Shinar are in disarray as they have lost their leader. The Nephilim under Ohyah have taken the opportunity to build a capital at Badtibira. They have the support of their kinsmen, the tribe of Tubal-Cain, son of Lamekk the Twice-Accursed.

Now, more than ever, I need your advice and your help. It is because of this that I have reinstated Afalo. His faith may yet be in question, but know that he has no love for the Nephilim who destroyed his father's kingdom and massacred his people. I want peace in our land. I fought in the first war with the Giants to overthrow Hishirash, and I know all too well the cost of war." The High King paused as he remembered the day when he and Mahalalel stood over the dying body of Pocabal, his brother's friend. "Still, we need to be ready in case war comes to us."

Ayrus waited until the High King had finished speaking, and then he rose to his feet. "I agree wholeheartedly when the High King says that we must prepare for war. I myself will lead a glorious campaign to rid the world of the Nephilim; however, I say that we must first root out all the messengers of the great enemy that have been allowed to enter our city. Only then will we be strong and pure and assured of victory against the Nephilim. We cannot defeat Hahyah and Ohyah with weapons alone; the history of our great city is a witness to this fact. In the past, whenever we held to the law of Yah, we prospered and our enemies were defeated. When we strayed from the law, we fell and our enemies prospered. We must cleanse ourselves and cleanse our city from unfaithfulness and disobedience to Yah." Many of the councillors in both parties murmured approval at this statement.

Ayrus paused and allowed them time to be silent. "Many years ago, my father made a very difficult decision to motion for the deposition of High King Kenan, a noble though flawed man who served Lhiosquor well in his time, and who is still beloved by many in Lhiosquor, even though he has chosen to leave our great city. Kenan transgressed the law of Yah by allowing Prince Yared, a man who had married a Cainite, to live rather than to punish him and his dark bride with death as the law decrees. Because of that sin, he could no longer be High King. When Konaryah discovered this transgression, Kenan was deposed and my father became the High King.

"Councillors and nobles of Lhiosquor, let us take into consideration the case of Afalo of Susa and our present High King. Although Kenan was deposed, the law that he received binds us for as long as the mountain on which he received it stands. The law of Yah that was given to Kenan on Mt. Tsayun declares that no one who follows another god must be allowed to enter the gates of the City of Lhiosquor. Konaryah brought the refugee Afalo into Lhiosquor with full knowledge of his family's apostasy from Yah. The High King did not make any efforts to persuade Afalo to forsake the false god Ea and turn to Yah; as a matter of fact Konaryah took it upon himself to change the very law of Yah so that Afalo and other followers of evil spirits would be allowed to live in the city. Konaryah even allowed the servants of demons to build shrines to their false gods where they could bow down to graven images. It was only when Afalo was to marry Astaris and become the Chancellor of the High Kingdom of East Threthoron that the High King made an attempt to persuade the son of Seuso to adopt the appearance of a believer.

"I believe that my father's crimes far eclipse those of Kenan, who allowed mercy to spare his grandson's life. Konaryah's edict allowed many who have abandoned the worship of the true God to take up residence in our city. Remember the warnings of the prophet Enoch who prophesied against Afalo and spoke of what would happen if we continued to neglect the law of Yah. I call on the High King to remove himself from office and relinquish his crown and title so that Lhiosquor will continue to be great."

At this, the High King rose from his seat in anger. "I have heard enough of your charges against me, insolent boy. Does the law of Yah not also command children to honour their parents? Yet, here you stand, proclaiming obedience to the law while you break the law by dishonouring me! I will remain king for as long as I live. I will not allow your political manoeuvring to divide my kingdom! I will have you executed and your body thrown to the eater lizards before I would give you even half of my kingdom."

Ayrus smiled placidly, "You have already given me more than that, father. You cannot have me executed; your armies answer to me. Don't you remember that I am the General of the armies of East Threthoron? I don't need you to remove yourself from office. I have given you the chance to resign gracefully, but now you leave me no other option." At the wave of Ayrus' hand, a guard standing at the council doorway entered, followed by a company of fifty soldiers. The soldiers seized Konaryah, Tarcheng, and Afalo as well as any others loyal to the High King who resisted, and escorted them to the dungeon under the High King's palace. Onlookers gathered outside the Royal Hall of Council on the Avenue of Justice were astonished to see their monarch and several of his closest advisors led away in chains. The people in the street began to panic, until Ayrus stepped outside the doors of the Royal Hall and raised his arms, motioning for everyone to be silent.

"Citizens of Lhiosquor, I beseech you not to be afraid. My father, the High King Konaryah, has transgressed the holy law of Yah passed on to us centuries ago. Not only did he allow unbelievers into our city, he even appointed Afalo the son of Seuso as his chief advisor. As your new High King, I promise to be faithful to the law of Yah and I will begin with the execution of Afalo the traitor in seven days. Lhiosquor will return to its former glory, and we shall march out against our enemies who creep ever closer to us. The City of Light will once again be the greatest city on the face of the earth, and our dominion shall encompass all nations!"

There were great shouts and applause when Prince Ayrus had completed his speech. When the noise died down, he dispersed the crowd and returned to the Royal Hall. Sumiseno, the servant of Prince Hebystos, had been among the people in the crowd. He went to Afalo's cell that very night and, as before, took a mixture of herbs to Afalo who was imprisoned in the same cell as Konaryah.

"Your Majesty, Chancellor, I have come to release you. Eat these herbs and you shall escape the dungeon."

Afalo turned to Konaryah. "This is the servant of your loyal son, Prince Hebystos, who helped me to escape before. He gave me these herbs, I ate them, and fell into such a deep sleep that the guards believed me to be dead. I was revived later at the western shrine once the guards had carried me out for burial. Sadly, there is but enough of this mixture for one person, and Lhiosquor needs you, o king. I beg you to eat these herbs and free yourself."

Konaryah thought deeply. "Thank you, my true friend. When I am free, I will make Hebystos my heir, and Ayrus will rot here in your place." Konaryah ate the herbs. They tasted bitter, rancid, but he swallowed them. Then he felt as if a fire had been lit in his stomach. He wanted to vomit up the herbs, but he could not.

Afalo and Sumiseno watched the former High King intently. Afalo then knelt beside Konaryah and whispered in his ear. "I knew that you would never name me as heir, so intent you were to place your own issue on the throne, cripple or not. I woke up from the herbs which Sumiseno gave me, but these herbs are different. You will not wake up from this sleep, but you will go to your grave. I will escape and wrest Lhiosquor from the hand of Ayrus, the hypocrite. I will have the honour due me as the son of a king. Farewell, great High King Konaryah."

Konaryah's eyes went wide. "What I did, I did for the good of Lhiosquor. Had I known you were ... a traitor ... I would have..." The former High King of East Threthoron collapsed dead on the dungeon floor. Sumiseno stood emotionless, and Afalo leaned against the dungeon wall with a faint smile on his face.

"You would have done nothing, old fool." he said. Afalo turned to Sumiseno. "You did well, my servant, and you will be rewarded. Now go, and make sure that the guards see you, but do not capture you." Sumiseno turned and left. As he went out the final set of double doors at the rear palace gate, he turned and looked in the face of one of the guards. Then he fled the city with unnatural speed.

Every night, the guards of the dungeon brought meals to the prisoners. Konaryah had eaten his heartily, as was his habit when he was distressed. Conversely, Afalo had eaten barely any of his meagre meal, as was also his habit when he was anxious. After Sumiseno had left the dungeon, Afalo inhaled the juice of an onion left over from his supper until the odour brought him to tears. He cried aloud, "Konaryah is dead! The High King is dead! Someone please come and see to his body!" Four guards in full plate armour came rushing to the cell. They eyed Afalo suspiciously.

"What happened, condemned one?" the guard in front asked, gruffly.

"Someone poisoned his food." said Afalo, feigning tears. "The High King ate his supper first, as he was distressed, and collapsed on the dungeon floor. I then tasted mine and knew that it had been poisoned, but I was too late. Please go and get linen for the body that it may be wrapped and prepared for burial."

The guards departed immediately, the gruff spoken one now behind the others. He glared at Afalo as he locked the cell door. "If you have killed the High King, you will face a worse judgement then the one you face now when you stand before Yah."

Later that evening, another guard returned with linen for the High King's body. "The embalmers will be here shortly. Rest and allow them to do their work unimpeded." The guard departed, locking the door behind him. When he had gone, Afalo quickly disrobed, removed the clothes from Konaryah's body, and clothed himself in the dead king's garments. Placing his own clothes on Konaryah's body, he carefully lifted it onto his own cot. Afalo then wrapped himself as carefully as he could in the linen cloths and lay perfectly still. After what may have been an hour, three embalmers came to prepare the body. They saw what they believed to be Afalo lying face down in the cot, and what they believed to be the High King wrapped in linen.

One of the embalmers turned to the other two. "It looks like the old snake wrapped the old High King himself. He did a messy job, not knowing anything about wrapping a body, but I guess it showed that he really did care for old Konaryah." The other two embalmers looked at each other blankly and said nothing, but picked up the body.

"Ugh, he's heavy!" complained the second embalmer. "He must have had quite a feast before they locked him up here!"

"Well, let's carry him out of here and get to work before he's too stiff to work with." said the third.

As soon as the embalmers had carried Afalo past the dungeon doors, he rolled out of the linen cloths and fled. Astonished, the embalmers cried out, but Afalo had already run too far and too fast for the palace guards to catch him. He fled Lhiosquor and hid in a dark and secret place where he planned his next move.

# CHAPTER 17

# JOURNEY TO UNUK
## (443 – 449 EC)

### 443 EC

Enoch and Mattu-Seth travelled to many cities in the years following their first appearance at Lhiosquor, bringing Yah's messages to each city. Some accepted their message and turned back to Yah, but most rejected them. Enoch and Mattu-Seth were often driven out of the cities that they visited, and they spent most of their time fleeing from one city to the next. On the seventh day of the third month in the year 443 of the Enosian Calendar, Enoch, Mattu-Seth, and their disciples were returning by ship from the far western city of Thyraquor on the northern bank of the Rahav. They stopped at the port of Yahbarinnos, which had begun as a merchant's village long ago. After the founding of Ahfeneyah, the Wise of West Threthoron built this fortress city which was situated across the wide Rahav River from the mouth of the Kapis River. The Nahla-Kapis river system and basin had all come under the dominion of Hurash, and General Mahalalel had rebuilt the harbour of Yahbarinnos into a naval base.

As Enoch's ship approached his grandfather's riverside fortress, he saw the Armada of West Threthoron returning to Yahbarinnos. Judging by the damaged condition of some of the frigates, Enoch surmised that the armada had returned from a fierce battle. Enoch hoisted the banner of Ahfeneyah, a white mastodon standing on a green mountain with a sky blue field behind, to the top of the main mast. The harbourmaster removed the chain that barred entrance to the harbour of Yahbarinnos, and the frigates of the Armada entered. Enoch's ship, the Eaglet, followed behind and sailed into the harbour. Enoch and Mattu-Seth had visited Yahbarinnos before on their journey westward, and their message had been well received by all. The harbourmaster recognized the <u>Eaglet</u>, and allowed them to dock in the harbour. Some of Enoch's disciples who had accompanied him leapt onto the dock to secure the ropes.

As Enoch stepped onto the dock, he saw his uncle Yahpettu, General Mahalalel's second son and admiral of the armada; disembark from his flagship, <u>The Sword of Truth</u>. Admiral Yahpettu was surrounded by advisors and commanders as he descended the ramp from his frigate. Yahpettu's glance rested on Enoch, and he motioned for his nephew to approach. Enoch made his way to where Admiral Yahpettu was standing, surrounded by his retinue.

"Come here, Enoch. There is something that you should be aware of."

Enoch wondered what his uncle was concerned about. "It is good to see you, uncle." he said. "What news do you have?"

Yahpettu looked straight at his nephew. "We have recently repelled an attack by the Nephilim against the region of Turvah. The enemy frigates had somehow slipped past us here at Yahbarinnos, but when we received word of them, we pursued them as fast as we could. We managed to defeat the Nephilim fleet, but at great cost. We were unprepared for the sorceries of Mahawai, a new Nephilim commander under Hurash. He seemed more of a magician or priest than a general or admiral, but those under his command followed him with zealous devotion. Mahawai hurled fire from his hands without the aid of a musket, called down lightning from the sky, and caused great winds to arise that capsized some of our ships. He calls on Hraw, Hishirash, and Ichsha, all the gods of the Nephilim, to help him defeat the followers of Yah.

"If we had not prayed to Yah to save us at that time, I fear that the sorcerer would have prevailed and destroyed all of us. After we prayed, God caused all of the sorcery of Mahawai to turn against the Nephilim while our ships were spared. Mahawai was both enraged and terrified to see his own curses coming back on himself, and he retreated swiftly. I believe that Mahawai caused a great fog to surround the enemy ships in order to pass by us to come to Turvah, just as he did when he cowardly retreated.

"Enoch, the Nephilim grow in strength, and we must strengthen our defences against Mahawai. I beseech you to pray to Yah, you and your disciples, for revelation as to how to overcome this new threat. I know that all of the faithful in Ahfeneyah and the regions under the dominion of our city will be praying as well. Will you intercede for us so that we will not be destroyed?"

Enoch's countenance became grave at the threat of this new menace, but he seemed to relax somewhat as he prayed silently to Yah. "The hand of Yah is stronger than any sorcery or any spirits from Lucifer. Even when victory appears impossible and all hope vanishes, He will prevail and rescue us with His mighty right hand. Even if all the other cities of the world fall under the shadow of the Nephilim, Ahfeneyah will not be captured. The City of the Wise will shine the brightest in the dark night like a gleaming star. Do not fear Mahawai; though his powers may seem great, his power has been stolen. All sorcery is stolen power. Mahawai can do nothing unless Yah permits it, as Yah controls everything that takes place upon the earth.

"Yah is sovereign. He allows man whom He created to make his own errors, and man must live with the consequences of his sin, however severe. Even still, the grace of Yah is never entirely removed from the earth, nor has He turned His face away from all that He has made, for He has compassion on all. Though we may have trials and suffer greatly, He will never give us more than we can bear if we seek Him and pray to Him."

Yahpettu stood amazed at the teaching of his nephew. "Enoch, I can truly hear the voice of Yah speaking through you. I ask that you would please go and return to cities that received you in the past and comfort them with this message that their faith may increase. As darkness continues to fall across the earth, those who believe in Yah must stand firm. Seth has said that a day of evil will come and we will need to do everything we can to stand."

"What the Patriarch says is true. Let us each continue to do what we have been called to do, uncle. As for me, I will pray regarding what you have told me, and try to bring comfort where I can."

"Thank you, Enoch." said Yahpettu. One of his advisors then laid a hand on the admiral's shoulder to tell him that he was needed elsewhere. Yahpettu embraced his nephew. "May the spirit of Yah go with you and protect you, Enoch. Be at peace."

Enoch nodded to his uncle and replied "Be at peace, Admiral." Then the admiral and his retinue left toward the inner fortress of the city. Enoch, Mattu-Seth, and their disciples remained for a fortnight before continuing on their journey.

## 449 EC

In the year 449, Enoch and his disciples travelled to Arattu, the city of Enokk once known as Turnienquor. Arattu had recently declared itself independent from East Threthoron, and now governed its own affairs. Enokk the firstborn son of Cain had a good relationship with Kenan, a testy but functional alliance with Konaryah, but had no tolerance for the new High King, Ayrus. Ayrus only saw Arattu as a buffer between himself and the Nephilim, and he cared nothing at all for the people of Arattu. He was so obsessed with tracking down Afalo and destroying him, that he wanted nothing to do with Enokk, and even suspected that the king of Arattu was sheltering the fugitive son of Seuso.

When Enoch and Mattu-Seth came to declare the message that was given to them from Yah, the people of Enokk jeered at them. "Yah has not helped us. Yah is Ayrus' god, and what has Ayrus done but accuse us? Ellil and Ana will save us. They are our gods. Be gone from here."

Enoch went to the entrance to Enokk's palace despite the angry crowds. "Before I leave, I have a message for Queen Neema."

The guard at the palace gate stood firm, his face set as stone. "You cannot pass here. What you would say to the Queen, say to me, and I will deliver your message."

"Neema, your father, Adam, misses you very much and prays that you are well. He hopes to see you again before the time comes when he will to journey to the place of the dead." Enoch turned and walked away from the palace gate. As he did so, six men seized Sinsil, one of Enoch's disciples, and began to beat him. Enoch prayed, and the men fell to the ground unconscious. His face and clothes seemed to brighten as the power of Yah moved in him.

"Hear the word of Yah!" he shouted. The people became silent and still with fear. "In the past, I delivered you from the hand of your enemies, and I protected you. Now, because of the way that you have treated My servants, your city will fall to the Nephilim after five years have passed. Because you would not listen, Arattu will fall under the dominion of the abominable ones. My hand is removed from you, and I abandon you to your fate." At that, Enoch and his disciples left Enokk and headed south over the Seven Mountain Ranges toward the cities of Shinar.

At length, Enoch, Mattu-Seth, and their disciples came to Unuk, where Enoch's family lived. The gatekeeper recognized Enoch and allowed the travellers to enter the city. As the large, iron doors of the northern gate were drawn open, the gatekeeper shouted through his window: "Thank you for these walls, Enoch. They have done well to keep out all who are not welcome here."

"I pray that they would continue to do so." Enoch replied.

The gatekeeper continues, "The enemy draws ever closer to our borders. Some days, we can see Giants and their armies moving in the distance, when we through the looking glasses that your father provided to the city. Still, be at peace, son of Yared." At that, Enoch and the others entered the city. The first new building that Enoch noticed as he entered Unuk was the new temple to the goddess Ana. It was a huge structure of several levels, each level smaller than the one below it. The levels were connected by four ramps, one on each of the temple's four square sides, two of which led to the small, square, topmost level. The entire structure was overlaid in gold and lapis lazuli. Enoch was grieved that Ana's temple seemed grander than the one he had built for Yah, and he wondered if he would ever have time to build a better one now that he had become a travelling prophet.

Turning away from that sight, Enoch led his disciples to his parents' house in the western part of the city. Along the way, they passed by the temple of Yah, a miniature replica of its illustrious predecessor. The temple appeared less used than Ana's, but there were always priests there to minister before the Almighty One. Yared was praying in the temple when he looked up to see his eldest son approaching. His face went wide with wonder and joy.

"The tales about you are true, my son. You have become Yah's prophet to all people. We have heard of some of your journeys in distant lands. What brings you back to Unuk?"

Enoch stepped forward and embraced his father. "I have not been to Unuk in all of my travels until now, as I go only where I feel the Spirit of Yah leading me. I have not been home in over thirty years since I left to attend the University in Ahfeneyah. There are many new cities in the northwest, west of the Great Plains of Jabal and north of the Rahav, where the herds of great horned armoured lizards roam. My travels will soon take me there, but first I must convince the cities of Shinar to unite against the Nephilim. Our enemies grow stronger as there is now a powerful sorcerer among them. The new High King of East Threthoron, Ayrus, is too busy hunting down Afalo son of Seuso to lead a force against Hahyah or Ohyah. King Enokk of Arattu has rejected my message, so our hope on the eastern front now lies in the hands of the kings of Shinar."

Yared's face looked grave. "What of the West? Are the Wise able to hold off the enemy?"

"The Nephilim have so far been unable to establish any foothold on the northern bank of the Rahav. Although we have not been able to gain any ground against them, we have been able to contain them. Pray that we may continue to do so, father. The new settlements being built constantly in the region north and west of Thyraquor require soldiers to defend them. The colonization of the northwest spreads our forces thinner each year. I do not know how much longer we can contain the Nephilim."

"I will arrange an audience for you with the king, my son" said Yared. "He is greatly concerned about Hahyah's forces across the plain in Badtibira, but Unuk does not have enough forces of its own to defend the city. It is only a matter of time before Hahyah attacks unless Unuk attacks first; a battle Unuk would surely lose."

A girl who looked like a younger, darker-haired image of Lilara, Enoch's grandmother, approached. She tugged on Yared's sleeves and asked him, "Is this my brother Enoch of whom you have told me?"

"Yes, Honaya, this is your brother." Yared turned to Enoch. "Enoch, this is your younger sister, Honaya, who was born to us sixteen years ago. She has listened intently to Niul as he has told her about your travels."

"I wish to go with you, brother. I want to travel to faraway lands and meet interesting people and see strange things. Can you take me with you?" Yared stood behind Honaya and shook his head worriedly.

"I and those who travel with me are in constant danger, Honaya. If you were to come with me, I could not guarantee your safety. You must remain here in Unuk for your own good".

Honaya sulked, "I can take care of myself!" she said, kicking the dirt before turning and going back to the house.

Yared smiled. "Your sister's heart is good and she is devoted to Yah, but she is also very strong of will." Yared paused before continuing. "Well, I had better get to the palace and tell Unuk what you have told me. Hopefully he will meet with you tomorrow."

Yared departed toward the palace, and Enoch went toward the house. Mattu-Seth and the other disciples followed him. Medgariva was changing flowers in a vase when she saw them. When she saw Mattu-Seth, she dropped the vase to the floor where it shattered into a thousand pieces. She walked slowly toward him as he approached the house. "It is you, isn't it, Mattu-Seth?"

The young man nodded slowly, unsure of how to react. "Yes, I am Mattu-Seth. Are you my grandmother, Medgariva?"

"Yes, I am. The last time I saw you, you were a mere infant. Now you are a grown man, and a great help to your half-uncle Enoch, from what I hear."

Mattu-Seth continued to stare quizzically at his grandmother, as if trying to find some distant memory of her. "That would explain why I cannot remember you. I have heard great stories about your travels, but my earliest memories were of living among the Jabalite nomads where your parents raised me as their own. Many Jabalites have since settled along the Bolkash in the far north where there is good land, but most still wander farther and farther from the lands of other tribes as new cities are built."

Medgariva turned to Enoch and embraced her son. "It is good to have you home, my son. It has been so long since I last saw you. I hope that you will not depart too quickly, but I know that you are called to a life of bringing the message of Yah to all people. For now, please come in and visit with your family, you and all your disciples. Your brothers and sisters and I would love to hear your tales first hand."

Everyone went inside into the common room of the house, where they reclined on large cushions arranged in a circular formation on the floor. Enoch told his family of his travels, beginning with his journey to Siaghlamh. Everyone listened with rapt attention as he described his appearance before Konaryah, then High King of Lhiosquor, and were astonished when he told them how the Spirit of Yah miraculously transported Mattu-Seth and himself away from Lhiosquor to Turvah before they could be apprehended by Konaryah's guards. The stories continued long into the evening, and Enoch was recounting his latest discussion with Admiral Yahpettu in Yahbarinnos when Yared came home.

"Enoch, I have finished speaking with Unuk, and he requests your presence immediately. We must go now, as he says the utmost haste is needed." Enoch said a brief farewell to his family, and accompanied his father to the royal palace of Unuk. Mattu-Seth joined them, but the other disciples remained at the house. Enoch's disciples numbered ten at this time: Mattu-Seth, Sinsil who was attacked in the city of Enokk, Garnan the cousin of Enoch, son of Enoch's uncle Soduryah (he was named after the Abbot Garnan), Anoria daughter of Unhir of Turvah, Temmuranda son of Ikarruella of Sippar, the brothers Mahalyah and Keneyah of Ahfeneyah, Teseria daughter of Quanahlon, a wealthy merchant of Thyraquor, and Yahban and Machik of Faoriquor.

Yared, Enoch, and Mattu-Seth were welcomed into the lavish palace of King Unuk by six lovely servant girls dressed in ornately woven gowns of red dyed linen and finery of gold and lapis lazuli. At the sight of the tall, fair-skinned, red-haired Yared, the servant girls giggled flirtatiously. They ushered the men forward into Unuk's throne room where he sat upon a throne embossed with jasper, chalcedony, and lapis lazuli. His eldest son and heir, Larak, stood at the king's right hand.

"Welcome to our palace, Yared the Wise, and welcome home, Enoch son of Yared. Your companion is also welcome here."

"We are honoured to be invited here, King Unuk." said Enoch, nodding deeply so that his chin touched his chest.

Unuk addressed them again. "Enoch, your father has told me everything that you have told him. I believe that it is the will of Ellil and Ana that the cities of the tribes of my grandfather, Irad, unite against the forces of the Nephilim. We are constantly reminded of their presence on our eastern horizon, and none of the scouts I have sent to determine their strength have returned. I am placing my son, Larak, in charge of the forces of my city, with orders to raise a great army. It is my hope that my uncle, Alulim, as well as the kings of the cities of Sippar, Shuruppak, Dilumu, and the smaller cities of Shinar will join us in this effort. I will send word to them immediately, and let us hope that the sons of Irad can hold off the Nephilim in the east as the sons of Seth in Ahfeneyah have managed to do in the west."

When Unuk had finished, Enoch addressed the king. "My kinsmen in West Threthoron will be thankful for any help that you can give in ridding the earth of the Giants. It is my fervent prayer to Yah that as Irad and Kenan combined their might to drive away the Giants in ancient times our peoples shall likewise labour together to free the world from the menace of the Nephilim."

After a feast with the king, his three wives, and his grown sons, Yared, Enoch, and Mattu-Seth returned to the house of Yared and retired for the night. That night, Enoch had a dream. In that dream, he saw the ruins of the temple on Mt. Tsayun. He saw the people of Tsayun enslaved and ruled over by a Nephilim sorceress who appeared to have the same bearing of power as Mahawai. In the dream, he wandered the streets of Yarku, now a city of slaves. A Tsayuni slave girl with long, black hair and piercing, black, sorrowful eyes saw him and approached him. She entreated with Enoch to come to her.

"Prophet of Yah, please come quickly to us and free the children of Tsayun from the hand of the sorceress Naphtassa. We labour and die under the hand of cruel taskmasters, and we pray daily to Yah for deliverance. Each one of us is a faithful servant of Yah, but we are not permitted to worship Him or utter His name." The girl walked closer and closer to Enoch as she spoke. She held his eyes with her penetrating, woeful gaze.

"The Nephilim have killed many who refused to worship Hraw, Hishirash, and Ichsha, the gods of the Nephilim. Please deliver us." When she spoke the last words, all that Enoch could see was the forlorn face of the slave girl, eyes wet with tears. He awoke with a start, surprised to find himself still in his father's house.

The sky was beginning to lighten in the east as Enoch looked through the window. The last words of the Tsayuni slave girl echoed in his mind. He knew that he must go to Yarku and demand that this Naphtassa release the people of Tsayun. He woke his disciples and his family, and told them that he was departing northwest. Enoch and Mattu-Seth bade farewell to Yared, Medgariva, and Enoch's brothers and sisters.

"Where is Honaya?" Enoch asked, "She was so eager to join me that I had expected one more attempt to persuade me to take her with us, but she did not even come to say goodbye."

Medgariva looked toward the house. "Honaya has probably gone off to the market early, before anyone else, to buy goods before the crowds arrive. She is averse to large numbers of people in tight spaces, and often leaves for the market early in the morning while the rest of the city sleeps".

Enoch gave no more thought to his sister, and departed with his disciples from his parents' house. At the gates of the city, they encountered a veiled merchant outfitting a runner lizard for travel. The merchant's unseen gaze followed Enoch as the prophet and his disciples climbed the ladder onto the back of a thunder lizard provided by King Unuk. A pavilion was tied onto the back of the gigantic beast large enough to provide shade for all eleven of the travellers. Thunder lizards were never in a hurry to get anywhere, but because of their vast size, the creatures walked in great strides and made good time.

After a few days they came to Shuruppak and stayed in that town for a night, allowing their beast of burden to drink from the Euphrates. In the morning, Mattu-Seth saw the veiled merchant from Unuk in the marketplace. He noticed that the merchant was watching him, turning away whenever Mattu-Seth caught him. He thought about confronting the mysterious merchant, but decided against it on the fact that Enoch and the other disciples were preparing to leave for the new city of Kish; the next stop along the Iradu Road. The Iradu Road followed the Euphrates from the city of Iradu at the river's mouth, up through the cities of Unuk, Shuruppak, Kish, and Sippar, all the way to where the Euphrates flowed from the Rahav. At that point, it met the Pilgrim's Road that led toward Tsayalam in the southwest and Turvah in the east. The Iradu Road avoided the Seven Mountain Ranges in the north, and was thus a much safer route to the Northern Kingdoms, but the Pilgrim's Road was no longer what it once was. One didn't need to travel far west along the Pilgrim's Road from the crossroads before coming to the immense, foreboding Nephilim fortress of Shiqar. Shiqar stood to guard the way into Hurash's empire from any who might dare to intrude.

Mattu-Seth did not see the mysterious merchant at Kish, but after reaching the city of Sippar, he saw the veiled stranger again, selling fruit in the marketplace. That was when he knew that he and those with him were being followed. He sought out Enoch, who was debating with some of the philosophers of that city over whether Yah or Ellil was the true God. As Enoch was speaking, he saw his half-nephew approach.

"Mattu-Seth, why are you in distress? You appear as if the peace of Yah has lifted from you."

Mattu-Seth was out of breath from running from the marketplace to Sippar's Court of the Philosophers. "Uncle Enoch, we have been followed. A merchant has been following us since we left Unuk. I saw him in Shuruppak, and again just now in the marketplace. I believe that the Nephilim have sent him in order to keep track of our movements."

Enoch thought for a moment, his face changing from deep thought and concern to a faint, placid smile. "Do not worry, Mattu-Seth. That merchant will not do us any harm. All things are part of Yah's great plan, as you shall see." And Enoch continued his debate.

Mattu-Seth wondered what Enoch meant by these words, but he kept watch for the stranger for weeks as the company of prophets journeyed northward and westward up the Euphrates River along the Iradu Road. Finally, one late afternoon, after travelling for two weeks along the River Euphrates, the Iradu Road came to an end at the Pilgrim's Road. When Anoria, who steered the thunder lizard, attempted to turn the mighty beast leftward toward the southwest, the behemoth sat at the crossroads and refused to move for four hours. Finally, she realized that the beast had stopped out of the fear of the Giants' realm and intended to go no further. The company of prophets then disembarked, determined to continue their journey by foot. The huge beast, free of its burden, stomped away eastward into the foothills of the Duobinar Mountains as quickly as its vast bulk would allow it.

Enoch led his disciples along the Pilgrim's Road, but before long, Mattu-Seth could see the menacing basalt towers of Shiqar rising against the last, dying rays of daylight, as if the black stone spires were reaching up to cover the sunlight that pierced through the Curtain of Heaven. The black walls of Shiqar measured an astonishing forty cubits in height, and the towers measured an additional thirty cubits from the top of the wall. The gate of Shiqar rose half the height of the wall and was set with two imposing doors of reddish wood. In front of these doors, sharpened iron stakes protruded from the stone at the base as well as from the gateway arch. They were each about twelve cubits in length, and they overlapped in the middle like the maw of a devouring monster. Engraved in the great arch of the gateway was an inscription which written both in Enosian and Tawthic, the script of the Nephilim:

LEGENDS OF LHIOSQUOR

The words, in both scripts, read the same as there was but one spoken language in those days. The Nephilim scribe, Tawth, had devised a different alphabet because of the Nephilim hatred of Sethites, Yah's chosen people, and to confuse anyone not knowledgeable of the new script who tried to read it. To create further difficulty, Tawthic script ran left to right, counter to Enosian script which ran right to left. This reflected Hurash's emphasis of the left side of a thing being superior to the right.

My apologies to the reader; I have digressed from the meaning of the inscription. For those who cannot read the Enosian letters and the Ancient Tongue, the inscription reads thus: "This is the fortress of Commander Shiqar, the left hand of General Mahawai. To all outsiders who enter here, prepare your bodies to be devoured and your souls for oblivion."

Now the fortress of Shiqar was set strategically in a place where the Pilgrim's Road passed between two mountains, in order to prevent any trespassers from entering the territory of the Nephilim along that road. As Mattu-Seth turned his gaze from the imposing structure before him, he thought he could make out the shape of a veiled figure almost hidden in the late afternoon shadows, keeping watch.

The mysterious merchant was not the only one watching the prophet and his disciples approach. Helmeted guards armed with muskets filled the tops of the towers, the sunlight gleaming against the hard steel they wore.

"Halt in the name of Hurash the Exalted and the Governess Naphtassa!" boomed an unseen Nephilim guard. "Return the way from which you came, or you will be put to death."

Enoch was wearing his hooded robe, so as not to draw camp followers from the countryside through which he and his disciples had passed. It seemed that wherever Enoch went, people were drawn to him from only Yah knows where to be ministered to, but now was a time of danger and Enoch did not want to endanger anyone who would attempt to follow his company into the lands of the Nephilim. However, he now removed his hood and addressed the guards. As he spoke, the glory of Yah filled him, and he shone as if he were a mirror reflecting the light of the sun into the faces of the guards. The guards squinted as their eyes adjusted to the light. "I come in the name of Yah, the Almighty Creator. Tell Naphtassa that the day is coming when the Nephilim shall again be destroyed and neither a trace nor a memory will remain of this fortress."

After he spoke, the bright light around Enoch faded, and the great iron teeth of the fortress withdrew into hidden cavities in the gateway arch and the stone beneath. The enormous red doors opened slowly as fully armoured guards wearing black-plumed crested helmets and mounted on flesh-eating speed lizards emerged from hidden doors within the walls of the fortress. Before Enoch or his disciples could do anything, the guards and their dreadful steeds surrounded them. Enoch and his disciples had no choice but to enter Shiqar in the custody of the enemy guards. They walked slowly in the centre of the circle of guards toward the towering stone gate of Shiqar. Hard, calloused hands grabbed their wrists and tied them together with rough-hewn rope.

As they passed under the great arch of the gateway, one of Enoch's disciples read the inscription engraved upon the archway of the gate of Shiqar and cried out in dismay. Enoch admonished him to be strong and to remember the purpose to which they had been called. He knew that they would not die, even as the foreboding doors of Shiqar closed behind them in the final rays of sunlight. Enoch's greatest adventures were still yet to come.

# EPILOGUE

Princess Astaris looked down from the top of the Tower of Might, the tower of the keep of Prince Afalo's palace. From her vantage point, she could see the entirety of Chintapiquor, the new fortress-city of her husband and captor. She could see the harbour of Karbolkash where Afalo's great battle frigates were sheltered. On the same day when Enoch and his companions were taken into Shiqar, Astaris stood and watched the last muted rays of sunlight dance on the western horizon upon the waters of the Sea of Arattu. She spent an inordinate amount of time in her private chamber at the top of the tower of late; sometimes by her own choice to escape her husband's madness, sometimes against her will when her husband was wroth with her. This time it was the latter. Ayrus had found Afalo's city and was coming to destroy him and rescue his sister.

Astaris longed to see her brother once again. She remembered her last day in the royal city of Lhiosquor when she received a letter bearing Ayrus' signature to meet him and his family for a day of relaxation and leisure in the Park of Victory, just outside the Ruwad district of Faoriquor. Faoriquor is the ring city that formed around the base of Mt. Threthor when the settlements surrounding the mountain, Ruwad, Cerchil, and the others, grew together into one city. The letter was written in her brother's style and had what appeared to be his seal on it, but when she arrived in the Park of Victory she was apprehended by two large and very strong servants of Afalo.

This happened in the year 434, three years after Astaris' father, the High King Konaryah, was slain by Afalo. Astaris had been blindfolded and placed in a carriage where a familiar voice spoke to her.

"We are together at last, my love." the traitor had said.

"My brother will hunt you down and destroy you, Afalo. He will not rest until he finds you."

"I know, but he will not find me easily. When he does, I will be ready for him."

Astaris realized that she was nothing more than bait to draw King Ayrus away from Lhiosquor into a trap. What kind of trap, she did not know, but she knew that she had to do everything in her power to discover this plan and get word to her brother. Afalo was a traitor, and so suspicious himself of treachery, but he had one weakness – his obsessive desire for Astaris. Astaris used this weakness to her advantage and, after living in Afalo's palace under guard for some time, she gradually became more co-operative with her captor. In return, Afalo gave Astaris more and more freedom in the fortress-city that he was building, although it was understood that she could never leave.

One day, Afalo offered to make Astaris his queen. She would have her own servants and as much of anything that she wanted. Astaris loathed Afalo, but becoming queen would help her to carry out her plan, and Astaris also – having being born into royalty – had a desire for power. Afalo and Astaris knew each other's weaknesses, and both used the arrangement against the other. Astaris sent letters through her servants to Lhiosquor, and received letters in return from the City of Light. Afalo's guards somehow never seemed to intercept any of the correspondence. A half a year ago, Astaris managed to get Afalo intoxicated with wine, and in his stupor he blurted out the location of Chintapiquor. Astaris immediately sent a letter to Ayrus, but this time the reply was intercepted. It was for this that Astaris was locked away in the Tower of Might.

On this evening during the 449th year of the Enosian Calendar, Astaris sat in the tower and watched the close of the day. As was her custom whenever she spent the night in the Tower, she lit a candle in the tower's westward facing window. As soon as she did so, she saw another light far off on the western horizon where the sun had just set. It shone for a moment and was gone. Astaris watched carefully as a contingent of Afalo's battle frigates hoisted their sails and left the shelter of Karbolkash. There was only one reason for warships to leave the harbour at night; Ayrus had come.

The light on the horizon was his signal to Astaris that he was coming. Apparently, the signal had not escaped Afalo's notice. Ayrus had chosen to attack Afalo by sea, sending his own battle frigates to attack those of his enemy. Afalo was more than prepared to defend his harbour and his fortress. As the sky darkened, Astaris began to see bursts of orange reflected from the clouds and the water of the sea. She could hear the distant boom of cannon fire as the two fleets fought one another. The naval battle raged for an untold number of hours, then sometime in the middle of the night, the flashes of cannon fire against the black sky ceased and the guns fell silent. Ayrus had lost, and retreated back across the Sea of Arattu. Princess Astaris would not be rescued tonight. In the dark hour of midnight, she wept piteously at her lost chance of freedom and made a vow to never rest until justice was hers.

Here ends the fifth scroll of the history of Lhiosquor. The City of Light did not reach the purpose for which the Creator had intended her. She became a pale reflection of her former glory, and the nobility of her sons was less than that of her fathers. Her doom had been foreseen by the prophet Enoch, but the tale of the fall of Lhiosquor will be told another time. There is also much more to be told about my great-grandfather, the blessed prophet Enoch; nevertheless the task of building a new world has fallen to me and my family. I, Noah, the son of Lamech, the son of Methuselah, the son of the prophet Enoch, will continue these accounts at a future time. It is my prayer that all who read these scrolls will take to heart the lessons learned through the history of our ancestors and seek to glorify Almighty God rather than themselves. May you build on the foundation of Yah and pray earnestly for the coming of the Blessed One who will undo the curse that drove humanity from Eden.

# Chronology of Major Events in After Eden – Book I

**40 AM** – The story begins with the exile of Cain.

**57 AM** – Enokk son of Cain journeys to the tents of Adam.

**130 AM** – Seth son of Adam and Lamekk son of Mathtu-Saol are born.

**170 AM** – Lamekk exiled from the city of Enokk.

**188 AM** – Hishirash, First of the Giants, is born.

**230 AM / 1 EC** – Cain is killed by Lamekk who takes over the city of Enokk (hence Turnienquor) in the first war. Seth marries Azura and they found the great city of Lhiosquor. This event marks the beginning of the Enosian calendar.

**6 EC**- Enos son of Seth is born.

**96 EC** – Kenan son of Enos is born.

**136 EC** – Kenan receives the Law of Yah.

**165 EC** – The Temple of Yah is dedicated on Mt. Tsayun.

**166 EC** – Mahalalel, eldest son of Kenan, is born.

**185 EC** – Konaryah, second son of Kenan, is born. Yah defeats the armies of the Giants at Mt. Threthor.

**196 EC** – Kenan is chosen as the first King of Lhiosquor. The allied forces of Lhiosquor and Arattu achieve victory at the Battle of Bariquor.

**201 EC** – Hishirash is defeated and the city of Enokk is liberated. Kenan is made High King of Threthoron and the surrounding kingdoms as they come under his protection.

**231 EC** – Yared son of Prince Mahalalel is born.

**238 EC** – Medgariva daughter of Madeg is born.

**281 EC** – Yared enters the Temple priesthood.

**288-292 EC** – Afalo and his companions circumnavigate the earth.

**290 EC** – Atalo takes Medgariva/Valiturnea as his bride and founds the Kingdom of Atalanti.

**299 EC** – The first of the Nephilim, the second generation of Giants, are born.

**339 EC** – The Nephilim take the Nahlonite city of Nubat and begin their empire.

**367 EC** – Ohyah's army comes against Tsayalam but is defeated.

**385 EC** – Having left Atalanti, Medgariva/Valiturnea journeys to Tsayalam and meets Yared once more.

**386 EC** – Yared marries Medgariva. High King Kenan secretly sends the couple away rather than execute them for mingling the bloodlines of Seth and Cain.

**393 EC** – Enoch son of Yared is born. Prince Konaryah learns of the High King sending away Yared and Medgariva. He forces Kenan to abdicate and becomes the second High King of Threthoron. Seth, Enos, Kenan, Garnan and several others are forced to depart and found the city of Ahfeneyah on Mt. Sentinel. The Kingdom of Threthoron is divided into east (Lhiosquor) and west (Ahfeneyah).

**400 EC** – Ohyah's forces capture Yarku and Tsayalam, destroying the Temple of Yah.

**423 EC** – Enoch is permitted entrance into Eden and receives the calling of a prophet.

**428 EC** – Enoch and Mattu-Seth appear in Lhiosquor and prophesy. Chancellor Afalo is imprisoned for the first time.

**431 EC** – High King Konaryah pardons Afalo. Prince Ayrus challenges his father, deposes him, and places Konaryah and Afalo together in the same cell. During his second imprisonment, Afalo kills Konaryah and escapes.

**434 EC** – Afalo kidnaps Princess Astaris, sister of High King Ayrus.

**449 EC** – Enoch prophecies to Enokk son of Cain and is rejected. High King Ayrus' attempt to take Chintapiquor – Afalo's fortress – by sea fails. Enoch receives a vision of Rehebeth praying for the deliverance of Yarku.

# APPENDIX B

# GLOSSARY OF PEOPLE AND PLACES

## PEOPLE – SETHITES:

**Afalo:** son of King Seuso of Susaron, twin brother of King Atalo of Atalanti. Afalo circumnavigated the globe and later became Chancellor to High King Konaryah. Afalo killed Konaryah and fled to the east. He also kidnapped the Princess Astaris, Konaryah's eldest daughter.

**Astaris:** eldest daughter of High King Konaryah and Queen Wolja, sister of High King Ayrus and Duke Hebystos. Astaris was captured by Afalo son of Seuso and forced to marry him.

**Atalo:** son of King Seuso of Susaron, twin brother of Prince Afalo. Atalo founded the kingdom of Atalanti on the distant island continent of the same name. He was the first husband of Medgariva / Valiturnea and fathered many sons and daughters. He was deposed by his son Ferdeo and sentenced to lifelong imprisonment.

**Ayrus:** third High King of Lhiosquor, son of High King Konaryah and Wolja. Ayrus was very handsome and charismatic, but also rather vain. Ayrus deposed his father for his oversight of the conduct of Chancellor Afalo. Ayrus disbanded the Royal Council and ruled as an absolute monarch. An austere, militaristic leader, Ayrus was at war with Afalo throughout his reign.

**Azura:** daughter of Adam and Eve, wife of Seth the Patriarch. Azura was one of the Fourteen Founders of Lhiosquor and held a seat in the Hall of Council in Lhiosquor, as well as a seat in the Council of the Wise in Ahfeneyah after the Wise left Lhiosquor.

**Enoch:** eldest son of the High Priest Yared and Medgariva of Uarga. The product of a forbidden mixed marriage, Enoch became the greatest prophet of the pre-Flood age. Enoch travelled throughout the civilized world with a message of repentance, exhorting people to turn to God and be saved from the dominion of the Nephilim.

**Enos:** eldest son of Seth and Azura. Enos was known for his great wisdom. He invented the Enosian alphabet and the Enosian Calendar, both of which were adopted throughout most of the civilized world due to the influence of Lhiosquor in its golden age. Enos also founded both the Enosian Academy in Lhiosquor and the University of Ahfeneyah.

**Garnan:** a companion of Afalo and Atalo on their voyage, Garnan settled in Atalanti where he founded a monastic order. Garnan and his monks accompanied Queen Valiturnea (Medgariva) on her voyage from Atalanti to Mt. Tsayun. He lived briefly in Lhiosquor where he married Yared and Medgariva/Valiturnea. Garnan was slain in secret by men loyal to Konaryah who set fire to his monastery.

**Hebystos:** Duke of Faoriquor, son of High King Konaryah and Queen Wolja, twin brother of High King Ayrus. Hebystos was crippled from childhood and deemed ineligible to inherit the Emerald Crown of Lhiosquor. He lacked his brother's physical beauty and oratory skills, but was extremely intelligent and shrewd, a master of diplomacy and espionage. It was the efforts of Hebystos that freed Chancellor Afalo from his first imprisonment and returned him to the favour of High King Konaryah.

**Hona:** daughter of Honos, one of the Fourteen Founders of Lhiosquor. Hona was the wife of Enos the Wise and the mother of High King Kenan.

**Honaya:** daughter of Yared and Medgariva, sister of the prophet Enoch. Honaya secretly followed her brother and his disciples to the Nephilim fortress of Shiqar.

**Kenan:** son of Enos the Wise and Honaya; first High King of Lhiosquor. It was Kenan who received God's law on Mt. Tsayun and ordered the construction of the Temple of Yah on the site. Under Kenan's kingship, Hishirash's Giants were defeated and the cities of Arattu were liberated. The rule of High King Kenan is considered to have been the golden age of Lhiosquor.

**Konaryah:** second son of High King Kenan and Muhalelet, second High King of Lhiosquor. He was deposed by his son, Prince Ayrus, and poisoned in prison by the traitor, Afalo son of Seuso.

**Lilara:** wife of General Mahalalel, mother of Yared. Lilara was known throughout the civilized world for her unrivalled beauty.

**Lognar:** a companion of Afalo and Atalo on their voyage to circumnavigate the earth.

**Magras:** the shipwright of Susaron, Magras settled in Atalanti.

**Mahalalel:** eldest son of High King Kenan and Muhalelet, general of the armies of Lhiosquor under his father's rule, general of the armies of Ahfeneyah thereafter.

**Muhalelet:** wife of High King Kenan, mother of Mahalalel and Konaryah.

**Seth:** third son of Adam and Eve, chief founder of Lhiosquor and Patriarch of the Wise at Ahfeneyah.

**Seuso:** friend and companion of General Konaryah of Lhiosquor. Seuso slew the Giantess Ichsha and founded the kingdom of Susaron.

**Soduryah:** a son of General Mahalalel and Lilara, younger brother of High Priest Yared and Admiral Yahpettu.

**Yahpettu:** second son of General Mahalalel and Lilara, admiral of the fleets of West Threthoron.

**Yared:** eldest son of General Mahalalel and Lilara. Yared joined the priesthood at Tsayun and later became High Priest. He made several important discoveries and inventions during this time and afterward. Yared resigned the priesthood to marry Medgariva of Uarga. Yared was banished from Lhiosquor for this forbidden union, and moved to the land of Shinar, where he continued his scientific endeavours.

## CAINITES:

**Adah:** first wife of Lamekk the Accursed, mother of Jabal and Jubal. Adah and her sons fled from Lamekk and were granted refuge on Mt. Threthor where they built the city of Shrivazh. She remained in Shrivazh until the early years of High King Kenan.

**Awan:** wife of Cain, daughter of Adam and Eve.

**Cain:** eldest son of Adam and Eve, founder and patriarch of the city of Enokk. Cain was slain by his descendant, Lamekk the Accursed who conquered Enokk.

**Enokk:** eldest son of Cain and Awan. Enokk was the only full-blooded Cainite ever to be allowed into the Great Forest. He escaped the conquest of the city of Enokk and later allied himself with Lhiosquor to retake his city. Enokk's kingdom became known as Arattu, and he was a vassal of Lhiosquor until the reign of High King Ayrus.

**Irad:** eldest son of Enokk and Neema, Irad escaped the conquest of the city of Enokk with his father, but set off toward the south across the Seven Mountain Ranges. Irad founded the city of Iradu in the plains of Shinar. He led the united armies of Shinar against the Nephilim, but was slain by Ohyah's forces.

**Jabal:** the shepherd, son of Lamekk the Accursed and Adah. Jabal sought refuge from his father on Mt. Threthor. When his people grew too numerous, he led them north to the Great Plains of Jabal beyond the River Gihon.

**Jubal:** the musician, son of Lamekk the Accursed and Adah. Jubal also sought refuge on Mt. Threthor until his people became too numerous. He left Mt. Threthor with his mother Adah and most of his people during the early years of High King Kenan.

**Kheruva:** daughter of Pocabal, the friend of General Mahalalel. Kheruva was the mother of Medgariva.

**Lamekk:** the Twice-Accursed, son of Mathtu-Saol. Lamekk was the first man to take more than one wife. Lamekk was banished from the city of Enokk for the murder of his brother-in-law, Machdal-Cain. He later raised an army of Giants, slew Cain, and conquered the city. Lamekk reigned in Enokk/Turnienquor until he was slain by his grandson, the Giant Hishirash, in a mutiny.

**Machdal-Cain:** son of Tophar-Cain and Rimlah, brother of Zillah. He was slain by Lamekk after being provoked into a fight.

**Mahu-Jaol:** eldest son of Irad and Eulla, father of Mathtu-Saol.

**Mathtu:** the Fisherman, fourth son of Cain and Awan. He was the first to break the law against eating meat. Mathtu built the first boats and founded the city of Mathtusekh.

**Mathtu-Saol:** son of Mahu-Jaol, father of Lamekk the Accursed.

**Medgariva/Valiturnea:** daughter of Madeg and Kheruva of Uarga, of the line of Nosjubal. First husband: Atalo son of Seuso. Second husband: Yared son of Mahalalel. When Yared entered the priesthood, Medgariva went on a journey to find the edge of the earth. She dwelt among the Harifa of the far eastern nation of Harifon who gave her the name Valiturnea. She then journeyed to Atalanti and settled there as Atalo's queen, but later fled Atalanti, returned to Yared and married him. Medgariva and Yared were banished from Lhiosquor due to their illegal union.

**Naamah:** daughter of Lamekk the Accursed and Zillah, wife and sister of Tubal-Cain. She became the mother of Hishirash and several other giants through the demon Hraw.

**Neema:** daughter of Adam and Eve, wife of Enokk son of Cain. Neema left Siaghlamh to marry Enokk and continue the line of Cain.

**Nehobal:** fifth son of Cain and Awan, he founded the city of Rethobal. Nehobal allied with the armies of Lhiosquor and his brother Enokk to overthrow the Giants and liberate the city of Enokk/Turnienquor.

**Nosjubal:** of the clan of Jubal. Nosjubal was a close friend of Kenan and even accompanied him for a stage of his journey in the year 136 EC. After most of the Jubalites left Mt. Threthor, Nosjubal remained behind and was appointed by the High King as governor of those Jubalites who had remained.

**Pocabal:** grandson of Nosjubal and childhood friend of Prince Mahalalel. Pocabal was accidentally slain by General Konaryah in the Battle of Turnienquor.

**Rimlah:** wife of Tophar-Cain, mother of Machdal-Cain and Zillah.

**Tophar-Cain:** father of Machdal-Cain and Zillah.

**Tubal-Cain:** son of Lamekk the Accursed and Zillah, brother and husband of Zillah. Tubal-Cain was the first to fashion weapons and other tools from bronze and iron. Tubal-Cain raised Hishirash and the other first-generation Giants as his own. Tubal-Cain founded the city of Badtibira in 214 EC.

**Unuk:** grandson of Irad, king of the city-state of Unuk. Unuk sought to unite the armies of the city-states of Shinar to combat the Nephilim threat.

**Zillah:** second wife of Lamekk the Accursed, Zillah was taken by force to be Lamekk's wife. She later became Lamekk's favourite wife.

## GIANTS/NEPHILIM:

**Gorgondish:** eldest son of Hishirash, chief of the Giants. After Hishirash's death at the Battle of Bariquor, Gorgondish briefly became master of Turnienquor until he was slain at the Battle of Turnienquor.

**Hahyah:** grandson of Hurash and brother of Ohyah. Hahyah was one of the three Nephilim generals. His capital is at Badtibira in the land of Shinar.

**Hishirash:** First of the Giants, born of Naamah daughter of Lamekk the Accursed. Hishirash was the mightiest of the Giants. After the Giants mutinied and Hishirash slew Lamekk, he became master of Turnienquor. Hishirash was slain by God during a duel with Seth.

**Hurash:** son of Hishirash and Ichsha, last of the original Giants. Emperor of the Nephilim, Hurash escaped capture by the men of Lhiosquor and secretly built up his strength in the Upper Nahla River region. Hurash's twenty daughters became the mothers of the Nephilim, the second race of Giants.

**Ichsha:** wife and sister of Hishirash, mother of Hurash. Ichsha escaped Turnienquor before its capture in 201 EC. She fled to the land of Harifon where she gave birth to Hurash. She was later tracked down and slain by Seuso of Lhiosquor.

**Mahawai:** Nephilim general of the Nahla river region and lands on the southern bank of the River Rahav. Mahawai is learned in the dark arts of sorcery. His capital is at Nubat.

**Naphtassa:** Nephilim governor of Tsayunos and Yarku, sister of Mahawai. Naphtassa is learned in sorcery like her brother.

**Okhar-Enokk:** Giant overlord of the region of Turvah. Slain by Kenan and Nosjubal in 136 EC.

**Ohyah:** grandson of Hurash and brother of Hahyah. Ohyah was one of the three Nephilim generals. His capital is in Susa.

## OTHER PEOPLE:

**Adam:** the First Father, father of all mankind.

**Cloys:** daughter of King Atalo of Atalanti and Medgariva (Valiturnea). Cloys fled Atalanti with her mother after being beaten threatened by her father.

**Dorro:** fourth son of Adam and Eve, patriarch of the city-state of Dorronquor, the Golden City.

**Eve:** the First Mother, mother of all mankind.

**Ferdeo:** son of King Atalo and Medgariva (Valiturnea), Ferdeo confronts, deposes and imprisons his father and founds the Republic of Atalanti.

**Hualichi:** the seventh son of Tsayun, first High Priest of the Temple at Tsayun. Hualichi appointed Yared to succeed him, but became High Priest again when Yared resigned from the priesthood.

**Mattu-Seth:** son of Cloys of Atalanti, half-nephew and disciple of the prophet Enoch. Mattu-Seth was Enoch's first disciple and has accompanied him since the beginning of his ministry.

**Nahlon:** a direct son of Adam and Eve, patriarch of the Nahlonites. Nahlon was slain by Hurash when the Nephilim first conquered Nubat in 339 EC.

**Quarro:** of Dorronquor. Quarro guided Kenan on his journey through the Great Forest.

**Shaochi:** fifth son of Tsayun, the shipwright and founder of Shaochiquor. Shaochi was the first to invent sailing ships.

**Sumiseno:** servant of Duke Hebystos, son of High King Konaryah. Also servant of Afalo son of Seuso. Sumiseno is skilled in stealth.

**Tsayun:** a son of Adam and Eve, patriarch of the Tsayunis.

## PLACES - CITIES:

**Ahfeneyah:** the City of the Wise. Ahfeneyah was founded in 393 EC by Seth and other members of the original Council of Elders from Lhiosquor after High King Konaryah deposed his father Kenan to claim the Emerald Crown of Lhiosquor. Ahfeneyah rests near the top of Mt. Chayat, known as Mt. Sentinel to Sethites.

**Badtibira:** the Nephilim capital of Hahyah, Badtibira was founded in 214 EC by Tubal-Cain son of Lamekk the Accursed after he left Arattu.

**Bariquor:** the fortress city of the Giants was taken by the combined forces of Lhiosquor and Arattu in 201 EC.

**Cerciann:** one of the daughter cities of Lhiosquor which sprang up around the base of Mt. Threthor. Cerciann was founded by Cerchil, one of the Fourteen Founders of Lhiosquor.

**Chintapiquor:** fortress city of Afalo, son of Seuso. Chintapiquor was built as a base from which Afalo could continue his civil war against Ayrus, High King of East Threthoron.

**Dorronquor:** the Golden City was founded by Dorro about eighty years before Lhiosquor.

**Faoriquor:** the Ring City is the result of the growth of the daughter cities of Lhiosquor situated at the base of Mt. Threthor. The cities of Cerciann, Ruwad, Triethu, Duirthan, Numeshad and Agrad had grown into a single ring of settlement by the beginning of Konaryah's reign.

**Harifon:** chief city of the Harifa, a tribe dwelling far to the east

**Iradu:** founded by Irad son of Enokk, Iradu is the greatest of the city-states of Shinar. Iradu sits where the Tigris and Euphrates rivers meet the Sea.

**Lhiosquor:** the City of Light. Lhiosquor was founded by Seth, his wife Azura, and twelve other sons and daughters of Eve. These became known as the Fourteen Founders. Lhiosquor was the most powerful and influential city in the world under its first king, High King Kenan.

Lhiosquor was the capital of the kingdom of Threthoron under Kenan and remained the capital of East Threthoron after the departure of the Wise divided the kingdom in 393 EC.

**Mathtusekh:** the city of Mathtu the Fisherman was conquered by Lamekk in 183 EC, then liberated by the armies of the Old Alliance in 201 EC after being abandoned by Hishirash.

**Nubat:** the chief city of the Nahlonites, Nubat fell to the Nephilim under Hurash in 339 EC, was liberated by the forces of Lhiosquor in 377, but then reconquered by the Nephilim again in 393. In the early fifth century CE, it became the capital city of Mahawai's realm.

**Pe and Dep:** twin villages along the Upper Nahla River which were home to the early followers of Hurash

**Rethobal:** a Cainite city in the Kingdom of Arattu founded by Nehobal, fifth son of Cain

**Ruwad:** a satellite city of Lhiosquor situated at the southern base of Mt. Threthor

**Shaochiquor:** port city of the Tsayuni people located along the southern bank of the Rahav River

**Shaol:** a village by the Burning Lake near the River Pishon where Lamekk was exiled by Cain

**Shinar:** the region between the Tigris and Euphrates rivers

**Shiqar:** a fortress guarding the borders of Nephilim territory in Naphtassa's province

**Shrivazh:** founded in 6 EC on Mt. Threthor as a refuge for the descendants of Adah fleeing the wrath of Lamekk. Most of its people left in 196 EC to find a land of their own.

**Shuruppak:** one of the city-states of Shinar

**Siaghlamh:** the town of Adam and Eve and their younger children. Siaghlamh is located within the protection of the Great Forest.

**Sippar:** one of the city-states of Shinar. Sippar was founded by Enmenduranna, a descendant of Irad.

**Susa:** founded by Seuso, friend of High King Konaryah of Lhiosquor sometime around 230 EC. Susa was conquered by the Nephilim general Ohyah in 418 EC.

**Thyraquor:** the westernmost free city in the known world in the fifth century EC, Thyraquor was a port city of the nation of Western Threthoron.

**Triethu:** a satellite city of Lhiosquor located at the southwestern base of Mt. Threthor. The military base of the High Kingdom of Threthoron is located in Triethu.

**Tsayalam:** the chief town of the Tsayuni people, Tsayalam is home to the Temple of Yah situated on Mt. Tsayun.

**Turnienquor (Enokk):** the first true city was built by Cain and named after his eldest son. When Lamekk the Accursed and his Giants conquered the city in 1 EC it became known as Turnienquor, meaning the City of Woe. The city of Enokk was liberated from the Giants in 201 EC and became the capital of Arattu, a vassal state of Lhiosquor.

**Turvah:** nestled between Mt. Chayat to the east, Lake Turvah to the south, the River Rahav to the west and the Kheruva Mountains to the north, Turvah is the chief city of the purple-skinned Turvese people.

**Uarga:** the remnant of the people of Shrivazh moved from the old town to the Common Fields and built this new town.

**Unuk:** one of the city-states of Shinar and birthplace of the prophet Enoch. Unuk was founded by the grandson of Irad of the same name. Enoch helped to build the walls of Unuk.

**Yahbarinnos:** the main naval port of the nation of West Threthoron, Yahbarinnos is a maritime stronghold against the powers of Hurash and the western Nephilim general Mahawai. It is situated on the northern bank of the estuary of the River Rahav.

**Yarku:** built as a fortress city to defend Tsayalam from Nephilim attack, the city of Yarku fell to the Nephilim in 400 EC.

## OTHER PLACES:

**Arattu:** the kingdom of Enokk, eldest son of Cain, Arattu was founded in 201 EC with the liberation of the older Cainite lands from the Giants. Arattu was a vassal of Lhiosquor until the reign of High King Ayrus.

**Atalanti:** a small island continent on the opposite side of the world from Lanti, the supercontinent

**Dilumu:** an island city-state located in the Bay of Dilumu south of Shinar. From the Lighthouse of Dilumu one can see the Outer Sea.

**Dry Lands of Nod:** situated between the Great Forest in the northwest, Arattu in the east, Mt. Threthor in the northeast, and the River Pishon to the south, the plains of Nod are mainly barren.

**Seven Mountain Ranges:** These separate the Northern Kingdoms of Threthoron and Arattu from the plains of Shinar and Susaron in the south.

**Euphrates River:** one of the four rivers flowing from the Forbidden Garden, the Euphrates forms the border between West and East Threthoron before continuing south to the plains of Shinar, and flowing from there into the Bay of Dilumu and the Outer Sea.

**Forbidden Garden:** the Garden of Eden from which Adam and Eve were expelled in 1 AM, only three men were ever allowed in the Garden afterward: Seth, Kenan and Enoch.

**Great Forest:** This forest surrounds the Forbidden Garden as well as Siaghlamh, Dorronquor, and towns of other minor tribes. It is protected by angelic beings known as Kheruvim and ringed about by the Kheruva Mountains. Cainites are forbidden entrance into the Great Forest.

**Inner Sea:** The basin of the River Rahav empties to the west into this body of water. Little is known of the Inner Sea.

**Kheruva Mountains:** These mountains form a ring around the Great Forest protecting it from intruders. Travellers from the west can enter through the city of Turvah. Those from the east may enter through the Pass of the Kheruvim which is guarded by angelic beings.

**Lanti:** the supercontinent where God gathered most of the dry land, with the exception of Atalanti on the far side of the world

**Mt. Sentinel / Mt. Chayat:** is located to the east of Turvah between the Tigris River and the Kheruva Mountains. Ahfeneyah, the City of the Wise, is situated at its summit. The Great Forest may be seen from its northern face.

**Mt. Threthor:** is located to the east of the Great Forest at the eastern edge of the Kheruva mountain range and is the source of the River Mashiren. Lhiosquor, the City of Light, is situated at its summit. Mt. Threthor was the centre of the High Kingdom of Threthoron.

**Mt. Tsayun:** is located southwest of Turvah and is the location where the Temple of Yah was built in 183 EC. The towns of Tsayalam and Yarku were built at its base.

**Outer Sea:** the body of water that surrounds the supercontinent of Lanti

**River Gihon:** This river flows north from the Great Forest into the lands of the Jabalites.

**River Kharkun:** This river flows eastward from the Duobinar Mountains past the city of Susa and empties into the Outer Sea.

**River Mashiren:** This river flows southward from Lake Cerciann at the base of Mt. Threthor to where it flows into the River Pishon.

**River Nahla:** this river flows northward from unknown lands into the estuary of the River Rahav.

**River Pishon:** the River Pishon flows southward from Forbidden Garden, through the Great Forest and the Kheruva Mountains before turning eastward. It flows to the south of the plains of Nod, continuing eastward past the city of Enokk/Turnienquor before turning northward. It runs past the Burning Lake and through the Lake of Refreshing before emptying into the Sea of Arattu.

**River Rahav:** this river runs westward from its source in Lake Turvah. It widens into a long gulf that eventually empties into the Inner Sea.

**Sea of Arattu:** this body of water is an inland sea into which the rivers Pishon and Gihon empty. It is northeast of Lhiosquor and north of Enokk/Turnienquor.

**The Common Fields:** a plateau on Mt. Threthor where the Colonial Council met. The town of Uarga was also built here.

**Tigris River:** This river flows from the Forbidden Garden, past Mt. Sentinel, through Lake Turvah, and then southward through the Seven Mountain Ranges into the plains of Shinar. The Tigris River flows past the city of Unuk before emptying into the Bay of Dilumu and the Outer Sea.

CPSIA information can be obtained at www.ICGtesting.com
Printed in the USA
LVOW06s1350270614

391901LV00001B/2/P